A ROAD UNCERTAIN

BY

HERBERT E. STOVER

CATAMOUNT
PRESS

an imprint of Sunbury Press, Inc.
Mechanicsburg, PA USA

CATAMOUNT
PRESS

an imprint of Sunbury Press, Inc.
Mechanicsburg, PA USA

For information about special discounts for bulk purchases, please contact Sunbury Press Orders Dept. at (855) 338-8359 or orders@sunburypress.com.

To request one of our authors for speaking engagements or book signings, please contact Sunbury Press Publicity Dept. at publicity@sunburypress.com.

FIRST CATAMOUNT PRESS EDITION: January 2025

Set in Adobe Garamond | Interior design by Crystal Devine | Cover by Lawrence Knorr | Edited by Debra Reynolds.

Publisher's Cataloging-in-Publication Data
Names: Stover, Herbert E., author.
Title: A road uncertain / Herbert E. Stover.
Description: First trade paperback edition. | Mechanicsburg, PA : Catamount Press, 2025.
Summary: Joel Pender always wanted to be a doctor, but the Civil War and the deaths of his parents disrupted his plans. Now he must avoid being drafted into the Army, or captured and tried for a crime he did not commit, while deciding whether to complete his medical training and becoming the man that Trudi Quinn believes he could be.
Identifiers: ISBN : 979-8-88819-268-9 (softcover).
Subjects: FICTION / Historical / Civil War Era | YOUNG ADULT FICTION / Historical / United States / Civil War Period (1850-1877) | FICTION / Action & Adventure.

Designed in the USA
0 1 1 2 3 5 8 13 21 34 55

For the Love of Books!

"I remembered (as rarely happens) a very fine line in the
Latin Grammar, whose emphasis and meaning is,
'Middle Road is Safest.'"

—R. D. Blackamore, *Lorna Doone*,
Chapter XXXVII, page 308

ACKNOWLEDGMENTS

The writer is grateful to the many who have helped in the preparation of this book. That is especially true of Miss Isabel Welch, Librarian of the Anna Holenake Library of Lock Haven, Pennsylvania. Miss Welch read and criticized the entire manuscript.

The State Teachers College Library, Doctor Gilmore Warner, was also extremely helpful, as was the Extension Division of the State Library in Harrisburg.

CHAPTER 1

JOEL PENDER WAS shaving when he heard the first light stirring in the dry leaves under the puncheon floor of the schoolhouse. When the sound came again, he smiled and put his razor back into its shagreen case. The morning had been good; it would be better if he managed to shoot the big blacksnake that lurked about the school property, frightening the children. He picked up his revolver and stepped outside.

Things happened fast, and there was no snake. He had just time enough to yank a gangling youth from his sketchy hiding place under the schoolhouse, listen to an incoherent story, and hide. He and the boy had crossed the narrow schoolyard into the shelter of the chinquapin thicket on the hill, when the three horsemen he had been told about rode into the clearing.

Joel dropped a reassuring hand on the boy's thin, trembling shoulders. A breath of breeze brushed both their faces with the softness of spring leaves. "Easy," he whispered. "Keep your head down, they won't find you."

Two of the riders dismounted. They entered the schoolhouse by the back room, where Joel lived. The third man rested the butt of his carbine against his thigh and slouched in his saddle. He appeared half asleep but didn't miss anything; not even the bird that fluttered out of a nearby butternut tree with a frightened chirp. Joel lay watching and thought through the boy's story.

"Hide me, Mister," he had begged. "Them's Shad Burley's folks after me, ketched me in Pap's corn patch. I slip't 'em when they watered the horses. Gonta sell me to the army fer fifty dollars hard money. I'd hafta say I volunteered. Did I make them liars they'd use a blacksnake whip on me."

Joel had moved fast. This type of story was becoming common, now that battles had so desperately depleted the gray armies. He could do nothing but hide the fugitive and send him back home when the horsemen left.

Trying not to alarm the boy, Joel eased the revolver from his trouser band and cocked it. From this point, he could look down over the hill to where the village of Talpo lay, a quarter mile off. The houses wavered along the wide road which was the town's street. Two cows grazed on the lush grass between the wagon tracks, but there was no one in sight.

"Indian town," people in the flat lands below the mountains called the village with disdain and hidden envy. Talpo was mostly Cherokee, with a few mixed families. No Confederate procurement officers bothered them about army service. There was peace here in the high coves, while North and South bled themselves white on a hundred battle fields. The recruiting service knew how much these Overhill Cherokees valued their peaceful lives and how hard they'd fight if their young men were taken away. So far, they'd stayed away.

The two guerillas emerged from the building in a few minutes and mounted. Joel shifted his revolver and reassured the boy again. "Easy, they're going." But he didn't feel easy. According to the boy, these were three hardened guerillas, less than half a gunshot away. A bird flew up, and the horses milled about for a moment or two.

Joel had ridden out a number of times, helping fugitive slaves and escaped war prisoners get north. He still had an incompletely healed bullet cut on his arm from one of these ventures, but he had never shot a man. In another minute, the choice would be taken from him; his first bullet must find the horse holder. In contrast to the slovenliness of his companions, he was neatly dressed, and close enough for Joel to see a scar beside and below his left eye.

Then the guerillas abruptly moved forward, riding side by side, following the cart track around the base of the hill where Joel and the boy lay concealed. It appeared that they had given up their present search.

The track would take them through the hills and come out on the road west of Talpo.

The shuffling sound of the horses' feet died away, and Joel let down the hammer of his revolver. He rolled over on his side and took a deep breath of relief. After a minute, he got up and spoke to the boy. "Come on down to my room. Let me look at your back. You winced when I touched you." There were four whip weals, none of them bad, and Joel dressed them with hazel salve. "How old are you?" he asked when the medication was finished.

"Goin' on seventeen, but I don't rightly know. Pop says he kinda lost track, a year or so back." His face was plaintive. "'Tain't far to the crick, mebbe a mile, where I kinda give them devils the slip. I figgered you Injun folks'd help."

Joel put away his medicines, then spoke sharply. "You get out of here, fast. Don't tell me your name, where you come from, or anything. That way I can tell the truth if Confederate soldiers turn up, looking for you. And—you don't know me, or where this schoolhouse is."

The young fellow stared for a moment, trying to understand. He drew a long breath as if he expected his talking to be a laborious job. "Mister, I gotta tell yeh. Shad Burley's a devil. Pop says as how it natcherly got too hot fer him in the flat lands west of here, and he come up inter our parts. Effen I had a pistol gun like you, I'd shoot the next 'un I seen." Then he ran like a startled rabbit.

Joel watched his visitor go down the cart track and disappear around a curve. He had a cold, uneasy feeling. Regular Confederate cavalry up here could be trouble, but guerrillas were unspeakably worse. Everybody in the hills knew about Shad Burley, the most evil of a devilish crew. Guerilla bands were outlaws, doing as they pleased—murder, arson, rape, robbery, and torture. Joel picked up the revolver.

A full minute passed before he put the weapon aside. In that thicket he had considered killing the man with the scar under his eye. It would be wiser, before getting into another tight corner, to talk with George Geis. The old man, though only half-Indian, through good judgment, kindness, and shrewdness occupied a position in the community like that of a tribal chieftain. He was always ready to help—with the sick;

about farming; hearing and settling disputes; or to point out the best places in the creek for bass fishing.

Joel looked about the little room for a moment, noting the places where he kept familiar things; pipes, his few clothes, and his books; then he went out and followed the footpath that led over the hill to the village. His mind was on what had happened, and he was moving fast. He almost collided with a man seated on a rock just off the track, around the first sharp turning. There was a gun across his knees. He looked up with a smile, followed by a wide gesture with a brown hand. It was George Geis, the man Joel wanted to see.

"Got out of breath," the old leader explained, "had to hurry home for a gun, when I saw."

Joel stared, surprised. Geis, with his high boned face and white hair falling straight to his shoulders, looked more typically Indian than usual. Also, he looked tired, mighty tired, all but his bright eyes.

"You saw?" George nodded. It was startling to realize how little the old leader missed, and how much the people relied on him. "George" had become like a title, used by everyone from children to adults.

"Yes, I saw the boy run, and who followed. I hurried home for this gun." His smile widened. "You worked fast, son. We'll make a Cherokee out of you yet, in spite of blue eyes and sandy hair." Joel took a seat on another rock, ready to tell all that had happened; but Geis had other ideas. "You like Talpo, friend?" The question was odd, but his friend often approached things sidewise.

"Of course," Joel answered. "I have since my father and Indian John brought me here, when I was a boy. When my folks died, and I learned how much they had sacrificed to send me to medical school, there didn't seem anything better than to come here. I was bitter, George, and wanted to get far away from home."

"Two years," George commented thoughtfully. "You've taught our school, ministered to the sick, rode with the boys helping escaped slaves and war prisoners—" He leaned forward and pointed at his companion. "You still have a bullet cut from the last run. Do you remember Doctor Kenny, the man you bandaged?"

"Of course. He had escaped from Salisbury war prison. George, I've been well paid for anything I've done. The boys here finished the training

Indian John started back in Hylersville. Look at the herb lore you've taught me. And my mind is more at peace, here."

The old man moved his hand in a wide gesture, and both his voice and manner took on the dignity of an orator. "You are young, like the leaves; and like them you will, and have, changed. Bitterness turned away to interest; from that to love of this place and its people. Yes, keep loving all, as I do: the yellow greens of spring, the russet of wheat in July, the tepee corn shocks in the fall. Do not leave out the hiss of snow on the hemlocks; and after it stops, how quiet the woods becomes."

His paused, then had more to say. "You seem to have hunted and found what I did after far wanderings—the treasured thing of the Cherokees—peace. Today, when trouble rode in on three horses, that is threatened." He rose stiffly and started toward the village with Joel walking beside him. Geis had done a lot of talking, none of it specific; and the younger man wasn't satisfied.

"You came out with a gun, George, should I have opened fire?"

"Who knows?" Geis shrugged. "If you had, it might have made the guerillas more wary. Or it could give them an excuse for a raid on the town, when any evil thing could happen. Once we take up arms to defend ourselves, the army will bring us into the war. Who knows, maybe they should have recaptured the boy; it would have been better for us."

"But not for the boy," Joel countered, and Geis studied him for a moment with his bright, inquiring eyes.

At the old leader's home, Joel apologized. George loved, and always used, the small amenities. "You will excuse me, friend. First, I must put this gun away before people notice and ask questions. I cannot say that I hunted ground hogs, for I have no game, and I always get some. Afterward, I must do some careful thinking."

"So, sir, you don't want me to mention the guerillas and the boy?"

Geis' wrinkled face came close to smiling. He reached out and tugged Joel's sleeve with a gnarled hand. "Friend, when there's danger or a quandary, it's no time for trumpets."

Joel walked on. George was right in not wanting to start an excitement in the village. However, it would be a sensible precaution to have every firearm in the town loaded and fit for action. Shad Burley could be planning a raid, and people should be prepared.

He always liked to walk through the village. A quiet, sleepy place, Talpo reminded Joel of his own home town of Hylersville. Like that, this Indian town was set in a framing of hills far enough away to be blue at times, or soft with haze, depending on the season. Winter winds broke against those ramparts, so the village was a sheltered place. The one sharp difference in the towns was that Hylersville houses were set in even rows, more or less, all about the same distance from the boardwalks and street. In Talpo, Indian builders placed their houses according to their fancies. Some were all but on the road, as if curious about passersby. Others were well back, with an air of secrecy.

Today, most of the men were out somewhere in the fields, and Joel did not meet anyone until he was close to John Quinn's General Store. A woman came out of a nearby house and stopped him. "Teacher, you cured my Betsy of her croup." Joel smiled and was about to walk on; but the stout matron wasn't satisfied. She came closer, pressing one hand into the palm of the other. "You'n Trudie Quinn give her medicine. If someday the child is sick again, she chokes, gets blue in her face. What is the medicine, Teacher?"

Joel rubbed his chin a moment while he thought. Betsy, a stout child who resembled her mother, had come down with the croup. Her mother, who could be troublesome, had been desperately frightened. He knew that if he told her the simple remedy, she would have no faith in it; and the child might suffer. To these Indians, a medicine had to taste abominably or smell worse to be considered effective. He held up one hand and ticked off items on three fingers.

"Take one tablespoonful of melted bear fat." Most Indian mothers used that foul smelling stuff for a dozen diseases, including croup. Something had to be added. "Mix the fat with twice that amount of vinegar, pressed out of the mother at the bottom of the keg; it's stronger, cuts the fat better." Mrs. Powers was closely mouthing the directions in a mumble. Joel added a third ingredient in a low voice. "Your Betsy turned a little blue. Add ten drops of elder juice pounded out of young shoots. And use the steam, as we showed you."

The stout woman beamed for a moment with her new found knowledge. Then, abruptly, she was embarrassed. "I forgot; I pay. Is two, quarter shinplasters at my house. You wait."

"No charge," he assured her hastily. "Just remember what vinegar to use, and the elder shoots should not be over a year old."

The woman scuttled away; and a chuckle from behind made him turn. "Joel, Joel Pender."

Trudie Quinn was laughing as she voiced his name, alive in every inch of her rounded body. Today she was all brown: soft hair with a wave, small curls escaping about her neck and temples; her eyes were brown, too, and they were laughing. The homespun dress she wore had been dyed with walnut juices to a shade that matched the tan on her hands. A white bow at her throat emphasized the brown.

"I didn't see you," he mumbled, wondering how much she had just heard.

"Shame, Joel Pender, to fool a poor woman. We just used steam on her Betsy. Grease, vinegar and elder juice; is that what they taught you in the two years you spent at Jefferson Medical College?"

There was no arguing with this girl when she was in such a mood. Joel wisely changed the subject. "That freckle on your nose shows today. On May first, before anyone is awake, walk barefooted in the dew. It never fails; freckles vanish."

Trudie put out the tip of her tongue at him, then caught his arm impulsively and squeezed it. "You were coming to the store?"

"Yes, for tobacco. Mrs. Powers cornered me."

Her father's store was a long, poorly lighted room with counters and shelves to the front; tables and chairs at the back where meetings were held. John Quinn, a small quiet man, was back of the counter. Trudie's mother, who looked much like her pretty daughter, was dusting shelves. Trudie told her parents she had been teasing Joel about his recommendation to Mrs. Powers.

He defended himself. "The bear grease and steam could have been enough, but her faith in me as a doctor, in recommending a common thing, would have gone into the air. I added the vinegar and elder juice for faith."

Trudie measured out Joel's tobacco. She took his money, then spoke more seriously. "There's something that'll keep Joel from being a successful doctor, Mother; he doesn't charge enough. Mrs. Powers offered him fifty cents. When I was up in Lancaster last year, a doctor would have charged a dollar for advice, and the drug store fifty cents, for even a simple medicine." She shook her head.

Joel filled his pipe carefully but did not light it. He liked the Quinn family. Kiley, the young sister, was the best pupil in his school.

Trudie had some news. "Pohasin's little girl isn't much better, Joel. I'll ride up after supper; it would be good if you could come, too. I may be there quite late. Besides, the child likes you."

"Yes," John Quinn commented, "see that she gets home safe, if you would. I don't like her wandering around in the dark, these days."

Joel thought about the merchant's remark as he walked back to his room at the schoolhouse. He could not help wondering if Quinn knew something about the presence of guerillas in the area.

CHAPTER II

JOEL LEFT THE schoolhouse at early dusk and walked up the track the guerillas had taken. There were plain horse tracks in the wagon ruts, and bits of half chewed leaves. It was quite evident the riders had been in no hurry. After a quarter-mile, Joel stopped abruptly, struck by a new idea. For kidnappers, the guerillas had shown mighty little earnestness. Their prisoner had slipped away from them in broad daylight, their search of the school property had been perfunctory, and they had finally ridden directly away from the area where their escaped prisoner might be expected to be hiding. He stood for a while, thinking; then he shrugged one shoulder, Indian fashion. He turned his thoughts to Trudie, and the evening ahead.

John Quinn was white, but one of Trudie's mother's ancestors was Cherokee. Trudie had a touch of Indian in her blood. When Joel had come back to Talpo she had been up north, staying with relatives in Lancaster, to learn about nursing. When she returned, and Joel came to know her, a new world had opened for him. They visited the sick together, took long walks in the hills, sat side by side on a creek bank and fished for bass. They had come to know one another well.

She opened the door of Pohasin's neat cabin and shook her head in answer to the question in his eyes. "Pretty bad, I'm afraid."

"I brought my spirits of niter, Trudie. Let's try some of that. Dad used it a lot."

After Pohasin's wife had died, a year or so before, the big silent man had tried hard to keep up a home for his small daughter and himself.

He led the way soberly to the split willow bed, where the child turned restlessly under the coverlet and muttered through dry lips. "My Mary fights the sick spirits."

Joel indicated a chair. "Sit down, Pohasin. We will give the child medicine, then wait to see the fever leave." He saw the doubt in the father's eyes and nodded gravely. "There is a spirit that watches over children. It will help your Mary, while the medicine works for the cure."

It was a long evening, with many intervals when Joel doubted. Occasional rational moments came to the little girl, and then she was frightened. Joel dropped to his knees beside the cot, touched the small forehead gently, then her hands. The child's fingers gripped his big ones spasmodically, and clung.

One hour passed, and part of another. Trudie moved quietly about the room. Several times she stood by Joel's shoulder, but he did not look up; his full attention was on the frail patient. The twitching and stirring stopped. He touched Mary's forehead with the fingers of his free hand and felt the starting of moisture. He drew a long breath of sheer relief. Without rising, he carefully freed his hand from the child's grasp. Candlelight made a fleeting bar of shadow across his bony face before he turned, smiling, to Trudie, and indicated the moisture beading on the child's forehead. "Guess I dozed. How long's she been asleep?"

Trudie carried her father's big watch in her dress pocket and had checked it every ten minutes for the last hour. "A good safe while, Joel. The fever started breaking half an hour ago. Go sit down, your knees must be stiff."

He went to a rickety bench which stood in the shadowed portion of the room and eased himself down. From there, he could watch. Pohasin kept his seat beside the bed. Trudie was moving about again, putting a chair in place, straightening the covers of the cot, doing other little things. From his vantage point, Joel wondered how the girl could make the room seem so much more comfortable and homey, just through the way she moved and touched things.

By now, he was bone tired. Looking around, he noticed a musket resting on a rack of deer antlers, over the front door. There was enough candlelight to show that the weapon was fully cocked, and that there was a copper percussion cap on the lock nipple. Beside the door was a long-handled ax, and the blade looked freshly whetted in the shine of the candlelight. Pohasin had been keeping two vigils that night. Did he know of the guerillas, or was he just alert for danger?

Trudie bent over the crib and carefully pulled the rag doll up until its head rested on the pillow. "The fever's broken, Pohasin. Mary will be well; but keep her covered. I'll come again tomorrow."

The Indian rose. Joel was always surprised at the man's height, a full hand's breadth over his own nearly six feet. The father's stoicism had broken, and profound relief marked his broad features. He pointed a finger at his sleeping daughter. "She will grow up, keep Pohasin's house. No more Mary, new name Trudie Quinn Pohasin."

Trudie smiled and touched the big man's hand lightly. "It is an honor—to have my name live on, after I am an old woman preparing for the spirit world. I thank you. Now, Joel will take me home; my mother will be anxious."

She caught a light shawl about her slim shoulders and walked to the door, followed first by Pohasin then Joel. He took a final glance at the gun as he went under it. If that heavy musket was loaded with buckshot, it would be the proper medicine for guerillas or other visitors who did not deserve welcome to this lonely cabin.

The feeble late-spring breeze had died sometime in the evening, and there was nothing outside but stillness and the fading moonlight. Even that seemed to give better light than the candles in the cabin. Pohasin loosened the Jimson mule's tie strap as Joel lifted Trudie up on the blanket pad saddle. The Indian was about to pass over the braided thong when he stopped abruptly. His big body was tense and alert.

A full minute passed until, as calmly as if there had been no alarm, he put the strap in Trudie's hand. "The child's sick time made Pohasin jumpy. He thought he heard a horse, and night roads are full of mischief. Trudie Quinn's father wants his friends to go home by the path."

Pohasin was dissembling; but Joel's sharp ears had also heard the sound, faint and far away, the fading echo of a horse's trot. He led the mule across the cart track, passing under the shadow of the big chestnut tree, into the path which led down the ridges to Talpo and Trudie's home.

Neither of them talked during the first half mile, for both were tired from the long anxious vigil. Joel's thoughts were with Pohasin, the guerillas, and the boy whom he had helped. Also, he thought of George Geis and his "no time for trumpets." Perhaps not trumpets—but Joel was sure it was time for loaded muskets, like the one back there in the cabin, over the door.

The Jimson mule was slow but counted two virtues: he seldom stumbled, and was easy to ride. In the shadows cast by timber and brush, the big animal was picking his way along with a care that would have done justice to a cat. His rider allowed her supple body to sway with the motion of the mule. Presently, there was the sharp odor of pennyroyal bruised by steel shoes, and Joel snatched up a small handful of the herb for his companion. "Your homesick weed, Trudie. Up home it's sweet fern."

"Pennyrile." She used the mountain name for the weed, then shot a question sharply. "Joel, why is Pohasin afraid? I saw the gun over the door; and you heard him outside."

"Not afraid, Trudie," he answered carefully, "just ready I'd guess."

"That's a poor answer, ready for what? The gun is cocked and ready."

"You missed the ax, Trudie. Well, war's been going on, on both sides of the mountains, for more'n two years. People in lonely homes have to be ready to defend themselves." Joel frowned, and was glad for the shadows. There he went again. Next, he'd be talking about the guerillas.

Trudie said calmly, "Pohasin didn't fool me, friend. I heard that horse, too." The dim oval of her face showed in the starlight and her voice grew more urgent. "Things are wrong these days, Joel Pender. Why not go home to Hylersville, work a while to get some money, then go back to Jefferson Medical School? You've had two years. One more and—"

The girl's voice choked; and the Jimson mule stopped. Joel stood looking downhill into a mass of shadows. Trudie had asked this same question before. Why couldn't she sense the real reason that kept him in Talpo? "There's no medical education up there waiting for me," he said roughly. "Just a shoddy uniform and a musket."

She reached out and touched his shoulder reassuringly, almost the same thing he had done to the frightened boy earlier in this long day. "You've been doing your part in the war. Remember how Doctor Kenny

praised the work you and the Indian boys have done. You've helped fu-
gitives get north, slaves and war prisoners. And when you dressed his
wound, he said you had the making of a real doctor. You're not an Indian
medicine man; look what you did for little Mary tonight."

"Not Mary—Trudie Quinn—remember the child's been renamed
for you. Me, I'm named for a Bible prophet—no wonder the child's better," he scoffed.

She shook her head, and the mule took a step at the motion of her
body, reconsidered, and stood still. Trudie mastered her irritation. "Yes,
my friend, there's something about those big hands of yours, and the way
you get close to sick folks, which helps heal them. We have dozens of our
people—old, sick, discouraged—whom you've helped. Don't throw your
gift away."

Joel looked up at her face, indistinct in the moonlight. "I had my
dreams, Trudie. My father knew he hadn't enough training; he wanted
me to be a finished physician. I've told you before. When I was finishing
that second year at Jefferson, he came down with quinsy. Too worn out
with work, he died. Mother had a bad heart; she nursed him; and when
she lost him, she died of shock. When I came home to bury them, I
found out they'd mortgaged their home, for me and that doctor dream.
And it killed them.

"Well, I remembered Talpo from a visit here when just a boy. When
my little world collapsed, this place was the only thing I wanted. Then,
the whole world went into turmoil. It's no time for dreams."

The mule pawed, and Trudie patted him. "Another thing, Joel Pender. Peace and safety aren't assured. You're a Northerner in the South. The
Confederate army won't bother our Indian boys, but you're white. One
of these days they'll grab you on sight and make a soldier out of you; or
hang you as a spy." When there was no answer, the girl lost her temper.
"There's more sense talking to Jimson mule than you! Actually, you're
getting lazy and shiftless, like some old Indian. Take me home."

His fingers fastened on the mule's headstrap. "Come on, Jimson, the
lady says home. Let's you and me oblige."

They moved on slowly through open places brightened by starlight,
then dark tunnels under trees. Joel whistled through his teeth occasionally.

Trudie muttered to herself. Finally, there was the village and the Quinn store tie rail. Joel tried to lift his companion from the saddle, but she slid from his arms to the ground. For just a moment, she was close.

"Trudie," he said desperately, "don't you understand why I don't want to go away, why—"

She lifted both hands, pressed them lightly against his chest, a hint of tears in her voice. "Maybe, Joel, because I'm part Indian—I just can't see you drift so far you can't turn back. I know too well how they get—old before their time, sitting in the sun, smoking laurel wood pipes."

He tried to interrupt but there was no stopping her. "Tonight, you came down a mountain with me. Why don't you find strength to climb your own mountain, alone or with—" Her voice caught. With a quick movement, she was under the hitching rail and running to her house.

Minutes later, in the stable, Joel spoke solemnly to the mule, already busy with his oats. "You and I are damn fools, Jimson, you for being a mule, I for hoping." The big animal paused in its eating long enough to snort, as if in derision. Joel slapped its shoulder and went out. He walked through the silent sleeping town.

The schoolhouse was dark. Joel undressed before the single window of his room, now just a lighter square against darkness. Naked, searching for his night shirt, a sound caught his ear. This time it was not far off or running; it was the slow plodding of a horse on the cart track. Joel crossed the room, opened the cupboard, and groped for his revolver. The sound passed. Finally, with a shrug of his shoulder, Joel replaced the weapon, found his shirt, and fell into bed.

"You came down the mountain . . . strength enough to climb . . . alone. . . ." What did Trudie want to add to her "or with?" He wondered, there in the quiet darkness, if he had the right to be hopeful, even though she wanted him to leave Talpo.

No answer came, of course, but heavy sleep did. He woke late, then dawdled through the remainder of the forenoon. He began going over his Cherokee translation of Red Riding Hood. He was using the alphabet devised by Sequoia, the ancestor of whom George Geis was so proud. Then he remembered how much Trudie had helped him with the idioms, selecting words children would understand. He slammed the pages together and dumped it all into a cupboard. He was pretty sure by now that the girl placed a low estimate on what he had been doing here for the past two years, and it hurt his pride. The worst was that he suspected she was correct.

". . . getting lazy as an old Indian . . . don't throw your gift away . . ."

Up north in Hylersville, he had walked away when the war clouds started, unmindful of anything but his own hurt. His mind showed those two lonely graves in the Lutheran church yard. They had dreamed for him; their pride in his small school successes was a precious thing to them.

Action might get him into a better frame of mind. The cupboard told him provisions were running low, but he wasn't going to the store. Trudie might think he wanted tobacco again. He started down the cart track with the wild notion of asking Mims, the tavern keeper, about the boy who had escaped the guerillas and the early morning horseman.

The weather had changed markedly. A few days before it had been springlike, now it was early summer. The dogwood petals were drifting down. Hollow places, where grouse had dusted themselves, showed in the cart tracks. Violets were still all about, but he passed one thicket where wild rosebuds had opened into blooms.

The cart track ran down to the creek ford. Most of Talpo's houses were built of whip-sawn lumber with planed window frames and doors, but Mims' tavern was a log structure, set back a dozen yards from the track. Back of the tavern were a number of big sheds, for Mims farmed some pretty wide fields and the bottom land was rich.

Joel knew Calloway Mims fairly well. He was a dour white man with a flat face, married to an Indian woman whom one seldom saw about the tavern. Their daughter, Laura, helped her father serve liquor and food to customers. It was fairly common talk that she was willing to entertain in other ways. She was popular with men when their wives were not present.

Mims had one Indian trait, dignity, and insisted on being called Mr. Mims even by young roisterers who frequented his common room. Only George Geis addressed the inn keeper as "Calloway." Geis sometimes held meetings in the tavern of those who helped runaways. Joel had dressed Doctor Kenny's wounds in one of the upstairs rooms. He turned in. The idea of getting information from the taciturn Mims was foolish. However, having come this far, and probably having been seen from the house, it would be suspicious if he didn't go in.

The big common room, with its tables and benches, and the bar in a corner, looked deserted. The door to the back rooms stood ajar; and there was a strong smell of soap about the place. Joel was crossing toward the bar when an exclamation made him wheel. Laura had been on her knees, mopping the floor behind some of the tables, and had stood up, calling his name.

There was nothing glamorous about the girl this afternoon. Her hair hung loose and uncombed, there were smudges of dirt on her face. She rubbed wet red hands against her skirt to dry them. It was not her appearance which startled Joel, but the look of fright in her eyes.

"Joel, Teacher, git out'n here. He won't be wantin' yeh round."

"I just wanted to buy some calamus. What's happened?"

She jerked a shoulder. "Git down back of the big shed afore he gits back. I'll come."

He turned slowly, looking over the room's roughly planed paneling, the tables, the benches. Something had happened here, something pretty serious to frighten a young woman of Laura Mims' experience. And she had been scrubbing just one corner, not the whole room. He made his way out.

Only a few minutes had passed when Laura came through the elder bushes behind the log shed. She had done something to her hair, and her face was cleaner, but the fright was still there. Joel led her to a log. They both sat down.

"Joel, yeh been good to me, never pawed like most. I'm scairt, gotta talk."

"Go ahead. Is it something about a boy, a day or so ago, Laura?"

She gulped and nodded. "Yes, Pa knowed him. He got away from Burley's men and stopped here a spell afore he started home. This mornin', a horse passed by early. Couple of hours after, this feller rid through the ford and wanted breakfast. Pa and me fed him, and he wanted likker. Pa motioned fer me to be nice. By and by he got to braggin', said nobody gits away from Shad Burley, claimed we could look under a beech tree down crick about five miles."

Joel felt a sick crawling in his stomach, remembering the fear on the face of the boy he had helped, and the whip welts on his back. He gripped the girl's shoulder with strong fingers. "Go on, Laura, what happened?"

"The feller went on braggin', said Burley heared there was a white doctor man in Talpo. One of these days he'd come fer him, said the Confederate army'd pay good fer such men. Joel, he was talkin' bout you." She paused to get her breath, then hurried on.

"Pa wan't much bothered 'bout ya, but he purely hates Burley, and thet boy was kind of kin. When I was gittin' pawed, Pa slipt round and kilt the feller with a club. He took him and the horse back to thet big sink hole, but the damn critter got away. He's wild." She jumped up. Joel was sure she meant her father was wild. "I gotta go now's you're warned like."

She took hold of Joel's sleeves. He could smell soap on her. "I never kissed a nice man, Joel. I wish yeh'd kiss me jest onct, seein' you'll be goin' away."

He was very gentle, holding her close for a moment, and turning up the tear-stained face before he kissed her. "I'll always remember, Laura."

Then she was gone, running through the bushes like a wild thing.

CHAPTER III

LAURA MIMS HAD asked no pledge of secrecy about the shocking things she had told; but Joel understood clearly enough about her father's attitude and actions. That sink hole, with a creek at its bottom, would erase all traces of the guerilla horseman. Calloway Mims was taking no chances of inviting a raid on the community by Shad Burley.

"Nobody gits away from Shad Burley." Laura's repetition of the dead man's boast brought the whole danger into focus. The guerilla leader was supposedly shrewd; if he told Confederate procurement officers that the Indian village sheltered murderers and helped draftees escape enlistment, the security of every young man in the community was gone.

Joel walked homeward, sobered and a bit nauseated by what he had heard and allowed his imagination to amplify. Sickness, death, poverty, ignorance, and heartache were familiar facets to him. But now murder, kidnapping, and threats of worse walked these quiet roads. He wasn't thinking much about his own peril, although he knew it could be very real; walking along he was wondering how he would react, if he was back in Hylersville and it was threatened this same way. There was a difference. In Pennsylvania towns there were laws, and officers to enforce them. Talpo was an alien community by race and customs, a small island of peace set in a sea of turmoil.

George Geis would have to know what had happened; there was no alternative to that. He might organize the community so it could fight for survival, and the Council of Elders might think that was the best thing. Council of Elders—Joel stopped short. He had often heard Geis speak of the Council, but in two years Joel had never seen this body, or heard the names of men who served on it. Now, here on this narrow road, he understood. There was no such body; George himself was the Council.

Minnie Dace, Geis's neat, middle-aged housekeeper, answered his knock; and she was both smiling and sorry. "Is away, Teacher, down country mebbe. Back tomorrow." Down country could mean anything. George might be sitting by a stream placidly fishing or he could be up in the hills, thinking. It certainly wasn't likely the old man would have taken a long trip into the flat lands.

Minnie sensed the irritation of her visitor. "He is like spring weather, Teacher, nobody is sure." She finished her remarks with a broad smile that showed excellent teeth, and closed the door quietly after Joel turned away. All the way back to the schoolhouse the feeling persisted that Geis was there in his own house, unwilling to talk. A white lie didn't mean a thing to Minnie Dace.

In the evening, Joel went up the hill to watch the lights come on in the village. A whippoorwill kept him company. High to the north and west, a dim star appeared and shone alone for a few minutes before the others appeared. The whippoorwill stopped and Joel stood up. Trudie was too sharply in his mind. They had often shared these lamp-lighting times, as she called them, and he wasn't going to sit here until tempted to go to town and see her. He went down to his room.

Joel was not quite sure when he had actually made the decision; but the next morning he began getting ready to leave. He had gone over the schoolroom and his own quarters, giving them a good cleaning. Papers and books were in place, benches neatly racked against the walls, and he was standing in the front door when he saw the mule coming over the path. Casper was a mean animal with one walleye, and ambition to kick at the lightest provocation. But he never tried his tricks on George Geis, who owned and rode him. Today, Joel did not leave the doorway while the old man clambered down, tied his mount, and walked slowly across the playground, where a few days before the horses of the guerillas had stood.

There was no greeting between the men. Inside, George seated himself at the teacher's desk. Joel pulled up a chair facing him and waited while George fumbled in a pocket of the long waistcoat he wore in place of a coat. The gnarled brown fingers found two worn gold pieces and laid them on the desk edge. "Going away money, friend, from the Council." Joel did not touch the coins. "What I have to say is not easy, friend Pender. You are to take this money and ride the Jimson mule northward. Wear your poorest clothes; nobody bothers a shabby man on a mule. It may be best to go at dusk." Joel smiled, his resentment against this old man fading as he remembered the kindness and counsel of two years.

"Shad Burley has taken over the old Heitel place, not over fifteen miles north and west, with as many cutthroats as miles. One of them is Lee Harne, from your own state, Joel. Kicked out by Mosby for brutality—" Geis took out a handkerchief, moved as if to mop his face, stopped and replaced the square of dark linen. "Burley lost a prisoner near this schoolhouse. A day later, after killing the escaped boy, one of his men was killed. Joel, the horse got away; it was still saddled. Pohasin, Mims and I searched for it. That's bad, it may go home."

Joel drew a long, involuntary breath and Geis continued. "Talpo has come to evil days. Son, no problem that concerns people is ever fully settled. Some are hurt, some are happy. I propose to get to the nearest Confederate army post and ask that officers come to our village. They will find here no one except Indian, or those of Indian descent. That could save us. The Staley boys live ten miles away; they are white and must take their chances."

"And I ride north on a mule." Joel said flatly, his resentment rising again, and Geis nodded.

"Perhaps only God knows the good you have done here, friend; but after you are gone, nobody in the village will ever have heard of a white man with big hands who taught the children, healed the sick, divided his little money with the needy." This time the handkerchief came out and was used.

Joel was again ashamed of his resentment. While his visitor recovered his composure, he stepped into his own room and returned, setting down a strapped bundle. Then he pushed the two coins back. "Keep the money, George, and I won't need Jimson. But I had made up my mind. Tonight, I go north, remembering you and Talpo. Both made a home for me when mine was gone."

George Geis, fumbling the coins back into the elusive pocket, got stiffly to his feet and said a single word. "Trudie."

Joel said slowly, "She said, I'd come down a mountain, and I must climb one alone."

The old man walked out the door, crossed to the Casper mule and mounted. The stubborn animal swung round close to the building where Joel was standing in the doorway. Geis' smile changed every grim line on the weathered face. "It is your mountain, son, and I am sure you will like the view."

Alone again, Joel walked out to where the guerillas' horses had stood. Well, he'd save George and Talpo some trouble; and Trudie might feel she had succeeded in stirring up his ambition. Actually, there was just one simple thing to do—find a Union army post and enlist, and that was the end of his dream. He could remember as a small boy, taking splinters from playmates' fingers and removing dirt from eyes. Medical school had been a great, challenging adventure. Then, here in the mountains, there had been Indian remedies so potent he almost ached to get them examined by real doctors. But a man didn't need an education to handle a musket.

At first dusk, he would strike north over the route they had used to get runaway slaves north. Going away when danger threatened the village looked a bit cowardly, but surely his presence there made that peril greater. Laura Mims' story proved that. And Trudie—he tried not to think how much he wanted to see her, if only for a few moments. The thing to do was remember how she had looked in Pohasin's cabin, pulling that rag doll out from under the covers, and smiling down at the sleeping child. There had been candlelight on her face and her soft hair had fallen forward as she bent over.

Two o'clock, three o'clock, Joel checked the time on the old mantel clock which served the schoolroom. It would be hours before dusk, and he was getting impatient; the reason for waiting to travel at night didn't seem important. There wasn't much chance of one man walking these lonely hills being seen. Still, he would wait a bit longer.

He was inside, settled in the chair allotted to the teacher; feet propped up on his own desk. He drowsed until a sharp staccato rapping at the door brought him up. The door opened while he was rubbing his eyes, to admit a small boy who spluttered excitedly in Cherokee. Joel could understand the tongue if it was spoken slowly but the boy was going too fast. He dropped on one knee beside the excited urchin and placed a hand on his shoulder.

"Slow, Aluns, talk slowly."

The boy spat on the floor and tried again. "Men come, Quinn's store, horses."

"What men?" Joel asked sharply. This could be the thing George Geis dreaded. Aluns, whose name meant arrow in English, shook his tousled head.

"Jake Lumb say run like hell, tell Teacher. Two, four men, Aluns count. One sit outside, watch horses."

Joel got up, knees weak and mouth dry. "Thanks, Aluns. Get home and keep out of sight till the men leave town."

The boy's bright eyes searched Joel's face. "You scared, Teacher?"

It was a good question, and Joel remembered it as he closed the building. To steady himself, he took time enough to lock it. If these riders were guerillas, God alone knew what might happen. It could be robbers, since Quinn was a prosperous man who had money. But the women, Mrs. Quinn, Kiley, and Trudie, were there; and John Quinn was not a fighting man. George Geis could make his plans; but Joel knew what he must do.

The path was the shortest way to the main village, and he compelled himself to walk fast rather than run. Thrust into his trousers band was the loaded revolver; guerillas would understand what it had to say. The wide street was entirely empty of living things except for the knot of horses at the store hitching rail and one man who leaned against a tree. Joel counted five horses. Four men would be inside, and the horse guard was half asleep.

He moved fast, but with the skill in stalking which he had learned from the Indian men. He took cover when there was any. The man moved once to scratch his head, pushing up a battered hat. Joel gained the corner of the Quinn house. The guard turned his back to watch up street; and dropped without a sound when the pistol barrel smashed down on his head.

Joel snatched up the fallen carbine, jerked back the hammer, and saw the weapon was capped, ready to fire. Then he stepped up to the store door, which was ajar, and waited a moment.

The voice wasn't loud, but it carried a nasal quality more irritating than the words it pronounced. "Like I said, I'm Shad Burley, workin' fer the Confedrit army. One of my folks is likely dead round yere. Couple of days back, one of yer people took a volunteer fer the army offen us." There was a moment of silence then the voice roared. "Dammit, I ast yeh enuff. I wanna know where's thet white doctor yeh got hid. Yer gonna hand 'im over or I'll jest nacher'lly raise hell with yer town—"

Joel pushed open the door. Against the wall stood George Geis, a trickle of blood showing at the corner of his mouth. John Quinn stood next, then his wife. Little Kiley, her dress torn from her shoulder, huddled against her mother. It wasn't hard to tell which man was Shad Burley. He sat on the edge of a table, a black hat pushed back on his rumpled hair. In spite of the warm day, he wore a canvas coat. Three other armed men lounged close to him.

Joel carried the carbine at his hip, ready for a snap shot. "All right, Burley, I'm the doctor. Get your crew out of here fast." The guerilla leader's small eyes narrowed. There was a weeks' growth of whiskers on his heavy face, but no sign of fear showed, although he could see the carbine was pointed at his stomach.

Burley slid from the table edge to his feet, hitching his shoulders under the heavy canvas coat. "Well, I'm pertickler damned! Yer him, and real mean-like. Guess we uns'll be packin, seein' yeh got the gun." His men were turning toward the front of the long room, coming closer to Joel. Then, all movement stopped at the sound of running steps. The door opened, and Trudie stepped into the room. For a second, Joel's eyes shifted from his target to the girl. He did not see the guerilla on his left come closer, nor hear George Geis cry his warning. A weapon crashed down on his head, and he collapsed to the floor.

Hazy consciousness came back to him for a few moments. Apparently, they were out of town, and there were more horses, more men. He was tied on a horse's back like a sack of meal. Carried that way through a nightmare of pain, discomfort, and semi-consciousness he traveled, while the guerilla cavalcade rode out the remainder of daylight into dusk. Occasionally, was aware of the rumble of voices, the jingle of equipment and the occasional clink of a horse's shoe against a stone. Once a hand yanked his body around, so it would not slide from the horse which carried him.

There was no way of knowing how much time had passed when they seemed to turn from a regular road into a lane so narrow bushes brushed the horses. In lucid moments, Joel remembered Geis saying Burley had taken over the Heitel place. The horses stopped, then milled about. There was the plash of running water; and he remembered that once he and some of the young Indians had visited the abandoned farm known as the Heitel place. There was a huge water trough fed by a wooden pipe from a nearby spring.

Rough hands loosed his bonds, and an impatient voice said, "Throw the damn fool into the corncrib." Two men took the order literally. Joel felt himself lifted. A door opened, screeching on unoiled hinges, then he was pitched onto a floor littered with corn cobs and trash, which reeked with the smell of rats and mice. He lay still, trying to ease the pain in head and body. Each time he moved dizziness gripped him. There was a stabbing ache in his side where he had been kicked. Lights showed about the place. Men unsaddled and watered horses; and the sound of the water was maddening, for Joel's lips were dry and his mouth felt furry. He could remember the cool brown depth of that trough, hewn from a big log.

Sleep came fitfully through the long night, and at first daylight men and horses were moving about once more. These guerillas were mighty careful of their mounts, but nobody paid any attention to the prisoner who had managed to put himself upright and lean against the slatted sides of his prison.

After the barnyard had quieted, a man, walking with long strides, came from the house to the crib. Joel saw, when he was close, that this was a very tall gangling boy, with a dirty face pushed out of shape by a big cud of tobacco. A heavy revolver was thrust through a strap belt, and he carried a huge brass key which unlocked the crib door. "Come out, Yank, and no funny stuff."

Joel half fell, half stumbled out of the door, and started toward the watering trough, paying no attention to the boy. Again and again, he thrust his still-aching head into the cool brown depths, the water stinging in the cut on his head but reviving him. Finally, he drank from cupped hands. For the first time, he could think clearly. The boy had the revolver clear of his belt. "Now step. Shad wants yeh. March."

Joel walked slowly ahead of his guard along the beaten path, passing through a picket fence where the gate hung by a single leather hinge, to the house door. The boy reached over his shoulder, unhooked the catch, and thrust his prisoner into what had been the farm kitchen. The place was filthy and cluttered with bundles of firewood, saddles, and battered furniture. Burley sat at the big round table eating from a skillet set before him. He held a piece of corn bread in his right hand and occasionally swiped it across the pan bottom, before biting off huge chunks and chewing them noisily. Beads of grease showed at the corners of his mouth. Without looking up, he jerked his free left hand at the boy. "Spit thet tobacco outside. It damn near makes me gag."

The youth obeyed promptly and was wiping his mouth on a dirty sleeve when he reentered the room. Burley had stopped his eating and was appraising his captive. "Damned if yeh look worth the ketchin'." His small eyes appeared to sharpen. "Funny them Injun folks was so close lipt 'bout yeh. Yeh are the doctor and teacher man, ain't yeh?"

Joel did not answer. His captor took a final swipe through the pan, chewed this last bite and finished by wiping greasy hands and face on a handkerchief. "So, yeh ain't talkin'. Thet's all right by me. Yer eddicated, I ain't." He gave the pan a shove, jerked back the chair and wriggled his shoulders into the canvas jacket.

"Some of the boys figger you kilt Jed Frein a while back. Well, mebbe you did. Me, I kin skin er hang yeh, dependin'." For a full minute Burley tried to dislodge a food particle from his teeth, using his thumb nail. "Either way yeh ain't worth a damn cent to me. Mebbe I kin sell you as a Yank spy, mebbe I kin git more for yer doctorin'." The guerilla was enjoying himself, studying his captive carefully. "God, them is big hands. Don't try runnin', the boys is pertickler hell on runnin' game."

Burley swaggered from the room. Joel saw that a second pan on the table was half filled with bacon, and he was hungry. His first taste told him the crisp slices were excellent, so was a lump of the corn bread. He ate greedily while his guard watched. "Shad says I'm your jail house man. I'll put a slug in yer guts, does you run."

Joel looked at the gangling figure. The boy was talking up his courage. "What's your name?"

"Tom Ellender. Gen'rally they calls me Tom."

Joel pointed casually to the big revolver. "There's no cap on number three nipple, Tom. Better fix it." The boy looked at his weapon in surprise. Joel knew this was his moment to overcome the guard, get the revolver and escape. There was no doubt in his mind that his position was a desperate one. But he did not know what had actually happened in Talpo. There could be other prisoners here on the old farm.

Ellender had recapped his weapon. "Yeh sure has good eyes, Mister." Joel half smiled at the confused look on the dirty face. "Say, yeh could hev jumpt me whilst I was fixin' thet cap."

"Yes, Tom," Joel answered quietly. "Just figure I wasn't ready."

CHAPTER IV

"NOT READY." Unconsciously, Joel had told the boy the truth. For the first few days of his captivity, his own pain and discomfort occupied his mind, but as he improved, the only thing which seemed to matter was whatever had happened back there in Talpo. He could see the store, four people ranged against the wall, blood on George Geis' face showing he had been handled brutally, and frightened little Kiley with her torn dress. The bitter thing was that he knew it was all his fault. His presence, a white man in an Indian village, had been the excuse these guerillas needed.

In sharp contrast to the general slovenliness about the farmstead, there was no carelessness in the way Joel found himself guarded. Most of the days, while Ellender worked about the barn, the prisoner was kept in the corn crib. Nights, he was locked in a storage room in the rear of the farmhouse. Its only window was boarded shut, but sun had warped the lumber until wide cracks let in sunlight or moonshine. If Joel tried, early in the morning, he could look into the barn yard.

Most of the time there appeared to be few men on the farm. There was a constant coming and going. Joel saw a good deal of the guerilla leader, who used the house kitchen as a headquarters; and from his room, he could often hear the rumble of voices in the kitchen. Burley did a lot of talking to a man he called Lee, who seemed to be second in command. George had mentioned Lee Harne. Joel had a fleeting glimpse of the man once and recognized the fellow who had held the horses at the school-house. A tall, sour looking man with a scar near his eye. It made the left eyebrow droop, which gave him a sinister mien not denied by the thin, straight lips.

On the fourth day of Joel's captivity, Shad Burley made an announcement. "Doc, we can't hev you eatin' us out of house and home without your workin'. Tom ain't really worth much as a cook. I figger yeh can't be worse."

Sharing household tasks relieved the tedium and improved Joel's relations with his personal guard, for the young mountaineer disliked cooking and hated dishwashing worse. However, under direction, he did help bring some order out of the slovenly kitchen; to the extent that stove wood was piled, not dumped in a heap, and saddles reeking of horse sweat and manure were placed on a side porch. Most important to Joel, his cooking furnished him with a weapon. Once a heavy butcher knife, it had been ground away in successive sharpenings until the blade was a sharp spear point. Burley had used the knife to spear bacon out of the pan; but it had dropped to the floor and got lost in the litter, until Joel found the thing and secreted it in his shirt.

The night of the finding, Joel lay on his corn shuck mattress, thinking. His prison door was secured by a big wooden bar, screwed fast to the lintel outside. With the knife blade the thing could be opened from the inside; escape would be easy, and he could get back to Talpo and at least find out what had happened. But Burley was a shrewd man; the moment he knew his prisoner was gone he'd raid the Indian village. There wouldn't be time to organize a defense. Once more, Joel knew, he would bring trouble to the people he loved.

When most of the guerillas were at the farm, there was usually a good deal of commotion about the barn and the outbuildings. This morning was like that. Joel and Ellender had finished washing breakfast dishes. The boy was sweeping with an improvised broom when there was the sound of a shot, followed by a scream, and a general hubbub of excited voices and oaths. Joel started toward the door, but Ellender stopped him. "Mister, don't go out there when they's riled up."

There wasn't any need. In a few minutes, Burley and another man, supporting a third between them, entered the kitchen. Without any sign of gentleness, they dropped him into a chair.

"Doc, by God, we got use fer you. Pistol blowed up in this here damn fool's hand." Joel could see the hand, dripping blood on the floor. A quick examination showed him mangled flesh and the white gleam of tendons. Burley had moved toward the big, locked cupboard. "Take the hand off, Doc. He can still shoot and feed hisself 'ith one."

The injured man started to whimper. Burley had opened the cupboard and Joel took a glimpse. Two modern carbines with packages of ammunition were inside, along with a braided and coiled blacksnake whip, and odds and ends of packages. Then Joel was startled, as the outlaw leader set out a small leather case easily recognized as the sort carried by surgeons in the field. He opened it and pulled out a small vial. Burley jerked his shoulder toward the shelves. "Got everything, 'nuff fer an army: quinine, laudanum, chloroform; hell, anything yeh need."

A supply of hot water still bubbled on the stove. At Joel's direction, Burley and his companion lifted the injured guerilla to the table. In minutes, under a heavy dosage of chloroform, he was breathing stertorously while Joel plunged the bloody hand into a basin of hot water furnished by Ellender. Burley kept peering over his shoulder while he made a quick examination. "Take off the hand, Doc. I want no gangrene in the place to scare hell outa the boys."

Joel had opened the surgeon's case. He wasn't too sure of anything: perhaps that amount of chloroform would put the injured man out forever. But the guerilla leader irritated him, and he wheeled. "Keep your damn hands out of this. Get me some balsam salve and brandy." Burley jerked back, then produced a small bottle of the liquor and a wooden box of salve. Joel poured brandy over the wounds, cut away jagged strips of flesh, then packed salve into each cut, finishing his job with a bandage taken from the big cupboard.

That was the beginning. Cal Horner started to recover in a few days, and other patients reported. There was an angry carbuncle to be opened, a swollen knee from the kick of a horse, and a half-dozen minor injuries. Finally, Burley had something else. "They's a feller up in the barn. Mebbe yeh'd look at him."

Most of the farm implements had been removed from the big building, but there was some hay in the mows, and rolled blankets marked sleeping places for the guerillas. Three or four men were lounging about, and they watched Burley lead the way to the locked door of the granary on the left side of the main barn floor.

The interior was semi-dark, and the place smelled musty, but Joel could see a dark form lying on a cot. There was the sound of heavy, halting breathing. "Get him out in the light." Burley hesitated a moment, then summoned two of the men who lifted cot and patient out on the lighted threshing floor.

The man was unconscious, matted hair and beard heavily shot with gray, hands and face emaciated. Joel bent over him, pulled aside the torn shirt, and lifted a mass of dirty bandage from the bony chest. The wound was there, a suppurating area as large as a hand. His searching fingers told him the pulse was very low. Burley pointed and his voice was a snarl. "Do something, Doc, don't jest paw the man."

Joel stood and faced the guerilla, savage anger burning in him at the inhuman treatment the man on the cot had received. "You foul brute, he's dying. Nobody but a beast'd shut up a sick dog like—" Burley's lashing blow sent Joel spinning. He stumbled and fell against the cot. Suddenly the sick man's eyes opened; he mumbled something incoherent. His breath rasped. Whoever he was, death must have been a relief.

Back in the house, Joel asked Tom Ellender about it. For once, the boy was forthcoming with information. "Thet was Old Man Heitel as owned this here place. Burley shot 'im when he come back to see what went on here."

Burley did not show up in the house until supper of the following day, and he had been drinking. There was a brown bottle thrust into the side pocket of the canvas coat. He finished his meal, leaned back until the old chair he occupied creaked, and belched. "Them was honest to God biscuits," he announced. "Tom, yer'n never was good. There was always horse taste in yer mixin'." He got out his bottle and took a long drink without pouring the liquor into a cup. This was the first Joel had seen the guerilla drink much, and he certainly was in an expansive mood. "Boys, I'm fixin' to be big. Git me suthin' fer all this ridin' and hellin' round."

Joel and Ellender kept their eyes on their plates, but Burley was bound to impress. His big fist thumped the table, making the dishes dance. "Three things is lined up fer me. Them damn army officers'll see Shad Burley's somebody. Next, I want lots of money, lots of it in chinkin' stuff, none of this paper. Then, I'll git me a woman, suthin real stylish."

He glanced round the room and became secretive. "Thet money pot's cookin'. It's rich, damn rich. Harne sez we cain't swing it. Hell, he used to ride with thet tony Mosby; I'll show him whut it means to ride with Shad." This time he half rose, then dropped back and caressed his bottle with thick fingers. "Know whut I aim to do atter I gits all thet money?"

He didn't get an answer but did raise his hand to his mouth to repress either a belch or a giggle. "I aims to marry with that chickadee I got cabined up in the holler. No sleepin' with her till a preacher sez his words, I promist. Either of yeh damn fools know why?"

Joel felt a coldness in his stomach—a girl in the hands of this beast with liquor drooling from the corners of his mouth. "She's got her a knife. But my time's comin', then I'll lick sense inter her."

Joel's big hands came up on top of the table where a frying pan, its bottom still covered by a half inch of hot grease, was only inches away. One hand was moving when Ellender jabbed him in the still sore ribs with an elbow. The shake of the boy's head was almost unnoticeable. Burley took a half sheet of paper from one pocket and threw it at Joel, who glanced at the scribbled message.

"Dear Shad:
    Goods at Hickory Crossing Thursday night.
    Bring your boys for the party."

The signature was a scrawl, but the name appeared to be Joe. The surname was illegible. Burley got up and took some writing paper and a pencil from the cupboard. "Now, Doc, you kin write good. I ain't much at it. Fix a letter like these army fellers has men to do fer them." He blinked his eyes briefly then dictated slowly.

"Dear Joe:
    Me and twelve boys will ride to yer place come Thursday.
    We'll do the entertainin'. Keep yer nose clean."

After another drink, Burley finished. "Sign it, boy, in big letters, Shadrach Burley." He grabbed the finished note from Joel, hitched his jacket round on his heavy shoulders, glowered at the two young men, and slammed out of the room.

Joel jumped up and paced back and forth. His mind wasn't on Burley's raid, if that was what the notes meant; it was on the girl in the hollow. He had a great lump of fear inside him that it was Trudie down there, the victim of the guerilla leader. The last thing he remembered of the scene in the Quinn store was when she opened the door and stepped into the room. Abruptly, he started and turned to face Ellender.

The boy sat with his face cradled in his hands; he had groaned. Now he was talking, desperation in his voice. "It's ketched up to me. I should hev kilt him long afore, long, long afore, when it happened to Molly."

Joel laid his hand on the narrow shoulders of the troubled mountaineer. "Talk sense, Tom. What do you mean?"

Ellender lifted his head as though it was heavy, and his eyes studied Joel's face. Suddenly he was pleading. "Mister, write me a letter. I ain't never hed time to learn writin' good. Mebbe I cud pay, so's yeh won't tell Burley—"

There wasn't time to finish, for the door was flung open, and this time it was Lee Harne who came in. Neater than his leader, the man was smoothly shaven and wore his clothes with an air. His face would have been handsome except for the drooping eyelid and the too-thin lips. Plainly, the man was angry as he came up to Joel. "Hand over the letter you wrote for Shad."

Harne's voice gritted. Joe laid down the crude lead pencil he had been holding and Harne grabbed his arm. The touch was too much. Joel remembered another frightened boy back at the schoolhouse, and a horse holder who waited nonchalantly, rifle ready to stop a running fugitive. He wrenched free. "Keep your damned hands off me, Harne. Get your letters from your boss."

Harne's lip twitched. His right hand moved swiftly, came up with a knife. Joel started moving round the table toward the frying pan. That would act as a shield against the steel. Abruptly, there was the sharp click of a revolver being cocked, followed by Ellender's drawling voice.

"Keep offen him, Lee, er I'll blow a hole thru yer guts. Shad don't want no meddlin'."

The outer door opened again. Not many minutes before, Shad Burley had seemed to be drunk. Standing there, taking in the scene, there wasn't a sign of intoxication about him. Harne sheathed his weapon, but Ellender did not lower his big gun. Burley's voice was low. "Thet's sure enuff," he commented. "Kinda mixt up, you are, Lee. Here's the letter you was worrit about."

Burley made a slight gesture with his hand. There it was, spread open, the note received from the man named Joe. "Lee, anybody gits hurt round here, it's on my say so. Lay off these boys and git out. I kin git real mean when folks is pryin'." Suddenly his restraint snapped, and he roared. "Yeh damned stinkin' Mosby man, get the hell outen here er I'll rip yer belly with yer own knife. This ain't Virginny and I ain't Mosby. Meddle agin with my letter writin' and I'll skin out yer eyeballs." Harne stiffened at the wild fury on his leader's face and in his voice, but he obeyed. After a minute or so, Burley followed him outside.

Joel turned to his companion and spoke quietly. "Thanks, Tom. Things look bad. Those devils'll kill each other. Let's get your letter written."

The boy walked to the door, opened it a crack to see if the two men were gone. Joel had seated himself with a piece of paper and the hard used pencil ready. "Mister, you write like I talk, er Molly won't think it's me." He took a long breath and talked fast, for him.

> "Dear Molly:
> Hits six months since they took me. I'll be home afore the baby comes.
> Don't be blamin' yerself none. Yeh couldn't help.
> We'll get us married up like nothin' happened.
> Sompin bad's comin' up.
> Atter thet I'll settle up fer yeh and me and come home.
> Tom."

It was a good letter. Joel could read between the lines as he wrote, and it was a story of tragedy. His respect for the gangling, tobacco-chewing boy went up. After Tom had taken the folded note, he remarked as casually as possible. "So, they picked you up, too?"

Ellender nodded and spread his hands in a gesture of futility. "They was mighty rough, first off, but I ain't mindin' thet too much. It's whut Shad did to Molly as makes me sick inside; and she no mor'n fifteen." His brown eyes took on a look of cunning. "By and by, I lets on as I wanted to jine up, drunk their likker, chewed my tobacco and set up their stories. All the time I been waitin' fer a night when the boys is in town and Shad gets him down in the holler to the girl he keeps. Thet night, Mister, I'll shoot his eyes out. I promist myself."

Joel felt a pulse beating in his own temple. Much of the uncouthness had dropped from the young mountaineer. He stood straighter; maturity showed on his thin features. Here again was mention of a girl in the hollow; and he remembered Kiley, back in Talpo, with her dress torn from her shoulder. His voice snapped. "Who is she, Tom, the girl in the hollow?"

"Mister, I don't know. Hit's jest one girl or another. He's got two Talpo boys lockt in the barn. Them I seen. But Shad'd shoot any man as stept inter thet holler, even was it Harne."

The fright which Ellender had shown earlier came back, and his jerking hands showed how greatly he was disturbed. "Worse is comin'. Hit's been cookin' fer a couple of weeks. Furst off, I figgered it was your Talpo town, but Burley sez there's no money amongst them Injuns. Hit's a paymaster wagon down west of here in the flat lands. Burley aims to bushwhack them folks and kill 'em off, no live folks left. Mister, I gotta ride with 'em, and it'll be plain murder. He told me, new fellers allus has to do the shootin'." The boy's eyes filled with tears, and he thumped the table with his fist. "Dammit, I talk too much. Burley'd skin me with a blacksnake if he knowed. Mebbe I oughta shoot yeh; claim you was runnln."

Joel looked at him and spoke quietly. "Did you ever shoot a man, Tom?" The mountaineer shook his head. "Better get that letter off if you've a way to send it. Maybe you won't hit anybody, if it comes to shooting." The advice appeared to quiet Ellender. He mopped his face with the ragged remnants of a handkerchief, then he drew the big revolver and examined it closely. "Who'll guard me when you ride off, Tom?"

"Old Ben Tunnis. He's damned stiff and ugly. Likes to see things squirm. He knowed Old Man Heitel'nd I figger he egged Shad inter shootin' him. Mister, hit's time you was lockt up."

Joel paid no attention but walked about the room searching for a weapon. The wall cupboard was securely locked, and there wasn't an ax in the room. Firewood was split outside. Of course, he could overcome Ellender and take the big revolver, but he had noticed the guerillas were in full strength lately. He followed Tom to the back room.

The next day was busy, men rushing back and forth. Joel was locked in the corn crib after breakfast and saw men grooming horses, working on saddles, cleaning weapons. The day after was a repetition; only early in the afternoon, a guerilla Joel had never seen took him from the corn crib to the storage room. "Boss wants you out from under foot a spell."

Joel tried to act casual. "You fellows going for a ride?"

The man grinned and became mockingly polite. "No, sonny. Word's jest come thet hell's froze over, and we all figger on taking a slide."

Less than an hour later, marked by the noisy clock in the kitchen, there was the sound of saddling and mounting. Joel watched through the chinks of the window boarding as a long line of horsemen filed past the house. He counted fifteen riders. Burley was keeping his word, sent on in his letter. This must be Thursday, or perhaps Wednesday, evening. Joel wasn't sure.

CHAPTER V

THE ROOM BECAME dark while Joel sat on his mattress waiting. The paymaster robbery didn't bother him much; if Confederate guerillas chose to rob a department of their own army, that was their problem. But, tonight, full dark was opportunity. He knew that the gnawing uncertainty of the identity of the girl in the hollow had to be settled. In all probability she would be some local slattern; yet Burley, hardened to such adventures, had been excited. Ellender had said there were two Talpo boys locked in the barn where Joel had seen Heitel die. Who they were was also a part of the night's adventure.

He had already started work on the door button with the knife when light and steps came into the hall; so he put the steel tool back under the mattress and waited, while fumbling fingers opened the door. The visitor was an old man who carried a lantern and a tin plate of food. A long flintlock pistol was thrust through his rope belt, and his only answer to questions was a shake of the head. When Joel finished with the bread, meat and coffee, the guard took the plate, backed out and fastened the door. His shambling steps died along the hallway, and the outer door of the house closed with a dull thump. Afterward the whole place was quiet except for the slow gnawing of a rat in the attic.

It was no trouble to get out. The short blade of the knife slipped through the door crack and upward pressure lifted the wooden button. The stable yard was empty and mottled with wide patches of shadow. Joel crossed to the barn and listened for a moment to the stamping of a horse. He went round the building to look in on the barn floor through the small door which opened through one leaf of the big doors.

To his surprise, the place was well lighted with lanterns. Beside the right-hand granary entrance, a man sat in a chair tilted back against the wall. There was a shotgun across his lap and Joel remembered Ellender's caution. "Old Ben Tunnis, he's damn stiff and ugly." The man sitting in there fitted the description, and that lantern light gave him a bright field of fire. Joel drew back. An unarmed man wouldn't stand a chance. Some other plan to rescue those Talpo boys had to be devised.

Joel knew, from his former visit to the farm, where the road into the hollow took off from the cleared land; but he had not been down it. The Indian boys had told him the road was washed badly and almost impassable. Joel started to hurry, stumbling on the bad going. Ben Tunnis might make the rounds later. There was a small stream to his left, making a clattering among the boulders and crowding the road round the tip of a low ridge. Having been in the dark all evening, except for when the man brought his supper, Joel could see pretty well. His heart leapt a bit when he passed through the dense darkness of a clump of pines and saw, a hundred yards ahead, the shine of a light. That would be the cabin, and someone was there.

He approached the small building with caution. Starshine showed him that the windows were boarded shut, and a heavy log prop was set against the door. He came closer, found a good chink, and peered through. A single candle set on a table furnished the light, and directly in front of him was the footboard of a bed, set at a slight angle. There was a woman on it, for candlelight shone on her hair; but he could not see the face clearly. Across the back of a chair was something he did recognize; a light, many-colored shawl, the one Trudie had worn that night coming down from Pohasin's cabin.

A sick feeling, close to a pain, so unnerved Joel that it was necessary to tug twice at the prop before pulling it aside. The door stuck a little, but finally he yanked it open and stumbled to his knees, and all but fell into the room. Still kneeling, almost as though begging to be mistaken, Joel looked up into Trudie's startled face. She was dressed in a long nightgown. Her bare feet showed under the edge, and a knife was gripped in her right hand. "Joel!" she cried. "He said they sent you north."

Standing, he looked at the glorious tumble of her loosened hair, the revealed ripeness of her body, saw her breath coming fast through parted lips; and his lips curled. "North, no. I've been locked in a filthy corn crib, and a room much worse. Two Talpo men are locked in his barn—"

"He promised," she interrupted.

There was thunder in Joel's head that beat on his ear drums so that he scarcely heard. This was Trudie, the "chickadee" Burley had cabined in the holler. Burley with grease running from the corners of his coarse mouth, the reek of horse sweat on his unwashed body and clothes. "You weren't kidnapped," he snapped, and she shook her head.

"He caught me, he said what he'd do to Kiley, and the town, unless I came with him. If I'd—if I'd—"

Joel leaned forward, teeth showing. "I heard him brag, Trudie, how a girl'd marry him, that she'd promised him." Trudie's eyes were wide with shock as Joel caught her by the shoulders, shaking her until the gown fell away from her shoulders, revealing the rich swelling of her breast. "Burley's woman, Trudie. You came away with that filthy beast. What the hell does a promise mean to him. He'll raid Talpo when he tires of you—" Beside himself with the warmth of her body and the sight of her loosened hair, Joel jerked her close. She was pulling away, but he paid no attention to her struggle until there was a sharp prick at his throat. Then he saw the weapon she had gripped when he entered the cabin, and her words lashed him.

"So, I have to use a knife to keep myself clean from brutes like him— and now, you, Joel. Yes, I took a chance to help my people, even you. At least I got his promise. All you did for Talpo was to bring him there. Whose fault is all our trouble, Joel Pender? Yours." Her eyes had become almost black with fury and the knife blade glinted wickedly in the candle light.

Joel, moving backward, stumbled over a chair. He did not understand what had really happened, only that he had hurt Trudie horribly. "Trudie," he said when he reached the door, "I can't ever make up to you for what I did and thought. But I won't leave this country until I've cut the heart out of the filthy beast who brought the trouble. Then, I'll come and get you out—" Abruptly he stopped, realizing. "Listen, put on your things, we'll get out of here."

Her lip curled. "Where could I go? He'd raid the town; there's Mother and Kiley."

There was only one answer. Outside, the big bar dropped in place as if it had always belonged there, and he stumbled away up the hollow. He didn't hear Trudie's low cry to him, or her sobbing on the bed.

Tom Ellender had voiced an idea. After a raid, the guerillas would go to town for an orgy of drinking and women. Burley would go to the cabin and his lovely prisoner. That would be the time; all a man needed was patience. Back in his room it wasn't hard to work the button into position, then Joel flung himself on the corn shuck mattress and groaned. There were small twitches about his body, a trembling in his big hands. He lifted one to his throat and took it away, sticky. That would be the blood drawn by Trudie's knife. Morbidly, he wished there had been more of it.

Not more than a quarter of an hour passed before there was tramping, and a light in the hallway. The door opened; the guard grunted at seeing the prisoner in place, then left. Burley's orders were being carried out.

Sleep was out of the question. The floor boards under the thin mattress creaked, the room was badly ventilated. But Joel almost welcomed physical discomfort, to keep him from thinking too much about Trudie. True, he had made his own coarse, brutal gesture; however, he knew the girl well enough to realize how completely she would sacrifice her well-being for her people and the village. And she blamed him for all the trouble which had occurred. Stubbornly, though, he reasoned that if he had left Talpo the morning after Trudie had given her advice, trouble would have come in any event, with an outfit like Burley's guerillas only a little over a dozen miles from the Indian village. He wished, desperately, that he could tell Trudie just why he didn't want to leave Talpo.

Joel got up and paced back and forth for a while. His jealous thinking had almost made the troubles Trudie's fault. A girl couldn't be held responsible for the folly of some poor devil who loved her too much to be wise about it. There was some dozing during the dark hours, but no restful sleep. It was close to an hour after dawn when the tired tramping of horses signaled the return of Burley's raiders. Through a crack in the window boarding, Joel watched the men dismount and off-saddle before watering their mounts. The guerillas moved with the awkwardness of the bone weary, and there certainly were not as many as had filed out that dusty farm lane.

Eventually the kitchen door slammed open, followed by the tramp of heavy booted feet and Burley's rasping voice. Evidently the hall door into the kitchen was open, for Joel could hear the excited words of the guerilla chief. "Well, Lee, we pulled it, and it's big, mebbe thirty, forty thousand. None of the boys seen how much. Now, do yeh figger it was worth the risk?" Harne's answer was a low mumble and Burley continued jubilantly. "We'll stack the boys up with a lot of silver and some gold. "Chinkin' money talks to them. The rest we'll hide."

Harne mumbled something, then his voice lifted. "Those guards had some warning, Shad. We lost four men, taking in Bill Shipley who died coming back. Tom Ellender, Shad—one of the boys claimed he saw him give Old Dan a paper."

Burley did not reply for a few minutes. From the sound, he was pacing back and forth. Finally, he gave his decision. "Lee, I don't figger Tom kin write. But he was shootin' in the air; I seen the flashes. Guess it's cheaper not to take chances, even if the men is edgy."

The pair clumped out and Joel hurried to his window to watch. Side by side, they stalked toward the watering trough to which Ellender had just led a horse. It was too far to hear voices. Burley grabbed the boy by the shirt, and Tom appeared to forget about the weapon in his belt, even though the guerilla whipped out his own. The boy dropped the leading strap, and Joel heard him scream, "Don't, don't!"

Three or four of the other men were near the scene of the altercation. Abruptly, two of them stepped forward and one shoved a revolver hard into Burley's ribs. Joel heard part of what he said. "Too damned much killin' already . . ."

Harne stepped forward, and the third man snatched a gun from where it leaned against a tree, holding the muzzle pointed toward the former Mosby man's stomach. There wasn't any more talk, but Tom was marched to the house between the two leaders. Burley's graveled voice gave Joel a crawling sensation. "All right, Tommie, my white-livered friend. The boys got yeh off this time but I ain't settled by a damn sight. You and the Doc's gettin' thick; but he was lockt up. Mebbe I won't shoot yeh right off. They say one of them guards got off. Does trouble come, Tommie, you'll hang from a rafter, and I'll poke yer guts with a pitch fork, whilst yeh kick."

After the tirade there was a heavy blow and a dragging sound. Joel's door opened and the unconscious young mountaineer was pitched into the room. "Comp'ny, Doc, 'nother damn sneak," Burley announced; and he did not forget to turn the button when he left.

Joel worked over the stunned boy for minutes, massaging the back of his neck and slapping his wrists until consciousness started to return, and he started babbling. "I ain't—I ain't sent no—" He struggled to a sitting position and stared. "Yeh ain't Burley, Mister—"

Joel shook his head lightly and spoke in low tones. "No, Tom, it's Joel. Tell what happened and you'll feel better."

Ellender was incoherent in the beginning, but as he hurried along, a fair account of the night's happenings came out. Burley's gang had ambushed a military paymaster's wagon. There was no attempt to hold up the officer; the guards and driver were simply shot down in cold blood. Yet there was return fire, after the first volley from the guerillas. Burley had lost some men. Now he accused Ellender of warning the paymaster, because of the resistance.

"Mister, I couldn't hev. Harne sed somebody seen me with thet letter to Molly." His voice raised. "Plain hellish it wuz, shootin', screamin'. I shot inter the air. Mebbe one got off, I seen him crawlin' fer the brush when I got on my horse. "Crawlin', all bloodied up, pushin' his face on the ground—Burley jest rid off, lettin' the dead folks and horses lay there. 'Buzzard bait,' he yelled at the men." His fingers clutched Joel's sleeve.

Joel managed, after a while, to quiet the all-but-hysterical mountaineer with assurances, remembering his own score with the guerilla leader. "Just wait, Tom. I want Burley, too; and I can open this door. Like you said, the men'll want to get to town, spend their money." Ellender did not appear to understand, just looked at Joel stupidly.

There was an immediate distraction, as men trooped into the kitchen, and Burley's voice was high over the din. "Line up, boys, and git yer money for tonight. They'll be more when it's spent. The Bee House's got three new girls. Old Ben and me'll hold the fort, and I got me some chickadee business o' my own. Lee'll be in town, case somebody gits in trouble or runs outta money."

Tonight. Joel touched the old knife hidden under his shirt. The men trooped out. Evidently Harne had remained. "You figger the men is satisfied, Lee?"

There was an edge to his lieutenant's voice. "They are, Shad, but I ain't, 'til we make the big split. Don't get any ideas."

Burley snorted. "Only idee I got is that wiffet in the holler. She'll come off her high horse er I'll take a whip to 'er. No woman's gonna string me along. You keep yer eyes on the boys. Likkered, somebody might do some braggin'."

Joel sat down beside his companion. "You heard, Tom. This'll be our night. I've got a knife. Your job'll be to get those two Talpo boys out of the barn. I'll go after Burley."

Ellender rose shakily. "No sir, Burley's mine. I'll git me an ax or suthin'. There's no call fer yeh to git all bloodied up fer the likes of Shad Burley."

Time dragged for the prisoners, but there was no use and much risk in making a move before most of the men had gone to town. Late in the afternoon, after a man had brought food and weak coffee, Harne and the men rode out of the farm lane.

Burley evidently remained in the kitchen, for he could be heard moving about and swearing at a razor. It was getting dark, and Joel's impatience was mastering him. He started opening the door with the knife, but Ellender caught his sleeve. "Wait till he goes out, Mister. Shad's jest plain hell with a pistol. It won't be long now."

After a bit the mountaineer said another thing which showed he was going along with Joel's plan. "'Twill be easy to fox ol' Ben 'bout them Talpo boys. I'll jest call him out fer a shot of likker, then knock hell out'en him. Ben was with them, that day Molly was abused."

The shadows deepened. Somebody had forgotten to wind the kitchen clock, for it no longer announced the hours; and there had been no sound from that room in quite a while. Joel could not stand the waiting. Warning Tom to stay, he slipped out and down the hall then stared in dismay. Burley wasn't there.

Shaving tackle lay on the table close to a smoking kerosene lamp; the whole place was in disorder. Joel's foot kicked against something on the floor under the table edge. It was Ellender's big revolver, dropped when the boy was knocked down, and unnoticed. He figured time desperately; as much as a half-hour could have passed since the guerilla leader had been grumbling; time enough for any deviltry. Joel hurried back to the room and gave the big revolver to its owner, who was delighted. "You stay back now, Mister. I'll do the shootin'. Gimme both jobs, then the fellers in the barn."

They were still in the hallway when the outside door opened with the familiar slam and Burley, howling curses, came in and made a beeline for the hallway. Joel and his companion had just managed to get back in the prison room and get the door shut, when the guerilla jerked it open. "Git out here, Doc, you'n thet damned boy."

Joel had the knife inside his shirt on the left side. There was a queer, new, unreasoning exultation in him, something unexplainable. The roaring man, who had just grabbed his sleeve, was about to die here in the half-dark. And the murdering devil hadn't been gone long enough to have harmed Trudie. "Get your filthy hands off me, Burley."

The guerilla obeyed in spite of his rage, but he did march his prisoner into the kitchen at pistol point. "Yeh damn sneakin' Yank, yeh was out last night." Joel noticed the twitches at the corners of the man's eyes and mouth. Trudie must have done something to him to provoke this insane rage. "Thet bitch knows too much," he yowled. "She won't talk, but she knowed you wuz here." He leaned forward. "How many men's in the barn?"

"Tom says two," Joel answered calmly. Burley rubbed his freshly shaven chin. Joel's eyes searched the room for another weapon, a chair or a club. The knife wouldn't be fast enough to beat a revolver, unless he was close. Burley stepped to the locked cupboard, opened it, and took out something which set a hard, cold knot in Joel's stomach. It wasn't one of the carbines, but a long, evil-looking, blacksnake whip.

Burley swung the thing out over the floor with a practiced hand. "Now, you damned spy, I'm cuttin' the truth outer yeh. Atter thet, the uppity bitch in the holler gits whut's comin' to 'er. Shad Burley don't share his women."

Joel slid his hand into his shirt to the knife handle. The table was his only barrier against the infuriated guerilla. Old Indian John, back in Hylersville, had given Joel his first lessons in knife throwing; the Talpo boys had done more. But the blade was short; it could be badly balanced

The whip hissed across the table, and the tip of the lash stung Joel's ribs like the flame of a match. Burley had the evil thing back for a full blow when he saw his victim's hand slide out of his shirt, cradling the pointed blade. It was too late for Burley to jerk the revolver from his trousers band, where he had thrust it so his hands would be free to use the whip. Joel's arm flew up. The knife, thrown with all the force of hate and loathing back of it, had been aimed at Burley's throat. Instead, its sharp point went through his wrist. Shad Burley, who had caused so much pain, screamed in agony and dropped his whip.

Joel found the big frying pan and started round the table to finish his man, before his antagonist could free himself from the knife and get his revolver. On the way he taunted, "You filthy body snatcher, I'm going to smash your head and slit your throat. You're the first and last man that'll ever touch me with a slavedriver's whip."

"Shad." The word was quietly spoken but it came with the force of a cry. Joel saw the leap of surprise and fear in the wounded man's eyes, and half turned to see Ellender, the big revolver coming up slowly. "Recollect the girl up in the hills thet you forct, Shad? 'Twas my Molly, and she screamed and screamed."

Burley's ashen face showed that he remembered. Tom continued talking. "I been a-waitin', Shad. Take this to hell with yer. I promist Molly to shoot out both yer eyes."

The heavy weapon roared and bucked in the boy's bony hand, and smoke filled the room. The revolver spoke again, seeming to slam the fallen man's body against the floor, his face a bloody mass.

Joel's limited medical training wasn't enough for the first brief moment when he looked down at the dead man; but he mastered the flutter of nausea in his stomach and looked at Ellender. Not long before, the boy had been upset when he babbled of the killings in the paymaster robbery; now he was completely cool. The loose lines of his thin face had hardened; it was as if he had just dispatched a dangerous snake in his native mountains.

Crossing to the open cupboard, he tossed onto the table the two carbines, their ammunition bags, two small powder canisters, and a ragged package of bank notes. Afterward, he picked up the revolver that had dropped from Burley's hand. "Keep this, Mister, it's the best on the place."

Joel thrust it into his belt and walked toward the door; but Tom stopped him, pointing to the table. "Thet powder, Mister, and the money."

"Keep it," Joel snapped, "let's hurry."

Ellender shook his head. "I'll clean Burley's pockets. Paper money ain't special where I'm bound."

The moon was high, lighting the farmstead. The two young men parted, Ellender going toward the barn, Joel to the hollow. He made good time over the rough going, trying to think only of Trudie, not the bloody scene in the farmhouse kitchen. Round the bend, he saw a light in the cabin. He took a long breath to fight back his excitement and broke into a run. There was no prop on the door; when he heard a groan, he smashed in the flimsy panels with his shoulder.

Trudie, trussed hand and foot, and partially gagged with a dirty handkerchief, lay on the bed. Her face was beginning to show the discoloration which comes from a blow, and her eyes were wide with fright and pain. Joel used an old pair of scissors to free her, but she kept gagging and trembling. Picking her up, he dropped into a chair and held her as one would a troubled child, stroking her soft hair with his big hand. "It's all right, Trudie, all right. Burley's dead. One of his men shot him, after I threw a knife."

"Thank God," she whispered. "He was a devil tonight after I asked the wrong question."

"I know," Joel told her. "Tomorrow I'll head north. The guerillas won't bother Talpo without a leader—"

She slid from his lap and faced him. "I'll go with you, Joel, to relatives up there. I can't go home. People will think—" Her frank eyes searched his face before she finished. "—what you did, Joel."

He didn't know how to answer, so he took her shoulders to shake her gently. "Trudie, I'm going back to see that those Talpo boys are set free. Then, I'm going to burn the place, wipe that infernal outlaw nest from the earth. Maybe that'll make it safe for Talpo."

He hurried back to the farmstead but stopped at the watering trough when three figures approached. Moonlight showed him they were Ellender, and Thad and Fred Sandys, white boys who lived close to the village.

"Fred, fire the barn, Thad and Tom, come to the house."

Thad Sandys just stood and gaped while Joel and Ellender broke open one of the powder canisters, made a black train to the door, and sprinkled the remainder of the flammable stuff about the room. Tom did the final thing and set the unopened second canister on the dead man's chest. As he left, Joel noticed the packet of banknotes and thrust it absently into his pocket. At the door, he touched a lighted sulphur match to the powder train.

Fred Sandys' job had been simpler, just to toss a match into one of the haymows; and the flimsy structure was already throwing out flames. The house was burning in minutes; the four stood watching. Heitel, the real owner of the farm, had died by Burley's bullet and neglect; his murderer lay dead in the old kitchen where the farmer had eaten his meals. Suddenly, from the house came a dull thud like a distant cannon shot, and the burning building disintegrated, sending showers of flames, shingles, and boards into the air.

Ellender moved close to Joel. "Mister, I thought I heard horses. Them boys could be comin' back. I'm pullin' foot." The mountaineer vanished into the shadows; at Joel's warning, the Sandys brothers trotted off up the lane, each carrying one of the carbines from the cupboard.

Joel stood for a few minutes watching the fire. Likely the blaze could be seen from town; the guerillas would be coming back; but unlike Tom, he did not hear horses. However, the thing to do was to get Trudie away quickly. He realized that the reassurance he had given her was empty. Harne would lead the guerillas now. Where the clump of pines made the way darkest, he stopped and listened. For a moment, he thought he heard horses.

Trudie, a small shape in the dim light, met him before he got to the cabin and asked about the fire and the noise. "No shooting, just a can of powder blowing up. The whole place is burned. Let's get into the cabin." The girl's few belongings, wrapped into two small bundles, lay on the bed. Joel picked one up. It was small, and he tried to put it into his pocket, but the packet of notes was in the way. He took it out. "Ellender found this in a cupboard and wouldn't take it. I picked it up just before we fired the house."

Trudie took the small packet and riffled through it. The money was all in old, worn bills, and it was United States currency. "It's a lot of money, Joel. Is this from the paymaster robbery?"

He frowned and shook his head. "No, couldn't be. Burley and Harne talked about hiding that. Anyway, it's not enough. A paymaster'd have a lot more. Come on, let's hurry." They put out the candle. Trudie followed Joel from the cabin. Abruptly, he realized he had no plans, and there was no finding a different path in the dark. Then, the night's silence was ripped apart by the short, brassy notes of a bugle. "Cavalry, Trudie. Ellender said one of the paymaster's men got away. They're raiding Burley's outfit. Come on."

When they reached the big turn in the rough road, caution asserted itself. Joel led his companion part way up the jutting hill. From this vantage point the farmstead, lighted by smoldering fires, was plainly visible. Things were moving fast. There might have been a score of troopers, all dismounted. Four tethered, hatless men were pushed forward against the corn crib which had been Joel's prison. An officer barked an order, carbines crashed, and the limp figures collapsed into a crumpled pile.

Joel could feel Trudie trembling at his side. "I ought to go down there, turn over the money, and tell them what happened."

She caught his sleeve, and her grip was surprisingly strong. "No, those soldiers'll shoot first and ask questions afterward. You wouldn't have a chance to explain. Wait, the time will come."

The cavalrymen were swinging into their saddles. The officer, pulling on a pair of gloves, walked to the horse held for him by an orderly, swung up into the saddle, and lifted his hand. He barked an order, and the column of horsemen, riding two by two, filed out the lane, past the smoldering house where Burley had shaped his big plans.

Trudie and Joel returned to the cabin. The guerillas were scattered or dead; there could be little danger before morning. "I'll have to sleep," he said apologetically, and she pointed to a big, rickety chair.

"I used that for two nights, Joel, try it." She gave him a coverlet from the bed, and he settled down gratefully, wondering at the overpowering feeling of weariness which flooded his whole body. Trudie watched him for a moment then blew out the candle. The bed creaked and the room was quiet. Joel slept.

CHAPTER VI

JOEL WOKE TO the improbable but comfortable feeling that he was still half asleep with no problems or compulsions to bother him. Turning slightly in the arms of the old chair, he caught the odor of cooking bacon and the fragrance of coffee. Trudie, walking quietly in her stockinged feet, was moving about, preparing breakfast.

"Put your shoes on," he greeted, "I'm awake."

She came over, smiling. "I know now what they mean by sleeping like the dead."

He stretched his long legs, sat up straighter and frowned. "Last night it looked as if I'd be doing just that," he commented cynically, and the smile left the girl's face. Joel got up and went out to the little creek to wash away the sleep with cold water. He shouldn't spoil the morning by thinking of the evil night.

Once they were seated, both young people ate with appetite. Joel was particularly hungry and couldn't really remember when he had eaten before. Trudie finished and began turning over a small iron spoon with her fingers. Something was bothering her.

"Joel, this puzzles me. That money's all United States currency. Why would Confederate guerillas have it?"

He rubbed his unshaven chin, remembering a fragment of conversation between Harne and Burley. "Trudie, Yankee money's just as good as gold, here in the South, war or no war. I think those bills were Burley's private hoard." Across the table, Trudie was looking at the spoon. One little curl had escaped from the tight knot in which she had done her hair. He helped himself to more bacon. "Let's not worry about the money. It was on the table, we were burning the house, and I picked it up without thinking. Eat your breakfast, Trudie, then we'll travel. Burn the money if it bothers you."

"Not three thousand, two hundred dollars, Joel Pender. That's too much to burn."

Joel whistled softly. "Three thousand, two hundred dollars, I never saw—"

Trudie's seat let her face the doorway. Joel's back was to it. He saw the surprised fear come into her eyes, and the spoon dropped to the table. He turned slowly, and the free feeling of early morning was gone completely. In the open door stood Lee Harne, a revolver held low and ready as he stepped into the room.

"Git the money, Yank. You've had your fun. Hand it over."

Joel read the danger in the guerilla's twitching eyelid, pulled down by the scar, and the little jerks given the revolver. The man would shoot at the slightest provocation. The packet of money was not in sight on the table. His own revolver was on the floor at the edge of the coverlet under which he had slept.

"The money," Harne snapped, "no stalling." His full attention was on Joel, disregarding the girl, who had jumped from her chair and stood beside it. With a quick sure movement, she snatched up her full cup of coffee and dashed the contents into the guerilla's face. Joel dived the few feet across the floor and snatched up his revolver. As he rose, his lucky snap shot knocked the weapon from Harne's hand as he clawed at his burned face. Next, he went down under a swinging blow from the barrel of Joel's weapon.

Harne was still partially conscious. Blood was streaming from his hand but, from the way he moved it, the injury was not very serious. Joel gestured with his gun barrel, and Harne stumbled out the door, down to the creek. Joel let him splash water on his scalded face and bloody hand. "Now, Harne, get out. Next time I'll shoot to kill." The guerilla lieutenant stumbled away up the road toward the farm, carrying his injured hand in the sound one. At the turn, he paused for a moment, and Joel sent his second shot over the man's head. Then he disappeared round the shoulder of the hill.

Back in the cabin, Joel snarled, "That damned money! There may be some more of those devils loose. Let's move, you won't always have hot coffee ready." There wasn't much more to do except to pack up all the remaining food, enough for several days' travel. Once outside the door, Joel made a final plea. "We can strike east a few miles to the trail we used to run escapees. But let me take you back to Talpo. The Burley gang's smashed; the village is safe."

She lifted her small head and held it proudly while her steady eyes met his. He could read the hurt and decision mingled in their brown depths, and his own eyes were first to fall. Trudie had nothing of which to be ashamed; he did.

"I left a note," she said.

"Suppose a guerilla finds it."

Trudie smiled. "You do not know George Geis. He'll have his boys look over each inch of this country, soon as the Sandys brothers get home."

They found the old Indian path north. Trudie proved herself an excellent traveler, and when they stopped for the night, both agreed that close to fifteen miles had been covered. Joel made a small fire, then built a lean-to shelter for his companion while she prepared a frugal supper. Afterward, they sat silent beside the fire before darkness came, and he took out the money packet. Impulsively, she reached over and took it from his hand.

"Listen," she said soberly, "I know you worry about the money. We'll share it for whatever it brings, good or bad."

Joel saw the braveness of the smile lines about her full lips. A spiral of smoke from the fire drifted by him, stinging his eyes. "Not the danger, Trudie, you've done—"

"Share and share alike, Joel Pender, including any danger."

Looking into her earnest face, he remembered a time when they had hiked in the hills too far and missed a meal. Trudie had found a lump of maple sugar in her jacket pocket and shared it carefully, making tiny morsels for two hungry young people. "Like that maple sugar we shared."

Her brows knitted for a moment before the smile came. "Bed time, traveler. Let's sleep."

He watched the dying fire a long time after she had gone into her lean-to. Reaction to all that had happened was sharp, so much so that his fingers fumbled with his pipe, which the guerillas had not taken from him. His mind was on the change in young Tom Ellender, turning him from a boy to executioner; and the scene in the farm kitchen was sharp in his memory, the report of the revolver almost a present sound.

Trudie's even breathing told him she was asleep, and he understood why she had insisted on sharing that money. Once more, she was willing to sacrifice herself, just as she had been to risk her lovely self into the foul hands of Burley for the sake of her family and the village. Suddenly he came to his feet, a tall gaunt figure with breeze stirring unruly hair above a lean face. His big hands opened and closed.

"Amount to something . . . climb a mountain. . . ." The sleeping girl had said it that night as they came home from the Pohasin vigil. For the moment, he wanted to shout aloud to the quiet hills that he would do as she wanted; that he would match her willingness to sacrifice. He *could* climb that mountain. A little shamefaced at yielding so much to emotion, he lay down to sleep. He thought of one of his father's sayings.

"A man's mind is a thing of many rooms. Be strong; and learn to close their doors at your will. That keeps good from bad, and a man can be sane, decent, and hopeful."

There was truth in the maxim. Love for Trudie was in one of those rooms. For want of closing a door, he had let his animal instinct for her lovely body master him for a moment, insulting her, making her think of him as she had of Burley. He wondered if he could ever humble himself, or do enough, to make her forget the weakness and beastliness he had shown. He slept.

The second day's march did not differ much from the first one, except that they made poorer time because of ridges and one wide stream which had to be crossed. Joel insisted on carrying Trudie over the creek. She actually giggled when he put her down. "You looked so desperate when you stumbled," she told him; and he frowned to cover the feelings her nearness had raised in him.

"And a different tune you'd be singing if I had fallen," he countered as they moved on. That night a light rain fell, but Trudie was safe under her lean-to, and Joel under a leafy chestnut tree. He overslept, and there was no sign of his companion when he wakened. The ashes of the evening fire were there; he pushed back his blanket, then stopped. It wasn't that he heard or saw anything; there was just a feeling of warning, and his hand went down under the blanket, found the revolver, and cocked it. He rose and stepped round the thick tree trunk.

Ten feet away, seated on a rock, was a big man dressed in a black suit and wide-brimmed dark hat. There was no mistaking the bronze color of his skin and high cheekbones. The newcomer was a Cherokee and a gun lay across his knees. Bright eyes were taking in all the features of the simple camp: Trudie's lean-to, Joel's rumpled bed, and the dead campfire.

"What do you want? Who are you?"

The Indian gestured with a hand as large as Joel's and spoke in excellent English. "One question at a time, my friend. I am Pohasin's brother, Jonathan, and I don't want anything. You do." He took out two gold coins which Joel thought he recognized.

"George sent me ahead with travel money for you and the girl. He comes slowly, but will be here in an hour. It is his wish that I carry you northward, taking the place of the Jimson mule. That is, I am to be your guide after George talks with you."

Joel smiled. It was hard to get out of George Geis' reach in these mountains. Trudie entered the clearing, wiping her wet hands on her skirt. Jonathan smiled at her. "Pohasin sends greetings to his friends, and says his little girl plays about the cabin, thanks to you both."

"Why, I know you," Trudie cried. "You're Trader Jonathan, the man of many travels, up north, in the deep south. Time after time you came to our store when I was small."

The big Indian rose, a powerful man like his brother, Pohasin. He bowed and took the girl's small hand. "True, and I come gladly to help, remembering the pleasant days. This morning, I am hungry, but I bring my meat." He picked up a package from behind the rock and gave it to Trudie. Joel built the fire; presently all three were eating hungrily, and they hadn't finished when George Geis rode into the tiny clearing astride the wall-eyed Casper mule.

The old man looked tired, all but his eyes, which made the same study of the camp which Jonathan had done. He refused Joel's assistance in dismounting from his tall mule, but he did take the food Trudie proffered him. When he finished, he was blunt. "First, Joel, go north. Your home would be best. Cavalry are going to hunt this region. They believe a fugitive has the paymaster money, and they want him." He frowned as if his statement had displeased him.

"Of course, ever since you and Trudie were taken, we have been scouting, gathering information. I knew about the paymaster robbery soon after it happened. Joel, you underestimated young Ellender. Happens I knew him, and he came straight to me from you, then went home before the cavalry got to Talpo. They came right up from the Heitel place, and the Sandys brothers walked right into those soldiers. They did a lot of talking, but I do not think they gave your name. Captain Munro of the cavalry tried to get that out of me."

"Sir," Joel interrupted, "I don't have the Confederate paymaster funds." He pulled out his battered share of the Burley money and George nodded.

"I know that. Close to forty thousand was taken. What you got, friend, was Burley's bragging money. Generally, he carried that about with him, to show off with it." Then, Geis was silent so long that Trudie, uneasy, moved closer to Joel. Jonathan, sitting on a big rock, appeared lost in a study of the far hills.

"Joel, the cavalry that wiped out the guerillas was blue. It was a Union paymaster whom Burley and his evil crew butchered."

All Joel could feel, for the moment, was numbness. Then Trudie slipped her fingers into his hand. Her small shoulders were set. "Well, George, it's nice there's only one army after us. Did you bring something from home? I ought to have a clean dress."

Jonathan smiled first, then Joel, and, finally, George, whose voice held relief. "Yes, young lady, there's a bundle for each, plus food." He took the packages from his saddle bags. "Just one thing more, Joel. There is no more dangerous place for you in all the world than these hills, so be careful."

Joel opened his package, finding some clean clothes and his shaving gear. He didn't say anything, but he wondered if George realized what Burley's camp had been like, and how close a captive there could be to an evil death

Trudie had taken her things and gone into the lean-to. Joel was glad to don a clean shirt. He threw the one he'd worn into the camp fire. The filth of Burley's hideout was gone.

Woman-like, when she emerged with her bright hair neatly combed, the girl had to examine the provisions of ham, bacon, dried fruit, corn-meal, sugar, and coffee.

"Your father thought of the coffee," George said; and Trudie's eyes filled.

"They each sent something. Mother my clothes, Father the coffee, and Kiley sent her special comb."

Jonathan was working skillfully and quickly, making up packs. "It's never too safe to linger over a breakfast fire," he smiled, "when you're on the run."

George had mounted Casper. There weren't any elaborate farewells, but Joel walked with him a few rods. "We are greatly in your debt," the old man said. "I will work to find the lost money and clear you, my friend. There is a Union officer named Colet who will help me, when I can locate him. It may take time." For a moment, the two men clasped hands, looking into each other's eyes. Geis smiled, and the look on his face brought a lump into Joel's throat. "I think, son, you will climb your mountain." The Casper mule went slowly down the trail. Jonathan had already shouldered his pack. Trudie had picked up hers, but she was wait-ing. Joel shrugged on his load.

They made camp after a hard day on mountain trails which Jonathan seemed to know well, and he permitted a small bright fire while daylight lasted. At his polite request, Joel filled him in on what had happened since little Aluns had come, breathless, to the schoolhouse with his warn-ing. Jonathan examined the currency.

"Old issues," he commented. "Likely the paymaster would have car-ried new paper money, at least. I have a notion your Burley might have double-crossed his gang completely, even Harne. Captain Munro said they had accounted for all the guerillas. He must not have known about Harne, maybe some others. There is no way to know how many were in that gang. When the farm burned, the hidden money could have, too. It is hard to say, from what is left.

"Harne didn't seem to think the money had burned," Trudie commented. "Now, let's talk about something else."

"It's a poor way to be going home," Joel said thoughtfully.

Trudie turned to Jonathan. "He's going to be a doctor."

Joel's look was expressive; he put in it all the hopelessness that possessed him, and the big Indian must have understood. "You are not at the end of the road, my friend. Young people are that way, thinking they are finished. Twenty years ago, when my blood was hot, a man up in your state died under my knife, and there was talk of hanging. I still have a good neck, and I have passed through that country since. No one blames me anymore."

The pattern of travel was repeated four days more, a steady march northward. Trudie and the guide often walked side by side for hours, talking occasionally. Joel found himself taciturn, and plodded along, busy with his thoughts. ". . . don't throw your gift away . . . lazy as an old Indian . . . strength enough to climb up. . . ." Trudie had said those things. He wondered if she remembered, and realized how futile such thinking was now.

They camped that night on the side of a low mountain, from which they could see a great valley studded by farms across which ran a railroad. "That's the Baltimore and Ohio," Jonathan explained. "Tomorrow, Trudie and I'll take a train for Baltimore. You go on, Joel, it's safe from here, only a few miles from Pennsylvania." Joel looked at him sharply. Trudie had walked to the edge of the little hill and was looking out over the flat land. "I promised her mother to take her to relatives." Far to the west the lonesome call of a locomotive whistle faded into the hills.

Later in the evening, Joel sat down by Trudie, who was looking into the fire. After a bit, he took out the worn coins George had sent with Jonathan and gave her one. "Share and share alike," he said, as she polished the gold with a small thumb.

"It's old money, Joel. I hate to spend it, and I do have some more, Mother sent it with my clothes." She glanced at Jonathan who was stolidly smoking and giving his attention to the stars. She leaned closer. "Don't try to find me. I'll reach you, if there's any news. Trust George to set things straight. Is it too much to ask, Joel, that you will always act as if I was with you, or near?"

He nodded because there was a lump in his throat, and she patted one of his big hands. "One fine day, Trudie Quinn will be so proud that she once knew Joel Pender, healer of the sick." Her voice was husky. After a moment, she added, "Perhaps someday we'll agree that it's better to be good friends than—what we both may have hoped for, once upon a time."

He had the good sense to get up and walk to the edge of the clearing. Trudie went into her small lean-to and pulled down the blanket screen which gave her privacy. After a little while, Jonathan came to him, and the two men looked out over the moon-touched valley. Farm lights showed here and there, and a distant dog barked a mild alarm. Presently, the Indian placed his hand on Joel's shoulder, and it was as if George was talking. "Don't worry. Both of you will be all right. Listen to the good voice she has left with you. Watch your temper always. Count ten before striking."

Breakfast was made up of all the odds and ends of provisions remaining. "Eat, gentlemen," Trudie said with a smile. "If you're tired of bacon, there is ham. Thank goodness there's plenty of coffee."

Joel made a small pack of his few belongings, some clothing, toilet articles, and the packet of money. On top he placed the revolver taken from Burley. He was tempted to discard the heavy weapon Harne had dropped. He turned it over, noted the letter H crudely cut into the walnut grip. Jonathan was watching, so he wrapped the whole in the light blanket he had been using. Later, Trudie watched as he tried to make his worn clothing more presentable.

"You look pretty fair, Joel. Turn around so I can see if there are any holes." He liked the touch of her hands, turning him slowly and brushing some dirt from one shoulder. She had the scissors her mother had sent, and with them, trimmed his hair. Joel could see how close tears were in the girl's eyes as she faced him. "All right now, my friend."

She came up on tiptoe, put one hand up on his shock of hair, and kissed him lightly on his lean cheek. Jonathan offered a hand which Joel gripped, then muttered his thanks and walked off down the hill toward the farmland.

He glanced back once, from the bottom. Trudie, a small figure beside tall Jonathan, was watching, but she did not wave. Joel walked on.

CHAPTER VII

JOEL WALKED THE entire forenoon, and well into the second half of the day. He had crossed the railroad tracks and was following a country road northward. At a little grove with a small spring, he turned off, took a good drink, and sat down on a log. Jonathan had managed their trip so well that traveling with him had not felt like an escape. Sitting there in the quiet, realization hit Joel sharply. Jonathan had taken Trudie to Baltimore because Joel Pender was a hunted fugitive. If he were picked up by the authorities, she would be involved.

He sat there a long time, thoroughly miserable. Trudie had understood and let him go his way, yet she and the big Indian had said many things. "Don't try to find me," meant he must keep away, lest he involve her. Then, "What we may have both hoped for," meant things were finished.

Jonathan had said "Both of you will be all right."

"Damn cold comfort," Joel said aloud, then looked about to see if, by any chance, he might have been overheard. The little grove was still. He rose and walked on.

Close to twenty-four hours after his disillusion with himself at the little spring, Joel walked into a small town. He felt hungry and reckless. This far from the Talpo country, it wasn't likely there would be a danger of being picked up by Union cavalry. There was a momentary feeling of satisfaction at being back in his home state after a long absence. However, the single street reminded him unhappily of the Indian village down there in the quiet hills where people had hoped for peace.

The changing scenery and the stiff exercise had kept him from thinking too much. His former home was a hundred fifty miles away, but there would be a train later. Just now, he wanted food. The town was awfully quiet, with few people about. Joel spied a general store down the street.

The sign read "Artlesburg General Store; A. Handy, Proprietor." The door was unlocked and a tiny bell tinkled as he stepped into the cool, semi-dark interior. A large yellow cheese under a glass bell stood prominently on the counter, flanked by a pile of linked bologna.

The door in the back opened after several minutes; and a thin, middle-aged man, with paper protectors over his shirt sleeves, came forward to meet his customer. His face appeared worried. Joel pointed to the cheese. "Half a pound of that, some crackers, and a link of your bologna, please." The merchant lifted the covering glass and cut a slice of the cheese with a long, heavy knife. "That's big enough for a corn cutter."

The storekeeper lifted the blade and stared at it as though he had just encountered a remarkable fact. "Yes sir, mebbe it is. But I ain't got no corn, Mister, not a stalk." He put crackers in a paper sack and wrapped the cheese and bologna separately, making a neat job of his work. He took Joel's few coins in payment. Joel had felt George's gold coin in his pocket, but didn't want to risk being remembered for such a thing.

"Town seems quiet." Joel remarked, taking his change.

"Finally!" The storekeeper's voice was loud.

"Has something been happening?"

"Mister, I thought everybody knowed; it's been going on most of a month. Army on the move—both sides, and strange riders, mebbe guerillas, been seen. Lee's in Pennsylvania, at the shoe town east of here, Gettysburg, thirty-some miles. The guns has been roaring three days past, since Sunday. Now, they're stopped. God knows just what's happened. Scared folks has gone through here, none of them knows much. Lee will take Harrisburg, Philadelphia maybe."

Joel shook his head, reading the dismay on the thin features. Without reason, he commented, trying to reassure the man. "No, they won't. No, our boys will turn them back."

The shopkeeper shook his head in turn. "Just kept rolling, them cannon noises. It was like thunder, only it never stopped. Mister, d'ye know how long it takes for a big army to pass? Fellow was by here last week, said he seen the rebels in the Shenandoah. It took full five days for that army to pass. All sorts of folks is on the road er hidin'. They're building forts at Harrisburg; out in Pittsburgh they give guns to the men folks. The rebels took all the money in York. Never thought I'd see a day when war come right to my door. When neighbors won't speak and everythin's unsure. And it keeps going on and on, worst and worst. Will it ever end?"

Joel picked up his purchases. "Have faith. We'll get through this. We have to. 'And I will restore unto you the years which the locust has eaten.' That's what the book says. We must believe it." He remembered Gettysburg, a sleepy little town which he had visited with his father. The place would be full of the broken and suffering. He knew now what he must do. "What's the best way to Gettysburg, Mr. Handy?"

"Bear right at the next cross roads to the Hagerstown pike. No, that'll be rebel country. Go north at the crossroads and work your way east." The shopkeeper looked appalled. "Mister, why in God's name do you want to go to Gettysburg?"

Joel was asking himself the same question. After all, he was a fugitive, what business had he on a stricken battlefield? His big hand dropped on the merchant's shoulder. "Maybe I don't rightly know, friend. Your guess is as good as mine. Could be, when I'm close, I'll be scared, too. But maybe I can help."

Heading out of town, Joel reflected that he had told Handy the exact truth. Armies march "to the sound of the guns." He knew he wasn't a soldier—it was the vague feeling that somebody needed him. And the need was whatever ability he possessed to relieve suffering. Excitement began to stir in him; he walked faster, eating as he walked.

A late afternoon shower drove him into a big red barn for shelter. All seemed abandoned. The farmhouse was locked. He found nothing about but two pigs and three sheep. When the rain let up, he fed and watered the animals and some frightened chickens which emerged from the wood lot.

He was up early from a bed in the haymow. He breakfasted on his dry provisions, cared for the stock, and was on his way. The morning was misty from the previous day's rain, and he had gone only a mile or so when a coming sound startled him into taking cover in a dense roadside thicket. In another minute, six men appeared, heavily armed and riding excellent horses. Each man sat his mount with the lazy ease of one accustomed to the saddle, and Joel's mind flashed back to the guerillas who had ridden into the schoolyard back at Talpo, when all his troubles had begun.

They passed, going in the direction he'd come. He waited in his concealment for a long time, then came the sound of a single shot. If it was at the farmhouse he had left, one member of that small livestock had eaten its last breakfast.

Guerillas. Joel's hatred for Burley and Harne seemed to come alive and tingle in his fingers. He opened his blanket roll and took out his revolver, then heard more sounds. A farm wagon drawn by heavy horses appeared, a slouched farmer on the seat. The body of the wagon was loaded with bags, pieces of furniture, and a boy's red wheelbarrow, roped fast on top. Joel put the weapon back and fastened the pack securely.

There were more and more people on the road, and Joel no longer took cover. Drivers and riders paid no attention to him. Nearly all the traffic was moving westward, in the direction of Artlesburg. Shortly after noon, Joel came out on a broad north and south highway. A sign board claimed that Bendersville was north, and Gettysburg south. The heavy traffic of wagons, buggies, and horsemen, now moving in two directions, raised clouds of the gray limestone dust which caught in a man's throat. Joel tried to keep to the side, walking in the already trodden roadside grass. He had gone a mile when a big, covered spring wagon drawn by a high-stepping span of bay horses passed him. SANITARY COMMISSION was lettered on the canvas top; and the driver, a man who looked no older than Joel in spite of a fringed beard, pulled up and waited. "Going to Gettysburg, Mister? Get in, give thy feet a break." His accent and the beard told Joel he was part of a German community.

Joel climbed to the high seat gratefully. The driver clucked to the horses and the wagon rolled. After his passenger was settled, the young man extended his right hand. "Shake hands with Jake Puffenburger."

"Joel Pender. Yes, I'm going to Gettysburg. My father took me there once when I was a boy." Puffenburger said nothing for a while, and Joel was increasingly aware of the devastation of the country through which they were driving. Once, this had been a neatly laid out and prosperous country side. Buildings still stood, but it was deserted, and littered beyond imagination. Broken down wagons and carriages were pushed to the sides of the road; fences were torn down; everywhere was the debris left by a passing army—clothing, broken muskets, cannon wheels, cartridge boxes, smashed canteens, and a wind drift of torn paper. Joel muttered, "The years that the locust has eaten, indeed."

Puffenburger waved his whip. "Couple of armies went through here. Just look how they dirty up a place. You won't know Gettysburg. Couple hundred thousand men fought over it, three days. Men clear beyont counting is hurt or dead. Doctors and them that can help hurt folks are mighty welcome in them hospitals. Meade, the Union general, licked Lee; and he's on the run south. But, what a God-awful lot of suffering he left behint." He slapped the horses lightly with the lines. "They tell there's more hurt folks then there is men, women, and children in Harrisburg city. There ain't ground enough to bury the dead decent."

Joel stared straight ahead, shocked at what he was hearing. The fact that Lee had been beaten seemed secondary to the misery his army had created here in this quiet Pennsylvania countryside. "I was studying to be a doctor," he told Puffenburger, "had close to two years in medical school before my parents died."

The driver jerked the lines and came close to stopping the team. He slapped his companion's knee. "Then do you forget for what you were coming down for. There's work, and plenty, and not enough folks. I carry a load for the Sanitary people, my second this here week. The Commission has sent stuff by the train load. Doctors from all around is down there workin'." The bearded young man was so pleased with his discovery that he took his companion's assent for granted. "When we get in, I'll see you are registered, they call it. All the names of helpers is on big sheets of paper. Does a doctor or some head nurse need folks, they pick from them lists. Like me now, it reads J. Puffenburger, Teamster, and I get hauling to do round the place."

When evening came, Puffenburger pulled his team into a small oak grove. The place had been used a lot as a camp, judging from blackened campfire remains and trodden brush and grass. Joel helped his host feed and water the team, and afterward the German shared his evening meal with Joel. They sat down against a tree, smoking an evening pipe.

Puffenburger confided, "This here army draft that's coming, all men is in it. We Puffenburgers don't hold with war and killing. Most of us live down Antietam crick way and there was a bad battle there. I ben driving for the Sanitary folks clost to two years; hauling shirts, bandages, powdered milk, and other stuff hurt men needs. I don't hold with carrying a gun to shoot folks. And I seen a lot of misery."

"Joel's answer came impulsively. "You've been helping; why should they draft you? Or, you could enlist as a teamster. The army must need lots of such men."

Puffenburger's face reddened. "Trouble is, when I talk with these war folks, I get all mixt up like and they say something about damned Dutch." Joel was unsure how to respond, and when the pipes were done, they were soon asleep.

The next day passed with increasing friendliness between the two young men. They talked a lot about the draft. Joel said he'd prefer getting into some medical unit, Puffenburger only wanted to drive teams. Traffic was heavy, but people passed each other without the usual nods or road courtesies. It was as if this shadow of war had banished all the small amenities.

Toward evening, down a long stretch of straight road, hundreds of lights showed. Beyond this would be the town. Puffenburger pointed with a sweep of his whip handle. "Them's the hospitals where the lights is; bigger'n the town. Course there's places for the doctors and such to live, but there's shacks and tents and houses, all full of hurt men."

Abruptly, the young German pulled in the horses and turned on his seat, so the strong lines of his thinly bearded face showed. "I got the solid feeling we're gonta be good friends. We'll pitch in down here, until it's done; then come on to Harrisburg with me, and we'll have us a long talk."

Joel just nodded and held out a big hand. There was a likeable honesty about young Jake Puffenburger, and perhaps more discernment than one would expect from his stolid manner. "That's a bargain, Jake. I was going to Harrisburg anyway; now I'm glad to be sure of company."

Puffenburger drove his wagon up to a long loading dock, and laborers promptly started taking the things out of it while the driver checked his lists. The work finished, he pulled over to a small grove and unhitched with Joel's aid. They took his horses to some rude, new board stalls equipped with feed boxes and water pails. "You and me shall camp in the wagon, Joel. Now, over we go, and sign up."

A lady whose brown hair was touched with gray took Jake's papers, smiling. Evidently, she knew and liked the young teamster. "Another load, Jake; now what else have you brought?"

"A good helper, Mrs. Tolfus, name of Pender. Is good with bandages and things."

The name was out. Joel looked sharply at the lady, but she just wrote it down, then started questioning him. He told her of medical school, and that his father had been a doctor.

"Mr. Pender, you're a real find. Lots of these so-called doctors haven't had half your training; I mean in a good school. We'll list you as a surgeon's helper, if you can handle chloroform?" He nodded, and she wrote that down. "I have it all. No, wait, I didn't ask you where your home is."

"Hylersville," he answered quietly, and stood looking down at the copperplate writing. Joel Pender, Residence–Hylersville. It was all there. Soldiers from all over the east had been on this great battlefield. Captain Munro's blue riders could have been among them. If his name had been picked up at Talpo—time enough to worry about that when it happened.

Puffenburger was hungry. Joel was glad to join him at the wagon and to eat by lantern light. Half an hour later they were well fed and were sitting beside the wagon, when a messenger from Mrs. Tolfus came. "Mrs. Lines at the church needs a couple of men for the evening soup detail."

"Come," Puffenburger said. "I know where the church is. It's real clost to here."

CHAPTER VIII

BY THE TIME the two had reached the small brick church on the northern outskirts of the town, the fact that he had given both his name and home address to the clerk at the loading dock did not seem either important or dangerous to Joel. When he was about to visit sick people, he felt a purposeful excitement and challenge. They found the wooden pews of the church set outside to make room for the wounded on the straw-covered floor of the building. Two soldiers had just set down a huge kettle filled with steaming soup. A small woman met them at the door.

"I'm Mrs. Jenner," she explained. "We've got to get some food into these boys before they die. Lots of them are so weak they have to be lifted to eat. Jake, go in to Mrs. Lines; new man, help me." She filled a pail from the kettle and, while Joel carried it, explained the patients were post-operative cases. Inside, they went to each blanket wrapped patient. Joel would slide big hands under the man's shoulders and Mrs. Jenner would spoon soup into his mouth. One big man, who had lost one arm and had the other bandaged, said, "Mister, them big hands of yours make a damn find back rest." Joel smiled, and the man apologized to the brown-eyed Mrs. Jenner. "Sorry, that cuss word jest slip't me."

She shook her head, and her smile was warming. "Swear all you like until you're good and better, but do swallow more soup."

The fourth and sixth men in the row were dead. Near them lay a pale faced boy who had lost a leg, and wore a heavy bandage across his chest that showed under his open night shirt. Joel knelt this time, and eased his hands under the bony shoulders to raise him so he could be fed. He could not be roused, and a last breath left him.

"Another," the woman muttered bitterly. "O God, how many more must go." Without thinking what he was doing, Joel held the dead soldier close for a long moment until the nurse touched his shoulder. Nodding to her, he laid the wasted form gently back on the straw.

The work went on through hours, under the light of smoking lanterns. When the feeding was finished, the dead were removed. Afterward the straw was stirred to make it springier. The women nurses were changed at midnight; but gray morning showed before Joel and Puffenburger were relieved. They stumbled outside, found the wagon, and tumbled into their blankets.

There was more work waiting in the morning when they reported. Puffenburger's team and wagon were to carry supplies to places in town and out along Cemetery Ridge. Joel was appalled at the number of wounded he saw, as they unloaded at the different hospitals. Jake couldn't keep his eyes off the burying squads, which seemed to hold a morbid interest for him. "Man that is born of woman," he kept mumbling. Then he caught Joel's arm. "Look, they ain't putting them plow-deep!"

Joel patted his shoulders. "Come on, man, the living need us."

Puffenburger was losing his appetite from the constant exposure to battle field odors. Finally, he was persuaded to use what most of the workers considered essential, a handkerchief soaked in cologne. When he described the remedy, he slipped deeply into the Pennsylvania German idiom. "It stops not the smell, chust gives someting new."

Work with the wounded passed its peak after six or seven days, with many thousands of the injured men evacuated by the railroad and wagon trains to the great base hospitals. But there were still hundreds so seriously wounded they could not be moved. Surgeons and nurses worked straight through most of the nights.

Puffenburger had gone to his bed in the wagon, but Joel was restless in spite of having worked hard all day. He was impressed by the real efficiency seen here on the edges of the battlefield, caring for the dreadful aftermath of the struggle. The surgeons' work fascinated him. This evening, he was thinking hard about the training behind their skills. Without waking Puffenburger, he walked over to the offices of the loading docks, where lights still showed. Mrs. Tolfus waved at him. "Pendon, one of the surgeons is asking for you. His orderly went out with a wagon load of wounded." She pulled her register over her plank desk. "Street A, fourth tent hospital. I didn't get the doctor's name."

It seemed like a regular summons, something which happened daily, even hourly, to any of the men and women who worked about the hospitals. Yet, as he walked through the poorly lighted tent streets for the first time in days, the feeling that he was a hunted person came to him hard. He was a man living and working in a borrowed freedom which could end suddenly. The thought of Trudie came as sharply as the dread. If he could talk with her for even a minute, things would be better.

Joel mastered his panic. The fourth hospital was a big one. He entered a tent which had its wide fly lifted to let in the thin breeze. There was just one man in sight; a large fellow bending over a plank desk, writing. Joel stepped closer, a mixture of eagerness and fright. The neatly tended hair, lighter than his own, the heavy shoulders—here was one man who could identify him. This was Doctor John Kenny, whose wounded arm he had bandaged in Mim's little upper room. Before he could speak, the doctor turned, and a broad smile of recognition lit up his strong face.

"Pender! So it *is* the Overhill Cherokees' medicine man." He was on his feet, offering a warm, strong hand. "I saw your name down there at the office, and just hoped it was the Joel Pender I knew, who fixed up my arm." He jerked back a sleeve and showed a scar. "Healed fine. That balsam salve's good but your sewing's bad. Look at those stitch scars."

There was so much friendliness about the doctor that Joel felt his misgivings eased. Kenny was explaining, "My orderly left with wounded; and I need a man because I must operate in minutes. The clerk showed me the names, and I picked you, hoping." His wide grin showed strong teeth. "Come on, we'll get ready for work. I'm in luck."

The doctor went on talking while they washed their hands well. He had served his hitch as an army surgeon, ending with his capture and time in Salisbury military prison. After the Talpo rescue, he had been mustered out and returned to Lancaster to resume civil practice. "All doctors marched to the sound of guns," he said soberly. "That's why I'm here with hundreds of civil practice men from all over the North; trying to put together what war has ripped apart. And you, Joel?"

The two faced each other for a moment. Kenny was the larger man, and older by ten years. His eyes, a deep blue, met Joel's gray ones frankly, studying the tan on the other's face, the unruly hair.

"I was in Talpo. Guerillas caught me, tried to put me in the Confederate army. Luck got me out of their clutches, and I was working my way home when this battle news reached me. A Sanitary Commission driver picked me up, and here I am."

Kenny jerked his heavy shoulders in the direction of the other tent. "Come on, Doc-to-be. Maybe you'll learn something. I'm supposed to be good." Joel was sure of that, despite Kenny's deprecating grin offered with his boast.

The young patient reminded Joel of the boy who had died in the church, the night of his arrival. He had suffered a deep shot wound in the left side, close to the heart. Kenny's fingers seemed like thinking things as they handled probes, forceps, and drains. Joel, handling the chloroform, watched in fascination until the surgeon finished, then flexed his tired fingers. "No more for tonight, friend. That was shaky business. I can use you, if you will. Tomorrow at seven, sharp."

Joel saw little of Puffenburger during the next two days, for operation after operation was the schedule in Kenny's tent. The evening of that second day, the surgeon had a message, then an announcement for his new helper. "I'm running up to Lancaster to see a critically ill patient; back in twenty-four to thirty-six hours. You're in charge, with Sergeant Bix to help. The Sanitary folks will help with the feeding."

Joel started to object, but Kenny had already turned away. Once alone in the big tent, with critically wounded men on every cot, panic came close to gripping him. Kenny had left written directions, but a slight slip meant life or death. Sergeant Bix helped carry out the exact letter of the instructions. Sometime after one o'clock in the morning, he clapped Joel on the shoulders. "Get some sleep on the Doc's cot." The sergeant gestured at the patients on the cots. "These are the lucky ones. Not many who were shot up like this, get care like the Doc and you've been giving them. Check 'em over in the morning."

Joel did not think he could sleep with the weight of responsibility upon him, but he dropped off promptly. He roused twice before morning and looked into the ward. The injured men were sleeping, Bix and the Sanitary women walking about quietly.

Kenny arrived ahead of time, looking drawn from lack of sleep; but he inspected things at once. "The men look good. Two more days and they can be moved to the base hospitals." He gestured, and spoke bitterly. "Half of those poor devils will carry a musket again."

The final day came. Soldiers were dismantling the hospital tent frames and floors after the canvas had been removed. In the evening when Joel and Puffenburger were finishing their supper, Sergeant Bix sent word that Doctor Kenny wished to see Joel before going home.

The doctor was quartered in a narrow story-and-a-half house directly across the street from where the field hospital had stood, and a fine-looking team hitched to a top buggy was tied up at the rail. Bix was standing by. "Doctor Kenny is packing, but go right in."

Kenny was in a bedroom and came out carrying a neatly strapped bag. "Take a seat, there's another bag to finish, then we'll talk." He was out in minutes, then straddled a chair, facing his visitor. "Forgive me if I talk fast, but there's an operation in my town tomorrow afternoon. Wish you could go along to help." Joel returned the pipe he had taken from his pocket earlier, wondering at the tenseness in Kenny's manner and voice. "First, I'm ten years older than you, friend. And I've practiced medicine and surgery a lot, which ages a man. My edge in years should carry weight with you."

Joel nodded, willing to go along with that. He respected and liked this man with the frank look in his deep blue eyes. "There was a hint, before I came down here, that you might turn up at Gettysburg because of your major interest; a doctor's business. At first, I was too busy to bother, then I found you. Later, I went back home, and now know your full story; why you left your home first, then Talpo and about the guerillas, plus this paymaster robbery."

Joel was getting up when Kenny's sharp gesture stopped him. "Men show quickly what they're good for; and I tell you the making of a fine doctor and surgeon is in your mind and those hands of yours. You have a sympathy for patients and a quickness to learn. When this war is over, every locality will have its broken and crippled ex-soldiers who will need medical care desperately. I say to you, Joel Pender, go home. Beg, borrow, or use Burley's ill-gotten money and get off to medical school for that third year. Then, come and join me in my practice. Don't squander your gifts hiding somewhere in the mountains."

Kenny took a long breath, jumped up, went to the door, and looked out. Satisfied that there were no listeners, he returned. "I'm risking the penalty of the law advising a man this way. Keep out of the draft which will put you in the army. Once in, that paymaster matter may catch up with you, and it could mean hanging. Or, what's almost worse, they may find out you can tie an artery and make a jackassed doctor out of you, finishing what rebel bullets started for some poor devils."

Joel's mind was racing. He wasn't contradicting Kenny or agreeing with him. There was only one person who could have given this earnest man his information; and he hadn't finished. "George Geis, in Talpo, may turn up that paymaster money. Major Colet of Intelligence will help him. He owes George help. What you took from Burley's cupboard is just some of his old loot." His lips closed grimly. "One more thing you must not forget. If you face arrest for the things that happened down Talpo way, or for draft evasion, get through to me—fast."

Both men rose, and this time Joel spoke. "Trudie Quinn."

Kenny nodded. "Yes, and the man who deserves and has her interest, ought to get out of himself all the timber will allow. She's in my town with friends. I telegraphed her that you were here and went up for the story. Anyway, it gave me a good chance to test you with my hospital. The girl's right, Joel, you do have the touch." He picked up his bags and turned from the doorway momentarily. "Don't fail either her or me. We'll be watching."

From outside came the sound of a buggy turning, then the clatter of hooves on the hard road. Joel was alone; and all he could think about, for the moment, was that final hillside camp and Trudie saying, ". . . better to be good friends . . ." Tonight, she wasn't much over fifty miles away, and a man in a hurry to talk with her and see her smile could get there in two days, perhaps a little less. He shook his head. She had urged him not to seek her out, and he realized again that the taint of his possible association with guerillas would bring danger to her. That was serious—military men hated those irregulars who rode by night, plundering, killing sentries, hiding during daylight hours. With them, the best thing to do when a guerilla was caught was hang him, then ask questions afterward.

Joel walked on, pulling his thoughts from Trudie to Kenny's advice. He was to go home then "beg, borrow, or—" A new idea came to him so suddenly that he stopped. When, down in Talpo, he had planned to go back to Hylersville, his reasons hadn't been very definite. He was homesick for the valleys, hills, and streams up there. Besides, it was the only place he knew to go.

Now, he saw something, a hard, sensible reason for getting back to the little town. After his parents' deaths, Squire Abel Wetwire had offered to sell the home and pay off the debts. The Squire was a good man with excellent business connections. Likely, there would be money left over; there could be enough for that final year in medical school. Joel was suddenly in a hurry and walked faster.

Most of the Sanitary people had left, but the loading dock area was still well lighted with lanterns. He stepped up on the platform and strode along, his steps sounding on the board floor. Abruptly, a big man in army blue, with sergeant stripes on his blouse sleeves, stepped out in front of him. He had been smoking a cigar and the aroma of tobacco was strong in the heavy, hot air. "Just a minute, young fellow. Guess you're in a hurry." Joel's throat went dry as the soldier continued. "Looking for a Joel Pender; man in the Provost's office wants him. I'm Sergeant Carter."

Maybe this was it, the way things moved when the army wanted a man, an easy casual manner that hid the iron hardness underneath. It would be possible to lunge forward and upset the sergeant, in spite of his side arm, but Joel knew the whole area almost swarmed with military police looking for skulkers and deserters. Jake Puffenburger, over there in his wagon, would help; but that would bring trouble on him, and the teamster had been a real friend.

"I'm Pender," he said. The soldier tried to talk as they walked along. Joel did not reply. It was one thing to be arrested, but a man didn't need to visit about it. The Provost office was a big shed, again lantern-lighted. The wide room was empty except for a man in shirt sleeves behind a littered table. "Mr. Agar, here's your Joel Pender."

The seated man fumbled in the paper litter and took out a sheet which Joel recognized as the roster Mrs. Tolfus had prepared. After a minute, he found the name and looked up. "Joel Pender, Hylersville, Pennsylvania, ten days, hospital assistant."

When he was answered with a nod, he lifted a hand and brushed long hair back over a pronounced bald spot. Then, from the table drawer, he counted out twenty dollars in silver and bank notes, and pushed the money across. "Sanitary Commission pays two dollars a day for volunteer helpers. Sign this receipt."

Joel signed with fingers which shook a bit; and was quite sure both men were smiling at him as he went out. Twenty minutes later, he shook Jake Puffenburger awake in his wagon bed. Relief had left him almost silly, and he was laughing and yelling. "Wake up, Jake. They paid me—twenty dollars!" He could just see the young teamster's face from the distant lantern light.

"Humph," the young German grunted disdainfully, "me they already did, but I gets a dollar each for the horses. Now, let's sleep. It gives a long drive, come morning." That was a good thing for a tired man to sleep on—a long drive in the morning, and it was north.

CHAPTER IX

PUFFENBURGER'S horses stepped out smartly. They had enjoyed a good rest and seemed to realize they were homeward bound. They two men sat on the high seat watching the country slip by. Even in a few days much of the former disorder had been set right; farms, houses, dooryards were coming back to normal. Puffenburger waved his whip. "Give the folks time, you won't know there was a battle in these parts. That's how it was down Antietam way."

Joel nodded. He was busy with his own thinking. Puffenburger was expansive; the horses didn't seem to be annoyed by his wide gestures with the whip. "Country like this is worth fighting for. But, once I went off to war, they'd read me out of the Church."

"Medical corps," Joel suggested. This time the whip flicked an imaginary fly off the near horse.

"I been asking round whilst I was in Gettysburg, Joel. Every regiment takes its own medical people. Mebbe it's somebody big in politics gets a place for a friend's boy so he'll be safe from bullets. If I went to somebody big, he'd just say, 'damned Dutch,' and that'd end it." He poked Joel's ribs with a far from gentle elbow. "Don't forget, it takes 'most as much spunk to say you won't fight on account of church things as to march all day and shoot a musket gun at somebody a quarter of a mile off."

Joel had to smile at the truth of that remark, but Jake's indirect reference to the draft was making him uneasy. The course Doctor Kenny had suggested could make a man as unpopular as any with religious scruples.

Jake turned from his own problem to that of his companion. "You could easy go as a doctor. They say lots of them surgeons in the army just got their trade working with another doctor."

Joel countered with real conviction. "Jake, so far my medical school work was mostly anatomy, that's the study of the body. The last year would be on symptoms of illness and medicine with some surgery thrown in. That third year—the others just lead up to it. I watched Doctor Kenny and maybe I could have handled his knife or probe. But I didn't know when or how deep to cut. You should have seen some of the messes of other doctors he had to fix up."

Puffenburger delivered himself of a considered opinion. "For me, I'd as lief have the powwow man as the regular doctor in our parts. Anyways, he ain't generally so drunk."

Joel had to laugh, and Jake joined with him. It was good to let go again after the grim horrors they had seen in the stricken town they had just left. But Puffenburger, who had once been laconic, went on talking, giving his companion practically no chance to reply, until they camped for the night in a grove of small oak trees a dozen miles from Harrisburg. Supper was over, pipes were lighted, the small fire had died to a few coals. Jake drew a long breath.

"Joel, I pretty near talked myself ragged. Mebbe I didn't want you to think much 'til I was ready." He leaned forward and his lightly bearded face was earnest. "You're a bothered man, been that right along. Last night one of the horses had me up; and I seen that sergeant wait for you, and you was scairt. You was both under the light; and you was figgering, 'til onct I was sure you'd cut and run. Afterward you come into the wagon and routed me out—" He stopped, smiled, and shook his head. "Nobody'd be that glad, just for twenty dollars."

The fire died lower, and Joel began to talk. He could trust Jacob Puffenburger, who was shrewd but entirely honest, after he had accepted a man. Joel's story took a good while, but it was finally all told, from the departure from Hylersville in bitterness to the final scene with Doctor Kenny. The only parts left out were Kenny's advice about the draft; and the ugly scene with Trudie in Burley's cabin when he cheapened the girl and himself.

Puffenburger scratched his bearded chin lightly. His next words were cryptic. "And it gives me yet another river." He saw Joel did not understand. "It's from an old camp meeting song. No matter how many troubles life gives, there's always another river to cross." He rose. "I think slow, Joel. Guerillas, house burning, money, it gives a lot to consider. Come morning, I might have something to say."

"Jake, you could get in trouble just hauling me around. Better drop me off before going into Harrisburg."

"Just like you had something ketching," the young teamster said derisively. "No, I want you to help me get up to Camp Curtin so I can get in the army as a teamster. If I don't carry a gun, the Church won't read me out. I hope. Afterward, you can go on home and get settled."

He didn't have much to say when morning came, except "Takes an older head, friend. I'm wishing you could talk with Grandpap up at Marysville." In Harrisburg, they reported at the Sanitary Commission headquarters, then put the team in a livery stable and spent the night in Puffenburger's comfortable room, which contained two beds.

In the morning, Joel prepared to head home. "I'll be going up past Camp Curtin, Jake. Go along and let's see what we can get for you."

The young teamster demurred. "Won't it be risky? Mebbe they might arrest you."

"Not likely. It'll take time for those folks down Talpo way to start a big search. Certainly nobody'd look for me in a recruiting office." He hoped that was true.

Jake gestured to the packet of old bills, "That'd send you off to school, Joel. You could go right down to Philadelphia."

"No. I thought about it, coming up here. It's dirty money. I just can't bring myself to use it. Maybe I will sometime . . ." He let the words trail away and finished making up the small blanket roll.

The lumbering north-bound horse car was empty, except for the two young men. Then at State Street an army captain, carrying his left arm in a black silk sling, got on and took a seat opposite instead of the many empty front ones. Joel glanced at the man several times, interested in the facial pallor which indicated he was not long out of a hospital. There was also a look of strain on the thin, smoothly shaven face. The officer's hurt could be more than just that arm.

Passengers both boarded and left the car during the next few blocks. One dignified gentleman with a full beard passed the officer and spoke. "Good morning, Captain Courser."

The soldier looked up, came close to a frown, and answered the greeting, and the bearded man walked to the back of the car. Joel imagined explaining his position to an officer like this man Courser. Jake commented in a low voice. "Not a friendly face, friend. Besides, his ears is too close to his head. A horse like that kicks."

Joel repressed a desire to laugh. Behind his sleepy manner, Puffenburger was a keen man, and his judgement was generally good. After a bit he did glance at the captain's ears, and they seemed all but pressed against the neatly barbered head.

The car stopped at the end of the line, just across a wide street from a railroad station marked in big letters CAMP CURTIN. The two friends got off and walked with other disembarked passengers toward the six-foot stockade of boards which surrounded a city of huge tents and wooden buildings. This was the gathering place and training ground for the great armies of Pennsylvania volunteers. The main entrance was wide, but it was guarded by two sentries whose bright bayonets glinted atop their muskets.

"Them knives on guns give me shivers," Puffenburger confided, as they came through the gates into a milling crowd in front of a row of low buildings, each marked RECRUITING OFFICE. The whole place was impressive because of its drab vastness. The enclosed portion with its tents and houses was only a part; beyond, on the flat land toward the Susquehanna, were long warehouses, and drilling fields on which men in uniform maneuvered. Armed sentries were in evidence, at tent street entrances, at each office, and a squad just inside the main gates. Joel turned in toward one of the offices. Jake took his small blanket roll from him. "Something in my hands helps when I'm nervous like. I'll carry this."

The big room was wide but shallow, with side doors opening to the other offices; and the man in charge was a young, pleasant-faced lieutenant, in back of a wide desk. The room was filled but not crowded, and most of the men were civilians. Joel saw the captain who had ridden up on the horse car, standing by a window. The lieutenant was speaking. "Yes, men, what can I do for you?"

"Information, sir," Joel said. "If a man with religious scruples about war enlists as a teamster, will it clear him with the draft? He's a good horseman, drove for the Sanitary Commission."

"Of course. The army's glad to get real horsemen. Have your man bring in his papers and we'll sign him. Real teamsters are scarce. Personally, I'd sooner face rebel muskets than a mule's heels—" The young lieutenant did not get a chance to finish. The captain had crossed the room.

"Lieutenant Waring, I'm Courser, temporarily with the Provost Office. I want that man." The long forefinger of his free hand was leveled like a pistol at Joel's trousers, given him by Doctor Kenny at Gettysburg. "You're wearing army property. What are you, a deserter, or just a thief of army equipment?"

Joel, expecting a much more serious charge, stared at his accuser not knowing, for the moment, whether to be amused or angry at the rawness of the officer's tone. A number of the bystanders moved forward. Joel turned from the desk and took a full step toward Courser, who snapped, "Speak up, where did you get those pants?"

"Gettysburg, Sanitary Commission stores."

"Damned unlikely story," the captain sneered, turning to the door sentries. "Take this man in."

Joel's lost his temper. He remembered the lantern light in those tents beside the battle field, the skilled hands of the surgeons, the patience of the wounded. He took another step, which placed him in arm's reach of his tormenter. "A man died in these pants. I worked in them. Where in hell did a man like you earn the right to wear your insignia and call himself a soldier instead of the bully you are?" Joel realized almost instantly that his reckless impulse had carried him too far. He was in a poor position to stand any sort of investigation. If only he had bridled his temper.

The guards were pushing through the knot of men who had crowded forward to hear better. Puffenburger got close enough to Joel to whisper. "Railroad station, out back." Then, apparently in a panic, he tried to get out of the crowded room. In his awkwardness, he got into everyone's way. He bumped into Captain Courser's good shoulder, throwing him off balance, and tripped one of the soldiers so he sprawled on the floor. Next, mumbling contritely, he attempted to get the man up, and upset a second man with the stock of the discomfited soldier's musket.

In all that confusion, it wasn't hard for Joel to slip through the door and mingle with the crowd. Holding to a casual walk, he reached the station, walked through it to the outhouse, and feeling sure he was not observed, plunged into a thicket of wild plum trees and blackberry brambles. The growth was on a bank; fifty yards away was a road. He sat on a rock, thoroughly angry; first at Captain Courser, and then at himself. Puffenburger had saved him, and he was concerned about what could happen to the young teamster. The likelihood was that he would be arrested. But for a man who hated war, the young German had shown a remarkable adroitness in creating a situation to his liking; and might get away. After a while, he felt better.

Less than a half-hour passed before he saw a man on the road, and recognized Jake, who came running through the brush at his friend's whistle. He wasn't even out of breath, and he was chuckling.

"Jake, how did you get away with it?"

Puffenburger slapped a lean thigh, delightedly. "Dutch, again. I made my apologies in the dialect, and that captain with the queer ears is likely still swearing at my clumsiness. The crowd helped. One man said he seen a man run off towards the tents; and our Provost man is hunting the whole army through after a fellow that wears wrong pants." They laughed.

A wagon rumbled along the road; a train stopped at the station then went on toward Harrisburg. Puffenburger said, "I been figgering. Even with the right pants, you wouldn't be safe clost to any army. Soldier folks is fussy." He stopped Joel's reply with a lifted hand. "Whilst I promist to think through your story, I didn't get any place. Let's get up to Marysville and see Grandpap. He'll listen good, maybe say something that'll help."

"Jake, my story's getting spilled around too much. You know it, Doctor Kenny does—"

"This won't be risky, Joel. Grandpap's old and smart. He'll figger something, even if it ain't more'n a good supper." Joel was under too heavy an obligation to the young teamster to put up more than a halting argument. Late in the afternoon, after a hard walk up along the great broad river, the two young men came into a town that was half village and half farm. Broad stone steps led up to Grandpap Puffenburger's white house; and the old man, a gray-haired giant with broad, stooped shoulders, welcomed them.

"Jakey don't come often. Now he brings a friend, and is double welcome. Come in, boys. It gives early supper and a dried apple pie. Maggie comes in soon." The big living room into which they were ushered was friendly with the late sun. Presently, without feeling he had been urged, Joel went through his story; and was not interrupted except when it was told that a Union paymaster had been robbed. "That iss bad. Money talks big."

Jake had something to add when it was finished. "Grandpap, Joel didn't tell you. He's had two years studying to be a doctor. Doctor Kenny, of Lancaster, was at Gettysburg, and says he'll make a good one."

The old man's face puckered, but out of it came a smile. "For a minute I didn't recollect. You mean the big man with the sharp blue eyes. Iss a wonderful doctor even if he does sometimes swear. Now, Joel, boy, tell me more about your folks."

He told briefly of his father's work up there in the hills, and how he had always been sorry for his own limited training. Sending his son to college was a natural thing, even if it had impoverished him. Joel wondered why he should tell this old man all his troubles.

"That's all. Father and I took a trip down to Talpo when I was small. When my folks died, I went there and worked with George Geis."

The old German rose and crossed to the west window to look out a while, then came back to his chair, which protested his weight with a creak. "This Talpo now. It's a funny world. When I lived down Antietam way on the farm, a man, half-Indian, called Geis, stopped a couple of times as he went through. I always wanted to see his mountains. He was a wonderful man. If he's down there, he will all unravel."

Joel could not share the old man's confidence, but he did not think this either the place or the time for a contradiction. Jake was fidgeting, occasionally rubbing his thin beard. "My grandson wiggles himself. Jake wants for me to talk like a gypsy fortune teller, and don't remember I am chust an old man with a wonderful appetite and, sometimes, sore feet. Yes, you did not get the paymaster's money; it would be ten times so much. And I am glad your knife did not kill this man, Burley." He flexed his fingers.

"This I would do like you planned. Go home, mebbe there is money coming to you. Get some work; don't spend Burley's money—yet. You been away a long time; could be the army's lost track of you for the draft."

He smiled paternally at the still impatient Jake. "When a man don't know what to do, is always best to do nothing. When Jacob was a little codger, he was by the south pasture when the bull got loose. I seen the red bugger go for the boy and there was no time for his Grandpap to do a thing, not even pray. Six feet off the boy, the bull stopped, snorted two times and walked off." He tapped his visitor's knee. "Mebbe the bull you see coming ain't too sure of hisself, either. Looks like he'd have ketched up by now, if he was real devilish."

Maggie interrupted everything with her impressive entrance. She was big, motherly, and noisy. First, she hugged Jake, then patted Joel's head; and departed for her kitchen, leaving behind promises that were well kept in half an hour when they sat down to a table strong with meats, sweet with pies and cakes, bitter with herb tea. Grandpap finished three cups of the medicinal tasting brew. Maggie did not eat with the men, contenting herself with walking back and forth from stove to table, keeping all dishes well filled.

Less than an hour later, after giving these hospitable people his promise to visit them again, Joel boarded a train at a flag station a quarter of a mile from the Puffenburger home. He was wearing a pair of Jake's drop front pants. Jake's honest face was worried. "Grandpap wasn't too clear, but setting still ain't such a bad idea. Mind you, don't get clost to a recruiter."

Joel grinned and slapped his friend's shoulders. "All I worry about is getting caught in a wind with these pants."

He dozed as the train chugged northward through the night.

CHAPTER X

WHEN LIGHT CAME, he watched the scenery. The rails followed the Susquehanna river, tree-shaded along its banks except for narrow boat landings. Two arks, cabins set on flat boats and used by raftsmen, were moored in one spot. Next spring, these clumsy crafts would be far up the mighty Susquehanna to meet the logs coming out of the woods on the spring freshet. He turned to look up the river, his eyes following the new line of railroad reaching up between the tumbled mountains. Joel had known nostalgia before, but his bitterness had lessened it during the early months in Talpo. Afterward, there had been work, and Trudie.

He tried to light his pipe and found that his hands were shaking. This was the country he loved, not the pennyroyal hills of the south. Here were the savage winters, the bursting springs, the droughts of summer and the great pines on a hundred mountains. His father and mother had been content with the place they had found. They had planned for him to take over. Now he was coming back, a hunted man. Likely there wouldn't be too much time until, wherever he lodged in Hylersville, there would be the tramp of horses outside, and a man in blue rapping at the door.

Joel let his eyes rove for a few moments. The rough hills they called Peter's Steps were across the river, and the tiny village of Rafttown huddled under the bluff. He wasn't going to admit it, but Joel felt as if he was saying goodbye. Back in Hylersville, there wouldn't be any chance for nostalgia; he'd have to be on his toes every minute.

The railroad station was deserted. There was the sour odor of tobacco spittle from the sawdust-filled boxes set about, a ticking of a telegraph instrument, and a tired calendar on the wall which tried its faded best to advertise BARKER'S LINIMENT, Best for Man or Beast.

He found the stagecoach station and took the stage to Colton. About noon, he knew he must take shank's mare the rest of the way. He began walking and took the winding road up the ridge. Halfway down the north slope he stopped and drank from the roadside water trough. Ready to start on, the memory of another place, where spring water flowed into a deep wooden container with a soft plashing, came to him sharply. Most of that first night at the Heitel farm he had lain, licking dry lips and listening to the sound of water.

He did not hurry. It was like the time his mother had sent him to his father, who was spending a few days with Indian John, fishing. Then, there had been a sore tooth. He knew he had to go but loafed along the creek road as much as he could. Today, he ate late huckleberries from roadside bushes, and found some blackberries in dark shaded places. The afternoon was almost spent when the narrow road passed the first open field, and he stopped for a look over the valley.

The village with its widely spaced houses, most of them half-hidden by trees, lay directly before him, a quarter mile to the north. Down there, the two valley roads met to form the town's single street. Far over the creek, along the ridge, there were some other houses set like watch boxes to guard the narrowing end of the valley.

But Joel's main interest was down the sloping road where, a full mile below the last house the mountains, kept wide apart so many miles by the valley, drew together to listen with friendly interest to the brawl of the creek between their shoulders. He could picture what those wooded mountains screened—long stretches of quiet water, then rapids where trout were less cautious about a fly. And two miles more along the road, a steep lane would take off to a tiny farm Indian John used to call High Valley, where the once-tilled fields were being taken over by encroaching jack pines.

Every boy in Hylersville knew the place. There they learned to shoot with bows and arrows, cooked over open fires, and listened to the old Indian's stories. John was gone now these five years, but his taught skills lived on with men who could hunt and fish expertly and care for themselves in the woods.

Joel rose awkwardly from his hard seat on a rock. There was no home to which he could go, except the farm which Indian John had left to him, but there was a boarding house in the town where he could live while his small store of money lasted. There was no purpose in putting things off. Standing at full height, he stretched his lean body, flexed his big hands, and started.

The sound of his steps on the village board walk annoyed him, but there was no one in sight, either up or down street, until he reached the tie rail in front of the two-story building which flaunted a crudely lettered sign.

Thaddeus Crisp
GENERAL MERCHANDISE
Produce bought and sold.

Crisp had painted and lettered that advertisement of his store himself, and his pride in his own workmanship would not allow a change in letter or line, even though the whole was sadly off balance. Uncle Thad, as he was known by the whole town, was sometimes a man of opinion.

This would be the storekeeper's supper time. Joel pushed open the door and a bell tinkled somewhere in the rear of the long room. There were no customers, and goods were neatly piled on the counters and racked on broad, heavy lumber shelves. Barrels of pickles, crackers, and oil stood in their accustomed places. In two years, nothing appeared to have changed, except that a new, brightly painted coffee grinder was set on a counter so that no one entering the store could fail to notice it.

A minute passed, then the shuffle of soft soled shoes, and the spare, neat figure of Thaddeus Crisp appeared from the back of the room. Joel could not remember when this man had not appeared old and feeble, but he'd always been spry. His coat was neatly buttoned and there was a black string tie at the collar of his gray shirt. His thinning hair was carefully brushed across a bald spot. The firm mouth was set in an apology, and Crisp was wiping his hands on a not-too-clean towel.

"Sorry, this was my supper—" His eyes widened in recognition of his tall, smiling visitor, and he sprang forward to grasp Joel's jacket. "Joel! Home at last. Son, I'd give up looking for you, months past."

Joel felt a smarting in the backs of his eyes and a lump in his throat. To cover his confusion, he hugged his friend and patted the narrow shoulders with a big hand. "Uncle Thad, you old dollar grabber, you've got a new coffee mill."

Crisp turned toward the red machine and touched a wheel pridefully. His voice was low and confidential. "Joel, four months, and I already have eight dollars profit with that thing. Folks buy coffee just to see it run." He waved toward the back of the store. "Have you et? Come and eat your supper with me. There hain't no customers, this time of day. We can ketch up."

Joel enjoyed the big helpings of bread and good butter, cheese and pickles. Afterward, Crisp poured excellent coffee, the beans freshly ground in the new machine. "Good, mighty good, Uncle Thad."

The merchant nodded and gestured with his hand. "Fresh grinding makes cheap coffee equal to the best." He poured another cup; and opened up. "We was looking for you. Still and all, I wonder that you came back, because things ain't good in Hylersville. The war's got work dried up here. Wetwire's running just one mill, farms is going to seed. Nine boys from our parts is in the war, mostly in the Seventh Cavalry."

"Nine," Joel whispered, trying to think just who those young men would be; and he realized that Crisp was watching him closely.

"That don't count four substitutes. Harry Sholes at the hotel hired the first, Ben Murth, that swamper of his'n, to go in his place. Harry claims he paid three hundred dollars to Ben's pap, who's been middling drunk ever since." He sat down and picked up his cup. "And, they're after the married boys now."

Joel set down his cup. The taste of coffee in his mouth had become bitter. He had not thought of the war's power to reach out into communities like this, hundreds of miles from the southern battlefields, and lay its young men dead or broken on alien ground.

Crisp finished his coffee. "They tell that deserters have been slipping back, some round here. I ain't saying any of 'em is our boys—but folks buy more groceries than they can well use." He waved the empty coffee cup. "Don't ask me where they get all the money. Them that pays, that is. I've got a lot out on tick."

"Uncle Thad," Joel interrupted the older man's talking and thinking, "you said you were expecting me. What did you mean?"

"Mebbe it was just a manner of speaking, son. War's got folks stirred up real mean. Lately, some said you'd run off south and wouldn't be back. Me'n Squire Wetwire claimed you'd turn up. Doc Pender's boy ain't a rebel. But you did walk off without an I, yes, or no—"

"This is for you, and maybe the Squire, no matter what the town thinks. I did go south for a while, but I haven't fired a shot in this war. I was in that Cherokee town with friends of my father. Uncle Thad, I'm not sold on killing people; I want to be a doctor and heal them. The past ten days or so I've been in the Gettysburg field hospitals, helping put the broken boys together again." Joel rose and paced up and down for a few minutes.

"But I don't know enough about using a scalpel or a probe. I came back to Hylersville. Maybe some way I can earn the money to finish at Jefferson. Listen, only God knows how many crippled men there'll be when the shooting stops. I saw it at Gettysburg—eyes, legs, arms, bodies ripped open until you could see the insides of a man. Uncle Thad, war is terrible."

Thaddeus Crisp was nodding, his eyes bright. Joel hurried on. "When I put a probe into a wounded man, after a bullet, I must know just where it's going, so it doesn't touch a nerve, or rupture another blood vessel. And, when I close the wound, I must know it's clean, no chance for deep festering that'll kill."

He stopped for sheer want of breath, and Crisp said, "That's what I told this Colet about you, week or so back. That you wanted to be a doctor since you could walk."

"Colet." Joel felt a stiffening run along his shoulders to the back of his neck, and his leg muscles tensed. Colet, friend of George Geis, government agent. Crisp saw the question forming on the young man's grim mouth and tried to explain.

"Oh, he was passing through. He knowed Indian John, and I guess he knew your father. Asked kinda offhand what become of the doctor's boy. Picked up some medicines, niter and Epsom salts, and the like." Crisp was trying hard to sound casual, but Joel knew the garrulous old man would've spilled anything he knew. Why was Colet here? He could not have had time to talk to George Geis. Joel was uneasy.

Crisp nattered on, "That Colet sure knows horses—did you ever see that mare he rides? He used to stop by here sometimes before the war." He cleared his throat. "Anyhow, there's a new boarding house in town. Mrs. Lisa Milburn, young widow-woman. She sets a good table. You can get a room there if you need to. Remember, the folks may be standoffish for a spell. But, after they see you round and hear you talk, things'll look different. This town was as proud of you as your folks was, when you went off to learn doctoring."

Taking his leave of Crisp, Joel walked over to the boarding house. Mrs. Milburn was well dressed and surprisingly attractive. Probably still in her early thirties, her heavy brown hair was drawn back loosely to frame a full face with loose, expressive lips and brown eyes that found it easy to smile. "Welcome, Mr. Pender. I've heard of your father and the good work he did in these parts." Businesslike, she quoted him her rates and accepted his payment, then smiled suddenly. Are you hungry? Come."

She led the way along a hall which opened into an immaculate kitchen dominated by a huge cast iron range and white work tables; and when Joel had taken the chair she indicated, served him a huge wedge of pumpkin pie and a glass of milk. Joel devoured every crumb. "Wonderful pie, Mrs. Milburn, best I ever ate."

She looked at him coyly. "Did you find southern cooking good?"

Joel resented her attempt to pry. "I didn't see much of it. But did you know, they make pies out of sweet potatoes?"

Refusing a second piece of pie, Joel was shown to a pleasant room at the head of the stairs. Mrs. Milburn was a lovely woman; her throat was smoothly turned, and she moved and walked with a grace that exploited her fine figure. There was even a touch of light perfume on her. She chatted casually, showing him a second door in his room that opened to a small balcony at the side of the house. Now and then she made a comment, like the one about southern cooking, and he knew she was fishing for information. She was clever. He'd have to watch his tongue around her.

That night, Joel lay awake, pondering. He had surprised himself with how intensely he wanted to be a doctor; and realized that his experience with Doctor Kenny had sharpened that desire. Throughout his professional life, Joel's father had deplored his own lack of formal training, and had tried to pass on to his son his respect for what real medical schools could give a man. He hoped he could find a way to finish his training. Hearing that Colet had been through, and asked about him, worried Joel. Sleep was a long time coming.

CHAPTER XI

JOEL WAS UP the next morning to a hearty breakfast, then went out to see how the town had changed. He stopped by the General Store. Uncle Thad was his usual talkative self, rambling on about the town and the war. His sharp eyes searched Joel, then, too casually, he asked, "At Gettysburg, son, what doctor did you help?"

Joel half-smiled, the old man's suspicion was so apparent. "Checking up on me, friend. Mostly, I was with Doctor Kenny, of Lancaster. You could write him a letter, any time." He saw that he had hurt the old merchant's feelings. "Oh, don't mind me, Uncle Thad. I just wanted to come home for a while. No place feels like home anymore, though."

"It has changed a mite around here. War'll do that. New folks in town—that Milburn woman that runs the boarding house, now, she's not all she could be. Keeps a clean house, and feeds her boarders well, from what I hear. But there's too much comin' and goin' at her back door, nights, for a woman who sings in the church choir.

"Then there's Harry Sholes—preaching Union but running to the Point Haven Copperhead meetings. And the gossips—" The old man had the grace to look ashamed for a moment, then talked on. "War brings out the gossips, meaner 'n ever. Folks natcherly like to talk, but they're ugly these days. The Good Book says, 'where the carcass is, there will the eagles be gathered together.' Some of these is more like vultures, and they don't wait for yeh to be dead, neither!"

Joel saw that his old friend was really bothered. He didn't want to pry. Turning the conversation back to himself, he said, "Listen, Uncle

Thad, I didn't get near the war until after Gettysburg was fought. When I left, bitter that the folks had gone into debt to send me to school, I went to the Cherokees. Part of the time I taught school. Evenings and spare time, I worked with the sick. Southern mountain people are as staunchly Union as folks here, maybe more. We did help some escaped war prisoners and slaves get away.

Well, I was a Northerner. When it looked as if the Confederate recruiting men'd pick me up, I started home—and stopped in Gettysburg." He could see relief on the thin face of his listener.

"Well, it's good you come home, boy. Don't mind them gossips, they ought to be doin' somethin' more useful. Soon enough they'll find someone else to carry on about. Now, you ought to get on over to see Squire Wetwire. He handled all your folks' affairs, you know. Sold up the house, and I believe there's some money left. There'd be more, but people kinda forgot they owed your pa, after he was dead. Shame on them." Uncle Thad looked both mournful and angry, like a hen whose eggs had just been taken. Joel just smiled and laid one big hand on the old man's shoulder as he left.

The single-roomed building which served Squire Wetwire as an office was unlocked, but the Squire wasn't in. He owned the big, two-story house next door, but was usually in his office whenever he was in town. Joel stood looking around. The desk top was littered with papers, the rows of calfbound books on the shelves undisturbed, windows robbed of transparency by heavy layers of dust, the floor unswept. The room hadn't changed since he had last entered it two years ago. Although the Squire grudgingly had a woman come in to clean the house, she was not allowed in his office. Joel glanced at the house, but it looked closed-up and empty. The Squire must be out of town today.

Back again at the boarding house, he informed his landlady that he would not return for the noon meal, since he was going out to his farm in the Narrows.

"That's a pity. I made fresh bread. I make my own jam, too, you know. What kind of jam did you get in the South?" Joel ignored this sally. "Oh, yes, the ladies of the church have a bake sale on in the old schoolhouse. It would be good of you to stop, since you will pass it on your way. There are some excellent cooks in this town. I'll let you guess what I contributed." She stood smiling as he left, positioned in a ray of sunlight, showing her figure to best advantage.

The old church had an annex building behind it. No selling would have taken place in the actual church, but this room was used for meetings and socials, sewing circles and the like. Joel was sorry the moment he entered the door. There were no men in the place, and six women by his quick count. One was coming forward, and there was no mistaking Mrs. Adson Fenemore, the most efficient news gatherer and trouble maker in the western end of the valley. Her dress looked like Uncle Thad's expensive calico and it took yards of the goods to properly drape her plump person.

"Why," she cried, "here comes Doctor Pender's boy. Jason, isn't it?"

"No, ma'am," Joel corrected, giving her proffered hand a limp shake, "it's Joel, Mrs. Fenemore. I am out for a walk, and Mrs. Milburn told me about your sale. Do I smell doughnuts?"

"Girls, we've a customer," she called. "It's Doctor Pender's boy, Jason, and he's hungry for doughnuts." Two of the ladies removed fly-clothes from the wares, but Mrs. Fenemore prattled on. "Yes, you went off to school after your parents passed on, didn't you, Jason?"

Joel was fussed. The big woman was all but barring his way to the table. She reeked of perfume, and she was hot on the trail of any news.

"No, ma'am, not to school. I went south to friends." He stopped, knowing that he had given the news gatherer something to go on. The other women were staring and obviously listening.

"Oh, I see, you were in the army like so many of our poor boys. Tell us, where were you, and what happened? We are so hungry for news." For the moment Joel disregarded his questioner, and stepped around her to the table.

"A dozen of those good doughnuts, please." The lady put the crullers into a paper sack, and Joel paid her. " No, Mrs. Fenemore, I wasn't in the army. I worked with an old doctor in the mountains. Then I came to Gettysburg and worked with Doctor Kenny of Lancaster until the field hospitals were evacuated. Now I should be going."

Outside, he was tempted to return to the room and tell Mrs. Fenemore to attend to her own damned business. He knew that his slip was dangerous. "Mind you, he was down south . . . not in the army . . . what was he up to . . . he ain't a doctor." That was the way the Fenemore woman would work.

The thought of Trudie came in a rush. She would have known what to say; or would have stopped him in time. *A man in trouble ought to have dodging practice,* he thought. *That, or somebody smart standing by.* His eyes narrowed. Mrs. Milburn had been coy in her curiosity, Mrs. Fenemore blunt. Uncle Thad had been a little ashamed. In their opinions, a man his age should have been in uniform, and they were suspicious of him.

He walked on. When he passed through the first defile of the mountains, following the creek, he had for the first time a real feeling of being at home. These hills were familiar from his childhood. In spring, the dark hollows would be the home of the first trilliums, and leeks would grow in odorous profusion. Now in summer, on all the hilltops goldenrod, known as mountain tea, invited late summer gatherers.

A narrow lane turned off sharply to the right up a steep grade to the level bench of High Valley farm. Grass grew in its center, and there were no wheel tracks. Joel came up slowly, feeling a rise of excitement. There appeared to be no changes; jack pines still crowded their way into once tilled fields; the chestnut logs of the cabin carried the neutral gray patina painted by the weather. One of the friendliest features of the building was the front porch, with its steps made of short sections of split logs, each adzed almost as smoothly as planed surfaces.

Indian John had had little interest in farming, other than to grow a little corn, some herbs, and a garden plot of tobacco so strong nobody else fancied it. He used wild herbs to make medicines, and Joel knew his father had used many of them.

Joel sat down on the porch steps and filled his pipe. Smoking and taking in the familiar view, he tried the doughnuts, which proved excellent. The road was screened out of sight by scrub timber, but he could catch glimpses of the distant creek and the hills beyond. Later, after a drink from the spring, he entered the cabin through the rear door, which was on the latch. Indian John had always welcomed anyone's use of the place, even when he was not there.

From the kitchen, equipped with a table and a woodburning cookstove, he could see the small alcove which served as a sleeping place.

Beyond that the living room that occupied most of the interior. Joel walked forward, surveying what he saw with pleasure. There was the field stone fireplace. John's small mattock, used for digging roots, his firestick, a rusted knife, and several bright quartz stones, still lay undisturbed on the wild cherry mantle. Wall shelves showed the backs of familiar books.

Dusty bundles of herbs, which made him think of George Geis, hung from the bed room ceiling; and he touched them with a fingertip as John used to make him do, as he identified them. Joel spoke the names aloud, and their uses. "Yarrow for a headache and a sick stomach, boneset for fever, lobelia as an emetic—throw-up medicine, John had said—horehound for a cold. Poke weed for red lips and a love potion."

He grinned at the old familiar game, and crossed to the books. They had belonged to his father; all were well thumbed, particularly the five heavy volumes of Tweedie's *Library of Practical Medicine*. Joel remembered they had been a gift to the doctor from his wife, who had saved the money secretly over a long period. He set the last of the five back on the shelf. Abruptly, his big hands knotted, something stirring in him of the bitterness at his parents' sacrifice that had come to him before he left home.

Joel did not return to Hylersville that night. The spell of the cabin and memories of Indian John were too strong. There were fish hooks and a small lump of rock salt in the kitchen, and bait from under the bark of a pine log back of the stable. In addition, he had late blackberries and high bush huckleberries. He fared so well that he did not return to his room in the Milburn house until the evening of the second day. As he mounted the stairs, the kitchen door opened a crack, and Joel knew his landlady was observing.

The room was comfortable and spotlessly clean. The little blanket roll lay on the bed where he had tossed it. The years in Talpo, where a man's property was inviolate, had made him careless. Inside that small roll of dark blue blanket was calamity. He should have taken it along. His fingers shook as he fumbled with the cord bindings and opened it.

Everything seemed to be as he had left it, his few articles of clothing, his razor and brush. He rubbed his chin; a shave was one item he could not manage at High Valley. The packet of old bills was wrapped in a piece of newspaper and appeared to be undisturbed. Finally, he picked up both revolvers, the light thirty-six caliber which young Tom Ellender had praised, and the heavier weapon taken from Lee Harne, with his initials scratched on the grip. Abruptly, Joel's hands stiffened. Both revolvers had been fully loaded, ready to fire, but now all the percussion caps had been removed from the cylinder loads of the weapons. Someone had searched his belongings—that could be curiosity, but whoever had handled those revolvers had something else in mind. For the first time he could remember, Joel fastened his door with the back of a chair set under the knob. The lighter weapon, recapped, was under his pillow.

When he stepped outside his room to go down to breakfast next morning, the maid-of-all-work was in the hallway busy with a dusting cloth. Joel greeted her, but knew it was unlikely she'd handled his things. Mary was not very smart, and painfully shy. There were three boarders at table when he took his place. The introductions were short. Miss Lulu Manner was a spinster of uncertain age and very upright bearing. Mrs. Fred Baskin, a widow, had a suspicious air about her portly person. The third, John Rider, a young man, dapperly dressed, was cultivating a new and small mustache. Of the three, he tried to make conversation, but it was a rather strained and pretty quiet meal.

Joel stopped by the store. Uncle Thad was eager to hear about his trip to High Valley, and tell him all the happenings of the past two days. He also related that Squire Wetwire had returned and would be in the office about ten o'clock. Joel was early, but Wetwire was already behind his desk.

The Squire wasn't tall but carried his heavy shoulders so erectly that he appeared to be taller. His heavy, smoothly shaven face and big nose were crisscrossed with red lines like those of an extremely heavy drinker. Joel knew though, as did the whole town, that the Squire never touched liquor. At sight of his visitor, his tired eyes lightened, and his thick voice held welcome.

"Well, I'll be damned. Here is our prodigal back. Sit down, Joel, let's talk." After a warm handshake, he cleared a chair by dumping the books and papers on the floor, then settled into his own hickory rocker. "Talk, Joel, tell me everything, where you've been, how you are. I'm just back, but the town gossips have new bait. They shot off about you whilst you were gone, now you can take your own part."

Joel fought back his resentment. He explained that he had lived with the Cherokees, until his presence as a Northerner might have caused embarrassment to his hosts. He explained his stay in Gettysburg. "So, I'm back, Squire. I want to go on and finish medical school, soon's I get the money together."

"You have no money?" Wetwire inquired.

Joel colored, more embarrassed than irritated. "No, less than twenty dollars."

The Squire frowned and leaned forward; his heavy face was grim. "That can be had. Your Father's account books are in that satchel." He indicated a big oilcloth valise. "By and large, the people of this locality owe him over a thousand dollars, by my reckoning. You can start collecting. Stop any man or woman on the street, and you can be damn sure they owed your father."

It was Joel's turn to frown. He hadn't even thought of those bills. He remembered his mother pleading with his father, "Most of those folks can afford to pay better than we, David." He couldn't imagine asking any of them for their old debts.

Wetwire continued, "That, and I have a plan. You've already had twice the medical training your father had, and he was a wonderful physician. We'll fix up an office, hang out a shingle, and I'll take care of the State Medical Board." He tapped the desk. "Another thing, I'll see the draft board keeps its fingers off you."

Joel was shaking his head before Wetwire was half through. "No, Squire. I've just worked with a man who knew medicine and surgery. I'm not doctoring until I know what I'm doing. There's no sense giving a sick man calomel if you don't know what's the matter with him."

Squire Wetwire shrugged his heavy shoulders. "Keep it in mind. Life is uncertain at best. You're close mouthed like all the Penders. Your story needs a lot of filling in, but it's your own damn affair.

"Let's talk business. Your father's books, medicines, and such, are out at High Valley. The account books and a few small things are in that valise." He unlocked a desk drawer, reached into the back and fiddled around. Joel heard a grating sound and click, and assumed there was a hidden compartment in the back of the drawer.

Wetwire brought out an envelope. Pulling papers and a small sheaf of currency from it, he said, "I sold the house and settled all the bills, including the mortgage. There's two hundred eighty dollars left. Here's the money; check over the bills and sign a receipt for my files. The house came to—"

Joel stopped the Squire with a gesture. "Never mind the bills, I'm sure they're right, and thanks for managing. Maybe one day I can forgive myself for the sacrifices my folks made for me."

Wetwire's rugged face broke into one of his rare smiles. "Son, you'll never understand until you've a boy of your own, what a privilege it is to provide for one. Mine died when he was fourteen, my wife a year later." He blew his red nose noisily.

"I'll talk with Thad, maybe between us we can dig up some work. Only one of my mills is running; things are a bit slow. You could teach school, couldn't you?"

"Yes," Joel answered, once again off his guard. "I taught a while with the Cherokees."

"We'll see, then. You're at the boarding house, I hear?" Wetwire picked up some papers, his mind obviously moving on. Joel thanked him, took the big heavy valise, and went out. Once in his room, he was delighted to find clothing in the valise; his best suit, still neatly pressed after its long stay in the bag, shirts, socks, underclothing. Some thoughtful, careful person must have packed these things after the Pender funeral. Joel wished he could thank whoever it was.

He had been sitting there some minutes, turning over in his mind what Squire Wetwire had told him. When he had gone away to school, the future was a thing crowded with promise. A man could do so much, conquer so many horizons. He didn't know it then, but he did now. When the small Indian boy, Aluns, had come with his word that the guerillas were in Talpo, all that had come to a dead end.

Abruptly, disgusted with himself for all this moody introspection, he got up to put the valise in the closet when there was a light rap at his door. At his word it opened, and his landlady entered. She extended a key to him. "Mr. Pender, you may want a little more privacy. Our people sometimes pass through your room to get on the balcony. With this, you can lock the door, and you will not be disturbed."

Joel eyes were hard with suspicion. "Thank you," he said, and put the key on the dresser scarf.

Mrs. Milburn made to leave, then turned at the door to ask, "You do not seem to like our little family. Has something happened?" When she was not answered, a flush of irritation showed on her neck and cheek. Joel stepped forward and held the door open for her. "I'm sure," she said slowly, an edge to her usually pleasant voice, "if you were more friendly, people would like you better, and be kinder."

"Yes," he answered evenly, "you may be right, madam. Thank you again for the key—and for thinking I might need it."

She very nearly flounced toward the stairway, leaving behind her that hint of perfume, the thing which did not go well with the landlady of a boarding house in the village of Hylersville. Joel closed the door thoughtfully; Lisa Milburn was a mighty attractive woman, and he felt her power to attract strongly. Yet, each time he had tried to meet her open friendliness, the hint of warning way back in his mind made itself heard faintly.

Someone in this house had tried to disarm him, someone knew a dangerous part of his secret, evidence that could mean prison. Abruptly, he wheeled toward the door and had it half open. Lisa Milburn had brought him a key. Was that her way of telling him she knew he had something to hide—the story back of a packet of used bank notes and two loaded revolvers? Something more than ordinary curiosity moved the woman.

He shook his head and closed the door again, a wry smile about his lips. If she had opened his blanket roll, being just ordinarily curious, she had found money. Perhaps she had removed the caps from the weapons to safeguard her establishment from an apparently dangerous young man.

CHAPTER XII

THE DAYS BEGAN to drag in a monotonous sameness. Joel had been away from the town most of four years. Young persons of his age had grown beyond his knowledge, and he was sensing the coldness of the older people. Those who recognized him gave only a limp handshake and scant words of welcome home. Each time he went into the post office or one of the stores where there were knots of people, conversation stopped.

One day near the bridge over the little brook which crossed main street, Joel spoke to a small boy who reminded him strongly of Aluns, down in Talpo. The lad stared back without answering until a sharp call came from a nearby house. "Henry!"

The urchin ran off, throwing backward glances at the tall man standing there, swearing under his breath. Joel knew that his father had probably brought that boy, and possibly his parents, into the world. Wryly, he wondered if they had a bill standing in that old account book down at High Valley farm.

"Damn it," he complained to Crisp, "folks act as if I'd just got out of jail, or had a touch of smallpox! Worst is, I see them look out from the sides of their windows when I pass. Hylersville's a town of squinting windows."

"That's clost to right, squinting windows," Crisp replied. The town's full of folks who'd risk one eye to see a murder or a fire. Guess they figger if they ain't caught looking, they're all right."

Joel filled in his days walking, going back and forth to High Valley, climbing the nearby hills, spending little time in the boarding house.

Now he carried the packet of bills with him, as well as the lighter of the two revolvers. When out at the little farm he counted the Burley money a dozen times. He was tempted. With it, and what Wetwire had given him from the sale of his parents' home, there was plenty to finance both finishing medical school and getting through the lean months when beginning a practice.

The quiet of the small cabin was suddenly oppressive, and as he stirred, the revolver bumped against the chair, so he took it out and laid the weapon on the floor. Bullets weren't likely to solve his predicament, however much the search of his room had frightened him. Somehow, without his own planning, he appeared to have come to a dead end.

"And it gives yet another river." Jake Puffenburger's remark seemed so real it was almost like a whisper in the cabin. The young Dutchman had hummed the song as he drove. "There's one more river, one more river for to cross." Well, the army could be another river; Joel should get into it, and accept whatever fortune turned up. If he was shot, that would yet be just another of Jake's rivers.

That evening he played checkers with Uncle Thad again. The storekeeper won all but one game. After the last game, he leaned back to talk. "How old are you boy? The way you act it's clost to a hundred, with troubles every year."

"Twenty-three, almost. Why do you want to know?"

"No reason in pertickler. I figger young folks don't look far enough ahead. That's what ails your checker game. The king row looks so far off you don't see it could be just a couple or three jumps when you're headed right. And, mind, if you watch the other player and keep your face straight when you're setting a trap, it's shorter."

"Like my coming home, Uncle Thad?"

Crisp's wrinkled face became as bland and expressionless as a washed dish, and his answer was in a tone of mild surprise. "What's checkers and your coming home got to do with each other?"

Joel frowned and tapped the table with a forefinger. "Don't fool with me. I don't like riddles, get what you've on your chest out in the open. It can't be worse than the treatment Hylersville's giving me."

Crisp eased his legs, cramped from sitting still so long. "No need to get mad. The town's not Hylersville no more. Boys is off to war, deserters in the brush, and folks is split up. Nobody comes out in the open, like you say. You're a young feller just walking about, and folks think you'll bear watching. They know you been down South and you're godsent to idee-starved gossips. Mebbe they'll make out you're a rebel general! They'd give angel Gabriel hisself hell, if he come and blowed his horn."

Joel picked up his hat from the floor alongside of his chair, and the two men walked out in the dimly lighted store. Joel let his big fingers touch the smooth flywheel of the new coffee grinder. There was a lump in his throat. Something of the strong lines in his face relaxed. He mumbled, "Good night, Uncle Thad."

He was near the front door when Crisp called, "I forgot, the Squire wants to see both of us, tomorrow about ten o'clock."

Abel Wetwire enjoyed a reputation for being on time or a bit ahead of it and was waiting in his cluttered office when Joel and Crisp came in, next morning. The two older men looked solemnly at Joel, and the Squire did the talking. "Thad and I've heard a lot of stories piling up about you, son. Folks have you guilty of almost everything from being a Copperhead to the man that stole Stonewall Jackson's prayer book. Some claim you're just two jumps from the sheriff."

Joel eased his length into a chair while the remark was running along, and he was becoming angry. The town's attitude was irritating enough, but it was worse being catechized by old friends of his father. Wetwire's eyes appeared to draw back into the caves made by his heavy eyebrows. "You been up and down in the Narrows, you see anything of deserters or any other suspicious thing?"

That question put things in a different light, and he tried to think. He shook his head. "Nothing about the cabin but two or three rabbits and a deer."

Wetwire opened his mouth, but Joel stopped him. "Except one thing. Somebody must have used the stable in the last month or so. The horse wore a small shoe. Of course that doesn't mean anything; Indian John used to say a man who refused to share his roof didn't deserve one."

The Squire was nodding a trifle impatiently. "Joel, you ain't been mixed up in anything serious, something you didn't tell us—a woman, money, or something?"

There it was again, something wrong, money—he thought of his bank roll and the revolvers and wondered what these men would say or think if he told his complete story. Serious—kidnapping, murder, house burning, money from a murdered paymaster—he doubted if anybody could believe the whole incredulous story. He kept his face straight and his voice controlled.

"Money—they're gossiping about that? Mrs. Daines was in the lower store when I went in for the tobacco Uncle Thad doesn't keep. I took out that rolls of bills you gave me, Squire, and she was watching me so close, her eyes popped."

"That old harridan," Wetwire scoffed, "nobody believes her. I'm concerned about Tom Hawks. Sober, he's all right; drunk he's mean, and he's been threatening you. What's Tom got against you?"

Joel frowned, trying to remember. "Haven't seen Tom in years. He does have an old grudge, some trouble between him and Dad. Tom's a few years older than I am. Well, I guess he couldn't take it out on Dad and picked me. We fought it out on the school ground one night. Neither licked the other. Dad patched me up, but was angry because I wouldn't tell him what had happened."

Wetwire picked up a pencil and threw it down, then spoke to Crisp. "Dammit, that's the way it goes every time I talk to him. It's either damn meanness or that Pender close-mouthed stuff. Likely he's been off in a Sunday School class—Mrs. Daines sees a few bills; Tom Hawks has an old grudge." He swung his attention immediately to Joel. "Maybe some of these stories could be true. You didn't spend two years without doing something, not with your temper, your brains, and those big fists. Could be, things got hot, and you came home. Dammit, I'm glad." His grin was sincere, but his eyes were on his visitor's hands. He pointed a pencil. "Whatever happened, if anybody went through those paws of yours, he would likely remember."

Joel shook his head irritably. "All I wanted, after I got over my bitterness at the folks making all that sacrifice to send me to school, was to earn enough to finish. It looks like the only way I've got, to get away from this squinting at me from around window blinds, is to join the army. Getting shot at can't be worse than being talked about."

"Getting shot lasts a man longer." Wetwire hurried on. "Not the army just yet, son. I guess I deviled you today to see how much fight is left in you. Thad and I are old men, and we figured you would blow up any minute. You want money. I'll get you a job, gossip or no gossip. Only keep your mouth shut. I'll do the talking."

Crisp hadn't said a dozen words. He made his excuses and left. A few minutes later, Joel and Wetwire walked down the street and turned into a neat front yard. Reuben Starr, who owned the lower store and two big farms, lived here. The Squire rapped on the front door.

Everything about the man who answered the door was sober and correct, from the trimming of his short beard to his neatly buttoned coat and carefully blacked boots. "Good morning, gentlemen," he welcomed, "come in and take chairs. Perhaps I can do something for you."

Wetwire was apparently unimpressed by the cordiality, as the three seated themselves in an over furnished living room. "Yes, Reuben, I'm sure you can help." The Squire spoke decisively. "Our school runs through August and the fall months before cold weather starts. It's been open part of a month, and John Darcy, the teacher, is already off on one of his drunks."

The Squire put the last statement brutally. Starr's eyebrows lifted and he glanced almost furtively at the door which shut away the other parts of the house. He spoke piously. "Yes, let's say John is indisposed, and he'll be down Point Haven way the rest of the week. Miss Talbot handles the smallest children, but we cannot ask her to take them all. John's students are not having lessons currently."

Wetwire leaned forward. "That's why we're here. I've found a teacher—this is Joel, Doc Pender's son. He's been in college, and he will take over the grammar school." Starr looked up at the ceiling, then again toward the closed door, but Wetwire didn't give him a chance to reply. "You, as the leading director, will be glad the children won't lose time—like they do every year. You pay John twenty-eight dollars a month. Pender, being a college man, will have to get a little more, say thirty dollars, and he'll start work tomorrow."

He got up, and Starr came out of his chair like a man half asleep. Joel moved toward the door, tempted to smile at the odd scene. "Another thing, Reuben. Suppose you pay Pender his first month's salary now. And take the time to get Darcy well."

It did look for a moment as if Starr would rebel at this final bit of high-handedness, but it was evident to Joel that here, for some reason, was a trapped man. Starr got the money from a tall secretary in the corner and laid the bills into the Squire's hand. Wetwire patted the director's stiff back. "Always a pleasure to do business with you, Reuben. You see the point so quick."

The two men walked some distance up the street without speaking. Joel was too dumbfounded by the whole occurrence, and the Squire was indulging in deep chuckles well down his throat. It was certainly evident that he had actually enjoyed baiting and crowding Reuben Starr. They stopped in front of Wetwire's office.

"John Darcy is Mrs. Starr's brother. Reuben has his reasons to jump when I whistle the tune. Believe me, Joel, I don't do such things often." Abruptly, he was savage. "Don't feel sorry for Reuben Starr. Men like that must know their masters, or the country wouldn't be safe. He'd scalp his own grandmother if there was a market for white hair." He ran a hand over his face, then said, "Go on over to the schoolhouse and acquaint yourself with things."

Joel cleared his throat, feeling he should have the luxury of one question. "Thank you, Squire. I'll be ready Monday morning—but won't this town raise hell when the prodigal starts teaching its children?"

"I shouldn't wonder," Wetwire agreed dryly, then turned and went into his office.

Joel did not like the way the job was obtained for him, but he was desperate with inaction and the money in his pocket felt good. He had no doubt about his ability to teach. He had done some tutoring at the medical school; and taught the children in Talpo. He thought of Trudie—here was one step, a crossing of one little river, which she would approve. There was no way of telling her, because he didn't even know where she was.

He had walked on, with no thought of direction, and found himself nearly to the bridge over the big creek, with Harry Sholes' hotel on his left. There were no shades on the lobby windows. When Joel, on impulse, stepped closer, he saw the huge bulk of the innkeeper seated in a low-backed armchair. Sholes was talking to a man who was trying to light a pipe, and waving his fat hands to illustrate something important. Finally, the smoker looked up, and Joel had no difficulty recognizing Tom Hawks, grown older of course. He appeared to be listening to Sholes, but not offering much in the way of opinion.

Joel turned to the school property. There were two buildings on the same lot. Mary Talbot, with whom he had gone to common school, taught the lower grades. She looked out her door when she saw him enter the unlocked building and gave him the briefest of nods. His mind went back to what he remembered of Mary Talbot. She was a careful, conscientious girl, doing the right thing, saying the right word. It would shock her to be working with a man of whom the town so openly disapproved.

The school room was in surprisingly good order, books in place, the floor clean, kindling and neatly piled firewood by the sheet iron stove for chilly days, a wooden blackboard newly painted. John Darcy might be a drunkard, but he was a good housekeeper; tomorrow, Joel knew, he would find out how well the man taught.

Excited by the prospect, he did not wish to sit down at the Milburn table and talk about commonplace things. He despised guarding, as he always had to do, against some statement which could be twisted or misconstrued. Rider always tried to get him to volunteer something about the war or its generals. The one thing the clerk never mentioned was the draft; his clever way of emphasizing what his suspicions must be concerning Joel. He was the sort of man who would stand by half-smiling when the debacle came, and his satisfaction would be *I always thought there was something the matter. Maybe it's good his parents aren't here to see. Doctor Pender was a fine man.* There were times when Joel wanted to get up and jam the young man's face deep down into a bowl of Mrs. Milburn's excellent chicken soup.

He walked back to High Valley, and had crackers and cheese and quiet for a while, but didn't stay. He returned to the boarding house pretty late. Hylersville retired early; the street was dark except for a light in Wetwire's office.

The front door of the boarding house was never locked. Joel let himself in. The ceiling light in the upstairs hallway shed a dim radiance down the stairway. It was Joel's habit to walk quietly, and the carpet helped. When he reached the top, he could see that the hall wasn't empty. To one side was a wide cupboard, and Mrs. Milburn had its door open, doing something to the contents. Joel was startled at what he saw over her trim shoulder, for the closet was crammed with men's clothing hanging from the walls and from hooks on traverse rods. She was so engrossed that she did not notice his presence until he noisily unlocked his own door. She wheeled, fury in her eyes. "You," she snapped, "don't ever sneak up on me like that." The closet door went shut with a slam, the woman's bosom rose and fell, while Joel tried to apologize.

"I didn't sneak, Mrs. Milburn, just came upstairs."

The landlady had herself under control as quickly as she had lost her temper. "I was foolish to be scared, but I did think I was alone. I was trying to plan some way to clean out that awful closet."

"Don't be afraid of me, Mrs. Milburn."

Her look became decidedly arch. "I'm not too sure, Joel Pender. Something tells me you could be a ladies' man." With that, she went down the stairs, the ring of keys in her hand clinking.

Joel went on into his own room and leaned against the door lintel for a few moments, thinking. There was real invitation, at times, in the landlady's smile and the way she carried the warm richness of her body. When he went to bed, he locked his door, afraid he might have a late visitor.

CHAPTER XIII

IT TOOK JOEL only a few days to learn that John Darcy must have been a fine teacher, with work planned ahead. Discipline was excellent, and apparently not obtained through whippings. The children at first appeared to be a little afraid of the tall, gaunt teacher who had taken charge so abruptly. Next, they were curious, doubtless because of gossip in their homes. Then they began to cooperate. Joel was delighted.

He began to feel relaxed for the first time in months. His new work kept him too busy to think about his own personal troubles, and time passed rapidly. Since he had begun to be regular about meals, living in the Milburn house was more friendly. John Rider's probing discussions of the war gave way to questions about the school and the pupils. Joel liked to talk about them. Overall, these youngsters were quicker in responses than the Indian children had been, and much better in expressing themselves. Joel knew it was because they spoke his language. Some of the Cherokee children had been very bright but had struggled with English.

However, the town did not relax its attitude. If anything, people were colder and more withdrawn. Joel realized that any outward protest against his teaching must have been stifled by Squire Wetwire's influence.

A month passed. Mary Talbot, the other teacher, had kept aloof. On a Thursday morning, she paid a surprise visit at recess time. With her was a small girl whose face showed the streaks of dried tears. "Bessie Breon," Mary explained. "Her sore tooth is loose, and her mother said I should pull it, but I can't."

Joel took the child out into the sunshine and carefully explored with a big finger. "Bessie, it won't hurt but a little, like a pinch. We'll make something to help." He put white oak cambium bark, from his small stash of herbs in his desk, and hot water from the kettle on the stove, into a cup. He prepared a mild effusion. "It'll numb the gums a little," he told Mary Talbot and Bessie, "and check the bleeding, if there is any."

Bessie cooperated willingly. For once, she was the center of the stage. Most of the other children had gathered round to watch. She filled her small mouth with the sharp oak tea, held it for a few moments, then spat it out. Afterward, there was a linen string, one big hand which held her head still, and a smart pull. The final touch for the child was being presented with the offending tooth. After that, scarcely a recess passed without some small patient reporting. Joel pulled teeth, removed specks from eyes, bandaged small cuts and knee burns.

One night Joel was playing checkers with Uncle Thad. The store-keeper said casually, "Well, son, you still don't know about that king row. I've beat you half a dozen times." He poked his visitor with a thin forefinger. "Folks say you're a good teacher, but some of 'em still favors running you out of town. Hiley Tufts, the barber, claims there ain't a kid in Hylersville that'll let anybody pull milk teeth but you."

Twice, Joel went to homes, to inquire about children absent because of illness. Each time, he was admitted to the house, saw the patient, but was chilled by the parental reception.

One afternoon, after school had been dismissed, Joel was sitting at his desk, looking out of the window, his mind on Trudie. In Talpo, she had visited the school often, helping with the smaller children and usually remaining after closing so the two of them could talk.

"Always act as though I were near you." Her phrase was running through his mind. He tried to keep the picture of Trudie before him. Lately, the sheer physical attraction of Mrs. Milburn was strong; and her attitude, now that he was about the house more, hinted that she would not repel any advance he might make. He shifted in his chair; there was the time two days ago when she had brushed past him in the hallway, letting her body touch him lightly. Today, after the other boarders had left, she bent forward over his shoulder to pour coffee.

There was more to warn him about the landlady with the come-hither ways. There was the search of his blanket roll, the removal of the caps

from the revolvers. If she had been the one who pried into his belongings, she was the one person in Hylersville who had something to back
up her suspicion. Joel got up impatiently. Too much thinking usually
ended in confusion.

There was a short rap at the door, and a man entered. He came forward with a smile about his deeply set dark eyes and a hand outthrust. The
newcomer matched Joel's height but was heavier through the shoulders,
and his unruly hair was rusty black. "I'm Jaynes, the local minister, come
to make my school visit. Forgive me for being so tardy about pastoral
duties. I had business out of town, and have just returned." Uncle Thad
had told Joel of the Reverend Samuel Jaynes. He had come to Hylersville
something more than a year ago, invalided out of the army where he'd
been a chaplain.

They chatted about the weather, the town, school, and textbooks,
and Joel found himself liking this man. Jaynes did most of the talking.
"We do this rather well, Pender. We've talked a full twenty minutes with-
out saying anything important. Actually, we've been sizing each other up.
Mayhap I'm looking for the horns and tail the town assumes you wear.
And you may be concerned about my halo, and the means of grace."
Both laughed.

"Actually, I have come to offer a fellow sufferer sympathy. Local gossips loosened my scalp close to two years past, and I was appalled at the
minor iniquities of which I was supposedly guilty. However, when a man
ceases to be talked about, either good or bad, he's dead."

The minister straightened his shoulders and took a coin from his
pocket. "Bessie Breon's father Jacob came to me, claimed he didn't want
to call on you himself, but that he pays his debts."

Joel took the heavy copper coin and examined it closely. On its face
was a woman wearing a liberty cap, some stars, and the date, 1852. On
the reverse was a wreath, inside which were the words ONE CENT. He
shook his head. "I don't remember ever seeing Breon, but he's trying
something that hasn't a thing to do with his daughter's tooth. That penny is the Copperhead coin. The Sons of Liberty, as they sometimes call
themselves, cut that LIBERTY head out, and wear it on lapels to identify
themselves to others of the same ilk. Breon's either a Copperhead or is

trying to insult me as being one. You ought to know which, since he's likely one of your flock."

The minister rose. "I don't know, to be honest. Come to church Sunday, meet Breon. Try to be charitable. Could be he sent you a penny, any penny he happened to have. If you get out in the community more, they'll see you don't have horns. Let them see who you are." He nodded and left.

Joel had liked the minister at first, but that Copperhead business irritated him, especially since the minister had his doubts. Instead of going to church, Joel left for High Valley on Friday evening.

As he walked, he thought about the southern sympathizers. Introductions to friends always went with the display of that offending bit of copper. The term Copperhead came from a penny, not the snake which already had a bad reputation for viciousness. Although the Knights of the Golden Circle, as they were sometimes called, had a reputation for viciousness too. Suddenly he wondered if Jaynes had been testing him. What if the man's secret sympathies were with the Copperheads? Joel couldn't believe it, but he wouldn't completely trust the man until he was sure.

At High Valley, Joel went to bed early and fell asleep listening to a whippoorwill and the monotonous crickets. It was still dark, in the early hours of the morning, when a loud thumping on the back door roused him. He took time to fumble for a sulphur match and to light the lamp, then opened the door to the sharp chill. A roughly dressed man, whose face showed days of going without a shave, said roughly "Mister, git your things on. There's a man hurt. We brought him part ways. Now, you'll have to git to him."

Joel ran his fingers through tumbled hair and started toward his bedroom. "I'm not a doctor, just a medical—" An all too familiar click made him whirl round. He was looking into the muzzle of a revolver.

"Stop talkin', I just ain't foolin'."

Five minutes later, partially dressed and carrying his father's small emergency case, Joel was walking ahead of his captor, following the old path which ran from High Valley back into the timber country toward the now abandoned Forbes lumbering camps.

It was getting lighter rapidly. The man with the gun was apparently a stranger to the country, missing the faint path several times. After a half-hour's going, he stopped to take his bearings. Joel turned clumsily, apparently caught his toe in a root, and bumped into his captor, half upsetting him. His big hand clamped down over the man's fingers and weapon. "Sonny," he said sarcastically, "you're no damn good with a gun. March ahead of me for a while, take me to this wounded man."

There was no protest. Another mile, and the messenger led the way into a small open glade. A clumsily built fire smoldered and a blanket-swathed figure lay on a pile of brush. Another man, this one tall and thin, stepped from behind a tree. "You took yer time, Casner. Dan's dead."

Joel knelt and drew down the blanket. The gray, drawn features told their story. He pulled aside the mass of bloody cloth to look at the wound. "I probably couldn't have saved him anyway. He was hit bad. Life just poured out of him."

The thin man's hand rested on his revolver butt. "Casner, cover him."

Joel had seen too much of guerillas to make any mistakes. The thin man made had made two. First, he hadn't noticed that his partner had been disarmed. Second, he was looking at the bloody body, not at Joel, who brought his weapon up. His voice snapped. "Get over there and drop the gun." The thin man's mouth opened in surprised dismay. "Which one of you killed him?" Both took a step forward in protest, and Joel cocked his revolver. "Talk, and make it fast, or I go to the constable."

Joel did not know why he had given the men an alternative; but he saw a number of things. All three men were younger than he had thought at first, and none of them were from Hylersville or the Valley. Also, they were plainly horrified at being accused of murder.

"No, mister," the tall man protested, "we didn't kill him. I'm Mort Brown from New York State, and he's Fred Casner. It's my brother, Dan, there. We're deserters, that's the worst about us. We never kilt anybody. They shot after us when we tried to get away, and Dan got hit."

It took time. Both Brown and Casner talked, taking turns, and Joel heard a story he would not have believed, except for the earnestness of these men. All three had been in General Milroy's army, which Lee's advance toward Gettysburg had scattered over parts of three states. They had been approached by a smooth-talking sutler. In exchange for whatever cash they'd saved, plus their muskets and uniforms, each had been furnished with civilian clothes and sent north through the mountains.

Finally, they had come to the Forbes lumber camp, which Joel recognized by the description. There was another smooth-talking man in the camp, together with about a dozen deserters. He had advanced the idea that the three young men re-enlist in Pennsylvania, picking up the bounties for doing it, then desert again. Casner and the two Browns had secretly talked it over and had tried to get away. That's when the shooting had started.

Joel had listened carefully. There was some excuse for desertions, but these men had held him at the point of a weapon. He gestured toward the dead man. "All right, bury him, then start running. Sooner or later the provosts'll get you." He could feel them staring after him as he walked away.

The peace was gone from High Valley. The deserters had brought home, hard, the threat which hangs over hunted men; and the chief part of that was not knowing when the ax would fall or who would wield it. He had little appetite for his noon meal. Early in the afternoon Joel was dawdling over one of his father's medical books, when the second knock of the day came on the back door. He opened it, sure who his visitors would be. He let them in and gestured at chairs.

"Mister, you scairt us about this running and about how a provost'd get us in the end." Casner leaned forward. "Man like you wouldn't know what it feels like to be traveling and watching all the time. You get all scairt inside. There's next to nobody you can trust. Mort and me is giving ourselves up. Mebbe, seeing you started it, you'd be telling us where to go."

Joel rose, walked to the window, and looked out and down over the hill. Through trees, the stream flashed in the sunlight. He wondered grimly what these battered, hard-looking men would think if they knew his story.

"Follow this main road north to the forks, then east to the county seat. Hunt the sheriff, who'll put you in touch with army folks. Take your revolvers, they're government property. Make up a good story about your uniforms and muskets." They were all standing. Joel frowned and fumbled in his pocket. "Likely you've no money. Here." He gave them each a silver dollar and divided his scanty stock of provisions. He went with his unwelcome visitors to point out the road.

Brown said, "Mister, we're obliged. Uh, we heard at that camp there was a man in these parts that managed things for folks like us, deserters. He fixed up bounties and kinda managed this part of—" He stopped, apparently arrested by the look on Joel's face. "No, mister, I didn't think you was him. You look honest. Just thought you might know somethin'."

He watched them go, down the narrow tree lined lane, two shabby figures going on to shake hands with trouble. Self-righteous, Joel told himself that these boys had brought their own worries on themselves. His problem had been forced upon him, by Shad Burley and his men. But he was still uneasy.

* * *

Back in town, Joel went to the store. Uncle Thad was willing to play checkers for a full two hours; Joel, as usual, was no match for him. Finally, the storekeeper put the pieces in their box. "You're just not a player, son. Half the time your mind's not on the game at all, and it's not too strong when it is.

"By the by, young Henry Meany is home on furlough from the Seventh Cavalry. Heard your buxom landlady you was hopin' to give a dinner for him." The old man looked up over the tops of his spectacles. "The Seventh has been in east Kentucky and Tennessee chasing guerillas and raising sort of Union hell in those parts. Henry's full of stories, his company was in an Indian village."

Uncle Thad was blueprinting his thinking, and it wasn't hard to follow. The Milburn dinner could mean anything, or nothing. It was generally known in Hylersville, by now, that Joel had spent time with the Cherokees in the South. Henry Meany had visited an Indian village. The dinner guests would listen.

Joel made no comment on the dinner. His pipe was drawing first rate. Uncle Thad had started to whistle soundlessly through his teeth as he replaced the wooden discs more carefully in the paste board box.

"Are all those deserters you talked about, soon after I came back, from around here?" Joel was sorry he had put the question when he saw the shocked look on his friend's thin features, and shrugged his shoulders to indicate the query was just casual. "You wouldn't have any way of knowing, of course. Only, if there are strangers in our hills and this country harbors them, who's the boss?"

It was plain that this question was even worse. Crisp's fingers fumbled then he picked up the checker board and put it away. "How would I know, like you said? Abel Wetwire's the big man round here, but it wouldn't be him. Sheriff Paul Randy's the political boss in these parts, the county, I mean."

Joel got up and found his hat. "Oh, never mind, Uncle Thad, I was just talking. The town's changed. Seems like I'm just dirt, to be peddled round by the women so their men will cold shoulder me. Gossiping in the street and squinting around the curtains."

Crisp recovered his usual aplomb but, after a moment, asked a question sharply. "Son, are you in real trouble somewheres?"

Joel half-smiled. He knew the old man was worrying. Next to his father, he loved Thaddeus Crisp. "When wasn't I in trouble, Uncle Thad? Barton's watermelons, fighting with Tom Hawks, putting water in Taby's kerosene—"

He wasn't allowed to finish; the storekeeper had a proposition. "I got five hundred dollars that ain't working. Take it and get off to school. With your house money, that'd give you a year."

Joel felt his throat stiffen and patted his friend's shoulders. "Thanks. Thanks a lot, Uncle Thad. Maybe I'll take that offer one of these days. But give me time. I like this school work."

At the boarding house, Mrs. Milburn met Joel in the hallway. "Come out in the kitchen and visit with me while I polish silver. I have to talk with you." She served him a piece of her excellent pie and a glass of milk. While he ate, she worked with spoons, taking up one, breathing on it, then using fine sand, very carefully, to bring out the polish. Casually, she told him about the dinner for Henry Meany. "Next Tuesday evening, you will come, won't you, Joel?" He nodded reluctantly.

"I'm worried about you, Joel Pender. Your being so close-mouthed doesn't help your friends."

He pushed aside the partly eaten pie and the glass, set his elbows on the table, and used the landlady's first name. "All right, Lisa. Thanks for your interest. What has your gossip circle cooked up now?"

She picked up another spoon, laid it down. "Everything. You've been down south with the war going on; maybe you're a spy. They say you have money and spend it helping deserters in the woods. Others are just as sure you're Union, looking for these same deserters."

Joel's long forefinger went out, touched her rounded arm, and he all-but whispered, "They're right, Lisa. I'm a southern spy trying to get the secret of your pumpkin pie for Jeff Davis. He's got a bad stomach, you know."

He heard her foot tap in exasperation, under the table. "Don't joke, it's serious and I'm worried."

Joel pulled out his wallet and showed the money Wetwire had given him. "That's what's left from my parents' home, Mrs. Milburn. I came back to earn enough to go on with medicine. You gossips wouldn't understand that. If you're worried about your board bill, the school wages are ample to pay."

Instead of being angry, she hung her head, fussed with the cleaning cloth, and her next statement surprised him. "Then, they say you're running with women, that awful Mrs. Docket, for one."

He realized that this woman with her soft brown hair and the smooth voice was playing a game, that this intimacy, her mock concern were all used so he would make a careless statement or grow confidential. He got up, fumbling in his trousers pocket. "Tell your ladies Mrs. Docket didn't charge me anything. I pulled her left molar, and she paid me fifty cents." He tossed the half dollar on the table. "Wages of sin, Lisa. Take it for the pie, the milk, and the news. Down country, though, you can sometimes get two whole pies for a quarter. And you'll never have to earn money as Belle Docket is supposed to do, for you can get to the city and get wages for your play acting."

He was out the door before the woman understood fully, and it was closed when the piece of silver she had been polishing jingled the panels. For the second time, Lisa Milburn was thoroughly angry.

CHAPTER XIV

ON MONDAY AFTERNOON, Joel's relations with his fellow teacher, Mary Talbot, came close to a real rupture. School was over and he came out of his building just as Mary appeared. They were going the same way, so he walked with her. Joel was still upset from his encounter with the deserters, and with Uncle Thad's perturbation about the questions Joel had asked him. He did not have much to say.

The girl was plainly uneasy and looked relieved when they came to her home. There was a neat picket fence about the Talbot lawn, and he opened the gate for Mary. She stepped through and paused irresolutely. "Don't worry," he assured her with some sarcasm, "I'm not coming in with you."

She stood for a moment or two, pushing the unlatched gate back and forth before offering a lame apology. "It's my father, Joel, he doesn't—"

He took the gate from her, pulled it shut until the latch clicked into place. "No need to explain, a fine girl mustn't let herself get involved socially with the town's leper. The gossips are too anxious to get a fresh crow to pick."

The bitterness in his voice seemed to hurt the girl, for her eyes showed a touch of tears and there was something genuine in her sympathy. "I'm really sorry, Joel, my father—"

He interrupted again, refusing to be mollified. "By the way, Mary, tell your father I looked through Dad's old account books. He pulled a tooth for him, three, four years ago. The charge was fifty cents, and it's never been paid."

Joel thought he felt better for as much as two blocks, before realizing his action in shaming this girl had been mighty cheap. Mary Talbot was a fine person, who meant to be kind. She was good looking in a wholesome way, and there was a touch of Trudie about her manner. Tuesday morning, a child from the other school building brought him an envelope. It contained a fifty-cent piece.

Joel was grimly ready for the supper that evening, and came down from his room shortly before six o'clock to meet the guests. The maid came in from the kitchen and whispered in her mistress' ear. Mrs. Milburn frowned, hesitated a moment. "Mr. Pender, Mary says a boy came to tell you, Mr. Crisp's sick and wants you."

Joel excused himself. Five minutes later, he entered the store through an unlocked door, passed through the dark store, and went up the steps to Crisp's bedroom. Uncle Thad, wrapped in a worn and faded robe, was sprawled in a deep chair. "Belly ache," he muttered, "throwed up twice."

The old man's pulse was normal, and he obediently put out his tongue for an inspection. Joel went into the kitchen. Over the sink was a tiny cabinet, and there he found the soda he wanted and mixed a strong dose of it. Replacing the box, he saw two things. One was a small bottle marked ipecac. The other was an iron teaspoon with a damp bowl.

The storekeeper took his medicine dutifully and Joel sat down beside him. When the soda took effect and Crisp belched loudly, he started to talk quietly. "Uncle Thad, it's funny about plants. Some kinds are found all over the world, and they've got different uses. Take the madders, depends where they grow, some places they're coffee, some just bedstraw, medicine in others. Our madder is a medicine. But take too much, and it'll turn you inside out—I mean the medicine made of the plant. We call it ipecac." Crisp sat a trifle straighter, and Joel grinned. "You old faker, half a teaspoonful of that stuff was your sick spell."

The old man covered his mouth with his hand and belched loudly while Joel continued. "You got me out of that dinner, Uncle Thad. Why?"

"Son," Thad's voice was speculative, "I just wonder what Lisa Milburn's got against you. It ain't that you chase her, she'd like that, for she hain't had a new boyfriend for quite a spell. But, she had things set up. Sister Fenemore to report to the public, Meany to talk, Reverend Jaynes to make things respectable." Joel jumped up. Crisp pointed a bony fore-finger at him. "Just for once, really listen to me. I figger they had you trapped, thought they'd make you talk. The women'd peddle the dirt, the men might work up to fireworks. Let Lisa Milburn finish her party. 'Thout you, all they have to chew on is vittles."

There wasn't much point in returning to the supper. Crisp had done a childish thing, but it had worked. The old man settled back, evidently ex-hausted by the wracking of his self-imposed illness. After a half-hour, Joel drew a thin blanket over the bony shoulders of the sleeper and turned the lamp low. Then he went downstairs and stepped outside. A dark figure crossed the wide street from the Milburn house into the field of the moonlight. It was Jaynes. "Mr. Crisp, Pender, he is better?"

"Yes. Stomach upset." Joel stopped there for a moment and added thoughtfully, "Perhaps it's dread of old age, he feels sick and gets scared."

"Yet it is the young man who is dying these days. The old cling on to the last of their thin days," Jaynes said philosophically and a bit cynically. "Come, Pender, walk me home, I've had a surfeit of excellent food and muddy gossip."

They walked along, each guarding against too heavy a step on the board walks which would disturb the sleeping stillness of the town. At the small bridge Jaynes stopped, and both men leaned on the railing, listening to the rattle of the water below them. "Pender," Jaynes said abruptly, "the town's given you a pretty rough time. Guess the prodigal has too many older brothers."

"And sisters," Joel said, "you ate supper with some of them."

Jaynes chuckled. "Friend, it was something. Those women pumped Henry Meany dry in the end. He's a nice, well-meaning boy, but he almost forgot his Bessie in telling about war, guerillas, Indians, moun-tains, robberies, and how the Seventh Cavalry rides forth like George of England to slay dragons. Crisp's illness was almost opportune for you, my friend."

"Why?" Joel demanded and Jaynes made a statement instead of an answer.

"When I came here some time back, I boarded with our hostess of the evening. She does nothing without a reason. Tonight, young Meany was a pretense. It gave them an excuse to grill you, thinking you trapped by gentility and the obligation to your hostess." Jaynes looked thoughtfully at Joel, who shook his head.

"They can't trap me that easily, friend. I know when to keep my own counsel. At times, I'd like to tell them all, and give them what-for, for their meanness and suspicion. But I know better."

Jaynes' hand came down on Joel's shoulder, shook him lightly. "You know something of the Bible. Many still speak of your mother's faith. Likely you know the passage, 'To everything there is a season, and a time for every purpose—'"

It was Joel's turn to quote, and he picked a grim portion of the pronouncement, "A time to cast away stones, and a time to gather stones together."

Jaynes shook him again almost affectionately. "Excellent, few persons quote that portion. But I was thinking of another verse. 'A time to rend and a time to sew; a time to keep silence and a time to speak.' That time will surely come, my troubled friend. Let's hope it doesn't come too late." With no other word, Jaynes walked off down the street.

So, Thaddeus Crisp's nervousness was noted by others, Joel thought. John Darcy was a good teacher, and a man like that didn't become a drunkard overnight. Back in the hills was an unmarked grave of a man cut down by a bullet. Hylersville, where the valley lost itself in the town streets, had lived from the grain, meat, and timber of a rich country. It had been warm and friendly. It had changed to a furtive place where women peered out at the side of window blinds when a stranger went by.

Joel, weary with what had happened and the talk of the evening, fell asleep quickly and knew nothing of the eight roughly dressed men who entered the village shortly after midnight. While two of their number patrolled, two of them stopped at each store, and the remaining couple knocked at the back door of the boarding house. Within a half-hour the men left town, leaving money behind at each place visited. Each carried a considerable load until they came to a waiting pack horse on a path which ran back into the hills.

* * *

In two weeks it would be Halloween, and the school children were excited about it and full of plans. Joel was regaled with stories of the high jinks played in the town and country side and already. Several small out-houses had been upset, a cow was discovered in the church, and someone had cut the school bell rope, having climbed to the roof to do it.

Joel's answer to the possibility of more serious damage was to spend his evenings in the schoolhouse. At any rate it was nicer to sit in the quiet of the empty room reading, than to be in his room at the boarding house. Two evenings passed without incident, then on the third, just after dark, there was an excited rapping at the outer door. It was jerked open before Joel could answer the summons, and little Fred Baumheit rushed up the aisle.

"Teacher, they're coming for you," the urchin panted. "I heard 'm out back of our barn and I run all the way."

Joel's mind flashed back to little Aluns, who had brought a message like this in far-off Talpo. Again, he patted the messenger on the shoulders and kept his voice steady. At any rate there could be no physical danger here, there were no guerillas about Hylersville. "Who are they, Fred, why are they coming?"

The boy shook his head vigorously and his small chest heaved. "I don't know, just a lot of men. I heard 'em say they was gonta give you hell." His eyes widened; Joel had stressed the matter of profanity among the children. "You don't mind my saying the bad word, Teacher?"

"No, I guess not. Now run home before your Mother or anybody else sees you. And thanks; I won't forget."

Alone, Joel stood staring down at his desk. Uncle Thad had been hinting, so had the Reverend Jaynes. Some of the lurking men in the hills could be in this, but that was doubtful. The trouble began and grew right here in town. Joel's face was grim as he took out his revolver. In Talpo he had brought the weapon to the school to kill a snake; here, a rat. It was going to be different this time, no lurking in bushes with a scared boy; here, whoever started something would get hurt.

The school shutters were always closed at the end of the day, and he locked the door after a short tour of the room. The mob might be a seasonal prank, but such things could be used to hide real violence.

A half-hour passed before he heard a low voice rumble outside and gleams of light filtered through badly fitted shutters. Peering out a crack, Joel saw men coming into the yard. A few carried torches, the others small wooden buckets. "Tar and feathers," he gritted under his breath. The noises were louder, and he picked up some words.

"Copperhead . . . damned rebel sneak. . . ." Joel was sure of one voice, that of Tom Hawks. Working swiftly, Joel placed the lamp he had been using on the entrance hall bracket. A mob was a cowardly thing. He turned the key, jerked open the door, and the light shone on the weapon in his hand. The crowd saw the glint of steel, and the foremost tried to push back. Joel stood looking at them for a moment. Then, very deliberately, he laid his revolver on the seat of a chair and started forward.

He forced himself to be steady and not hurry, though the impulse to run was almost overmastering. The yelling stopped, so did the swinging of lanterns; and he walked through the aisle which opened to him. There was a prickling at the base of his neck; at any moment someone might muster courage and attack, then they would all be upon him.

Scarcely seeing that he had passed through the mob to the edge of the school yard, he walked into a group of hurrying men which closed round him. Squire Wetwire with a shotgun was there, Thaddeus Crisp carrying a cheese knife like a sword, and the Reverend Jaynes holding a heavy cane in a business-like way. The other three men Joel did not know, probably they were some of Wetwire's mill operators. No one said a word until they were in front of the Milburn house. There, Wetwire spoke for the rescuers. "We offer the apologies of our town, Joel. This thing grew out of Harry Sholes' free whiskey and Tom Hawks' big mouth. Something will be done about both."

There was no sign of Mrs. Milburn or any of the boarders when Joel entered the house and clumped up to his room. Sleep came slowly, and two names the Squire had mentioned kept running through his mind— Tom Hawks and Harry Sholes. The other men out in that schoolyard could have been riffraff, but they had been led.

Up early, Joel went down to the schoolhouse and found the room a mess, with books, paper, and dirt thrown about. His revolver was gone. By the time the children came, the place was presentable enough, and beyond some looks of curiosity, the whole day passed peacefully enough. This was Friday, and good behavior earned an earlier closing. There was no lingering on the grounds, as was common on other days.

Joel walked slowly down the hill. Before he had slept the night before, he had made up his mind. He had been pushed around for months on end, in Talpo, on the Heitel place, now here in his home town. As he walked, something close to elation tingled in his mind and sent touches of tenseness through his muscles. Tom Hawks, Harry Sholes.

When he reached the hotel, he did not enter the main building but slipped back of it to a woodhouse which housed fuel on the first floor and stored things on the second. It only took five minutes; there was the tar barrel from which Sholes sold the stuff to use on old-fashioned wagon hubs. Mixed with tallow, it acted as a long-lasting lubricant. Beside the barrel were five small buckets still filled with the viscous black liquid.

Joel walked up the hotel steps, one of the wooden buckets in either hand, and luck was with him. Harry Sholes was back of the bar, half-asleep. Tom Hawks sat at a table, scowling down into a glass of beer. Neither of the men had seen him yet. Joel studied them curiously. Sholes wore pink garters on the sleeves of his dirty shirt, Hawks' hat was pulled far forward on his head. Behind Sholes was a neat pyramid of glasses, set in front of a big frowsy mirror.

Joel half-smiled at a boyish memory. He had been in this room before, on an errand for his father, and had wondered how it would be if someone threw something at that pyramid of glassware. He hurled his first bucket and saw the whole carefully set structure explode into flying shards mixed with tar. Sholes yelled, dodged, and came up with a bung starter. He was too late; the second bucket grazed his head, and the big mirror was completely smashed. Sholes, bar, and floor were plastered with the sticky black stuff. The hotel keeper was moaning and trying to grub tar and glass fragments from face and shirt.

Tom Hawks was up, glaring, then he rushed forward. Joel sidestepped the big man and thrust out a foot, sending Hawks sprawling. Before handling the tar, he had pulled on a pair of old buckskin gloves. He waited. Tom came up, wild with rage, hat gone, big hands knotted into fists. Even the hair which showed at the neck of his open shirt appeared to stand up like the ruff of an angry dog. He was swearing viciously, mixing names into his profanity. Once he used Uncle Thad's name, but Joel wasn't listening too closely. He knew he should end this thing as quickly as possible. Hawks outweighed him by a good twenty pounds and his big body would absorb terrific punishment.

Joel's first blow that went home made his arm hurt clear to the shoulder; it was like hitting a wall. "Tom, I'm going to close your filthy mouth for you." Tom's roundhouse swing grazed him and sent him spinning.

Luck was with him; right after he had gritted the words, Joel's gloved fist went home on the broad, heavy lips and Hawks' knees buckled. He jerked back his head, trying to draw breath through his smashed mouth, and Joel's full blow went straight for the upthrust Adams apple. From there on it was just brutal savage punishment, the leather of the gloves cutting Tom's face again and again. He went down in a heap, got back on his knees, took another blow just under the temple and spread out on the floor as if he had thrown himself that way. Thin trickles of blood began to spread out on the dirty boards.

Joel looked at his prostrate adversary and knew he had not been hitting Tom Hawks. The man typified everything unpleasant which had happened since he came home—the gossip, the squinting windows, the warnings, the dead deserter in the woods, and the mob with its feathers and tar. His fists knotted, and for a moment he hoped Hawks would try again, but the man lay still. Joel turned his attention to Sholes.

The tavern-keeper came around the end of the bar, waving a revolver. But he was too slow. Joel rushed him like a Cherokee, jamming Sholes' huge stomach against the corner of the bar. The man grunted in agony. Joel snatched the weapon away. "My revolver, Harry, you damned thief. Tell me, can you take as much as Tom?" Sholes' heavy face was a mask of fright studded with gobs of black tar. Joel brandished his weapon. "Get a basin, wash up your partner."

The fat man worked on his knees, turning over Tom's heavy body and swabbing the battered features far from gently. Hawks revived and pushed Sholes away. Joel, from his seat on a chair, kept both men on the floor, the revolver dangling but ready. "Get the message, my tar-and-feathers experts? Make one more move, spill one more story about me—"

He stopped and shrugged his shoulders. "Hell, what's one more killing? Both of you'd be easy to hit, even in the dark." Joel stood up. He had seen something in Tom Hawks' eyes. It wasn't fear, it seemed more like wonder. There was one small mirror close to the end of the bar which was still intact. Joel picked up Tom Hawks' beer glass, measured the distance carefully, and threw. There was a satisfactory crash followed by the tinkling fall of shattered glass.

"Good shot," he advised himself pleasantly, and walked out.

This time, when he returned to the boarding house to get his things for the weekend at High Valley, Mrs. Milburn, her face tear-streaked, met him in the hall and led him into the empty kitchen. "Joel, I'm scared. Two nights ago they came. Talked pleasant enough, but they were afraid I'd be burned out if you stayed here. Now there was that mob. What shall I do?"

He looked at her, remembering so many things—the blanket roll search, taking the caps from his revolvers, her prying, and the Meany supper. "Just play out your hand, Lisa," he said sarcastically. "How dumb do you think a man can get? You're playing both ends against the middle."

Her tears dried almost instantly. Again, as in the hallway before the open cupboard that evening, she was blazing with anger. "You. Why should I bother? You're everything they say—thief, spy, maybe murderer."

"And you, Lisa, are likely what they say you are. Do you want me to use the word?" His big hands dropped to her shoulders and he shook her lightly. "I'll leave your house soon, but don't worry. Your two playmates, Sholes and Hawks, will be busy for a while." His hands slipped from her shoulders. She was very close and there was that perfume. Her soft brown hair had been loosened, framing her face softly, and her full lips were parted. Joel shook his head. "It might have worked, Lisa, but it's too late." He wasn't quite sure what he meant, as he left the kitchen, got his things from the room upstairs, and left for High Valley.

CHAPTER XV

JOEL HAD PASSED the Reuben Starr house. On impulse, he retraced his steps and knocked. As then, Starr opened it. Nothing about him had changed; he appeared to be wearing the same suit, the same necktie, but this time he wasn't cordial enough to invite his visitor to enter the house.

"Mr. Starr, this is my notice. Have John Darcy report for work a week from Monday."

The man in the brown suit, standing there in his own doorway, gave no indication of how he felt about the announcement, except for one quick breath. He appeared to be waiting for his visitor to make an explanation. When none came, he cleared his throat. "In that case, I'll pay you. Your month will be up a week from today."

He left Joel waiting on the step, but was out in a few minutes with three ten-dollar bills. When his visitor took the money with no thanks or comment, Starr paused, then said, "I wish you good evening," and Joel could not help but smiling a little.

"Yes, thank you, Mr. Starr, there appears to be a lot of it." He did not look back as he walked toward the Narrows. But he was sure someone else had joined Starr, and there was no sound of the door's closing while he was in earshot.

John Darcy. The teacher's name kept running through Joel's mind as he walked and was there occasionally during the weekend in the cabin. Darcy was an excellent teacher; the school had borne out that fact in the way children responded, and their mastery of work covered, under the man who was supposedly a sodden drunk for months. John Darcy and his brother-in-law, Reuben Starr—there must be some driving reason why Starr should finance the drinking. Jaynes had hinted that he did.

The town was quiet during that week, and Joel thought it was a trifle friendlier. Everyone must have known, by this time, the story of the abortive mob attack and what had happened in the hotel. Mrs. Genevieve Conant, one of the more vicious of the village gossips, encountered Joel in the store and actually wished him the time of day, civilly enough. From back of the counter where he had been working, Thaddeus Crisp took in the scene and kept his face straight. Afterward, he commented.

"So, one of the eagles flipped a feather at you, son."

Joel grinned. "Uncle Thad, Mother had a cat one time, that'd scratch at the same time that it purred."

Crisp snorted, but he was smiling as he went about putting things in order on the shelves.

So far, Harry Sholes had done nothing, at least openly, about the damage to his bar. Joel encountered him late one afternoon. There was a muddy place, bridged with two planks laid side by side, affording only room enough for one person. Sholes had actually started across when Joel arrived on the scene, and he stepped back and waited for the younger man to cross. "Don't press your luck, boy."

Joel did not answer the half-expressed threat. A few days later, he had a brief encounter with Tom Hawks. His face still in pretty bad shape, Hawks entered the store while Joel was in the back of the room. While Crisp waited on his customer, Tom looked about and glimpsed his antagonist. This time, unlike the look he had given Joel from the tavern floor, his eyes and set lips showed pure malice.

There wasn't much left of daylight on the fall evening when Joel left for High Valley. He was carrying his mother's big valise, in which were his few clothes and the blanket roll, and a clean grain sack partly filled with provisions. Squire Wetwire had merely snorted when told that Joel was turning over the school job to Darcy. Mrs. Milburn had taken the board money with polite thanks, and had been tactful enough not to express any pleasure at her difficult tenant's leaving.

The walk through the lower portion of town wasn't pleasant, since there was enough light for people to watch. Joel plodded along, feeling he was giving the squinting windows a good show. In an hour there would be talk all over the village.

"Mind you, he quit," some would say; others, "well Reuben Starr got rid of that man, at last and good riddance."

He walked on. With something close to a childish gesture, he walked slowly, granting everyone their look. Even the Conner dog had its chance, barking loudly, then accompanying the walker for a hundred yards before turning back.

It was quite dusk when he reached the big creek bridge, and dark by the time he had turned the shoulder of the first mountain. He stopped to rest, seating himself on a roadside boulder he remembered, rather than saw. None of the usual night noises had begun, but suddenly there was the light, metallic clink of a horseshoe against a stone in the road. Joel, startled, listened intently to learn the direction of the animal's movement. The sandy road muffled most sounds.

Minutes passed, then it was quite clear; a fast-stepping horse was approaching from the direction of Hylersville. Screened by heavy pine shadows, Joel was sure he could not be seen. Rider and mount came closer, passed. He smelled the sweaty odor of the horse, heard the light creaking of saddle leather. He had smelled tobacco as if the rider had lately enjoyed a cigar. When all was still, he went on.

He had gone a full half mile before he stopped and set his valise down. Not many local people rode, most of them preferring buggies, carts, or wagons. Joel did not remember any Hylersville animal that picked up its feet like the one which had passed. He was surprised that he had not heard it crossing the plank bridge. The trampling of hooves would have been drum-like in the quiet of the early night.

He thought for another few minutes. Well, he was in no hurry. The cabin would wait, and so could the identity of a man riding a good horse. Joel resorted to the habit he had started In Talpo, shrugging one shoulder, an effective answer to a problem when one didn't have a solution.

Indian John had lived by a set of his own rules. Invariably on leaving his home, he bolted the front door from the inside, went out the back, and left that unlocked. Visitors were always welcome unless they left a door stand open as an invitation to a curious skunk, a snake hunting shade, or a porcupine searching for a board with salt soaked into it.

Joel found himself remembering these things with a smile as he entered the little building through the back door and set down his burden with some relief. It had been a little chilly outside, however, it was comfortable in this small interior. His sulphur match smoked at first. When it gave off a clear flame, Joel lighted the wall lamp in the living room.

There were pine kindling sticks in the fireplace; it took only a moment and a second match to have them alight. He stood with the dead vesper in his fingers and frowned. Likely the mob business had made him nervous, but he remembered that that lamp chimney had seemed warm in his fingers, when he raised it to get at the wick. Of course it was warm now. There was no way to check, and the kitchen stove was cold.

The fire, helped out with split birch sticks, began giving real friendliness to the room. Joel settled himself, eating some of Uncle Thad's cheese and crackers which he had brought. Naturally, he remembered what the old man had said, almost word for word. "Too bad you quit the school when, mebbe, you had the town coming your way. You cleaned up Hawks and Harry Sholes. I figger the town thinks that mob stuff was going too far."

Joel recalled his own cynical questions. "How far's too far, Uncle Thad? How'd you like to take my chances in these parts?"

The merchant rubbed a stubble-covered chin thoughtfully. "'Fore God, boy, I wish't I knowed."

Joel finished his cheese, then started counting his money. What he now had was all he would get in Hylersville. He paused, laying the thin packet of bills on his knee. In all, there had been the money from his parents' home, his earnings teaching school, and the twenty brought with him, making nearly four hundred dollars. But there had been his board at twelve and a half cents a meal; the rent of his room; what he had spent in Uncle Thad's store; thirty dollars Crisp had turned over for him, anonymously, to Reverend Jaynes church fund; and ten more to fix up his parents' graves. There was less than three hundred left.

Money. He got up, opened the valise and the bed roll. Burley's bragging money was there. Only God and the dead guerilla knew how much misery and how much bloodshed had gone into the amassing of the sum. There was just one thing about it of which Joel was sure: it wasn't the paymaster's roll. Temptation was here, ready to hand. He had counted the worn money often enough since Trudie had divided it back in the hills. It was surely more than enough to finish medical school and open an office afterward. The sobering thought was that it was enough to hang him, if arrested and charged with working with Burley.

His big fingers gripped the packet; the fire was bright. If he tossed the money in it, there would be nothing but clean, fleecy ashes lifting in the smoke up the wide chimney, and some measure of safety.

"That's too much to burn . . . for whatever it brings, good or bad." Trudie had said those words so long ago. It seemed like years since he had looked into her eyes and heard her insisting that they share and share alike. Trudie, holding that sprig of pennyroyal the night they had come home from Pohasin's, Trudie brushing his clothes before they separated. He jumped up, crossed to an old fishing creel which hung on the wall, and buried the money under the dried grass which lined its bottom. He had just returned to his chair before the fire when there was a rap on the front door.

Joel's hand covered the grip of his own revolver, which lay on the table. There had been no other sound outside, no steps on the gravel, just this summons. His quick glance reassured him that no one could have spied on him while he handled and hid Burley's money. The revolver barrel slipped under his trousers band, and the skirt of his jacket covered the walnut grip, as he opened the door.

There was the bulky outline of just one person on the porch. Joel gave no invitation, but the man stepped into the room as if there had been one. He was smiling, with wide-set eyes above cheeks and chin partially covered with a neatly trimmed beard. His hair, when he removed his hat, was streaked with gray. Joel, taller, lean and smooth shaven, kept studying his visitor, noting the boots innocent of dust, the string tie at the throat of a fresh-looking shirt. His first conclusion was that this man was a soldier. The newcomer was holding out a hand.

"I'm Joshua Colet, one of Indian John's friends who has used his place often when I came through. You, young man, would likely be Joel Pender. Once I had the privilege of meeting your physician father; and John often spoke of a boy."

Colet—this was the officer George Geis had mentioned. Joel offered no comment and no friendliness. His present problem was what to do if this man had come to arrest him. The revolver was still in his belt, he had heard no sign of other men outside.

"Yes," he said, "I am Joel Pender. Can I do anything for you?"

"That has been done already, Pender. I stabled my mare in your barn and fell asleep on the hay. When I woke, your light showed. Now, I would like a bed for the night. John used to put me up, guess I made stopping here a habit."

So far, the visitor had showed no signs of menace, and his story could well be true, for Indian John delighted in hospitality and had had many friends. There was something likable about this stocky, bearded man with his air of quiet confidence and being at home in the cabin. Only one flaw appeared in his story—the fact that, although he had slept in the shed for a while, there was no hay dust or dirt on either his jacket or trousers. Joel removed his revolver from his trousers band and laid the weapon on the table.

"Sorry, sir. I don't usually arm myself against visitors, but recent experiences have made me cautious."

"Deserters?"

Joel frowned at Colet's word, which could have been either a question or a comment. His visitor drew a revolver from under his jacket and laid it beside the other weapon on the table. "No apology needed for arms in these troubled times. I travel a long road and try to be ready. I see you like a thirty-six caliber, too. Maybe they won't stop a man, but he'll know he's hit."

"An odd thing—over in Point Haven the other day, two deserters walked in and surrendered peaceably. Both had been with Milroy's scattered army. They'd been on the run for months. However, both had good uniforms and their issued muskets. You can't stay that neat hiding in these hills."

Joel merely shook his head. His mind was on the three men who had escaped from the Forbes camp a few miles back in the woods. And if these men were the pair who had been in this very room, they had been in ragged civilian garb, and armed with revolvers, not muskets. Maybe they had located the big man they had talked about.

From then on, the conversation was casual. Joel wanted to know if the highway running through Hylersville and this Narrows was really the old Philadelphia and Erie Turnpike. Colet talked history. "Guess my mare, Katy, and I've traveled most of it from Erie to the Susquehanna. The government used it a lot in the war of 1812 but the hard grades over Rattlesnake Mountain, west of here, make stretches of it lonely."

Joel was tired and Colet suggested bed. In twenty minutes, both were on their cots and from the horseman's breathing, he was asleep in ten minutes. But there was a lot to consider. George Geis had suggested that this man could help. Doctor Kenny had said a man named Colet was an intelligence officer. Could Joel trust him?

And there had been a few queer things—there had been the horseman, earlier in the evening, and no sound on the bridge, the absence of hay dust on Colet's clothes and his quick mention of deserters. Joel laid awake so long thinking that he overslept and, when he woke, his visitor had breakfast ready. Colet had been out of bed for some time, having fed and groomed his mare. He'd made coffee, and Joel wasn't sure if Colet's quiet movements or the good smells had wakened him. When the two men had eaten and disposed of the dishes, they went to the stable. Katy was a fine, light-stepping mare. When her halter was slipped, she trotted about for a moment then rolled in the dust, after which she came up to her master and daintily accepted a small piece of loaf sugar. There was pride in Colet's voice. "More of a friend than a horse, Pender."

"Sure-footed at night," Joel said grimly, and pointed to the animal's left front leg. The morning curry comb had missed one place where the hair was matted. "You didn't cross the bridge, Colet. There's a ford just above it."

The visitor stroked his short beard for a moment and half-smiled. "Exactly. Trust a man with medical training to be observant. Let's get back to the house and talk." The weather had turned mild, so they sat on the front porch steps and Colet pointed to a glimpse of the road which showed through the trees. "Used in two wars, friend; once to serve a hard-pressed country, now it's a highway for drugs smuggled from Ontario to the Confederacy. Deserters use it like the slaves did. Both had help. The south knows damn well that desertion hurts armies more than killing men in action. So, there's organization and money. There's still some Southern cash. Northern people up here furnish civilian clothes to deserters. Of course, a few have funds, and they pay their own way, footing the bill themselves. Right through Pennsylvania, clear into Virginia, a rebel thoroughfare with its way stations like the one about here, somewhere. Horses, clothes, drugs go south, deserters and bounty hunters come north."

The horseman jumped to his feet, tramped about for a minute then pointed a forefinger at Joel. "Maybe fifty thousand deserters are hiding in Pennsylvania alone, along the river, up the big creeks. You've seen the wreckage of battle, Joel Pender. Oh, yes, I know most of your story. I know you're not involved. But I want to wake you up so you'll see that Hylersville and these hills hurt our cause as much as one of Lee's regiments."

Joel was riled. "Listen, Colet, don't ride me. I took enough since I came home. If you're a Provost officer, arrest me. There isn't one damn thing of which I'm ashamed."

Colet's grimness dropped away like the taking off of a mask. "Yes, yes, no doubt you're right, but I was getting to this—you came back home, folks can't account for you. Copperhead or Union, they're scared. One thinks you're for the Union, the other sees you a southern spy. Come on." He led the way to the shed, where he saddled his mare and strapped on his saddle bags.

"Pender, don't leave this country. There is work for you here. When chance comes, I can help you. Forgive me for tormenting you. Actually, I was trying to learn something about you and your reactions." He swung up into his saddle and his smile was real. "I'm Trudie Quinn's uncle. She's in Point Haven working with army convalescents. She wants to see you. And, Joel Pender, I privately had to know if I wanted you to see her. It's just possible you deserve that much; but be careful. Don't involve her."

He cantered off down the lane. Joel barely noticed. Trudie was close, and she wanted to see him. At the moment, nothing of the bitter months in Hylersville mattered. An hour later, having taken time to shave carefully and to dress as well as his meager wardrobe permitted, he was on his way.

He reached the county seat fairly early the next morning and went to a barber shop to have his hair trimmed and his shave checked. There was no other customer, and the proprietor offered to brush Joel's worn coat and trousers. Finally, he had a look at himself in the big mirror and turned with a grin, offering the barber a quarter. He took the coin, handled it a moment, then gave back a dime in change. "You get a special rate, friend, for what you've got in your eyes. Just for a while, you made me feel young and eager again."

The address proved to be a square two-story brick house on Water Street. There was a small porch with wrought iron grills on either side and a white china knob on the door lintel with the word RING lettered just below it.

"Miss Trudie Quinn," Joel told the severe looking woman who answered his ring. "Tell her, please, that Joel Pender is here."

The landlady inspected the caller carefully, missing nothing from worn coat to battered hat. It was quite evident that she wasn't pleased. "What do you want to see Miss Quinn about, young man?"

Joel had a hard time concealing the flash of temper she evoked. "About nothing that would interest you, madam. Tell Miss Quinn I am here."

A long ten minutes dragged by while he waited in a badly lighted parlor, furnished uncomfortably with horsehair upholstered chairs and settees. But, when a door opened at the far end of the room, there was no mistaking the figure which appeared, nor the leap in his heart. He met her more than halfway across the big room and gathered her fingers into his big palm. "Trudie, Colet told me you were here, and I came right off."

She left her hand in his like a child, as he led her to seats near the front window. "And you walked, Joel," she said teasingly. "There was no Jimson mule, and it's a long way."

"No," he said, trying to be exact and not sensing her mild raillery, "not all the way. A man gave me a lift for a few miles. I couldn't believe you were so close."

Trudie explained her presence in Point Haven rapidly, filling in the background. "Jonathan took me to Baltimore, then I took a train to my mother's sister's home in Lancaster. Doctor Kenny is a family friend; and he told me he was going to Gettysburg to help with the wounded. It's queer, but I was sure you'd show up there and I told him some things about you. He made a trip back, and I told him the rest. Doctor Kenny thinks you have great promise; he'd take you into his office as an assistant right now, if you had finished school."

Joel started to interrupt but she smiled and held up her hand. "I did some nursing in Lancaster, then Doctor Kenny sent me up here, because there were so many convalescents in this town, and so few doctors or nurses. When Uncle Josh stopped to see me, I—"

Joel did interrupt her, this time. "Trudie, never mind how much you told him, can I trust him? He's a government man."

Her frank eyes were troubled. "He's close-mouthed and trusted greatly by lots of important people, mostly his superiors. He's fair and wise; and George Geis knows him. Uncle Josh was in the cavalry earlier in the war but resigned because of a wound. Joel, I'd trust him."

Perhaps his doubt showed on his face for she nodded her small head emphatically. "Yes, trust him. He already knew some of the things that happened to you; and told me. You see, I know about the mob and the cold shoulder the home folks gave you. I felt like going down there and giving those people—" The look on his face stopped her for a moment. Then she hurried on, "Uncle Josh feels you can put confidence in two Hylersville people. One is the minister, Mr. Jaynes. I met him once, in Lancaster. The other is Thaddeus Crisp. He doesn't want you to go too far with Mr. Crisp, because he's old and talks when he's worried.

"Joel, this is the worst. Jonathan got through to me, and tells that the soldiers in the Talpo country have your description—height, weight, color of hair and eyes, even the size of your hands and your temper. The only thing the Sandys brothers didn't give was your name. Those soldiers know you fired the Heitel buildings and that you came away with money. Also, Lee Harne and one other guerilla got off and out of that country."

Abruptly, the girl was on her feet, and for the first time since he knew her, Joel saw real fright on her features. He got up and rested his hands on her slim shoulders, shaking them lightly. It was his chance to reassure her as she had so often done for him. "Don't be afraid in the dark, Trudie. Nothing that amounts to much has happened, so far. Above everything don't let anybody, not even Colet, know you have half that money and so drag you into this mess." He smiled down into her eyes. "So long as you're safe, Trudie, I'm not afraid of anything."

The hint of tears was there. "Joel," she whispered, and his arm was slipping about her when she drew back and gestured toward the door through which she had entered the room. "My landlady's watching. Her hearing is bad, but she sees more than any two women. I've more news; this good, Joel. Doctor John McColl from Lancaster is moving to your country, place called Camar. You are to work with him. Kenny says it will help toward your degree."

Trudie smiled at the mounting excitement on his face. "Doctor Mc-Coll has some drawbacks. His wealthy wife likes men and whiskey. The doctor merely likes the drink. But Doctor Kenny says he is very competent. Remember, the draft won't bother either a doctor or his helper."

"Thanks for making me a bomb proof, Trudie. McColl will be a Godsend. Our folks need a doctor more than they have any idea. As for me, I'd get along with the devil if he taught me some medicine."

Some of Trudie's earlier hurry returned. "Go home, Joel, and be careful. Uncle Josh thinks you could be in real danger, but he didn't know exactly of what. I'll be so glad when you're working with McColl." They walked together to the entrance hall. The hint of tears was suddenly back in the girl's eyes. She raised to her tiptoes and kissed Joel's cheek. "Goodbye, for now. Be careful. Remember as Doctor Kenny put it— we're bound to make a doctor out of you."

Out on the porch, he thought of a dozen questions he might have asked, and a dozen things he might have told Trudie, but it was too late. Several blocks up the street he noticed the way passersby were staring at him and smiling. Then, he saw that he was carrying his hat before him in both hands, just as he had taken it from Trudie minutes before. He knew he also must be grinning widely.

The last of the second day's light was fading when Joel reached his cabin and stood, leaning against a porch post for a while before going in. His mind was on Trudie—the way her soft hair framed her face, the touch of her hands, and more, the soft, warm kindness of her kiss. There was strength in him now; she had renewed it.

Pieces of bark from the porch post stung his face and neck before the report of the rifle reached him. Joel pitched himself forward and crawled to the door, thankful that he had not barred it in his hurry to be off. He pushed it open and got inside. With his revolver, he went out by the back door and circled the cabin warily. There was no sign of powder smoke, the breeze would have dissipated that quickly. The three shots he drove into the brush brought no reply and no sign of any movement. That night, he barred both doors. The bullet had struck a foot above his head and his judgement was that it had been fired to frighten or warn him. Mountain men would not miss that badly, if they were in earnest.

CHAPTER XVI

HALF-ASHAMED AT his precautions, Joel sat before his fire. The room did not heat up well, so he went to bed to get warm, and as was his custom, lay thinking. The shot did not disturb him too much; somebody out there in the brush was trying to frighten him into leaving the cabin. Hylersville, with unfriendliness, the mob, and veiled warnings, had tried to do the same thing. Even Uncle Thad had tried to loan him money so he would get back to school and so be away. Only Trudie and Colet wanted him to stay. He rolled over in bed and thought of his father.

David Pender had lived out most of his life in these hills, and Joel wondered what the kindly, devoted physician would think of this situation. He finally slept, without resolving anything in his mind. He hadn't slept long when he was roused by someone stumbling up the front steps. A light shone through the cabin's liberal cracks. Revolver ready, he yanked open the door.

"What a road, what a road to Jericho," a deep voice grumbled.

"Jaynes," he called in some relief, "come in and shut the cold out."

The minister set the lantern he carried on a table, and his sharp eyes did not miss a thing. He pointed to the revolver. "Are you nervous, or don't you like visitors?"

Joel let down the hammer of his weapon, picked up the lantern, and showed Jaynes the bullet scar on the post. Inside again, he had a sarcastic question. "Just tired of playing sitting duck for a poor shot, Reverend. By the way, as a part of your pastoral duties, you didn't fire that shot, or did you?"

The minister shook his head. "No, this doesn't happen to be my week for attempted murder. Actually, I haven't shot at a man since Shiloh, and I'm in the Lord's army, not Grant's. Anyway, the man missed. I don't think a rabbit worries about the shot that misses him. He just goes on about his business of being a rabbit."

Joel's scowl met Jaynes' smile. "Being an army chaplain makes a man hard. Don't mind my levity. I came for you because a man's hurt and folks suggested strongly that you could help. Either his arm's broken or dislocated, and the pain's bad. Put on a pair of pants and come along. There's a horse and buggy on the road, waiting."

Joel glanced down at his bony legs, then went into the bedroom and dressed rapidly. Jaynes had his jacket ready. A broken or dislocated arm wouldn't be too much of a problem. Joel had helped his father, then George Geis, with a number of breaks; and he carried the old physician's emergency bag.

They were half way to Hylersville before the minister commented. "There are signs of a good doctor about you, friend." Joel grunted and Jaynes chuckled. "So far you haven't asked the name of your patient but just came along. And you forgot your revolver. It's back on the table. Pender, your patient's Tom Hawks. Shall I take you back?"

Joel swore under his breath. "Suppose you get a little speed out of your horse. Either a break or a dislocation will swell up like a poisoned pup."

Tom Hawks lived with his wife and two children in a house directly north from Crisp's store, but across the creek on the beginning of the ridge road. It was only a short distance from the hotel. A group of neighbors had gathered in front of the place, and a lighted lantern hung from a porch rafter. A man came forward to tie the preacher's horse and commented, "He's pretty bad, Reverend."

Joel, carrying his bag, got out and started for the house without speaking to the onlookers, who stared at him curiously. Some of the men could have been with Hawks the night the mob came. There were low murmurs. "That's the teacher . . . old Doc Pender's boy. . . ."

Neither Jaynes or Joel paid any attention, and the door was opened by a small woman whose hair was liberally touched with gray. She was wiping her hands nervously on her clean but faded dress and spoke to Jaynes. "He's in bad pain. Tom's never been sick before."

The minister patted her shoulder. "Pender's here to help, Mrs. Hawks."

Evidently the woman had not taken a look at her other visitor, but at the mention of his name, her eyes widened. "That's the teacher man. Tom had—"

Leaving Jaynes to make any comment that occurred to him, Joel stepped past her and crossed the room in three strides. He pushed open a door which was partially ajar and saw his patient. The big, twisting bulk of Tom Hawks sprawled on a bed, badly rumpled by his tossing. He sat up with an effort at the sight of his visitor. "Get to hell out of my house, Pender. If I wasn't helpless—"

Joel paid no attention to the injured man's roar. He set his bag on a chair and pulled off his jacket. The wife crossed to the bedside and pushed her husband back on the bed. "Be still, Tom. This man came to help, and he's the only one in these parts as can."

"But, Allie," Hawks protested, "he ain't, he'll—"

Joel eyed the heavy muscled torso and spoke to Hawks. "Yell and swear all you like, but the more that arm swells, the worse it's going to be. Jaynes came for me, I'm here. You're going to be treated whether you want it or not."

Mrs. Hawks bustled about, bringing hot water so Joel could wash his hands, and a bundle of soft cloth for bandages. The powerful left arm of the man on the bed made a grotesque angle and sweat stood out on Hawks' forehead when Joel rotated the injured member. "Mrs. Hawks, the arm's dislocated, not broken. I'll need all your cloths and hot water." The kettle must have been on the stove. In minutes, Joel had hot compresses on the shoulder and upper arm. He had seen his father do this same job; the things he needed were in the bag.

"Hawks, this pill is morphine. Chase it with the brandy." The patient dutifully downed the medicine. Beads of sweat stood out on his forehead, either from pain, or dread of what lay ahead. Jaynes, his coat off, stepped forward and waited for instructions.

"On your right side, Hawks." The big man on the bed hesitated before complying but Joel seized the work hardened hand on the left arm in his own left, placed his right on the elbow while Jaynes held the heavy torso still. Like many big, powerful men, Tom Hawks did not react well to pain, and he groaned as the arm rotation started, then bellowed as the jerk came. Joel released his grip. Mrs. Hawks wiped her husband's forehead with a corner of her apron. Joel held out a piece of paper. Hawks reached for it with his right hand. "No, use the left, the hurt one."

Hawks' eyes widened with surprise, and he yelled, "Allie, look, I used my hand!" Joel finished his work swiftly, bandaging the injured arm to the side. The morphine was working, Hawks was sleepy. "Let him rest until noon, Mrs. Hawks. Keep the bandage on two days, use hot compresses if the pain is great."

Hawks fought off the sleepiness. "What do we owe you, Pender?"

Joel was pulling down his shirt sleeves and fastening the wrist bands. He stepped close to the bed and stared down into the relieved face. His voice was harsh. "Not a damn thing, Hawks. But I guess you're not the fellow who shot at me this evening."

The man on the bed was too groggy to understand, but the wife glanced uneasily from her husband to the tall young man walking from the room followed by the minister.

The group of neighbors in the yard had increased but Joel walked through it without speaking and climbed into the buggy, not offering to help Jaynes untie his horse. The minister clucked to the animal and drove on up the hilly ridge road. Joel's mind was on what he had done in the Hawks home. He was pretty well satisfied, even to the use of morphine. That would keep Hawks quiet until the wrenched muscles had a chance. The minister's deep chuckle startled him.

"A pretty good job back there, friend. But, I am afraid your bedside manners are pretty rough."

Joel snorted derisively. "The patient was rough first. He's been sitting in Shole's tavern bleating about me ever since I came home, and you know he was in that tar-and-feathers crowd. That's squared since I pounded the devil out of him."

Jaynes slapped his companion's knee smartly. "If you were one of my church flock, Pender, I'd say you lost a fine opportunity to forgive, which in your present state of mind, doesn't look like the Christian virtue which it is. Thomas Hawks has more dislocated than his arm. Basically, he's a good sort—fond of his wife and children, works whenever he can find a job. Outside of that, he's devoted to Thaddeus Crisp, watches over the old man like a good hen does for her chicks."

Jaynes took the buggy whip from the socket, then put it back. "The odd part is that Crisp appears to resent Tom's interest. That's another Hylersville mystery along with who's shooting at you. Pender, your next call's the one which really bothers me."

"Next call," Joel remonstrated. "It's late, people will be in bed. Don't use me as a doctor; all I am is a fair to good first aid man—"

The minister interrupted. "Doctor, indeed. You should have seen some of those hatchet-and-saw men at Shiloh. This is first aid, and as long as we're out—Michal Metz cut himself with an ax. He's a young hill farmer with three little girls, all under ten. And he's been called in the draft."

The horse stopped, and Jaynes, leaning forward in his seat, urged it on. "Here's one of the many cases where this army draft hurts. Michal goes in two weeks. I wonder if it's evil to wish that ax had crippled the man. My young friend—"

"Young friend, indeed," Joel snapped, exasperated. You're not much older than I am."

"Seven thoughtful years, Pender, old enough not to be stubborn about what I can or can't do. Listen carefully. Dora Metz is all right so long as her husband is here—a good wife and mother. But she had a past in Point Haven, before marrying Michal. When he goes off to war, there will be mighty little money coming in, and Dora won't see her girls suffer. She'll make money in the only way she knows." Jaynes stopped talking and cleared his throat. It was quite plain that he was greatly concerned. "The only way out is mustering three hundred dollars for a substitute, and there's no one to back the Metz family. At times, I almost wish I could swear away my exasperation like Tom Hawks does. Give me some tobacco."

Jaynes crammed a small handful from Joel's pouch into his mouth and chewed hard until he could spit over the side of the buggy. "Chewing's a hoggish business, but it steadies me like no pipe or cigar does. Three hundred dollars—a hundred apiece for three little girls, one of them crippled. Why are the concerns of war greater than that of children? Get up, horse, let's get this stubborn man to the Metz house and try his soul."

There was no group of neighbors about the farmhouse, but light showed from the front windows. A little blonde girl answered Jaynes' knock and invited them to enter. Like the Hawks home, this one was neat and clean. Two other light-haired girls ranged themselves along the wall; and a big, well-formed young woman, who had been working at the stove, came over to welcome the visitors. Jaynes apologized for the late hour.

"It's all right. Michal couldn't sleep, so we all are sitting up with him for a few hours. Mr. Pender, you're the schoolteacher. I'm Dora Metz, these are Laura, Jenny, and Susan." Each child acknowledged the introduction with a smile and a bobbed head. "I'll call Mike, gentlemen. Excuse me, please."

Joel glanced toward Jaynes, but he was busy talking to the children. A tall young man, walking with the aid of an improvised crutch, entered the room. "Welcome, friends," he said. "We're having a crutch party, as Susan calls it. Sit down, everybody."

Jaynes shook his head. "We can't stay long. Pender, here, will look at that cut foot. He's a medical student, his father was a doctor." There was a bed in one corner of the room. After Joel had washed his hands again and Metz was lying down, he made his examination. The cut was badly in need of attention.

"I'll need to clean that out, Mr. Metz, and there'll have to be three or four stitches." Here was one case where Joel was sure of his ground, and he worked swiftly, aided by Jaynes and Dora Metz, with plenty of hot water in which to sterilize his needle and sutures. When he was done, he gave the wife a small bottle of the balsam bud tincture made by Indian John. "Keep the cut damp with this, and don't tie up the bandages tight. He'll be around again in ten days or two weeks."

Metz glanced at Jaynes and mopped his forehead. It had been a pretty severe ordeal, but the young farmer had met it better than Tom Hawks. He sat on the edge of the bed. "Dora, have Doctor look at Susan's knee."

She turned, and the curly-haired oldest of the children came forward, walking with a slight limp. Joel felt his heart sink. Here it was, something beyond the reach of his limited training, a difficult diagnosis and still more difficult treatment. The eager light in the parents' eyes, and the child's shy smile, hurt. He drew a long breath and found a chance to scowl at Jaynes.

First, to see if there was a noticeable spinal curvature, he had Susan stand on her good leg, supporting herself erect by use of a chair. Next, he had her sit down and went over the small leg and knee with his big, incredibly gentle hands, testing, feeling, kneading lightly.

"Mrs. Metz," he said, when he stood up, "there could be a shortened tendon or muscle in that knee. They tell me a regular doctor is coming to Camar soon. I'll bring him here. Maybe Susan can be helped." He frowned, looked at the child sitting there so quietly. His hooked finger gesture called the mother over, and he knelt again. "Massage that knee a little, each day. Use a circular motion." He demonstrated and noticed that Jaynes watched closely.

"I saw my father do this to children and it helped. Put a little grease on your hands if they're rough and don't use liniment; it will burn the child's skin and won't help, anyway." He patted Susan's curls as he rose. She looked into her mother's face for permission and hurried from the room.

Outside, it was Joel's turn to be distraught about the Metz family. "Dammit, Jaynes, don't push me into such things and get folks' hearts and hopes up. I know anatomy but I'm a greenhorn about things like Susan's knee. Kenny, in Lancaster, could cure her. It might take a knife to loosen tension. Also, it could be bone tuberculosis and no hope. Did you see the parents' eyes?"

The minister did not reply, and they were headed downhill when he asked his own question. "What did you think of the mother, Pender?"

"Only that I liked her, and she knew how to help."

"Exactly," Jaynes said with something like a groan. "Most men like her. I know the life from which she came, and where she'll land with Michal off to war and no money for the children. So, we've got to fight a war and see a woman flung to the devil for her children."

Most of the long drive back to High Valley, Jaynes chewed tobacco and Joel smoked. Neither man appeared to want to talk much; Jaynes appeared busy with his driving and Joel because he felt a thrill of elation. Tonight, he had put two men well on the road to recovery, and a child had challenged his sympathy and training. If he could get in touch with Doctor Kenny or Trudie, there might be help for Susan.

Jaynes stopped his horse at the entrance of the steep lane. "This night, Joel Pender, I had a tempting thought—to desert my calling and make some money. Three hundred dollars would save a home and children. A hundred more and a child would walk freely." His hand reached out and touched his companion's shoulder. "Oh, I've prayed a lot, and the Lord always sends comfort. But he's a might slow about cash."

* * *

Close to four o'clock the following day, after little sleep and a lot of thinking, Joel presented himself at the small house where Jaynes lived by himself. His welcome was warm, in fact, the minister almost pulled him into the house. "I was thinking of you, Pender. Mrs. Jim Cardy sent me half of a roasted ham; a small one, it's true, but enough for two hungry men to share. You will stay to supper."

Joel tossed his hat on a sofa, fumbled for his pipe, and took the offered chair. "Yes, I'll be glad for a supper I haven't cooked myself. But—I warn you that you'll be eating with a sinner, a man with a past, as Hylersville would have it."

Jaynes frowned at his visitor but spoke quietly. "A better man than either of us could hope to be, did that often."

Joel's face was earnest. "Sam, that little girl with the game knee bothered me ever since I left you. The way she looked into my face reminded me of another child who was sick. She got well, and Susan deserves as much—at least a chance." Jaynes settled back in his chair, sensing a story and lifting his hands so he could make a tent of his fingers. Joel went on.

"Two days ago, a friend told me there was one person in Hylersville I could trust—you. I hope that's true, but it doesn't matter too much. The fact is, I have in my possession a lot of money belonging to a dead guerilla. No, Sam, I didn't kill the man. Another who had a gun beat me to it. The house, this guerilla's headquarters, burned. Just before, the money turned up in a closet. It came away with me." Joel leaned forward and shot a question. "How much was it, Sam? I think you know."

"Yes, I do know, Joel. Over fifteen hundred dollars. Our mutual friend—and would be mutual temptress—Lisa Milburn, told me you had that much in your blanket roll. With it, you had two revolvers, both loaded."

Suddenly Joel wanted to laugh. Lisa Milburn had the gall confide in her minister that she had gone through a guest's things.

Jaynes was nodding. "Yes, friend, Lisa likes to confide in young men. Let me confess that, when I first came, she came close to giving me the "mild course in iniquity" they say a young minister needs. The woman could be a siren, given the opportunity. She has the equipment for it. She lacks one thing."

"What?"

"She always feels sorry for her victims." Jaynes dropped his light manner and settled deeper into his chair. Deep lines showed on his face. With heavy brows drawn down, his strong features were stern. Joel reached into his pocket and took out the sheaf of worn currency. He slapped it on the table. "There it is. God knows how much blood was spilled; how much evil was done getting that hoard together. Bragging money, the guerilla called it."

Joel strode to the door and opened it, and after he had looked round, returned to his host. "Mark this well, Sam. I'm not handing over the money because it could hang me if I was caught with it; I have the notion that if it was put to work for good, it could wipe away—" He interrupted himself to snatch up the money and slap the table with it again. "Take it, Sam. Make it work. Get Metz's substitute, arrange for Susan to be taken to Doctor Kenny. Maybe you can find a place for whatever's left over."

The minister took a long breath, and dampness showed in his eyes. "Lord, let thy manna fall." He snatched up a piece of paper and made notations.

> Item one—substitute for Michal Metz, three hundred dollars.
> Item two—surgery for Susan Metz, one hundred dollars.
> Item three—Bring back Peter Blooner from the poor house,
> to die in his own home, eighty dollars.

He stopped writing and looked sharply at his visitor. "Forgive me, Joel. Have you set up some conditions?"

"No. Well, just one. Nobody is to know where you got it, the money. Especially Lisa Milburn—"

"Will hold her peace, that's a promise I can keep." Jaynes' comment surprised and intrigued Joel.

"And, Sam, if officers came and asked you about the money, what would you do?"

"It's a donation, anonymous, and I do not have to tell all I know. At any rate, the money would be spent. Now, a question for you, Joel Pender, son of a physician. Your whole ambition is to become a doctor. I've seen you work, and believe you have the gift. You lack money. Why didn't you use this?"

Joel answered carefully. "I wish I could bring myself to tell you my whole story. Let's put it this way; I'm willing to see the money working for others; for myself, knowing what I do, I couldn't take advantage of it. Even so, I feel as if I'd loaned a friend a dirty shirt."

Jaynes jumped up. "No further discussion of scruples. We will visit the sick, help the needy, and now, eat good meat. Let's to supper." The two young men ate to repletion, and when they had finished there was a cigar apiece.

The minister wanted to take Joel home in his buggy, but he preferred to walk. "Do me good, after all that ham," he assured his host. He swung along light-heartedly. So much had happened in the last few days. Chief among them was his visit with Trudie. Then, he had helped sick people, and finally, was rid of that money. Even now, in his mind's eye, he could see the littered table in the Heitel place and the greasy packet of money on the table close to the cast iron skillet.

Outside his back door, Joel paused for a little, thinking of Lisa Milburn. Jaynes had told him a lot about the woman, more by inference than actual statement. How could he keep her from talking? What hold could an honest man have on a woman of her stripe? For no reason, Joel thought of her that evening, standing in her hallway before a closet crammed with men's clothing; and her bitter anger at being discovered. The implications of that little scene were too absurd to credit. This was central Pennsylvania, not a Maryland or Virginia locality where such things could be true.

Some time in the night, he wakened, as if at a sound. There was no wind stirring, no sounds about the cabin, but he lay listening. After a few minutes he heard it again. He crawled out of his bed and went to the front door without lighting a lamp or candle. Down there on the highway, horses were passing. He tried to count, and made it six animals, at least, proceeding at a measured walk as if burdened. They were moving up the creek in the direction of Hylersville.

The night chill touched his bare feet and shins sharply, but he stood listening until the last sound was lost, up the sandy road. Joel was cold when he crawled in under warm blankets again, but he had not forgotten to bar the front door.

CHAPTER XVII

SHARP WEATHER AND a need for provisions took Joel to town in the morning, and Uncle Thad was unusually glad to see him. "Just heard about your doctoring, son. Tom Hawks is talking sense for once. Then, you was up at the Metz place."

"Do you know the family, Uncle Thad?"

"Sure, best-behaved children in these parts. Mike's having a hard time making things go with that hill farm." He scratched his chin. "Joel. I been thinking hard. Move in with me, hang out a shingle, and start doctoring regular. You'll have enough money for school, come spring."

Joel leaned against the post which supported a counter end, and looked at his friend with something like a frown. "Don't tempt me; nothing else in the world would suit me better, but I'd come up against things that only a real doctor could handle. You remember the oldest of the Metz children, the one with curly hair?"

"Susan, sure, the one that limps."

"Uncle Thad, that's it. A man like Kenny could make that child walk. I wouldn't touch a knife to her knee to save my life. Let's forget the shingle and talk groceries."

They were filling out a list of things needed and arguing about the value of lemons for colds, when a sound outside stopped them. It was the tramp of many horses, coming up the road from the bridge, the rattle of accoutrements and the sharp command to halt, just outside the store. The two men stared at each other. Joel was fighting a tearing excitement so keen he could not think of any action. Crisp was close to panic, and his alarm helped steady the younger man.

"Cavlery," the storekeeper whispered.

A bold front was the only thing which could offer any safety. Joel went out, followed closely by the old man. A long file of blue-clad horsemen, in a column by twos, had halted in the street. Each man sat his McClellan saddle stiffly, but with the ease of a veteran horseman. Each uniform was buttoned neatly, each trousered leg had the yellow stripe showing from jacket bottom to boot top. The only noticeable difference among the soldiers was the individual way in which they wore their flat-topped forage caps. Spencer carbines rode in leather boots, each man carried a holstered revolver, and sabers were thrust through blanket rolls strapped on the back of saddles.

People were emerging from houses up and down the street and staring curiously at the horsemen. The lieutenant, riding up front with the guidon carrier, swung off his mount, handed his reins to the flag bearer and dusted his uniform with gauntleted gloves. He had the young-old face of one who had endured the shock of battle too much, and he was studying the two men in the store doorway. "Which of you is Thaddeus Crisp?"

The storekeeper cleared his throat, tried to speak, but could only manage a nod. "Lieutenant Cord, Seventeenth Pennsylvania Cavalry. I'd like a word with you, Mr. Crisp, inside."

Joel could not help a selfish feeling of relief. Uncle Thad was nervous, but surely he hadn't done anything criminal. The troopers, once their officer was in the building, relaxed. However, none of them paid the least attention to the increasing knot of townspeople across the street. Lisa Milburn, with a shawl thrown over her lovely hair, appeared on her porch. Joel was tempted to cross over and speak to her, but she went inside almost immediately. Two troopers dismounted to rearrange saddle blankets; some of the men swung legs over their pommels so they could sit more at ease. One, who was chewing tobacco, spat down into the dust, careful not to touch his horse with the spittle.

As much as fifteen minutes passed until the door opened a scant foot, just enough for Crisp to summon Joel. A stiffness passed through his body. Down south in the mountains there had been blue-clad squads riding, hunting. Joel could not forget how they had settled things with the guerillas in the light of the burning Heitel place. The lieutenant greeted him crisply. "You are Joel Pender?"

"Yes."

"Mr. Crisp informs me you live in the Narrows below here. Have you noticed any unusual night travel lately?"

Joel saw the pleading in Uncle Thad's eyes. Crisp wanted something and was hanging on Joel's answer. For the moment, he had forgotten the horses that had passed the night before. "My place is off the highway, Lieutenant, and I am afraid I sleep very soundly." The storekeeper's face showed so much relief that Joel was afraid the officer would notice.

Lieutenant Cord hadn't finished. "Nothing out of the ordinary then, Pender?"

A perverse impulse stirred Joel. It might be a good thing to break through this officer's assured crispness in dealing with civilians. "No. Somebody shot at me the other evening, though; probably just a local way of showing me I'm not welcome in these parts."

"Why?" The cavalryman's word snapped, and his sharp eyes searched the lean features of the younger man for mockery.

"I wouldn't know, sir. You'll have to ask the village gossips, they keep informed."

Cord was a wise man. His hard face showed both impatience and caution. When he spoke again, it was a complete change of subject. "One of my men has a boil on his arm. Mr. Crisp says you could lance it for him." He didn't wait for any agreement; the trooper was called in and Joel washed his hands while the cavalryman got out of his jacket and rolled up his sleeve. After cleaning the angry sore with whiskey, which Crisp furnished, Joel took his father's spring lance from his pocket. He sterilized it with the liquor, set the instrument, and tripped it. When the pus was washed away and the arm bandaged in cloth Crisp furnished, Joel gave directions.

"Keep that clean until it heals over. Be careful in grooming your horse for a few days."

Cord had watched every move, especially the care to keep everything clean. He smiled. "I didn't expect to find a real surgeon, Mr. Pender. Our thanks to you." He was following the soldier toward the door when another question occurred to him. "Does either of you men know a horse trader who travels through here, short, bearded, neatly dressed—"

The storekeeper was shaking his head. "Lotsa folks look like that. They all stop here, too. Best store in town. Why you ask?"

Cord looked hard at both men, then shook his own head. He started to speak, then turned and went back outside.

Once he and his men were gone, Crisp walked back to a chair and dropped heavily into it. He wiped his forehead with a dirty cloth. "Pour me a little snort o' that whiskey, Joel. Get some yourself." Joel was startled, knowing the man rarely drank, keeping the stock for paying customers. They didn't speak for several minutes, then Thad got up and began working around the store again. Joel tidied away the whiskey and glasses and joined him.

The old man stopped fussing with a roll of cloth and pointed a shaky finger while the cunning look returned to his rheumy eyes. "Son, Reverend Jaynes was in here and settled some bills folks has owed a longish time. Where do you figger he gets his money?"

Joel was startled. He hated keeping things from Uncle Thad, but the old man talked to everyone about everything. Carelessness would not help him. "Well, what does the preacher say, ask him?"

The storekeeper snorted. "I did, and he claims he got it from the Lord. Mind you, he really says that."

"Well," Joel commented carelessly, as if he had little interest in what Jaynes did, "likely he's better acquainted with the Lord than you or me. I suppose it must be good money, the Lord wouldn't use Confederate or counterfeit."

"Looks good to me," Crisp said, jerking open his cash box and taking out a twenty-dollar bill. "All I can say is the Lord uses his money hard, judging by the wrinkles."

* * *

That night, a light snow fell, followed by three days of mildness which turned it into mud. Joel spent the time replenishing his woodpile and putting the cabin into condition for winter. He liked using an ax and saw, and ate his meals with appetite. Usually, he would tumble into bed too tired to indulge in his usual thinking. The fourth night following the visit of the cavalry, he was roused to a heavy thumping on the front door. It was Tom Hawks, who made no apology for the late visit. "Somebody hurt Uncle Thad, bad. You come, fast."

Hawks had brought a buggy; and put his attention to making speed rather than conversation. Yet he told enough. Crisp's light had gone off at the usual bed time. But when Hawks went outside later, the light was on again and did not go off. Uneasy, he had gone over and found the store door partially open. The old storekeeper lay back of a counter, unconscious. The store was a shambles. Tom had carried him upstairs. "Somebody purely knocked hell out of him," Hawks concluded grimly.

Roused neighbors had undressed the injured man and put him in bed. Mercifully, he remained unconscious as Joel's big hands went over the horribly beaten, frail old body. When he stood up, he knew there was no chance of recovery. Both arms and one leg were broken, so were a number of ribs. Deep gashes in the scalp accounted for much of the blood.

"Nothing to do but watch," he told the neighbors, "Tom and I'll sit up with him until morning." With the first of the dawn light showing, the injured man appeared to rally and regained partial consciousness. Both men leaned over him as he tried to raise a hand. His eyes were wild.

"Don't . . . come back . . . Joel . . . didn't tell . . . where you. . . ." With that, he was unconscious again. Joel turned to Hawks.

"Look if the store was robbed." Hawks returned, carrying the cash box always kept under the left-hand counter.

"Clean empty," he said laconically, and kept moving about the room a few minutes before settling down. "Doc, I got to do some talking. Mebbe I ought to keep my mouth shut on account of my family, but I gotta talk."

Joel had lived long enough among the Indians to be able to wait for a slowly unfolding story. Hawks glanced at the man on the bed, then back to his listener. "Them soldiers as talked to Uncle Thad had a fight with bounty jumpers and deserters. It was out on the edge of Miller's Kettle. The cav'lry kilt three of 'em and took two prisoners. Folks say they hanged them, but I doubt that."

Joel's jaw set. So far, he had been too shocked to do much speculating. The old man's injuries roused a fury in him, covering a growing grief. This was Burley's brutality all over again. Hawks continued. "One of them dead boys was from these parts, up the valley a ways. Uncle Thad knowed a lot about deserters. I figger he just fed them and their families out of the goodness of his heart. He wa'n't agin the government and I know he didn't tell them soldiers a damn thing."

Hawks leaned over carefully and looked into the face of the man on the bed, his own heavy features bleak. "Mebbe you didn't figger what he said, Doc. He didn't tell the devils as kilt him where you was."

Joel was on his feet, big hands knotting, as understanding hit him. Hawks continued. "Folks thinks as somebody is after you, Joel Pender. Thet devil knows now that you was in the store with that lieutenant. Uncle Thad was first, likely you'll be next. And, my place'd be burnt if these damn woods lice thought I was talking."

Hawks turned away, crossed to the window. He returned to the bedside in a moment, as if he didn't want to be far from the dying storekeeper. Joel could tell the big man was sincere, but he was hiding something; whatever it was gave him a sense of guilt.

"You don't trust me, Tom. Uncle Thad and I didn't talk about any of this. He always ran away at the mouth, yet he was keeping secrets, even from me. I wish he'd trusted me with it. You can, you know. I've kept a lot of secrets."

The big man waited a moment or so, then delivered a noncommittal answer. "I jest don't know. Folks has talked about you being a government man, or somebody from the south. Nobody knowed where you stood. I figgered you was running, and was mixing Uncle Thad into helping you." Hawks shrugged his big shoulders.

"I ain't saying I didn't take vittles and clothes to the poor devils half-starved in the brush. But there wasn't any mean stuff then like this, fighting soldiers or hurting Uncle Thad. Doc, whoever did this, I'll break his neck. Sumpin' devilish queer has hit folks lately—"

Joel stopped the man with a gesture and pulled out a wrinkled dollar. "Tom, I know you hate to leave; but Uncle Thad won't wake up again. Say your goodbyes now. Take this money, lay in a stock of powder and bullets. Get out to my place where you'll find two revolvers. Keep the big one and wear it like you do your pants. Bring the other to me. If somebody jumps you let him have it; likely it'll be the man or men that did this."

Hawks took the money. His lips moved wordlessly to the still form on the bed, then he turned and went out, his steps light on the stairs to the lower floor.

Squire Wetwire came at nine o'clock and watched his old friend a long time. He did not volunteer any suggestions, just nodded to Joel and left. Two neighbors offered to spell Joel for an hour or so. Hawks returned at three; he and Joel went into the sick room and Tom passed over the lighter revolver. It had been freshly capped. "I draw'd them loads and recapt her," he said. "She'll shoot."

They sat together in silence. A few minutes before four by the wall clock, Crisp moved slightly and drew a long breath. A few moments later, he died.

* * *

Sheriff Paul Randy, a fat pompous man, was loudly sympathetic, but made something less than a perfunctory investigation, putting the murder down to tramps who had robbed the store. Hawks, when questioned, kept his own counsel, just stating that he had found the dead man and knew no more. Thaddeus Crisp was buried in the cemetery a short distance from the store where he had lived and worked his entire adult life. The village people had turned out en masse, and Reverend Jaynes officiated.

Joel, sick at heart, was thinking hard, even during the funeral, trying to remember the young men from this locality who might be deserters. Even so, he could not think that anyone who knew the old man would hurt him, much less commit such a brutal killing. Even Harry Sholes was at the funeral, and his eyes had not been dry. Again, he thought of Burley, and the brutality that was part and parcel of guerilla life.

Tom Hawks' statement about Crisp helping deserters was probably true; the old man would not have turned away a hungry or hunted man to save his own life. Thaddeus Crisp, like Joel's father, was unable to say no. Wetwire had been his partner, keeping track of the money and debts for his friend. The hard thing to understand was the storekeeper's nervousness which became real fear when the soldiers came.

The funeral over, Wetwire had settled the dead man's affairs. The sheriff had put down the murder, almost casually, as the work of tramps.

Joel wanted to get away from curious eyes in Hylersville, his own problems lost in a swamp of bitterness about Uncle Thad.

He was walking down the street and came to the little bridge. There
was just one man in the village entirely trustworthy. Impulsively, Joel
turned left, and in ten minutes, was knocking at the door of the minister's little house.

Jaynes was at home and welcomed his visitor cordially, insisting that
he take the deep arm chair and accept a cup of coffee just brewed. "Sam,
it's partly my responsibility that Uncle Thad is dead. If I had talked out
when Lieutenant Cord's men were here, they'd have caught these woods
lice before the murder. I was cowardly, afraid of getting involved, I kept
my mouth shut and Uncle Thad died."

Jaynes finished his coffee and set the cup down with a care. "Friend,
just now there's a pistol under your coat. Your thought is to find the
murderer and be judge, jury, and executioner. I tell you, man, that'll land
you in a Federal prison or worse." He frowned and shook his head in
dissatisfaction. "Forget that. Tell me your whole story, everything since
you first left Hylersville, and maybe we can find some light."

Joel studied the craggy face of the minister. There could be no doubt-
ing his full sincerity. Besides, having turned over the money, it was all but
imperative to tell how he came by it.

It took time. The wood fire in the heating stove burned out and there
was a chill in the room when all was finished, down to the story of the
dead deserter in the hills and the passing of the horses that night. Jaynes
heard it all, leaned way back in his chair. After a minute or two, he shook
his head, jumped up and rekindled his fire. It was crackling by the time
he spoke.

"It's almost incredible—murder, arson, kidnapping. George Geis—
I've heard of the man in connection with that Cherokee alphabet. Colet
I know; and, my friend, I have met your Trudie." Suddenly he grinned.
"One great thing in your favor; for a man apparently dressed in the full
panoply of crime, you have picked your friends well, including your present company." He took time to rub his chin carefully. "But, did I pick
you or you choose me?"

"Lisa Milburn brought us together on common ground," Joel said
with mild sarcasm.

"She sitteth at the door of her house—" Jaynes began, then a knock at the door drew him away. He listened intently for a moment, then turned back to Joel.

"You have your bag with you? There's work for us; powwow stuff. Old Ab Hillis is up to his mumbo jumbo; his nephew John's wife is sick. Now the old charlatan is going out there. I don't care if he pretends to cure warts and small things, but he could be dangerous."

Joel did not hesitate. Powwow doctoring had been one of his father's pet hates. "My father hated witch doctors, tried to laugh it off, or drive it out of the community. He'd be glad to know it's illegal now, since '58."

"Yes, but that doesn't stop Ab Hillis, and there are always people who want to believe. After your father died, he was all there was around here for years, I understand."

After a short drive, the two men entered a farm kitchen. A small, bald-headed, bearded man bent over a sick woman on a bed at the far corner of the room. With one dirty hand he pointed toward the ceiling, with the other he was holding a fry pan full of live coals close to the woman's face. She was moaning and trying to writhe away from the terrible heat.

Joel crossed the room in three long strides and forced the man to set the pan on the stove. "Ab, you damned fool, are you trying to kill that woman?"

The little man hopped like a fighting cock. "Gimme that pan, Pender. She's got Saint Anthony's fire. She'll die of it if sumthin' ain't done!"

Joel seized the would-be healer and thumped him down, hard, in a chair. He turned to the patient. One side of the sick woman's face bore angry scarlet blotches, the other cheek was about as bad from Hillis' savage attempt to cure. Joel touched one of the scarlet blotches, watched it disappear, then return in a moment. "This is erysipelas." He pulled some bromine from his bag and began applying it with a clean cloth. Angrily, he lectured the sullen powwow man. "We know you can stop blood, sometimes. Maybe you can take off warts—but you could have killed this woman. A man like you ought to be tarred and feathered out of town."

Hillis was mopping his face and head with a big red handkerchief and was suddenly so contrite that tears showed in his eyes. "She's a good woman. My nevvy called me and I did what—"

Joel was relieved to see that the heat had not burned the woman's cheek, the redness was fading. "If I catch you doing any powwowing again, Ab, I'll make sure you leave town and don't come back. If you don't wind up in the jail, that is." The sound of Hillis blubbering mixed with the slowing sobs from the woman on the bed.

Jaynes stepped in. "Both he and his wife are good at nursing the sick, Joel. They help out a lot, when a neighbor needs it. It's the powwow stuff which he needs to quit. Ab has a good heart."

The door was flung open and a little woman rushed in, followed by a younger man, who stopped at the sight which greeted him. The woman bustled forward, clucking her tongue. "Ab Hillis, I told you and told you—" She turned to the woman on the bed and gathered her into her arms. "It'll be all right dear, the doctor is here now. Did Ab hurt you very badly?"

The sick woman was crying again. Joel turned to John Hillis. "You and this lady take turns keeping damp cloths on your wife's face until morning, then use wet bran."

Joel spent the night at Jaynes' house. He wanted to check on his patient early the next day. Near dawn, someone came to the door. Jaynes left, but didn't ask Joel along, so he thought it was probably a spiritual sickness, not a physical one. He was walking toward the Hillis house when he met the minister coming back with the buggy. Jaynes' face showed a mixture of excitement and chagrin. "I stopped at Hillis' house on my way home. That woman is sitting up and claims she's hungry. Could those wet cloths cure that quickly?"

"No, the disease would run a week, anyway."

Jaynes shrugged his heavy shoulders. "It'll take us years to stop Old Ab, now. He'll claim it was his treatment which worked."

Joel grunted. He was even more puzzled than the minister. He remembered a number of times when his father had encountered similar happenings during his long practice and how he would sit brooding or grumbling about them. The really bad effect of such procedures as the powwow men used, was to shake the faith of people in the regular practitioners. He headed back to High Valley, where he took out his irritation at his wood pile.

CHAPTER XVIII

THE GREATER PART of a week passed before a shortage of food drove him back to town. He was headed to the store when the maid from the boarding house appeared and beckoned. When Joel came up to her, the girl looked up and down street furtively before confiding her message.

"She seen you. Go in the house so you two can talk."

Mrs. Milburn had dressed with her usual care, letting her brown hair frame her face and her house dress do the same for her full figure. Today there was no sign of coquetry in her direct manner as she took her visitor into the small sitting room and came to the point.

"You'll have to get away from Hylersville. I talked with the Squire, and he agrees. I've got three hundred dollars saved; it's a loan to help you through your schooling. It'll be business like; I'll take a mortgage on High Valley. You can pay when you're practicing."

Joel looked at her with surprise and read the seriousness in her eyes.

"Lisa, I'm grateful, of course, but I can't—"

Her fingers were twisting a fold of her dress. "The Squire said you'd be stubborn but, after what's happened—" She stopped, and her eyes widened. "I'm scared they'll kill you, and the talk is worse. They say you struck John Darcy down, tried to kill him so you'd get the school job back, and they hint you had something to do with Uncle Thad's death. I sent Mary for Tom Hawks."

Joel stared at her in surprise. "John Darcy?" He was interrupted by heavy steps in the hallway. Tom Hawks entered the room and Joel turned to him. "Tom, what's happened?"

Hawks eased himself into a chair, and Joel noted that he was careful of his left arm. "They came back to Uncle Thad's store. There was talk about town as how he had money hid, and I guess that word got into the woods. Three men walked in on John Darcy, who was redding up. He yelled for help afore they knocked him down with a club, most like they did to Uncle Thad. This time I heard, and when I come runnin', they took off, three of 'em, and I follered after. Crost the crick they started shootin'. I got nicked a bit in the arm." The big man's face was grim.

Joel stood up and motioned for Hawks to roll up his sleeve. The bullet burn was shallow, but in a spot which would hurt whenever Hawks moved his arm. Someone had applied a neat bandage and some sort of grease. Joel hoped it was clean. "Did you hit any of them, Tom?"

Hawks frowned, glanced at Mrs. Milburn, and answered unwillingly. "I guess so, they carried one man off, up the Dog Run path. 'Course, he could have stumbled or sumthin'."

"John Darcy. Tom, did Darcy say I was one of the men?"

Hawks shook his head. "He was knocked out and they took him to Starr's. I reckon Reub and his missus told what he said."

Joel slammed out of the house, evading Lisa Milburn's grasping hands. Tom caught up with him. "Joel," he demanded, "why in hell did you make me say that about shooting?"

Joel stopped and frowned. "I see, Tom, they'll be after you now?"

The big woodsman nodded. "I ain't afraid for myself, it's what they might do to my family. My figgering is, the one I hit is dead."

"Tom, I want to talk to Darcy and Starr. We'll put our heads together later."

At the Starr home Joel strode up to the front door, rapped once, then opened it and walked in. John Darcy, his head swathed in a bandage, lay on a couch. His sister, Mrs. Starr, sat in a rocking chair, basket of sewing on her lap. Surprise, distaste, and anger showed on her thin face at the intrusion. Joel stood over Darcy and kept his voice down.

"John, why did you say I struck you down?"

"I didn't." Darcy eased himself painfully to a sitting position and turned toward his sister. "Carrie, is that what you were telling Lizzie Fenemore in the next room?"

The rocker stopped, and the thin woman seemed to be shrinking inside her voluminous dress. "John, he made me do it. He told Sholes and the minister, Reuben did—" Starr walked into the room and, this time, there was no urbanity on his face as he glared at his wife and Joel.

Darcy gave him no time to say anything. "I said, and I remember clearly though half stunned, that the man was tall, like Pender." The schoolmaster's face was grim below his bandages. "It's time for a reckoning, Reuben. This house is mine. Carrie's money has kept you going. You hated Doctor Pender and have tried to take it out on the son. I suspect you were back of that mob."

In spite of his strong words, Darcy was out of strength. He lay back against the pillow, and his sister began to fuss over him. Neither of them paid any attention as Joel gestured at the door. Starr mechanically obeyed, and the two men walked out of the house to where Tom Hawks still stood. Joel stepped close, and his powerful right hand gripped Starr's vest and shirt front. "How much did you pay Sholes for the mob, Reuben?"

Starr struggled. "Twenty dollars."

"And his damages?"

"Yes."

Joel released Starr and stood looking at him. The man's Adam's apple bobbed up and down as he swallowed. Obeying the habit of years, Starr's hands came up and tried to pull coat and vest into some order. Joel could beat the man to within an inch of his life, or he could march Starr down to the hotel, force him to make a spectacle of himself. Starr began hiccupping.

"You're a sick man, Starr. I've seen you crawl twice and it's not pretty. Go and hide somewhere until you feel cocky again." Joel turned and strode away.

Jaynes was at home, and his welcoming smile changed to surprise as he looked into his visitor's grim face. "Sam, why didn't you tell me what's going on? What'll this town do next?"

"Give you another river to cross, I suppose. It depends some on how you take this."

Joel stepped forward. "What kind of answer is that? What ministerial counsel do you give a man that Reuben Starr smeared?"

"This town blows hot and cold because it's scared. A few days back it would have gone hard for you, if you'd come to town. By now, most folks know Starr stretched things. And you've already done a lot of good, Joel Pender. Teaching, and helping the sick—people can see what kind of man you are." He pointed a finger. "Someday you're going to know that whenever you helped anybody else, you helped yourself more. And, by the Lord Harry, I'm going to see you learn to take it with a grin. It's my notion that Hylersville, in its crooked way, has been good to you."

He seized his visitor by the shoulders, shaking him lightly. "Joel." His voice was like a bugle call. "Come with me, will you? See a patient. Sallie Briller is sick." Jaynes picked up his hat and coat. "Do you know her?"

"I think she was in school with me, a few years younger."

Jaynes harnessed his horse and hitched it to the buggy. "Sallie is shunned by most of town. Her daughter, Lucy, is about three. Sallie never married. She picks up whatever work she can find. I don't know how she keeps them fed. The good women of the town would rather see them both starve than help them." Jaynes' voice was bitter. "I heard the child had had a fever. She seems to be recovering, but the mother looked poorly yesterday."

Sallie lived in the tiny, unpainted house which her parents had occupied up until their death. A single room comprised the whole lower floor of the building. Lucy, a small, sober, dark-haired child, played with a rag doll near a stove that sent out but little heat. She had a thin woolen scarf pinned over her dress, but her small hands looked blue. A woman, on a bed at the far side of the room, tried to smile as the two men walked toward her.

"Sorry," she croaked. Jaynes touched her forehead, telling her not to try to talk. Joel checked the child over first. She didn't look strong, but had no fever and only a minor cough.

Jaynes fixed the fire. "There, Lucy, you and your doll can get warm." He poked the fire, worked ashes away so there was a draft, laid what little wood there was on the coals. "I'll gather some more wood." The minister went out, and the child crept closer to the blaze.

Joel crossed to the bed, smiling. "I'm Joel Pender, Sallie. Maybe I can help you."

"We called—you Doc," she panted, "in school—Joel. Did you—?"

"No more talk. Yes, that's what they called me. I took a splinter from under your nail and remember you yelled murder. I did two years of medical school." His examination was quick but careful. He touched forehead, testing for fever. He listened to her breathing. Finally he excused himself to get something out of the buggy and Jaynes followed him.

"Sam, she needs a nurse, someone to care for her. Is there anyone who will?"

"Well, Ab Hillis and his wife are kind to her. The wife is good with the sick. Ab would be too, if he'd forget his powwowing."

Joel shook his head, but said, "Go see if they'll come. I don't think we should try to move her." He went back in.

"Don't try talking," he advised the sick woman. "I'll leave some medicine, and somebody to help out until you're well." Sallie's eyes were grateful, and, worn out, she slept fitfully for a while. Jaynes arrived with the Hillis couple.

Jemima Hillis bustled around, wrapping her own shawl around the child, and setting on water for hot drinks. "Ab, lay in more wood, and bring in that basket from the buggy."

"No powwowwing, Ab. None." Joel's voice was firm.

The wife glared at the little bald man, then told Joel, "I'll not let him use anything you have not told us to. There'll be no foolishness."

"I won't say no words," the little man promised. "I'll keep up the fires and run errands."

"Can you trust them?" the minister asked as they drove away.

"Probably not. But who'd walk into sickness like that? For a fallen woman?" Joel's voice was sharply cynical. "Sam, we'll have to get a doctor, soon. I can't do much better than Ab Hillis. Even Dad had trouble with high fevers. Even if I had the medicines regular doctors use in such cases, I'd be afraid to prescribe such strong stuff."

"Do you know what it is?" Jaynes looked wary.

Joel shook his head. "I have suspicions, but won't say for now."

Jaynes pulled in his horse and pointed. The hilly, rolling fields showed, here and there, some light dusting of snow. Dozens of crows were congregated in every big tree. At some unseen signal, the black birds swung abruptly into the air, moving toward a wooded hollow a quarter of a mile away. "They're making sure of a warm bed in the hemlocks. Crows have sense. By the way, did you know a south wind has been blowing toward the northwest for the past three days?"

"He that observeth the wind shall not sow," Joel quoted, but his attempt at humor fell flat.

"Influenza weather, my Bible quoting friend," Jaynes said. "We're bound for the Millheits. I fear influenza, grippe, lung fever—whatever you call it."

Joel didn't argue. The Millheit home and property was in sharp contrast to Sallie's sad little home. There was a picket fence, and the house was freshly painted. They were admitted by a maid, and the interior was heated with a coal burner. Joel remembered a thin, determined woman who always spoke of herself as April Millheit, as if reluctant to own herself a wife. Today, she was dressed in a warm flannel gown and lay on a wide bed in a well-heated room. Her husband was also wrapped in a flannel gown, sitting in a deep wing chair near the bed.

Joel started an apology. "I've come to help, if I can, but you should know I'm not a registered, trained doctor."

Millheit broke in. "We know all that. Neither was your Pa, but he was a good man. However, my wife and I just have a chill."

"Yes," Joel said, nodding, as he looked at the flushed faces. Husband and wife glanced at each other, and the woman spoke in a choked voice.

"It feels like water touching my back and my neck's stiff. My husband complains of a sore nose when he uses a handkerchief." Excited now, she sat up in bed and delivered her bomb shell. "This morning, I spit blood."

Joel walked over to the bed. He had heard his father speak of influenza; and he had studied it briefly in medical school. There was a touch of fear at the base of his neck, almost as sharp as if he had been prodded sharply with a pistol barrel. This overheated, too comfortable room was full of threat. "No, madam," he said carefully, "likely it was just colored mucous. It's a symptom, but don't get frightened."

"Get us a doctor," Millheit demanded, "send to Point Haven, we can pay."

Joel studied the now anxious face, the labored breathing, the high fever flush. "Yes, Mr. Millheit, we'll get a doctor, if we can. You may both have influenza. Keep warm, drink lemonade, lots of it. I'll leave some niter for the fever."

* * *

The sickness of Sallie Briller and the Millheits was the beginning. The weather, after a two-day snow, turned cold. Tom Hawks was sent to Point Haven for medicines and a doctor. Joel was tempted to ask him to learn if Trudie was still in the town but didn't. Hawks returned with some niter and ammonia which Joel was afraid to use. Point Haven was already in the grip of the disease; all doctors busy, medicines running low. Hylersville was alone in its threatened extremity like a beleaguered city.

At the end of a week, there were eight cases of influenza and April Millheit was the first death. Fear of contagion was so great that Joel and Jaynes had to help dig the grave. However, fear did not prevent the spread of the disease. In ten days, so many were ill that, with the help of Tom Hawks, the two young men carried out slops, kept up house fires, and fed those unable to care for themselves.

Sallie Briller lingered, becoming steadily weaker. One evening, Joel felt the frail fingers in his hand relax and he took her pulse quickly with his free one. In a moment, he laid the wasted hand on the coverlet. He placed his things back in the old black bag, noting as he did so that one of the seams was breaking.

Drab, gray days dragged themselves through the second week of the epidemic and the double strain of work and anxiety began to tell on both Jaynes and Joel. Neither ever got a full night's sleep, they ate irregularly, and there wasn't even much chance to change clothes or clean up. Generally, in the evenings, they brewed teas for the sick, drawing on Indian John's supply of herbs—boneset, horehound, wintergreen, and yarrow. Both knew that the worse a medicine tasted, the more faith it brought to the patient.

Three more, one a child, died. Old people appeared to be immune to the disease, but it hit the middle aged and young hard. Wetwire worked as a grave digger, Ab Hillis and his wife made an excellent team, as did Tom Hawks, his wife, and oldest boy. On the fourteenth day, Doctor Clarence Mulvay from Point Haven came and spent several hours with

Joel and Jaynes. Surprisingly, he approved the herbal remedies, and the dosage used.

"Nothing cures this thing, men. Most anything in the way of medicine that keeps up a patient's hopes is good. The depression which comes with the disease can be a death warrant. Pour soup, wine, beef tea into them when they get better. I'll send help, so soon as we can spare anybody in Point Haven."

The doctor had brought a welcome supply of quinine and niter. When he was gone and the young men were finishing a sketchy meal of hard bread, rye coffee and dried beef, Joel pushed back his plate and made an announcement. "Soup, beef tea, maybe whiskey."

The minister chewed slowly, favoring a sore tooth, then said, "What?"

"Get soup, beef tea, chicken broth, rice. We've got medicine now; but we can't keep up the fires, cook, dose, dig graves much longer. Everybody in town's turned in what they have. The Crisp store's been open day and night with John Darcy handing out what's there and never a nickel paid. Even Reuben Starr furnished this dried beef and the ham Mrs. Fenemore's boiling into a stew. Yes, sir, my ministerial friend, we're going to let a man cast his bread on the waters. Mark you, it will be well buttered. We're about to let a fat man into the lodge of do-gooders."

"Harry Sholes," Jaynes said in amazement. "If you mean him, he'll throw you out of his place."

Joel was pulling on his worn jacket. "Implement my faith, Reverend. Tell Tom Hawks to meet me at the hotel in an hour."

The big lobby and barroom combined was empty, except for a man asleep with his head on a table, and the rotund proprietor back of the bar. Sholes took one look at his visitor and grabbed the limber handled bung starter. "Get out of my place," he roared, "or I'll smash you with this."

Joel walked closer and Sholes backed into the shelf behind him. "You're too fat to run or use that club, Harry. So, listen. Twenty-two people, counted since noon, are down sick; and ten now have died. The sick folks and those getting well must be fed. They need soup, milk, whiskey. The last is the kind you drink yourself, not the stuff you sell over the bar—" Joel put both big hands on the polished wood and leaned forward, "—and send out to the deserters in those little kegs. The government ought to know about you, and the town can spare you any time the cavalry comes back."

Sholes stared, small eyes almost hidden in rolls of fat, then had enough courage to snap out a scornful comment. "Soup, milk, whiskey, who's to pay?"

Joel studied Sholes for a moment. Profit was this man's god, the only thing he either loved or respected. Burley's money was in the minister's hands. Joel had bought medical supplies from his own pocket; and he and Jaynes had paid for burials. Finally, he took out a five dollar note and tossed it on the counter.

"That's for one week. Tom Hawks'll be here in an hour, for all you've got cooked. After the week, it won't matter to you. I suppose you know you have a fever now."

Sholes started to lick his lips nervously and Joel nodded. "That's how it starts, dry lips and a little fever. Your nose burns when you blow it." The hotel man fumbled for a handkerchief and Joel pursued his advantage, making his tone casual. "Influenza's hard on fat people, Harry. By the way, if you stop sending the soup and other food, take a bottle of your rot gut up to bed and drink yourself to death. Who in hell'd care? I solemnly promise that if you don't help this town, no medicine'll get to you."

Joel took out a small vial filled with quinine pills and rattled the contents. "Pills for influenza, sent over by Point Haven. Taken in time, they help."

Sholes shot out a fat hand, fingers hooked. "Gimme some. My head and throat hurt. I'm a sick man, Pender."

Joel counted out two of the gray pellets. "Take one now, one at bed time. How about the soup?"

"I'll call the cook now. We had a boiled dinner. Soon's Tom comes, I'll have a load for him."

When he was back in Jaynes' house, Joel was impatient and disgusted with himself. "Sam, I've sunk pretty low, scaring a fat man out of two years of his life. You see, I didn't know until we began to talk that Sholes has a morbid fear of this disease. Maybe it was whiskey, but I let on his color was due to fever, and worked on that. He's turning over what we want. And, Sam, he'll keep furnishing things if I have to break the whole book of medical ethics."

CHAPTER XIX

HARRY SHOLES furnished food, but even the hotel's supplies were limited. All work in and about the community had come to a stop. Occasionally a farmer would drive in with a load of provisions and leave what he brought at the Crisp store, where John Darcy tried to ration the limited supply. One man brought in four hams; that night the store was raided and the meat taken. Tom Hawks had chased three men back into the hills and had fired a shot to halt them without result. The big man, along with the minister and Joel, were getting desperate, for the convalescents were even harder to serve properly than the sick were.

Joel walked slowly down the street toward the main bridge and the hotel. Sholes had taken influenza after all and was bedfast; and it was surprising to see a smart spring wagon and another heavier one at the hitching rack. Two women alighted. One hurried into the hotel, but there was no mistaking the other in her knitted hood and blue coat.

Joel started to run. "Trudie," he cried, and she turned. Her eyes widened and she hesitated a brief moment before smiling and coming to meet him, one mittened hand extended.

"You must be Mr. Pender, sir. Mrs. Blanche Driggs and I, Trudie Quinn, have been sent from the county seat to help."

Joel took the extended hand, felt the fingers under the wool grip his fingers hard. Trudie was still smiling but she was whispering. "We mustn't know each other, Joel. Trust me. Lieutenant Cord's in Point Haven; he knows I'm from Talpo. He's tried to question me."

"Mr. Pender, both our wagons are loaded with supplies. Come, meet Mrs. Driggs," she said in normal tones, and Joel followed her. A moment

later, he was presented and was shaking the hand of a rather plump woman with a delightful smile.

"We've heard wonderful things about you, Doctor Pender, from our
Doctor Mulvey."

"Not a doctor, Mrs. Driggs," Joel assured her. "All we have here is one
minister, one good driver, and a quack. Lord, but it's good to have you
and Miss Quinn here. Even the hotel man is in bed. Let's go up and see
him. He'll want the privilege of putting you both up, for your stay."

Mrs. Beryl, the frightened housekeeper, took them upstairs to Sholes'
room, but before they entered, she pulled Joel aside. "Will he die, Doc?"

He patted her plump shoulder reassuringly. "Sure, Mrs. Beryl, we
all will, eventually. Harry has a good chance to get well, if he doesn't get
hold of too much whiskey. We'll go in." Joel got a glimpse of Trudie's
face, and thought she smiled.

Sholes lay deep in a feather bed with a tick of the same material over
him. His eyes were uneasy as Joel took his pulse and tested his forehead
for fever. "How am I, Doc?"

"A little better, Harry. And now we have help. These ladies are
Miss Quinn and Mrs. Driggs. They'll need rooms." Sholes pudgy hand
emerged from the covers and pulled Joel closer.

"Tell Beryl to put 'em in three. It's got a stove, and she's to feed 'em
good."

Joel pulled the covering tick back into place and bent low to whisper.
"Damned if you're not getting human, Harry. Keep trying."

Trudie organized the campaign along lines suggested by the Point
Haven doctors. There were two teams, one Trudie and Reverend Jaynes,
the other Joel and Mrs. Driggs. Tom Hawks and his wife were to manage
the food. Organization began to tell, inside a day.

Joel got no chance, at all, to talk to Trudie alone. In fact, he saw little
of her except for brief times in the hotel when all four were present. The
schedule she had worked out provided sleep and rest for the overworked
men and both began to feel better.

One day, Joel saw Jaynes and Trudie emerging from Mrs. Milburn's
boarding house and it angered him. Later, when he had a few minutes
with his friend, he demanded roughly, "Why in hell did you take her in
there, Sam?"

"You mean why in Hylersville, my friend. Our business is to visit all the houses and, it is my Christian duty to call on the widows and the fatherless."

"She's no widow," Joel snapped, and Jaynes dropped his flippancy. "She ought to be, Doc, she ought to be," he said cryptically, leaving Joel to wonder just how much this close mouthed, able man knew. Wishing that a woman should become a widow didn't fit properly into the minister's usual outlook.

Abruptly, Joel stopped what he was doing at the moment. Trudie, had he mentioned her when he told his story to Jaynes? He closed his eyes and tried to think. She was always in his mind; his story would not have been complete without her part in it. But he couldn't remember, and it made his head ache to think. So many things had happened, this desperate struggle with the epidemic, the deaths, the burials. What a man said, even a few days ago, didn't seem to matter.

Harry Sholes was doing better, and there were no new cases. A week saw things so improved that Mrs. Driggs returned to Point Haven, leaving Trudie to finish the work. Joel walked down the hill again, thinking of what a shock it had been when Trudie had not permitted him to show he knew her.

At the hotel, Joel found his convalescent patient in bad shape, his fever up, his throat bad. He lay on his bed, fighting to breathe. From his breath, it was apparent that he had been drinking. Trudie and Jaynes were somewhere uptown. Joel worked alone, lifting the gross body so Sholes could breathe easier, and fanning him. After midnight, he was breathing better and resting easy, yet Joel remained another hour before summoning Mrs. Beryl and placing her in charge.

Joel's head was aching again as he stepped out into the cold darkness of the early morning, which was relieved a little by a light skiff of snow that had fallen during the night. For the past few days, a general lassitude had been bothering him; he had set that down to the strain he and the minister had undergone. His evening meal had been tasteless. The chill air made him so dizzy there was difficulty getting down the broad porch steps.

No one else was abroad at this hour. Joel had the feeling he was plodding through a great emptiness where silence was the only thing of substance, and it had to be pushed aside with all a man's strength. By the time he was walking down the hill once more, every step demanded effort so great that he had to stop often to get his breath.

Now that rationality had deserted him, he was drawn along by a queer homing instinct that found him, in gray morning, entering the Narrows. There were many times when he fell and lay for a time before struggling to his feet and going on. It was close to midafternoon when he crawled up the cabin steps, pushed open the unlocked door and, fully dressed, sprawled on the blankets of his bed without consciousness enough to draw them over his chilled body.

Hours later, Trudie and Jaynes found Joel tossing on his bed in the icy cold cabin. His face was flushed, and he was babbling a confusion of all but meaningless words and phrases. His two friends listened for a moment in shocked silence.

"Burley . . . Tom . . . trouble on horses . . . Trudie . . . not a doctor . . ." The sick man opened his eyes and appeared to recognize his visitors, but what he said showed he was still delirious. "Can't . . . child's knee . . . straight . . . Sallie . . . damned deserter . . . tablespoons whiskey . . . Harry."

Trudie turned to Jaynes, started a question, but he stopped her with a shake of his head. "No need to cover up with me, Miss Quinn. Between us, I know his whole story. Yes, he's in danger—but never more so than now. Build a fire while I undress him."

Two brisk fires, one in the cook stove, the other in the field stone chimney, heated the small interior in a short time. Trudie turned the sick man over, tapped smartly between the shoulder blades, and saw the involuntary shrinking that indicated pain. She turned to the minister, tears starting in her eyes. "He's bad, awful bad. I'm going to try the Indian remedy. Get me lots of hot water and plenty of hemlock browse."

She worked fast. In an hour, Trudie had the patient under a blanket tent, and Jaynes kept her supplied with hot water to steam the hemlock browse and keep the tent filled. Jaynes noticed that she added leaves from a dried plant that hung from a rafter to the hemlock infusion. In addition to frequent doses of the bitter stuff, Trudie kept hot cloths on her patient's chest through the night. Jaynes, watching anxiously. "Does this sweating always cure?"

The girl glanced inside the tent, then dropped the blanket quickly so heat would not escape. "Indians use a tight willow hut, so the steam gets a good chance."

"Does it cure?" he demanded, and Trudie lifted a hand to her face. Her answer was blunt. "Not always. What other chance do we have?"

This time, it seemed to work. The tent came off at dawn, and Joel was conscious about noon. He smiled weakly at his friends and tried to speak, but Trudie stopped him with fingers across his lips. Afterward, she gave him a tisane of herbs and nodded when he shuddered at the taste.

Tom Hawks showed up in early evening with provisions and a lot of questions. Jaynes cautioned, "We better not tell folks Pender's sick. People get scary if there's no doctor about. Miss Quinn and I'll take turns to stay with him. Can you manage in the town?"

The big man made no comment, just stood there a minute or two as if expecting something, then nodded and left. Jaynes noticed that he carried a revolver thrust through the waist band of his trousers.

The two friends took turns watching throughout the second night. Joel was definitely better, but very weak and burned out from the fever. Trudie explained that these symptoms showed the danger of the sweating treatment. "He needs liquid to replace the sweats. You go back to town, Reverend Jaynes. It will be the truth to say I've left town. And I can manage, if you'll run out now and then. Check with our sick."

After they were alone, Joel talked in snatches. With Trudie bustling about, it was like the old, kind days in Talpo when they were out with the sick. He was too weak to rationalize; once he went over the details of a picnic, again of a search for roots. "They looked like human bodies, Trudie," he said weakly, and she answered indulgently.

"Ginseng, Joel. Stop talking and drink this tea."

He swallowed the pungent dose obediently, gagged, and caught her fingers as she took the cup. "Feathers," he mumbled, "bring me feathers." She looked at him curiously. He seemed rational, and was grinning while he pointed to the cup. "Indian medicine, now feathers . . . war bonnet."

When Joel wakened, his head was clear. He had been asleep for hours. The bedroom alcove allowed one to see into the living room. Trudie was in there, close to the fireplace. She seemed startled, and one of her hands was hidden by the folds of her dress. In another moment Joel heard steps coming up on the porch, then the front door opened.

In sick surprise, he recognized the taller of the intruders; the man he supposed was far away in the southern mountains, the man who had held the horses that morning by the schoolhouse. There was the black hair, the drooping eyelid. This was Lee Harne, and he was grinning.

"Well, well, Shad's little chickadee. And so far from home." The second man pushed the door shut and set his back against it, and Harne's voice went hard. "Money, girl, I've come a long way for it. Step aside. Your schoolteacher friend'll come across this time."

Joel heard the edge of savagery in the former guerilla's voice and knew what the man was capable of doing. Using all his strength, he tried to raise his body and swing his legs off the bed. He fell back, gasping. Joel knew Trudie could shoot as well as any man he knew, but he had not seen the weapon until her hand whipped up from the fold of her dress with the revolver. The roar of the shot seemed to tear the room apart, muffling Harne's howl of pain and surprise. There was a second report, then a third, as the two men tore open the door and jumped off the porch into the darkness. Joel watched Trudie push the front door shut, drop the bolt in place, and lean for a moment with her back against the panels. He tried to move again but was too close to the edge of the bed and fell to the floor.

Somehow, the girl found strength enough to drag Joel's inert body back on the bed. She had scarcely finished before there was the pounding of heavy feet on the porch and a jerking at the door. "Tom Hawks!" a voice yelled, "open, quick."

After the big man was admitted, he shoved a heavy revolver into his trousers band and almost tiptoed to the bed. He swore softly, under his breath. "I knowed I oughta watched, Miss Quinn, seein' I heard things, rumors, around. Did they shoot him?"

Trudie shook her head. "No, I shot one of them. Help me with Joel."

Again, there was an all-night session with the sick man, but he was conscious at dawn. Trudie reassured him when he tried to talk excitedly. "It's all right. Tom Hawks is here."

Joel's eyes lightened and some of the tension left his drawn features. "Thanks, Tom. I'll sleep a little, now."

The big man turned away, walked to the front door then returned to Trudie. "I misjudged him onc't, on account of Uncle Thad. It's gonta take a long time to make it up. From now on out, I'm watchin'."

The big man meant what he said. When Joel was more comfortable, he reloaded the revolver, cautioned Trudie to keep the doors locked, and left for town. Returning several hours later, he brought his wife, a shotgun, and supplies.

"You take care of the sick," Mrs. Hawks assured Trudie, "I'll manage the house, and spell you; and Tom'll stand by."

Joel mended rapidly. When Trudie sat beside his bed, he talked quietly of many things, none of which centered on their present situation. He was savoring fully the joy of having her close, with her quick smile, and sometimes, the far away kindly look—as if she, too, was remembering the goodness of little Talpo and their friendship there.

With Hawks to play nurse for a short time, his wife insisted Trudie walk with her for some fresh air. When they had gone, Joel beckoned the big man over to the bedside. "Where are they, Tom?"

The two men had come to understand one another, and his answer came quickly. "Six, seven miles back, the old Forbes lumber camps. They's mebbe ten to a dozen of 'em." He got up, crossed to a window to check on where the women were, before continuing. "Doc, I don't believe there's a damned Valley or Hylersville boy with thet crew, though I couldn't get clost enough to see 'em all. These is furriners, likely bounty men thet come and go. They enlists, gets the bounty pay and deserts, lies low, and does it all over agin."

"Harne?"

Hawks took another precautionary look for the women. "I told you onct there was somethin devilish loose. It's him, sent in here. Doc, Harne butchered Uncle Thad."

Joel nodded soberly, then put out a hand and touched the sleeve of this man who had become his friend. "You see him alone, Tom, shoot him, and just let him lie. When I'm better, there'll be two guns after him."

The women were coming up on the porch. Hawks nodded and Joel saw the quick flame leap into his dark eyes. Murder for murder looked out for a moment.

Then, there was an afternoon when the Hawks had gone into Camar, at the foot of the Narrows, for supplies; and there was time for uninterrupted talk. Joel went over everything which had happened since he had come to Hylersville. "So, you see, Trudie, I've been lying here, thinking, Colet gave me a half promise, told me to stay round here. Why doesn't he do something about this rat's nest in the woods, round up men like Harne—"

"Perhaps he has, Joel. Don't be impatient. There are other localities all over the state. Harne'll be quiet, there's a bullet in him somewhere. Your business is to get well and work with Doctor McColl, when he comes."

Trudie got up, went to the kitchen and returned with a cup of Indian John's goldenrod tea. Her patient drank most of it.

"Trudie, let's face it. I'm a hunted man and it's about time I was on the move. They'll know you nursed me and that you're from the South. This talk of doctoring or going back to school is just wind in the brush. If George Geis can't straighten out that paymaster matter, I may hang. Tom Ellender could help, but he shot Burley and wouldn't talk."

Joel shifted his shoulders against the piled-up pillows. "Tom Hawks and I'll have to get Harne out of this country or there'll be more murders. Then, I'll walk into a recruiting office and get shot at respectably, not from the brush. I want you to get back to Point Haven, young woman, and forget you ever knew a gangling, would-be doctor who came to you in the pennyroyal country."

Trudie reached forward, both arms toward the big pillow. Joel leaned forward a bit so she could work with it, but, instead, her strong fingers caught his bony shoulders and pushed him back sharply. "Listen to me, Joel Pender. You can no more dodge being a doctor than you can fly. It's in your blood, even if you don't realize or appreciate your gift with the sick. Something makes you a healer. It was that way with little Trudie Quinn Pohasin that night and with the people here in your home town. Added to it, you make the right friends, like Doctor Kenny and Reverend Jaynes. My friend, if you weren't so soaked in self-pity, you'd know that things will work out. Actually, you've just kept a whole town alive."

Trudie got up, walked to the front door, and let in cold air, while she looked out a moment before returning. "Reverend Jaynes says my share of that money would be enough—" Joel came to a sitting up position with a jerk, his bony feet protruding from under the blanket.

"Trudie, for God's sake, I didn't tell him about that. You mustn't be involved. How did he find out?"

"I told him," she said calmly; "he knows everything; but all you know about him is that he's a kindly minister, working for his people."

Joel pointed his finger. "So, you took the final risk, Trudie. Are we bound to go on trusting him, crossing the rivers he suggests?"

She nodded. "Joel, Reverend Jaynes has always been a minister. A wound, taken in a skirmish in the west, took him out of the army. Stonewall Jackson had his younger brother hanged. The boy was out of uniform calling on a girl. Nobody we know wants the North to win as much as our Sam Jaynes. But he came here, trying to work the bitterness out of his mind and soul, and he walked right into this mess of deserters, bounty jumpers and murderers. Perhaps he is helping Colet. He's seen something in you, Joel. Trust him, do what he says."

Trudie jumped up, impulsively, breaking the tension. She flounced out into the kitchen and started rattling pans and dishes in preparation for a meal.

"By damn," Joel growled in his best voice, "I'm an important man, not yet twenty-four years old and already the army wants me to pack a musket. Intelligence wants me for robbing paymasters and burning houses. Sam Jaynes and some others want me to practice medicine, when I'm still too damn dumb, professionally, to tell bees from beeswax. Fact is, everybody wants me except the fair village of Hylersville, and a girl named Trudie Quinn. Nurse, get my clothes. I'm moving to Sam Jaynes' house 'til I'm strong enough to shoot rattlesnakes."

She obeyed without comment, tossing his clothes into a pile on the bed. "You might shave. That way you'll look better to the folks that want you."

Left alone while she went into the living room, Joel dressed with fumbling fingers and went to the kitchen to shave. The mirror gave him little comfort. His high cheek bones were sharper and there were shadows under his eyes that made him look older. He remembered that Sam Jaynes had not addressed him as "young man" in some weeks.

Tom Hawks agreed to take Trudie to Camar where she could get a stage to the county seat. She was all ready to go; blue coat, mittens, and the knitted hood over her bright hair and, for these moments, they were alone.

"Trudie," said softly, "maybe someday there'll be one of Jaynes miracles and we—"

"Yes." For the second time she came up on her toes, her breath touching his face as she kissed him lightly, this time on his lips, chapped by fever.

Hawks was back at dusk and delivered Joel and his scant baggage at the minister's house, probably thinking that anybody would be safe in such quarters. Jaynes was out, but a note on the table said he would be back in two hours. Joel made himself at home.

CHAPTER XX

AFTER A FEW DAYS, Joel went out with Jaynes in his buggy, and waited outside while the minister made his calls. The town, hard hit by the epidemic, recovered very slowly from its depression. Work had been at a standstill; food was poor and scarce, and houses showed the lack of repair or pride in them. Hylersville did not begin to show real life until a mercifully early spring announced itself with red on the maples, and the powdery flaunting of catkins on the poplars. Bush willows displayed their wooly promise of leaves, and the single horse chestnut tree in town, the one near the Crisp store, was covered with sticky buds that seemed to yield hourly to splitting from the growing force within them. People began to rouse to the challenges of the season. Men talked of trout fishing; some started spading up garden plots, while women grumbled about the labors of spring cleaning.

Both young men read a great deal, and they had acquired the companionship which did not need to express itself with much talking. Joel took longer and longer walks, strengthening himself for his return to High Valley. One evening they talked briefly about Thaddeus Crisp, for Joel had put up a board marker on the old man's grave that day.

"He wasn't actually a blood relative?" Jaynes asked.

"No, no family connection at all, but we were close since my boyhood. He was murdered in cold blood; the county authorities did nothing, and I've done no better, toward punishing his killers."

"No use reminding you whose business vengeance is," Jaynes said, smiling. "We all loved the old man, and both of us worried that he might have been involved in something dangerous. His killers likely thought he furnished Lieutenant Cord information. Say, I wonder where Squire Wetwire is, these days."

Joel felt irritated. Jaynes had made a statement that brought in the Bible and Squire Wetwire. Trying to distract him? It was too involved to straighten out; he continued about his old friend. "Thad was either worried or scared. It showed, especially when Cord and his troopers came. If this epidemic hadn't hit I'd have scouted the hills looking for these deserter hideouts. And it's worse now that Lee Harne's in the country."

Jaynes adjusted the draft on his stove before returning to his chair. "One thing, if Crisp was really involved, he's safe now. One of these days there'll be a roundup of these criminals, and I'd hate to see a man like our friend dragged into that mess."

"Roundup." Joel tensed. There had been a night when he had seen how troopers do a thing like that. That night was still sharp in his mind's eye. He went to the door, while Jaynes slumped deeper in his chair. "Sam, I keep wondering what sort of soldier I'd be. War looks like the poorest way to end an argument. We take a man, get him shot, then put him in a field hospital to patch the bullet hole. It's such an abominable waste of blood, pain, and tears."

Jaynes' eyebrows went up. "We will presume, however, that you do not expect to set up a field hospital for Lee Harne."

Joel went out; there was no use arguing with the man, or even trying to imagine what was actually back of his ready words. Mrs. Milburn was on her porch, and insisted on his coming into the boarding house, where she served him a cup of tea and a piece of apple pie. Neither mentioned their earlier quarrel. "It's been a long, awful winter," she commented, "folks died; you were sick, yourself."

"But it's past," he assured her, "and the new doctor's coming to Camar. No more epidemics."

She frowned. "I'm not concerned about him, Joel, it's you, and when you'll go back to school where you'll be safe. Tell me, you are going?"

"No, Lisa, not just yet. I'm to work with the new doctor a while, until he gets started. Of course, that experience will count toward my degree." Joel kept his eyes on the final bite of pie on his plate. It seemed foolish to be sitting here with this woman, exchanging polite talk with her. When he did glance up, it was in time to catch the frantic look in her eyes. She covered it by rising and pointing to his worn coat.

"I just thought of something, and you're about the size. Excuse me a few moments." She was back too soon to have gone upstairs, and she was carrying an excellent brown coat. "This was in the hall closet. I was cleaning yesterday. Maybe you could use it. I hate to see it wasted. The ladies of the church will make rugs of the other garments. Dear me, that place should have been redd out years ago."

"Clothes for deserters" was something Colet had said, and the phrase was in Joel's mind as he took the coat. Surely a man didn't need to be suspicious all the time and of everything, his own mother had had a closet crammed full of such things.

"I'm in your debt, Lisa, for the pie, the tea, and this coat. My clothes are pretty shabby, and I don't seem to get the chance to get to a clothing store." He smiled, and suddenly believed what he was about to say. "Someday, maybe I'll be able to buy you a brown dress to go with your lovely hair."

To his surprise, the woman's mood had changed. There were tears in her eyes, and he laid his big hands on her shoulders. Next instant, she had crowded close. "What's wrong, Lisa?" Her clenched hands came up, pressed against his chest.

"Everything. What does a woman do when she's caught with something and can't get loose. I keep telling you to get away, but—"

Joel stopped her with his question. "Tell me, Lisa, why are you scared? What do you know?" She twisted free and left the room without answering. After a few minutes, he picked up the coat and stepped outside. The promise of spring did not move him as he walked slowly back to the minister's house.

Jaynes was out, having left the usual note pinned to his door. Joel wrote one of his own and, minutes later, carrying his meager baggage which included the new coat, was on his way to High Valley. Perhaps there, alone, he could think things through.

Early in the morning of his first full day at the cabin, Joel set about the reconnoitering he had promised himself to do, since Tom Hawks had mentioned the old Forbes lumber camp as the hangout of the deserters and other riffraff. In a half hour, he passed the place where the deserters who had surrendered themselves had buried their companion. There was no sign of the grave; melted snow had dampened the ground and the matt of old leaves until there was no sign the ground had been disturbed. He turned away, depressed. Thaddeus Crisp slept in a marked grave, later there would be a stone there with his name neatly chiseled on it. There was nothing for this boy.

Joel remembered this country pretty well, and by noon, was on the edge of the big clearing where the three dilapidated buildings, which had housed the lumbering crews and their horses, stood. The site was a natural clearing, with a small brook meandering through it. To one side there were old stumps and a few outcropping rocks. Smoke was lifting from the chimneys of two of the buildings which had been the bunk houses. A sudden metallic banging startled him until he realized it was the call to the noon meal. The lumbermen must have left their triangle in one of the houses.

Three men emerged from brush along the little creek, two more came out of the stable and a sixth man appeared on the far side of the clearing from Joel. The man who had sounded the call would be the seventh, and Joel wanted to know, desperately, how many more men had been in the building when the call sounded.

A thin wedge of fairly thick brush to his right thrust its way into the clearing. Beyond its point were several gray boulders. A man who was careful could get within twenty feet from the bunkhouse, and he had played this game of stalking with the young Indian men at Talpo. The single window, high on the side of the log building, was the final temptation.

He slipped through the brush carefully and gained the cover of the first big rock. He had been too slow, for a man carrying a gun came outside and methodically searched the whole clearing with his eyes. Minutes dragged; Joel knew the men in the bunkhouse would finish their meal in short order, and his chance for observation was slipping away. He pulled off his hat to wipe his sweating forehead on his sleeve. Something of his movement must have shown; a gun cracked and bits of stone stung Joel's face. That rifle would be a muzzleloader; crouching low, he turned and darted for the brush.

Men boiled out of the building, shouting, and the marksman called to them. "Must have been a deer, next time—"

Joel spent the better part of two more hours, this time watching from a safe distance and a good route of retreat. In that time, he thought he counted ten men, though there might have been several more. Also, he figured out the lay of the land. An old woods road ran from the camp, down Cherry Run to the highway, a distance of ten miles or so. And there was a path over the mountain to Hylersville. This camp wasn't over three miles from the village, itself.

He went back to his cabin knowing that he "had a bear by the tail" as woodsmen would say. One man or two, counting Tom Hawks, couldn't do much here. The only feasible thing was to try to contact Colet. He'd have to see Trudie, and it wasn't too big a risk—after all, he'd visited her in the county seat before.

It had been almost dark when he reached High Valley and he was hungry, since his lunch had been nothing but a lump of corn bread carried in his pocket. It took time to get fires and lamps lighted. That done, he set out some food and noticed the water bucket was empty.

He picked up a wooden pail; and left the back door open so the lamplight would guide him on his return. He had almost reached the spring when a blanket, reeking of horse, was pitched over his head. His feet were kicked out from under him, and men were forcing his body down. They tied his hands and feet with rope in spite of his struggles. Helpless, he was dragged into the cabin living room and the blanket jerked aside. Joel looked up into the snarling face of the man he hated. There was the slit of a mouth and the drooping eyelid.

"Harne," Joel gritted, and spat blanket fuzz from his mouth.

The guerilla spoke to his companion, a stocky, bearded man. "Poke up the fire, Bill. I may need it, if he doesn't talk quick." He swung round to his prisoner. "Once, I promised to work you over. Tonight's the time unless you dig up that thirty thousand dollars. Federal money it was, me and Burley checked it over, on our way back to that damned Heitel place."

Joel glared back at his captor. "You filthy, murdering coward, I should have killed you that morning."

Harne gave him a staggering slap across the face. "To hell with your mistakes. That old storekeep wouldn't talk, wouldn't even tell where you were. But there are ways. You ain't spent none of the money; where is it?" The second slap almost knocked Joel from the chair where they had seated him. Harne had worked himself into a fury; grabbing Joel's hair, he spat into his face and the prisoner's jerk brought him nearly to his feet. The second man slammed him down again.

Joel twisted and tried to get some of the spittle from his cheeks by shaking his head. The shorter man was watching him closely; he might be tempted. "Bill, listen. Your boss is murder crazy. I never saw Burley's money. Search the place."

Harne struck him again. "You got a lot of debts to pay, teacher; the boys shot at the Heitel farm—and you can't keep your hands off women. I'm going to make you crawl and beg fer a bullet. Then, look for a club-bin' like that damned storekeeper got."

He snapped an order at his companion. "Stick the ramrods into the fire. Tonight that bitch ain't here to slip a bullet into me." Harne paced back and forth while Bill thrust two iron musket ramrods into the fire. The guerilla glanced at them occasionally, but the other bandit stood, bearded face expressionless. His right hand hovered close to the butt of a revolver thrust through his wide leather belt. Harne strutted in front of his victim.

"I'm a full captain now, sonny. I'm not Burley's man any more. Damn the man, I aimed to kill him for the money, but you stole it. You Yankees are dumb. We got close to an army in the brush, up and down this state; enough to take Pennsylvania out of the war. Hell, we'll do it, one of these days."

Joel wasn't following the ranting too closely. He was sure Harne was touched by insanity and might make a mistake, open up some chance. At the Heitel farm, he had wanted to use a whip; here, it was fire. Bill watched the heating irons closely. Harne joined him, and while their backs were turned Joel tested his bonds desperately, using all his strength.

"Ain't hot enough, Bill," the guerilla commented, "but we've got all night. You can write with those things when they're really hot. I saw Burley use one once."

His companion had begun edging toward the front door. Suddenly, his nervous hand dropped to the butt of the revolver in his belt and strain pitched his voice high, like a woman's. "Lee, I come to git word outer this man but I ain't got the stomach fer a burnin'. Hell, I ain't no Injun. Now, I'm gitten back to camp where I can't hear thet poor devil holler."

Harne gaped in surprise. When he took a step toward his companion, Bill's hand moved, and his weapon came out smoothly, the hammer snicked back. The man's voice had become normal and steady. "No closer, Lee, er you'll git it in the guts. I kilt men afore, deader than the old man you clubbed." Bill had reached the door, his revolver flicking up and down like a snake's tongue. Temper took control of his voice again. "Damn you, Lee Harne, it was peaceful round these parts 'til you come. Now I'm tired of takin' orders from a lousy Secesh. Mebbe the Provost wants me fer shootin' an officer, but I ain't ever burnt a man." He opened the door, stopped, took a step back. "Mebbe I ought to finish yeh here and now. Yeh sure as hell been ripe a longish time."

Joel held his breath, hoping, but the door slammed shut, boots drummed on the porch, and the place was quiet except for the snapping of the fire. Harne appeared to have lost all interest in his prisoner, his concern centered on the defection of his henchman. First, he tiptoed to the kitchen and returned with a carbine. Next, he peered through a crack in the front door, then slammed it, tiptoed through the rooms and left the cabin by the back, carrying his weapon at full cock.

Alone, and desperate for time before Harne returned, Joel searched the room with his eyes. The ramrods glowed cherry hot in the fire. His revolver, half hidden by the doctor's bag, was less than six feet away. Then his heart leaped—his double-bitted ax, its blades razor sharp, stood in the corner. The whole tool rested on its wide, four-pound head, handle sticking up.

He hitched himself into a fall from the chair, fearful lest the thump warn the guerilla outside. Crawling frantically, he reached the corner. The first trial cut his wrist, but the second brought the thin rope across the ax edge and it parted, freeing his hands. He had only seconds to cut the rope on his ankles, but he had been tied very tightly. He stumbled as he tried to reach the shelf. He fell heavily, but had his revolver in his hand when Harne dashed in.

The first shot spun the guerilla around, the second dropped him in a heap, half-supported by the side wall. Joel, breathing like a half-spent runner, stood over the prostrate killer. Obviously, he wasn't dead, but blood oozed from one shoulder and there was a livid weal across the side of his head. Joel was fighting with the nearly impossible urge to shoot again, to end the life of the man who had murdered Uncle Thad in so terrible a fashion. Before, back there at the cabin in Burley's hollow, he had spared Harne's life; and the man had gone on to more murders and violence.

He paid no attention to the sound of horses on the road, nor the drum of feet on the gravel and then the porch. The hammer of the revolver came back; the copper sight steadied on the break between the unconscious man's eyebrows.

The door crashed open, and Tom Hawks had again come at the right moment. Jaynes, Wetwire, and the Squire's sawmill boss, Jim Turley, were with him. Joel pointed, and gritted through set teeth, "Drag that beast outside before I blow his brains out. He killed Uncle Thad."

Joel offered no protest when Jaynes took the revolver from his grasp. His lips were bleeding from the slaps, and Harne had kicked him twice in the side when they had him down. Wetwire produced a bottle and handed it to Joel. Jaynes and Hawks straightened the wounded man's body, and the minister looked at the shoulder wound. Just then, Tom, who had straightened up first, saw the ramrods in the fire.

"Good God," he said, and for a horrified moment or two, the newcomers stood in shocked silence.

"Preacher," Hawks said softly, "give Joel back his gun, or should I shoot 'im?"

Wetwire's hand went out and covered Tom's. "No, the man dies on a rope. Let's not get smeared in any more killings."

Jaynes had not risen, but he had removed Harne's coat and loosened his shirt. He beckoned to Joel. "Come on, friend, give him field hospital aid. He's bleeding pretty badly."

Joel got off the chair where he had been sitting, and moved with the faltering steps of a sleep walker to the side of the minister. He dropped to his knees. Wetwire handed over the doctor's bag, and Joel opened the instrument roll.

The bright gray steel of a scalpel glittered in the lamp light, and, for a moment Joel held the keen blade within inches of the prostrate man's throat. One flick of that blade would end the career of the guerilla's murdering and torturing. The irons were still red in the dying fire. Jaynes was waiting. Joel laid down the knife and picked up a probe. "Get me hot water."

A scowling Tom Hawks held the basin steadily enough. Jaynes' lips twitched as the thin sliver of steel explored the wound. Joel laid down the probe and picked up a lint pad and some bandage. "Bullet went through," he explained laconically. "There may be a concussion from the head wound, but that takes a surgeon. He'll live to hang."

Wetwire spoke. "Doctor McColl arrived in Camar two days ago. We'll take this brute down there." He frowned at Joel as if trying to control himself. "All right, son, Tom got us out here as soon as he knew you were alone. Seems he saved your hide once before. From this same man, Harne. What's the man after?"

Joel carried the basin to the kitchen, poured out the bloody water and washed his hands with a clean supply. He knew he could not tell the real story of Harne's vindictiveness. "Robbery, I guess. There was another man with him, and they fell out when Harne wanted to use torture so I'd give him money. He boasted he'd do the same to me as he did to Uncle Thad."

"Harne, you said, how did you know his name?"

"His boasts, claims he's a rebel captain, mixed up with deserters."

Jaynes had remained silent. Wetwire took charge. "All right, men, we'll take him to Doctor McColl, then on to Sheriff Randy, if he can travel."

Hawks stepped forward and yanked the wounded prisoner to his feet. "You're damn right he can, Squire. The bastard's shamming, his eyes flicked open when you talked."

Wetwire walked to the door. "There's enough of you boys. Joel will go along to make charges. McColl's office is in the Denver place. Some of you know where that is."

After Turley had led Harne from the room, Joel turned to Jaynes and Hawks. "Tom, I have you to thank again—"

The big man shook his head. "Why, the Squire lied. I was coming later, but he rounded up me'n the preacher. He drove like blue blazes, getting here."

The gray of morning was showing when Hawks' spring wagon stopped at a white house, set less than a dozen feet from the creek in the village of Camar, and Jaynes did the knocking. After some minutes, a man answered. He wore his night shirt stuffed into the top of his trousers, and carried a lamp with a smoked chimney. He listened to the minister's explanation of their presence. "Yes, I'm Doctor McColl. Bring the patient in."

Joel watched closely. Harne pretended to be unconscious again when they stretched him out on a table. McColl had sharp lines about mouth and eyes, which denied the open friendliness of the remainder of his features, and he worked swiftly. "That's a good bandage. Is one of you a doctor?"

Joel colored a little and nodded. "I'm a first aid man, sir, and I put it on."

McColl jerked a thumb into the air and his voice was edged as he spoke to Harne. "My stupid friend, you're shamming. There's no concussion. The shoulder wound knocked you down, likely a bone was nicked. Get off that table, it's not a lounge."

He turned to the others while the guerilla complied. "Gunshot wounds have to be reported. Take this man to the sheriff. He has another partly healed wound on that same shoulder."

That was from Trudie's bullet; none of the three men explained. McColl shook hands with Joel. "I'm glad to meet you, Pender. They tell me we are to work together for a while."

Joel liked the quick sure grip of the doctor's fingers but the opening of a door in the rear of the room made him look over McColl's shoulder. A tall woman stood there, dressed in a wadded gown with a thick braid of yellow hair over her shoulder. "Did you call, John, is something wrong?"

"No, Sarah, it's all finished. Go back to bed."

"What an unholy hour," Joel heard the woman mutter as she went out.

Sheriff Randy showed little enthusiasm at the capture of the man who had killed Thaddeus Crisp, but he had a turnkey take Harne away.

"I'll file the complaint," Joel said, "attempted robbery, threat of torture, murder."

The sheriff took out papers and indicated where the complaint should be signed. "Who shot the prisoner? What evidence or witnesses have you for the District Attorney?"

Surprisingly, it was the usually laconic Tom Hawks who answered the sheriff's question and did it roughly, even savagely. "Randy, we all seen the red-hot irons this Harne was planning on using on Pender. The rope he tied Joel with, too. Thet devil bragged that he kilt Thad Crisp, and remember, you didn't do a damn thing about thet murder but drag your fat bottom in and out'n your buggy and bawl a bit at the funeral. You keep this Secesh skunk tight 'til trial time."

The sheriff edged away from the furious woodsman while Joel and Jaynes signed the paper forms. The minister was not satisfied. "Sheriff Randy, we're filing another report with government people, telling that you have a Confederate spy under lock and key. Provost officers will want to see this man."

"File ahead," the county officer snapped, and Jaynes smiled, entirely without mirth. He had something to add.

"Don't make any more mistakes, sheriff."

Joel's friends waited while he hurried to Trudie's boarding house. Her grim landlady seemed to get pleasure in announcing to her shabby caller that the girl was away, and would not return for two days. She waited impatiently while Joel wrote a brief note. "Tell Colet to come," he had written.

He looked at the tall woman, his dislike showing. "Of course you'll read the note, Madam, but don't forget to give it to Miss Quinn."

CHAPTER XXI

HAWKS WENT ON up to Hylersville, but Joel was pleased when Jaynes announced that he would spend the night at High Valley. Both men busied themselves putting the disordered cabin to rights and then settled down to enjoy a cheerful evening fire. Jaynes watched the little flames curl round the birch logs and nodded when there were tiny pops.

"Air pockets in wood," he explained. "Hemlock is really noisy, keeps a man awake."

"And red oak smells," Joel said a trifle impatiently. "Sam, we've got Lee Harne in jail, but think of what the man is telling, to receptive ears."

"Yes," the minister said thoughtfully, "I've crossed that bridge a half dozen times. However, you can't let a mad dog run loose, even if our sheriff isn't to be trusted. Harne will accuse you of murder, arson and robbery. Sheriff Randy's ears will prick up at the word that you have thirty thousand dollars hidden. If—"

"If Harne'll trust the man that far. My guess is that the guerilla won't open up unless he's out of that jail." Joel booted a stick of cord wood nearer the fire. "I should have killed Harne that first morning at the Heitel farm and saved Uncle Thad's life. I should have shot him in this room or let Tom Hawks do it. Maybe I'd have saved my own neck, that way."

Jaynes made a tent of his fingers. He spoke carefully. "It's one thing to kill a man to help others, or maybe, in self-defense—"

He broke his tent long enough to wave both hands in an including gesture. "If you'd have been a better shot, things would have worked out fine. I've no brief for keeping men like Lee Harne alive. But, and it's a big word here, the man was helpless, already cut by two bullets. Joel, I've watched you in a lot of trying situations; you are not a person to act as judge, jury, and executioner even to save your life." He shook his head.

"I didn't stop you from pulling that trigger—you did. Thank God for the decency bred into you. Go to Trudie someday with clean hands, or to prison with a clear conscience. Colet will be here, soon. Perhaps all this has hastened the showdown."

The minister's rugged features appeared to stiffen as he used a poker to open better draft between the burning logs. "Once, I hated a man enough to make me feel like killing him. Well, a year or so later, he was killed in battle. No, I'm not conceited enough to think the Lord aimed that bullet for my personal vengeance, but things do just balance out. Colet's working for you, so is George Geis. More than either, so is Trudie."

He grinned and leaned toward his friend. "Tell me, my perplexed pilgrim, having crossed another river—what does a girl like Trudie Quinn see in you?"

Joel had to grin at Jaynes' manner. "I don't know, Sam, I really don't." He wasn't quite sure what his friend meant, but he was becoming increasingly aware of the minister's ability to get under a man's skin.

* * *

Doctor McColl surprised the region by moving from Camar to Hylersville before he actually got his things unpacked, giving as his reason that living by the creek side annoyed him and his wife. Joel made his call on the man with whom he was to work, and the blonde woman admitted him to a bare waiting room. She had not closed the door behind her, and after a minute, Joel heard her talking. "That Pender man is here, John. He's shabby, even needs a haircut. For pity's sake let him drive your horses but don't let him meddle with your practice."

What seemed like a long moment passed before McColl's steady, low-pitched voice answered his wife's comment. "Sarah, I don't care a damn about the man's clothes or his haircuts. This boy keeps his hands clean, and that bandage he put on Harne's shoulder the other night was a professional job. It's my notion that he's a little better than good; and, my dear, you will treat him civilly."

A mirror across the room picked up Joel's reflection. It gave him no comfort, since it told him Mrs. McColl's comment had been, to say the least, accurate. His hair hadn't been trimmed for a month, there was no tie at the collar of his dark shirt and his worn coat was short in the sleeves and tight over the shoulders.

McColl's greeting was cordial. After some general talk, he tactfully drew out his visitor about background and training. "Very good, Pender. No doubt you could get a license to practice now. However, I understand you want your degree, first."

"Yes sir. I've seen so many things I do not understand; and I'm wary to prescribe medicines and use instruments."

The doctor smiled. "There should be others—" McColl shook his head in interruption of his own statement. "Who am I, to discuss professional ethics. Pender, something interests me. They've told me of that man's attack on you. What would you have done, if he had actually used those hot irons?"

Joel rubbed his chin; he was trying to remember who had told him that a rabbit doesn't worry after being shot at and missed, he just keeps on being a rabbit. He grinned. "I don't know, sir, you see, I didn't have the money he wanted."

McColl rose, pulled on a coat, and picked up his hat. "There's a little girl, bad leg, suppose you take me to see her, and any other patients that might need me."

The new doctor greeted Mrs. Metz pleasantly, and the child's knee interested him. He was very gentle and reassuring. "Yes, Mrs. Metz, and Susan, this trouble can be corrected, I believe. We can take her to Point Haven. Mrs. Driggs will go with her to Lancaster and Doctor Kenny. She'll run like any other child, afterward."

Susan looked up into his face, she was frightened but, childlike, she trusted this new acquaintance. "Will it hurt?"

Impulsively, McColl swung her up in his arms. "No, Susan, they will put another blue ribbon, like the one you're wearing, on your hair. Then you will go to sleep. When you wake up, there will be a little cut,

After that heals, you can come home, and visit me. You'll have to do your exercises, and make that leg strong, you know." He smiled down at her.

"Have you a little girl, Doctor?"

"I had, Susan, but she went away." He set her down. "Mr. Pender and I'll have to go now."

Joel accompanied Doctor McColl through the community. Over the next days, he came to like the physician better and better. Mrs. McColl was, as she had been directed, civil.

One day, when Joel arrived, Mrs. McColl had been resting. She did not rise to greet Joel. As the doctor gathered his medical bag, a bottle on the kitchen table caught Joel's eye. He made no mention of it, just followed the doctor out. Once in the buggy, McColl abruptly said, "My wife has had her troubles. Life is not always easy. She cannot be blamed."

After a moment, the doctor continued, "My wife is a mild alcoholic, Pender. I see that she is safe. Should you see me drinking, don't worry. I never prescribe or diagnose when I am not myself." They fell into a silence, and no more was said of his or his wife's troubles.

* * *

Jaynes was always pretty busy with his calls and seldom at home, but Joel did find him in one afternoon. "Sam, when will Colet come?" The minister shook his head and Joel hurried on. "Harne really believes I have that paymaster money. Suppose he tells Sheriff Randy; what would the man do? He winked at Uncle Thad's murder."

Jaynes frowned. "It could be that our esteemed public officer senses there is a showdown coming. He could be busy, covering his own tracks." He stopped his friend's unspoken question, with a raised hand. "Don't ask me what I know, it's little enough, but Colet could be setting the stage for his roundup. Meantime, just go on doctoring."

"By the way, John Rider has been gossiping. He says the new doctor drinks, so does his wife; who is also a loose woman. I suggest you talk to John; just talk, I mean. McColl's in for the usual Hylersville treatment."

There was no one who understood the "Hylersville treatment" better than Joel. Luck was with him. In the Crisp store, he heard his one-time fellow boarder talking to Mrs. Fenemore. "A shame the man came to our town, even though we need a doctor; and his wife—"

That was all Joel heard, for Mrs. Fenemore saw him and moved away. Rider looked embarrassed. "John, I've been looking for you these past two days," Joel told the nervous clerk. I have to see you about something. Come outside a little, where we'll be alone."

He made his tone confidential. Rider followed him out the back door, and they walked between some ranks of firewood. He was getting nervous, licked his lips and made a shaky comment. "You heard what I said, to, to Mrs. Fenemore."

"Yes, John, what you published. That biddy's poison. Now, here's something you ought to know. You're a stinking, prying, peeping piece of filth. I know you look in bedroom windows. Get your coat off, John, I'm going to knock hell out of you."

John Rider was big enough to defend himself, but he had no stomach for battle. He ran, only to be promptly tripped so that he fell sprawling. Joel pulled the squirming man across his knees and grabbed a piece of board. Rider moaned and sobbed for mercy, but the board rose and fell mechanically until Joel was tired and allowed the beaten victim to rise. "Keep your tongue clear of the McColls after this. Remember, John, you searched my room, right after I came to town."

Rider nodded soberly. "I knew you blamed me for that, but I never went in your door. I saw her—"

Joel stopped him with a gesture, having no desire to hear more, and Rider was glad to get away. After a little, Joel went out to the street and walked off. He didn't feel very proud of himself. The fact was that he was getting jumpy and vicious.

* * *

On the seventh day of a dragging week, McColl was nervous and irritated by the condition of a patient. A boy who had stepped on a rusted nail had been treated by his parents with the local cure-all for such hurts—a piece of fat, salty meat bound on the wound, resulting in a bad infection.

"Red streaks on his leg, Pender. I'm going home, have a drink and some rest. Amputation may be necessary. I hope not. I'll drop you off at your cabin."

Joel walked slowly up his steep lane. Halfway up, he saw the neat hoofprints, as identifiable as if the mare, Katy, had written a signature. Colet was cooking in the kitchen and greeted his host with a smile that Joel found hard to return. After a brief handshake, the older man seemed to understand the lack of cordiality. "I came as soon as I could." He pointed to the bubbling on the stove. "That's army potato soup, dosed up a bit with some of Indian John's herbs. We'll eat our soup, dunk our doughnuts, then talk."

Both men ate with good appetites; Joel was usually hungry, and Colet was proud of his cooking. The soup, which was almost a stew, was excellent, and so were the doughnuts. When the meal was finished and the dishes washed, they went into the living room. Colet had cigars, but Joel preferred his pipe. A few minutes passed while the visitor fussed with a match and arranged the small logs in the fire.

"Luckily, Trudie got back to Point Haven in time to prevent your landlady spreading your note all over town." He frowned. "There are those in Point Haven who know I am Major Colet, once in the Seventeenth Pennsylvania Cavalry, now on detached service."

"Provost," Joel snapped, and Colet waved his cigar.

"Not exactly, friend, say army intelligence."

Joel was thinking about his note. He knew at the time that it was indiscreet, but there had seemed no other way. "Lee Harne was in the jail, sir. I wanted you to talk with him. Sheriff Randy's not to be trusted."

Colet nodded. "Too bad. Lee Harne escaped three nights ago. Randy was struck over the head, making him more unconscious than usual. The ex-guerilla's likely well on his way to Virginia. I was just too late."

"As you and your men were, when Uncle Thad Crisp was murdered?"

Colet was trying to hold his temper, but he did throw a half-smoked cigar into the fire. "Joel Pender, listen carefully. I'm not God, just an army man under orders. I'm here, not because you sent for me but because the jump off, or roundup, whichever you call it, comes in three days; and it's state wide. East of the river, a whole battalion moves into a valley after deserters and riffraff. Lieutenant Cord will be here, with troopers. Your job will be to take him to that old lumber camp. My men and I'll clean the town; and your eyes will pop when you see what we've turned up. Randy's the first in Point Haven. This is a clean-up."

Colet was on his feet, striding back and forth. When he took his chair again, his voice was kinder. "For Trudie's sake, I became interested in you, else you'd have had that trial months ago. You got away with *some* money; that, in these war times, would be enough to hang you. I have promised her, and I promise you—after this mess is finished, I'm being sent to what is now West Virginia, and I'll see George Geis and this Tom Ellender, the mountain boy. We can clear you if we can find, or account for, the paymaster money—thirty-two thousand, seven hundred dollars."

Colet had lighted another cigar. "You've surely helped here, as I thought. People watched you, but not my men. Sure, you've had a hard time; but think, every day hundreds of boys your age die on the battle field. And you'll live to be a damn fine doctor. Trudie had faith in you, and I guess I ought to, as well. Now, I'm going to bed."

After Colet had gone to his bunk, Joel stepped out on the front porch. Toward the highway, the leaves filtered the thin moonlight down to the shadows of the tree trunks. The creek's chuckle and rattle always seemed muted in deference to the usual night stillness. To the right, the fireflies made themselves into a searching party over the weedy field.

Every detail of that night at Pohasin's came back to Joel vividly—the tenseness of the big Indian as he listened; and the nearness of Trudie with her breath touching his face now and then. For a moment, the memory was so vivid, he thought he heard the distant sound of a horse's hooves, and smelled pennyroyal. It called him back to reality. He went inside.

Colet was up early, and had breakfast prepared when Joel roused and went to the kitchen. "Got to be moving, Joel. Katy's fed and rubbed down." When they finished, Colet apologized. "The dishes are your job, son. I have to hurry." As he swung aboard the little mare, he said, "There's one thing. Colonel Clary, my chief, knows about your work with the epidemic. In recognition of your service to the community, you can clear any one of those we arrest, provided he's done no murder."

Joel stared, not fully comprehending the offer. Katy nuzzled his hand. Colet leaned from his saddle. "Cord will have his orders. One is—to do what you should have done and shoot Harne on sight."

Three days, that was too much time for thinking. At any rate, Joel's mind wasn't very clear whether the time began when Colet rode away, or the day before. Colet, like Jaynes, had a way of being indefinite and irritating, when he chose.

"Clear any one we arrest, provided he's done no murder," that would have saved Uncle Thad, if he was alive and entangled in this affair, or Lisa Milburn who had all-but admitted that she was entangled. There wasn't any sense to such a promise. It probably wouldn't hold.

Abruptly, Joel was suspicious. If he cleared anyone who worked against the Federal government, he would entangle himself. . . .

Damn Colet, the promise to see George Geis might mean nothing. Yet this same man had told him whom to trust in Hylersville and his advice came through Trudie. Thinking of her made him pace back and forth as her uncle had done the night before. Joel could not remember when he wanted to see her more; for reassurance, advice, or just to hear her voice, and if he was lucky, see her smile.

Next morning, Doctor McColl had come to the cabin, driving his team. "There's work for us, Pender. Two men routed me out of bed asking me to come to Kettle Valley. There's a farm up there and a man hurt. Do you know where it is?"

Joel knew, and it took him only minutes to get ready. He was thankful for something to get his mind off Colet's plans. The doctor drove. At the foot of the Narrows, they turned left, following a rough, narrow road which passed through mountain defiles before emerging in a small bowl- shaped valley. Another half mile ran through the timber into the open where fields overgrown with weeds, a pole barn, and a ramshackle house indicated a farmstead. Joel tied the horses to the hitching rail while McColl got out with his bag. Three roughly dressed men had come out of the house and a stocky, brown-bearded man was the spokesman.

"I'm Wash Tibs as sent for you, if one of you's the doctor." McColl nodded. He had already started toward the house, the others following. "Blanche is inside with Bowder. He's been mighty bad all morning," Tibs volunteered further.

The only furniture in the room they entered was a broken rocking chair, and a rumpled bed in a corner on which a man lay, breathing heavily. An inner door opened and a tall woman, with a thin braid of blonde hair hanging down her back, appeared. "Blanche," Tibs pointed to McColl, "this here's the doctor. I got him soon's I could."

Joel was close enough to see her venomous look and her gritty whisper. "Like hell you did."

The doctor had paid no attention to the interplay but went to the bed and pulled down the blanket. The injured man's eyes were closed; his face was covered with several weeks' growth of dark beard, but both the blanket and the brown nightshirt were surprisingly clean.

McColl's examination was mercifully swift and thorough, but he lifted the matted bandage from the right leg just once; long enough for a quick glance and to note the familiar, sickly-sweet odor. He turned to the woman who stood watching. "You his wife?"

"Not exactly."

McColl's snort covered a wealth of opinion. "Any relatives here?"

"He's got a kind of cousin outside," Tibs said. "I'll call him in." The youth who entered reminded Joel a little of Tom Ellender, except that there was a vacancy in the light blue eyes. McColl faced the group. He pointed to the bed.

"That man's dying. Gangrene. You damn fools just as good as murdered him by not getting me here days earlier. The leg'll have to come off, but the operation's likely to finish him." No one said anything. Blanche shot another ugly look at Tibs. The doctor's voice was hard. "It's a bullet wound, you know. Why didn't the one who shot him, give it to him in the head? Now, get out. You, Blanche, hot water and lots of it, and a basin."

Ten minutes later, coat off, with Joel handling the chloroform, Mc-Coll set to work without removing the old bandage. His hands moved with a deftness which amazed his helper. This surgeon was as good as Kenny. He began to talk in a low voice.

"Good lesson here, Pender. Speed is the essence . . . flaps long . . . too short . . . another amputation. Poor devil's dying . . . flaps won't matter." He finished, stood erect. "How long, Pender?"

"Close to fifteen minutes, sir."

McColl snorted. "A little slow. Did it in the army in eight minutes flat."

Joel's fingers moved to the patient's wrist, to confirm what he already knew. He looked up at the surgeon's drawn face and took a long breath. McColl answered the unvoiced comment. "Yes, he's dead."

He pulled the blanket over the dead man's face, picked up the basin and pitched the bloody water out a window. Using fresh, he washed his hands and gave Joel a turn at the basin. The doctor then rinsed and dried his medical equipment and put it back into his bag. He pulled on his coat. "Anyway, Pender, you've had a good lesson in amputation. Life and death, they're so close to each other I wonder they don't shake hands." They walked to the group waiting just outside. McColl announced bluntly, "The patient's dead, the operation came too late."

The doctor was walking toward the buggy, carrying his bag, when the youth who had been called into the room earlier let out a howl. "Them damn butchers kilt him, I knowed they would." He broke through the group, a cocked, sawed-off musket in his dirty hands, and ran toward McColl. Joel was the nearest man; his hand shot out, grabbed the gun barrel, and twisted it upward, just as the weapon roared and sent its vicious load ripping into the tree tops. Thrusting his foot forward, he sent the youth sprawling. Two men held him down. Joel stepped off the porch and smashed the musket stock against a rock. Blanche appeared and snarled at Tibs, who stood with his mouth open.

"Pay the man, you damned murderer. Give him some of that Secesh gold you're so stingy with."

Tibs scowled at the woman. Without a word, he laid a ten dollar gold piece in Joel's hand.

Neither man had anything of moment to say until they were back on the Narrows road. Joel gave the doctor the money, and McColl grinned. "That's a bad sign for a beginning doctor, my friend. You're too good at bill collecting."

The horses trotted along, Joel driving. He was thinking of Colet, and realized they had just come from a deserter hill pocket. McColl was mumbling details of the work he had just finished, writing in a notebook he pulled from his bag. "Leg amputation . . . posterior flap long . . . anterior . . ." A few miles farther on, he closed the notebook, and justified the finish of an operation on a dead man.

"No matter how close to death a patient may appear to be, it's the surgeon's or doctor's business to keep doing all he can, like we did back there. Any medical man, as you will learn some day, Pender, knows that the day of miracles isn't past."

At Joel's road, McColl settled himself into the driver's seat. "Pender, I figured you had some troubles of your own, and might like to work with me to get your mind off them. Good thing I did, or I might not have come back. I'm obliged."

Joel waited until the fast-moving buggy disappeared round the turn. Once again, he had gone through a moving experience with a surgeon whose every movement was a challenge. He was thrown back to the time with Doctor Kenny in the field hospital at Gettysburg. He walked up the steep lane, trying hard to fasten in his memory every phase of McColl's technique; and for the moment he forgot the threat which hung over him.

CHAPTER XXII

TENSION RETURNED sharply on the second morning of the wait for Colet's plan to come to a head. In early afternoon, Joel tried to relieve it by calling on Jaynes, who was cordial but could not entirely conceal his worries. He did listen politely to the account of Doctor Mc-Coll's visit to Kettle Valley.

"The man's good as Kenny in some ways. I've worked with both and I think I know a surgeon when I see him in action."

"Likely you do know, friend. But now, how about whiskey, and gossip about Rider's backside?"

Joel had to smile, but he did not feel proud of what he had done to the clerk. "Rider had it coming, Sam, but he was too cowardly to defend himself. About McColl's drinking—not many men are as good sober, as he is with a little whiskey under his belt. I've no comment to make on his wife. Rider should keep his mouth shut, now."

Jaynes shoved the tobacco jar across the table. His next interrogation touched the thing which was really bothering his friend. "Colet gave you the chance to save somebody in this raid. Have you made up your mind?"

Joel scowled at the minister. "If I knew just what trap the Major is setting for me, it wouldn't be hard. He's sitting back, licking his chops, until I show him how I like the bait."

Jaynes' fingers shook as he tried to cram tobacco into a pipe, which he didn't light. "Colet and I have been in touch a long time, Joel. Remember I was once an army chaplain and am not yet officially mustered out of service. Frankly, this newest of our worries is making a trembling old man of me. These are my people, Joel, and the raid'll tear the town apart. While I have my suspicions, I'm not sure where the ax will fall; except, of course, on the leaders."

He held up a finger and gestured with it. "No, the Major's not setting a trap for you; but no man should be put in the position in which he has put you. Like I said, before, one person should not set up as judge, jury, and executioner. If you don't make a choice, you'll send some one to prison or the gallows. The thing works both ways, punish or save."

Joel shrugged his shoulders. "It wouldn't work out. No officer short of a Major General could make good on a promise like that. Colet is just talking."

"Young man," Jaynes' voice was stern, "Joshua Colet has enough influence with the higher-ups to declare a state holiday for deserters in these parts, if he so chose. The man's a quiet, hardworking power. Don't underestimate him, ever."

They talked of other things for a while, then Jaynes walked to the street with his guest. "When it's all over, friend, I'm coming out to High Valley for some retirement. We can read, fish, talk, rest our souls, and forget. Above all, we'll try to reason out the prophet's statement: "Neither shall they learn war anymore.""

Joel walked slowly back to High Valley. He had liked the sound of Jaynes' quotation, but the times didn't seem to indicate that men were even trying to learn that promised lesson. It was full dusk when he arrived, the hills had lost sharpness of definition, and the creek sounds were muted. No whippoorwill had begun his advice. Then he saw that he had a visitor. Seated on the top step of the porch was Squire Wetwire.

"Sorry I wasn't here, Squire," Joel greeted. "Come on in the house, I'll have coffee on soon and can rustle up supper for us."

Wetwire declined almost curtly. "Eating can wait, but we'll go in. I want to talk about a lot of things, mainly what's about to happen."

When the lamps were lighted, Joel was shocked to see the deep lines on his friend's face. He pushed over his most comfortable chair and, when his guest was seated, sat down facing him. Wetwire took a long breath and started talking. "Joel, I was doing well financially when the war broke. Then, things went downhill fast. You couldn't hire men, and the lumber market was bad. Deserters came into our mountains, about a month after the fighting started. They came to my camps, wanting to buy food, clothes, anything we had. From then on, it was downhill: drugs, clothes, and liquor were sent south over what they call Deserters Road, something like the old Underground Railroad for slaves. I used some of my horses and friends. The South gladly put money into what became a real business. Our goods came in from Ontario, down over the traces of the old Boone Road. My worst mistake was getting some things from Uncle Thad. He didn't fully understand, but he knew something fishy was going on."

Joel tried not to look at the stricken face of Uncle Thad's best friend. The Squire was staring at the floor as if trying to marshal further facts of his story. He glanced up at his listener. "You came, and things hadn't become really bad, yet. Gossip started. I was scared, as a keen young man might easily catch on to things. Also, I wasn't too sure you weren't a government man. Anyway, it looked wiser, and I really meant your good, to get you off to school."

There was no use commenting. Now that the Squire was telling his story, things began to fit together. Squire Wetwire had always been, so long as Joel remembered, the big man of this community and in most parts of the county. Even if people had been suspicious of him, they would have hesitated to say anything openly. Wetwire half rose, then sank back in his chair; and his hands were clenched.

"Then, that damned Harne appeared. A Southern captain, he took over. Our local people were too tangled to do anything. He started working with deserters, having them re-enlist for the bounties, then desert. At least two men were shot because they wouldn't go along. Two things more. Uncle Thad was killed because Harne thought he gave information to the cavalry. And I learned that Harne was after you, Joel, something about money, guerilla money." His lips twisted. "I tried to kill him but I'm not much good with a gun; and Lisa Milburn, who was once Harne's wife, warned me to keep away from the camps. Then, I tried to circulate an offer of three hundred dollars to anyone who would shoot Harne."

He shrugged his shoulders. "Not much use of telling more. Lisa Milburn was really anxious to save you from her husband. Believe me, Joel,

so was I. She's gone now. Lisa used to handle the clothing for the deserters." He smiled at Joel's surprised and stricken face. "The government
raid's coming. While I can't go to the camps, the county organization's
information keeps me posted."

The Squire smiled again. "Maybe you'll understand. Your father was
a friend. I loved Thad Crisp, and I saw you grow up."

Joel was on his feet; he struck his fist into his palm. "Squire, I can get
you off, Colet promised—"

"I even know that, Joel. No, I'm guilty, and I'll take my medicine
with the others. The old Forbes camp is headquarters. Keep out of this;
let Colet's man and the cavalry handle things. All I want now is to settle
with Lee Harne or see him dead." He rose. "Reuben Starr's coming out
for me. It's time to go."

Joel had to ask. "You people know the raid's coming, why don't you
all get out of here, go South or some place."

Wetwire smiled indulgently. "I guess you don't really know Joshua
Colet. When he's after you, there's no place to go. This thing they call
Deserters' Road is just a hundred-fifty-mile gauntlet. We've got a choice,
son, jail or a Spencer bullet." He offered a hand diffidently and Joel took
it promptly, shocked at how wasted and cold it had become, since the
time he had held it a year ago. He walked partway down the hill with
Wetwire, then turned back, knowing the man wouldn't want to be seen
going into custody.

After the sound of a buggy turning down below on the road had
passed, Joel sat a while on the porch step. He felt numb. So many
things had happened, since he had pulled that youth out from under
the schoolhouse down in Talpo, that he had become almost inured to
shock. Almost. It was quite clear that war does not claim all its casualties
at the battle fronts. A young deserter was buried in an unmarked grave
just a mile or two away. Uncle Thad had been brutally murdered. Lisa
Milburn had slipped away. Squire Wetwire had built the machine which
was about to destroy him.

When Joel prepared to go to bed, he noticed the brown coat on the
wall, Lisa Milburn's gift. She had cried when he suggested that someday
he'd buy her a brown dress. He hadn't worn it yet.

"Anxious to save you," Squire Wetwire had said of the woman who was Lee Harne's wife. His lip curled. She had searched his blanket roll and would have recognized her husband's revolver by his initials scratched on the stock. He stood up suddenly as another realization struck him sickeningly. Lisa Milburn had counted his money, but she had not told her husband that Joel didn't have anything like the amount taken from the paymaster.

Lieutenant Cord, Sergeant Mathers, and twelve competent troopers arrived the next forenoon. "Colet had to change his deadline a bit, Pender. We hit Kettle Valley yesterday afternoon. One soldier's dead, another wounded. We move tomorrow morning."

Joel stared at the officer. Kettle Valley was where McColl had performed the amputation. "What about the deserters?"

"Clean house," Cord said cynically, "seven of them dead."

"There was a woman, lieutenant. Doctor McColl and I were there. He operated on a man who died."

The officer merely nodded. "They put up a fight from the house. The woman was in it. A Spencer bullet doesn't pick its target. Seven, I said, that includes her."

No tents were pitched but the cavalrymen made themselves comfortable in the old field just beyond the barn. A half hour after their arrival all of them, including Joel, were eating a noon meal; and the horses were munching oats at their tie up.

Cord was impatient to reconnoiter. Leaving the sergeant in charge and taking two privates with him, the officer followed Joel's lead back over the hills to the Forbes camp.

Men were moving about the three buildings. While the lieutenant studied the place through his field glasses, horses were led out to water, and one man split firewood, while others loafed and smoked. Joel's concern was about Harne, even though Colet had hinted that the ex-guerilla would be half way to Virginia after his jail break. But none of the men they could see answered the description of Burley's lieutenant.

Cord finally closed his glasses with a snap. "Close to a dozen men down there, four horses in the barn. No good cover in a hundred yards."

"Sixty, sir," one of the troopers corrected, pointing to the rock Joel had hidden behind.

The lieutenant paid no attention. "Small and Stane, stay here. Look for the rest of us about dawn. Take turns sleeping, and don't expose yourselves or do anything unless you see signs they could be pulling out. If they do, start firing. I'll have a man posted on a hill who'd hear, and we'd come."

He looked at Shane, a smoothly shaven trooper probably younger than Joel. "Which gun do you have, your Spencer or the Sharps?"

"The Sharps, sir."

"Good, that'll cover any long-range stuff, come morning." Joel took Cord back by following the old logging road which ran down Cherry Run to the highway. Horses could use that. They returned to High Valley in time to eat supper, after which the soldiers settled down to sleep until time to march.

They moved quietly through the pre-dawn light. "Pender, I see you have a revolver. Leave the shooting to my boys, if there is any. Here's where they get their chance to come peaceably." Cord had snapped out his direction and Joel was irritated. He had served the purpose of leading these soldiers to their prey, but he was no part of them; he was Joshua Colet's creature, something to take orders.

"Lieutenant," he said, in an edged voice, "next time you or Colet want a bellwether to lead you into the brush, get somebody else and be damned to you. I came for a chance at Lee Harne. Brass buttons and a blue coat won't stop me from shooting, if that murderer shows."

Cord half-grinned, and an odd light leaped into his eyes. "Stane has an extra carbine, Pender. It'll beat a hand gun." He made sure all his men were in place, then drew a white handkerchief from a breast pocket.

Joel had no chance to reply. The officer, walking stiffly, paced out into the open. Jerking out his revolver, he fired one shot in the air. Keeping his leisurely, military stride and holding up the handkerchief, he went forward. Fifty yards from the still quiet buildings, he stopped and yelled. "Come out and surrender. You're surrounded."

There were minutes of almost complete silence except for the loud breathing of Stane, next to Joel, who now had his carbine. "Damn fool," the trooper muttered under his breath and his thumb brought back the big hammer on the Sharps rifle.

The crash of a rifle shot from one of the buildings tore apart the silence. Smoke bloomed for an instant at a high window. Cord pitched forward, the handkerchief he had carried falling from gloved fingers.

There was no need for the sergeant to order firing. These men were battle-seasoned troopers, they had seen their commander shot down, and the Spencers opened with the crash of a volley, then the men shot at will, ripping window frames and doors with bullets. On three sides, watching their cover, troopers edged forward as their fire was returned.

Joel did not stop to reason things out. A man was down; he might not be dead. He found his wedge of scrub oak brush, went through it, then dived into the open, sprawling forward to the shelter of the rock which had sheltered him before. Once again, a bullet from the log house chipped bits from the rock. Cord lay ten feet away. Joel threw himself sideways like a scuttling crab, reached the prone officer and dragged him back of the rock. There was a livid crease on the lieutenant's temple, but his eyelids were starting to flutter with returning consciousness as Sergeant Mathers joined them in a diving rush. Under a heavy covering fire from the troopers' carbines, they dragged Cord to the shelter of some pine trees off the clearing.

"You have any whiskey?" Joel asked, and the sergeant reached for a hip pocket.

"Not that the lieutenant knows. I just pack it for snake bite and sometimes to kill the smell of sweat."

While Joel worked on his patient, two troopers had gained the side of the log bunkhouse and were raking the interior with their murderous fifty-six caliber slugs. Two men dashed out the front door and went down, riddled by a cross fire.

There was no more shooting from the camp. The cavalrymen stopped and waited while four disheveled men emerged, holding a dirty white rag on a stick. Minutes before, they had violated such a truce sign, now they were trusting the men who had whipped them to have a higher moral standard.

Mathers reported to Cord, who was sitting up, stimulated by the sergeant's whiskey. "Sir, four prisoners. Six or seven dead, all theirs. One of our boys is nicked a little. Shall we string 'em up, right off?"

"No, sergeant, the Provost will want to ask questions. Search the buildings."

While that operation was going on, Joel walked down to the buildings and checked the dead deserters. Dejected, he went back to Cord. "Harne wasn't here."

"No, Pender. Colet told us you wouldn't guide our column unless you thought we were after Lee Harne. The man's originally a Pennsylvanian. Locked up for robbery, he killed a guard and went south. Surely that's what he's done again. If Mosby would have him. If not, someone else would. Sheriff Randy was lucky, he wasn't killed, but lived to confess he was hand-in-glove with the man."

The search showed that one of the bunk houses was a storehouse of clothing, drugs, food, and whiskey. Among the drugs was a supply of morphine and chloroform, so much needed that they would sell to the Confederates for more than their weight in gold. The last item turned up was a case of percussion caps.

They made the rough trip back to High Valley, prisoners shackled and walking ahead of the troopers who rode, in spite of the brush. Cord was still shaky but anxious to report. Mounted, he leaned from his saddle.

"Pender, a Provost squad'll come out and take care of things in the lumbering camp."

Joel did not reply. The lieutenant continued.

"You don't like this work. Don't be a damn fool enough to think I do, except on orders. When this turn's over, Colet promises I can rejoin the army. Come along with us, Pender. The Seventeenth can use a man of your nerve and temper."

He was extending a gloved hand, and Joel saw the livid welt across his temple and the twisted smile. Maybe the lieutenant was offering him the only sensible way out of his dilemma. He gripped the offered hand, hard. Cord's horse was turning but he had a final word.

"Don't put off joining too long, Pender. I might get a worse headache than the one I'm not enjoying now."

Sam Jaynes drove out in his buggy the next day and negotiated the steep hill with the rig. "Vacation," he announced. It took them a full quarter hour to unload books, supplies, and horse feed. When they were settled, he supplied details of what the raid had done, in the village. "The town's just ripped apart. Colet used plainclothes men. Mrs. Milburn had skipped out; they padlocked her house. Wetwire, Sholes, and Starr were taken over to Point Haven. The sheriff was already in custody. The detectives are still rounding up people and taking statements. What about Harne, did Cord's men get him?"

Joel frowned. "No, he wasn't among the dead or prisoners. I did think Bill, who was with him the night they tried to burn me, was among the dead, but a bullet changes a man's face a lot."

He closed his eyes for a moment and the scene came back to him so vividly that he shook his head. There was the lieutenant, neat, precise, walking forward, holding the clean handkerchief. Then the quiet of the morning was ruined by the shot from the bunk house, followed by the carbine volley. The troopers had fought like machines.

The friends settled down to a quiet good time together. Jaynes did most of the cooking, which pleased Joel. They tramped over the hills, did some trout fishing, cleaned up about the cabin and spent long hours reading or just talking. Somehow the young minister's company made Joel feel whole and new again. In that strength, he was beginning to have some faith that things would come out all right. For the first, in weeks, he allowed himself to hope about Trudie. One evening they discussed the raids again. Joel brought in Harne's name.

"I keep wondering if Lisa went away with him. It's my notion that the murdering devil will come back. We seem to be tied together, better or worse stuff."

"No, he's finished in these parts. The Secesh deal 'round here is dead. Colet put such a fear of the law in these hills you can cut it with a knife, and down in the village it's even sharper."

Joel did not argue but he did not agree with his friend. Lee Harne wasn't easily scared; and he would be as vicious as a wounded rattle snake. There was also the lure of the money.

* * *

The morning of the fifth day of Jaynes' visit, Doctor McColl stopped. He had an operation to perform and needed help with the anaesthetic. It was a long drive to the house and things went slowly with the patient, so it was late in the afternoon when they came past the High Valley lane again. Joel had been telling McColl that the minister had tamed a rabbit enough to come at his call.

"Come up and see the beast, Doctor. Sam'll get us a good supper. And your team was fed at the farm. They'll take no hurt for the wait."

They went slowly up the lane and topped the grade in sight of the cabin. McColl grabbed Joel's arm and pointed. Sprawled on the edge of the porch and partly on the steps lay what looked to be a pile of rumpled clothing. Joel had seen enough of such uncouth heaps on the Gettysburg battlefield. He ran.

It was Jaynes, body and head on the porch, long legs dangling over the steps. His face was turned toward the edge of a pool of blood. McColl saw Joel's panic and took charge, turning over the body, finding the pulse. "Still alive, help stretch him out."

The minister's eyes remained closed, but there was a faint groan as his body was handled. McColl was working swiftly, cutting away, coat, shirt and under clothing. ". . . lots of blood . . . bullet high . . ." he muttered, then cried out, loud, "Glory, Hallelujah, it's high, missed the lungs."

He turned, glared at his stricken helper, and his words were pure poison. "Haven't I taught you anything, you big ox? Heat water, fix a bed, rustle blankets."

Joel needed that jolt to put him into action. Jaynes had a pot of water heating on the stove, preparatory to getting supper. It wasn't long until the wounded man was stripped, the blood washed away, the bullet hole probed and bandaged, and his body swathed in blankets, stretched out on a cot. Then, McColl grinned apologetically at Joel.

"That's the first I've seen you knocked out, friend. I just had to give you a jolt so you could help."

"Thank you, Doctor. I was hit pretty hard. Guess I'll step out and get a little air."

The clothing McColl had removed or cut away lay where it had been thrown. Mechanically, Joel wadded up the torn shirts, reached for the coat, and stopped. For the moment it was as though a cold hand had touched him, checking his breath. Realizing that he had already lost his head once, he took the garments and went inside.

"Doctor McColl, that's a coat Mrs. Milburn gave me some time ago." He pointed out the brown pattern with his finger. "Somebody shot Sam, mistook him for me, somebody who knew that coat."

The doctor stared for a moment, then went to the door and looked out. When he turned, he was very cheerful, very professional. "Both you men are lucky. You were away, Pender. The preacher, here, has been hit by a small bullet, and the lead went on through. The wound's clean. Also, we got here in time, so he didn't bleed too much. I wager he'll be moving about in a week or less."

McColl strolled about the rooms restlessly, sniffing at bundles of dried herbs, handling some of Indian John's curios, eventually coming to a stand beside the cot where the wounded minister lay.

"We'll have to move him back to town, say in three days. You have the damnedest friends, Pender. One of them might come back, shoot you, and Jaynes would die from lack of care. I'll send a man out, soon's I get home."

Jaynes was beginning to stir and mutter. He was coming back to consciousness as McColl walked off the front porch.

CHAPTER XXIII

TOM HAWKS REPORTED at the cabin before a full hour had passed, having been met by the doctor on his way to the village. The Reverend Samuel Jaynes was a strong and tough-minded man. When he became fully conscious, he proved that he had not been frightened by his experience. Joel held a full cup of Indian John's blackberry wine to his lips and waited until it was swallowed. The minister's face twisted into a wry grin, and he voiced his dislike of the medicine.

"A vile Indian decoction," he whispered. "My mouth has been set for tea. Don't let the pot boil over."

Joel stopped him with a hand pressed to the forehead. "Stay quiet for a while, Sam. Doctor's orders."

After an hour's sleep, the wounded man had rallied so much that it seemed better to let him talk. Joel propped him up with pillows and let him tell what had happened.

"Not much to it, friends. I put water on the stove for tea. It was chilly so I donned your coat, Joel, and went outside and sat down on the steps. Everything was quiet and serene until something hit me like the kick of a mule, and I blacked out."

Joel listened to the bald story and offered reassurance. "McColl says the wound's clean, the bullet went through. It did nick your collarbone, that's why you dropped."

"Thanks for the news," Jaynes said wryly. "Tell your good doctor to remember the ministerial discount when he sends his bill."

McColl made his call early in the morning and did not hide the fact that he was more concerned for his patient's safety from another attack than about his physical condition. He announced that he had changed his mind, and would take Jaynes to Hylersville himself, at once. He directed Tom Hawks to get his rig up the hill, and to pad the seat with blankets. Joel had a moment alone with the physician, in the kitchen, and remonstrated.

"He'd be safe here. Whoever fired that shot meant it for me, the man expected to be wearing Mrs. Milburn's brown coat."

"Exactly," McColl agreed, "and you're going along as nurse. I don't want any more patients with bullet wounds something less than a half inch from the lung cavity. Pender, some of them damn things can kill a man."

Joel and his patient were scarcely more than settled, when the village became aware of what had happened. Visitors, women, came by twos and threes, bearing dainties like jellies, homemade wines, cakes, and ready cooked meals. Joel was pleased at the outpourings of practical sympathy for his friend but glad when the minister was well enough to greet and thank his own visitors, because he noticed something unpleasant. When he opened the door to a caller, no matter who it was, there would be a look of surprise on the face. The recent raid had not added to his popularity, which had been all but nil. Jaynes saw and understood, making a brief for the town folk.

"They're really good people, Joel. If they're standoffish, it's because they're scared."

Joel filled and lighted his pipe. "Sure, Sam, good people, dealers in tar and feathers, cold shoulders, and black gossip. I'll work with them when they're sick, teach their children, clean their messes, but I don't have to love them."

"No," Jaynes agreed in a mild voice. "But, under that hard front you wear like a vest, from what I've seen, I wouldn't be surprised if you really did."

Colet arrived on the eighth day of Jaynes' invalidism and, for him, was almost effusive. "You did a fine job, Joel Pender. Lieutenant Cord, in his report to the War Department, praised you highly."

"War Department," Joel said and was silent for minutes. He had done a lot of thinking and there was no friendliness for this man who had used him, even if he was Trudie's uncle. "Fine," he continued savagely, "but why in hell didn't Cord send for a rope and be done with it? No, that's wrong—in effect, he did, Major. Why didn't I let his blue-coated majesty lie out there under fire? Then, there wouldn't have been any report. When your War Department people put things together, they'll know who I am, and where I live. *Any money,* you said, could hang me. Well, I had it, Shad Burley's bragging money."

Colet's face showed that he was hurt but there was apology in his tone. "Rescuing a valuable officer under fire cannot pass without notice. However, I came to tell you that I'm bound South and may get into Talpo after a month. Just now, I'd like a short visit with your ministerial friend."

Joel went out to the garden, picked up a hoe and started to work. Inside, soldier and minister greeted each other, then watched him. Through a window they could see the tall man taking pains with a row of cabbages. Colet turned away with no comment, but Jaynes spoke soberly. "He had the right to think the rough stuff was over, and he's bitter. Josh, I'm sure he wouldn't have minded much if that bullet had hit him. He feels guilty because the ambusher shot me."

He frowned. "It's that brown coat which Mrs. Milburn gave him. We know she's Lee Harne's wife. Is the man really out of this country?"

"Yes, Jaynes, I'm sure he is. The man who shot could be a deserter who escaped the roundup, and thought you were Joel because that was where he lived. It could have been an enemy of your own—"

The minister looked startled. Colet raised a forefinger in emphasis. "The shooting isn't too important, but this is. I ripped the office open, getting that permission to free somebody. Why, in the name of all that's holy didn't that boy out there see the light and grab it for himself? That's what I had in mind. Guilty or not, nobody could have touched him, ever."

The ghost of a satisfied smile played round the minister's strong mouth. "You and I'll never really understand Joel Pender, probably because he doesn't understand himself. It never occurred to him to free himself. The man's a doctor at heart, forgetting his in other people's needs. I saw him do that day after day during our epidemic."

"Well," Colet commented, "I'll do all I can for him in the south. If I fail, what'll become of him?"

Jaynes reply was carefully made. "There's nothing to hold him here. He'll go away. He won't go to Trudie and involve her. My guess is the army. However, my friend, I have the feeling that he will be cleared; and one day our proudest boast will be that we knew that hard-headed, close-mouthed, soft-hearted boy with the big hands that heal."

Joel did not see Major Colet leave, and Jaynes made little mention of the officer's visit other than to pass along what he had learned about Lee Harne.

"Colet thinks he went straight to northern Virginia where he used to serve with Mosby. His wound could be troubling him, too."

* * *

In ten days, he was back in High Valley. Dried blood stains still showed on the porch, but he paid little attention. His mind had been made up days ago; he had only waited until Jaynes was fully recovered. In Talpo, Trudie and George Geis had believed his presence there would bring trouble to the village, then Burley had ridden in. Here, in quiet Hylersville, Uncle Thad had been brutally murdered and a minister, the best friend of the community, shot. Both crimes pointed at him; his homecoming had been a tragic mistake, and his dream of becoming a doctor a dangerous nightmare.

Armed with hammer and saw, his pocket full of nails, Joel went over his place, nailing the barn doors shut after wrecking both the horse manger and feeding trough. In the cabin, he piled his books and other treasures on the floor, spread a tarpaulin over the pile, and nailed the cover to the floor. He burned the brown coat in the fireplace.

Everything was finished. The cabin doors and shutters were nailed tightly; he stood on the front porch, the hammer in his hand. It would take a carpenter with a pry bar or a man with an ax to gain entrance to the once hospitable cabin. Joel stood, remembering what a mecca this cabin had been in boyhood. With a quick movement, he snapped the hammer up over his head and let it fly into the bushes. Being careful not to look back, and carrying less baggage than his small blue blanket roll had contained when he had come home to Hylersville, he walked down the stony lane to the road.

Point Haven was quiet, with few people on the street. Nobody paid any attention to a tall young man, dressed shabbily, who bought a ticket for Harrisburg. He went out of the station and sat on the edge of a baggage truck while he waited for his train.

Camp Curtin was different this time. The recruiting offices were still there, but the armed guards were gone from the gates, and there were no crowds, just a few civilians and four or five soldiers in undress uniforms moving about. Joel entered the same building where he and young Puffenburger had walked into trouble about a pair of pants, a year past, and enlisted as a private in the Seventeenth Pennsylvania Cavalry for a term of three years. He had been thinking of the elder Puffenburger and his story of the bull which changed its mind, when the officer, writing at his desk, asked about a preference as to outfits. Recalling Lieutenant Cord's invitation, Joel had named the Seventeenth.

The medical examiner was a physician beyond middle age, and he had time to go over Joel's lean body carefully, missing nothing. He touched a scar on Joel's arm.

"Bullet cut," he said, and waited for an explanation which didn't come. That was the slight wound Joel had received on a trip north with the Talpo boys, taking some runaway slaves to the next station. The doctor finished with a comment. "Those hands, young man, if I had been so equipped, I might have been a great surgeon instead of a country doctor."

The recruiting officer had him stand at attention and take the military oath. "You are now a soldier of the United States, subject to regulations and orders, together with a pay of seventeen dollars a month, beginning today." He leaned forward over his desk. "Pender, this is a personal question you do not need to answer. I heard the doctor mention a bullet scar, yet you have no service record. This is the query, why are you enlisting at this late date?"

Joel took his turn smiling. He felt a certain exhilaration at having broken all his ties, of having turned over his effects and money to be kept for Reverend Samuel Jaynes in event of death. He rubbed his chin thoughtfully.

"I'm afraid, sir, I don't really know. Maybe in a month or so I'll be sorry."

The officer laid down his pen and took a long look at the new soldier and said, dryly. "It will be a little late then, friend."

Joel and five other recruits for the Seventeenth were equipped with uniforms and equipment. They were kept under close watch in a barracks for three days until they were entrained, in the care of a corporal, and taken to Baltimore. There they joined a company of twenty more replacements and were sent westward over the rebel-harassed Baltimore and Ohio Railroad. The whole outfit detrained at a station called Monocacy, a few miles south of the city of Frederick.

The new soldiers had entered upon a scene of what looked like complete confusion. There were loaded freight trains on each of the sidings, and docks were piled high with mountains of supplies. Lines of horse or mule drawn wagons loaded and left, without seeming to make any dents on the vast array of boxes and bales.

The recruits, always under surveillance of hard-faced sergeants, were herded into an empty warehouse where all doors were guarded by soldiers with fixed bayonets on their muskets. They were very well fed. A dour named Wilcox grumbled, "Thet coffee was fine, strong enough to bear an egg. Back home we're damned glad for rye coffee. You like it, Pender?"

Joel was watching a newcomer who had entered and just grunted. The man wore the hashmarks of a sergeant. His short jacket was neatly buttoned, his boots polished, his gloves folded and passed through his belt. He was smooth shaven, and his cap was tilted at a precarious angle on bright, closely clipped hair. "Men, I'm Sergeant Sney. On your feet, form up outside."

The recruits made a fairly good line, along which the sergeant walked, checking names. He stepped back and turned to give a smart salute to the officer who appeared from around the corner of the building. Joel recognized him at once. He was standing close enough to see that the livid weal across the temple had just about given way to a very definite scar. It was Lieutenant Cord.

In the Camp Curtin recruiting office Joel had chosen his outfit without much thought. Certainly, he had not expected to come under Lieutenant Cord's command because such a regiment of a thousand troopers would have scores of officers. At the moment when the man who had led the attack on the Forbes lumbering camps appeared, he was neither glad nor sorry. The thing to do was wait.

Cord talked crisply and to the point. "You are replacements for the Seventeenth. It's a veteran regiment, and you'll need all the training that can be crowded in. We'll have to do the work of months in two weeks. Things will be hard, but every man of you will be glad for what he's learned when we join the main command."

Sney dismissed the company, and Cord spoke as Joel was about to pass him. "Glad you're with us, Pender. I hope you like the army." The nearest of the recruits looked startled. Joel managed a passable salute and entered the warehouse.

Training quarters were three miles from Monocacy, on a farm. Cord had brought with him a couple of sergeants plus four veteran enlisted men. For two long weeks, it was drill eight hours a day and guard duty at night for three more. Joel liked the hard grind, for it kept him from thinking. He was so tired at night that he "went dead" when he lay down. There was riding, caring for horses, target shooting, military evolutions, care of uniforms and occasional lectures on outdoor cooking. The grumbling of the first few days lessened as the new soldiers found themselves improving. There was more spirit in the work. Cord proved a very capable officer.

"A trained soldier is a safe one, men," he kept emphasizing. "Drill is for you, not just to bedevil you. It's the one thing the Johnnies lack, and the thing that'll win this man's war. Wait until the Miniés sing and you'll be glad for anything you know."

Sergeant Sney formed the squadron standing to horse on the final afternoon. Men stood holding their mounts' bridle rein four inches from the bit, sabers hooked high on their belts, carbines against their legs, backs straight. The little sergeant walked along the line, then faced the men and made his pronouncement.

"Damned if I don't think you'll make soldiers; say in six or seven years. Stiffen up a bit, here comes the lieutenant."

Cord rode up, swung off his horse and tossed the reins to an orderly. At his nod, Sney mounted the squadron. Then, the officer snapped his order. "Prepare to dismount. Dismount."

The recruits came off their horses with snap, but Cord's sharp eyes had caught something. "Wilcox and Biel," he said in a conversational tone, "you hung up a bit. Be sure to get your feet clear of stirrup irons quick, or a scared mount might drag you.

He paced the line, talking. "You've done well in a short time. Crabb and Fallon are mighty good field farriers. Jones mends leather well, Biel looks like a gunsmith. I saw him dismantle a Spencer the other day. Each of you has his gifts." His eyes ran over the men again.

"We move out with full equipment tomorrow morning. All officers taking men into the Shenandoah are directed to caution their men not to trust any local people, on account of guerillas. The farmer that lets you water your horse at his trough may slit a sentry's throat at night. Straggling is sure death in the Valley."

They crossed the Potomac in the morning and reached hill country by evening after a stiff day's march, pitching camp on an abandoned farm where all the buildings had been destroyed by fire. Cord was a careful man, directing that the horses be corralled inside the standing walls of the barn. He put one of his veterans on watch with each recruit who had guard duty during the night. Sergeant Brown ordered, "Sleep in all your clothes with carbine magazines full. Anything happens, shoot at gun flashes. Don't get any of them new uniforms spoilt by rebel bullets."

As they settled into their bedrolls and first watch took up position, the night quieted. The occasional stamp of a horse accented the night insect sounds. Joel had finally found a comfortable position when the Lieutenant came up softly and squatted by him. "Pender."

Joel half-sat up. "Sney saw some signs on the road, thinks there are guerillas not far ahead of us. Go with him to scout ahead a bit. Quiet like an Indian." The man's teeth flashed in a sudden grin, and he left, as quietly as a cat in the still camp.

Joel joined Sney at the edge of the camp. The little sergeant had him leave his carbine, lest the ring rattle against the stock. He checked his revolver and knife, and they stole away down the dark path without a word. At a spot where a small, nearly dry rill crossed the road, Sney indicated by hand signals that he was going to follow it, and join back up with Joel up the road. He slipped into the brush with barely a sound, and Joel waited a moment until the night noises resumed. A rabbit thumped once in the bushes. A mosquito bit his ear, and he moved on.

After a bit, the road turned sharply, following a looming ridge. The fitful breeze brought a scent of horses to his nose, and he slid deeper into the shadows and stood a moment, listening. A movement caught his eye, and Sney slid out of a shadow. It took the little man a few seconds to find Joel in the shadows, and he nodded approvingly. Holding up one finger for silence, he led the younger man around the bend. A clearing widened off the road, with the spring which fed the little creek they'd crossed. Several horses were picketed to one side, and bedrolls ringed a small fire. Men sat among them, checking weapons and obviously waiting for something.

Sney pulled Joel back, and they hurried off down the road as silently as they could. Back at the camp, they informed Lieutenant Cord of what they'd seen. "They know we're here, and they're comin' for us, sir," Sney told the officer. "They're just waitin' until they figure we're sleepin'."

"Yes. This is what we'll do. Wake the men quietly. Roll the blankets to look like sleeping men. Take up positions in the woods." They barely had time to put Cord's plan into place. Sney had taken up a position along the road, just outside the camp. He would fire as the guerillas passed.

Suddenly it came, the spang of a carbine, then the drum of running horses coming straight at the camp. The guerillas were making a wild charge with a narrow front, yelling and firing their revolver shots into the bedrolls on the ground, as they rode them down. Cord's whistle shrilled and the carbines crashed as the hidden cavalrymen sent shot after shot into the mass of riders. Horses screamed as the force of the charge broke into a milling of frightened animals and shouting men.

The camp was a shambles with six horses down and twice as many riders. Two guerillas dodged out from the shelter of the barn walls, trying to escape into the brush. Sergeant Brown lifted his carbine, and it cracked twice. Cord came over. "Where's Sney?"

"Haven't seen him, sir. There are no prisoners," the sergeant reported. "Fallon's dead, Biel's nicked."

Fallon was buried carefully. The dead guerillas were dragged into a small depression and covered pretty lightly with ground. Brown and another man scouted up the road, and returned to the camp, carrying Sergeant Sney. The little man was conscious, but fought back a scream when he was laid down on his back.

"Guess it's broke," he whispered when Cord bent over him. The officer opened the short cavalry jacket. He drew back a hand covered with blood.

"Pender!" Joel had just finished bandaging Biel, the trooper who had been nicked by a bullet. He walked over to the knot of men gathered about Sney. "See what you can do, Pender."

Joel frowned at the officer, then knelt by the wounded man. They removed his jacket and pulled aside his shirt. Joel saw a wound along Sney's side and began testing with his fingers.

"No ribs broken; help me turn him, lieutenant." Sney's body was thin and bony. Close to the prominent spine was a bluish lump; and the little man groaned when it was touched.

"Get a razor," Joel demanded. "There's a box of salve in my saddle bag." He inspected the razor, wiping it off with a few drops from a flask. "It's not bad, sergeant. Hold steady, half a minute."

Sney bit his lip, and Cord held him in place as Joel made a quick slash across the lump. The bullet rolled into his hand. Cord supplied a clean handkerchief, which Joel used as a pad to hold salve against the cut, finishing the whole job with part of a torn shirt tied about the bony waist.

"Help him up, he can stand, now."

There was a wild look in the little sergeant's eyes as two troopers held him. He took a step and yelled. "By God, he's right. I can stand, and I thought my back was knocked off!"

Joel grinned and turned away. The pistol bullet had been half spent, creasing along the ribs and ending in the heavy back muscle, near some nerves. Sney's number had been almost up, but he'd been lucky, and he'd be well in days. They tidied the camp, recovering what they could. Some blankets were much the worse for wear from the horses' steel-shod hooves. At dawn, they rode out.

A few days later, Cord led his replacements into the vast encampment of the Army of the Shenandoah, halfway between Halltown and Berryville. His men rode with the assurance of veteran cavalrymen. They had fought a battle, had looked on their dead and driven off the enemy. Caps were worn rakishly, horses handled smartly. They had become soldiers.

CHAPTER XXIV

AS THE DAYS passed, Joel could not stop wondering about the great city of war into which he had come. At Monocacy there had been confusion of materials; here was order for men, beasts and war. Tented streets stretched out in compass-straight lines. Thousands of horses picketed on ropes fought flies; smoke from farriers' forges and cooking fires lifted into the still air. This was the Army of the Shenandoah, becoming stronger each day as replacements came in, a war hammer in the hands of bandy-legged Philip Sheridan to smash the long valley that fed Lee's armies.

Sergeant Sney had adopted Joel. They stood one afternoon at a cavalry mount tie up. "Mister," Sney declared gravely, "when Sheridan led that cavalry corps, it stretched thirteen miles on the road. Yessir, thirteen miles and there's more here, right now." They mounted for drills.

Blandy, a recruit, rode beside Joel. "Pender, war's a damn big thing. We got so many fighting men here you got to count by hundreds. Do that one by one and the war'd be over before you got done." His mount nudged Joel's horse. "What bothers me'n some of the boys is how these here men can shoot guns all at one time without killing each other. We was figgering; give each man five feet, lined up, and they'd stretch out to forty miles. God Almighty, where'd they get them enough rebels to put up a fight?" A bugle blared a command, and both men rode forward into column.

Later, when they were off duty, Sergeant Sney overtook Joel as he was going into a sutler's tent for tobacco. "Come on, mebbe I can show you the general." Main headquarters, a farmhouse with a wide veranda, was close; and the two soldiers were in luck, for a man walked out on the broad porch, evidently waiting to meet somebody. "Sheridan, that's him," Sney said, pointing.

The commander in chief of this great army had the head and torso of a big man, but his legs were absurdly short; and the odd, flat-topped hat he wore did little for his dignity. Later, when Joel saw the general mounted, he felt him an impressive figure; but here on the porch it was different.

"Them's the damnedest legs," Sney said, "but the General's a man. I rode with him over most of this damn state. First off, when he come here from the West, the men didn't give much for him, 'til they got to noticing. When he overtook a column on a narrow road 'twas the General who'd ride off into a field. He'd just as soon eat his supper with an enlisted man as a brigadier. Onc't I seen him help a private with a sore hand fix his saddle blanket."

Sney stiffened. "There comes two more. The one with the curls is Custer, t'other is Wilson." Both cavalry generals were young. Wilson, the slighter of the two, was uniformed in the conventional manner but Custer, with yellow curls falling from under the brim of his wide hat, wore a plum-colored velvet jacket, well laced with braid, and his soft leather thigh boots glittered from polish as he strode along. Joel's thought was that he'd prefer Wilson as a leader. Sney spoke again. "Hell's gonta pop in this valley when them three fighting generals get together. Bet you a week's pay they're cooking something."

Three days later, Joel was alone in the tent he shared with a trooper named Wilcox. So long as he was actively engaged in the hard work of exacting drill—horsemanship, target practice, field maneuvers—army life was all right. It was when he was off duty, as he was this afternoon, that depression rode him hard. By this time his small circle of friends, Trudie most likely of them all, would know he had joined the army, which meant that he had given up his dream. Trudie. He had not seen her for months, but she was the final thing in his mind at the end of each waking day. He closed his eyes now, trying to visualize her face, but it wouldn't come. He could see the red curving of her lips, the soft framing of her hair and searching of her eyes, the rest was misty. By now, she would be sure he had failed her dream for him.

Pushing the tent fly aside, he stepped outside. Sergeant Sney came around the corner. The dapper little soldier was in a hurry, and most military, as he approached Joel. "Private Pender, the lieutenant directs you to report to his quarters. Follow me."

"Yes, sergeant." He followed Sney through part of the great dusty camp, past huge wagon and horse parks, then through brushwood and timber, to a small house dwarfed by a tall yellow pine which leaned over it. Lieutenant Cord had a big room which took the entire first floor of the house. There was a wide table desk littered by papers and, to one side, a neatly blanketed cot.

"Glad to see you looking so fit, Pender." Cord swept a quick glance over the tall figure in its neatly fitted shell jacket, the close-fitting breeches, and the varnished half boots, then grinned. "I've a notion Sergeant Sney's been looking after you."

"He has that."

Cord indicated the chair, and sat down back of his table. He cleared his throat. "Pender, Major Colet felt he should tell me your complete story, including the paymaster business. He's gone south to look into it at the village of Talpo. Both of us are in Intelligence. If he can't straighten you out, it will be our duty to bring you to trial, in spite of what we both owe you, personally."

Joel felt his temper rising, but did not speak. "We know, just Colet and I, that you divided the money taken from Burley's house before the fire. What did you do with your share?"

Joel's lips twisted. Jaynes hadn't talked. "It remained in Hylersville; put to good use there."

Suddenly, Cord's eyes widened and he chuckled. "So, that's where he got the money. Yes, Pender, I'd say it was well used."

Joel wasn't completely mollified by the officer's approval. His voice went hard. "If you and Colet are really so damned eager about that paymaster robbery, why don't you catch Lee Harne who was in it? He attacked me twice, he murdered Uncle Thad Crisp who was sheltering me, and ended by shooting down my best friend in Hylersville. That's why I enlisted; I had become a danger to my friends."

Cord nodded and shifted a bit in his chair. "I didn't bring you here to threaten you, Pender. Colet and I know your ambition to become a doctor. I wanted to be a lawyer, now I chase guerillas, deserters, and bounty jumpers. When you operated on Sney's back, my decision as to how to use you was made. Colonel Kellogg concurs." He glanced at a paper on the desk. "You are hereby transferred to Headquarters Company with the rank of corporal, two dollars more a month. That outfit, Pender, isn't just a bunch of body guards. It does all sorts of mean jobs, dangerous things like getting inside rebel lines occasionally. The commander is Sergeant Joseph McCabe. If I was in a tight pinch, he'd hearten me more than a full squad of cavalry." Cord handed over a paper. "You'll be a field medic a good part of the time, Pender. You're a good scout, but medics—especially good ones—are few and far between. Take care of those big hands."

He returned to his paperwork. Joel snapped a salute and left. It took no time at all to gather his things from his tent. Wilcox, who shared with him, just shrugged. "I hope the new man doesn't snore."

Joel found his way to Headquarters Company, looking for McCabe. A couple of men were loafing about, and he had just asked them when a tall man, wearing a nondescript jacket, a battered felt hat, and infantry trousers, rode up and slid from his saddle.

"I'm McCabe," the newcomer said in a low voice, "heard you asking for me. If you're Pender, I was expecting you." Taller than Joel, the sergeant carried his shoulders in an apologetic stoop. A straggly mustache softened the grim lines of his mouth and only the steely blue eyes indicated the fighting man. He shook hands gravely.

"Glad you're with us. Cord said he'd send you. The boys'll fix you up with a first aid kit, a horse and anything else you figger to need."

The first week was disillusioning, for all the troop did was ride back roads and raid two tiny whiskey stills which were destroyed. The Virginia countryside, softer than the hills of Joel's home, did little to suggest hidden danger. Farmers the troop met were quiet folks, neither civil nor uncivil.

One Friday the company raided a farmhouse, finding a store of whiskey which they destroyed. The farmer, a man named Breen, was sullen. After his men were mounted, McCabe stared down thoughtfully at the man.

"Breen, I still got doubts about you. That was a goodish lot of liquor."

The farmer spat tobacco juice at a burdock stalk. The sergeant leaned down until his face was only a couple of feet from the sullen man's, and his voice carried all the warning of an aroused rattlesnake. "We'll watch, friend. You get night-riding ideas and I'll guarantee to stretch your neck."

The raid had been made early in the forenoon. About midafternoon the troop was in rougher country, mostly woods and brush land, with an occasional field fenced with stone. The weather had been hot, and even the grass was turning brown. McCabe called a halt in a grove of young white oaks through which a brook flowed. Back of them was a stone-fenced field where corn ears drooped on stunted stalks. Some of the men had gone over there to get fodder for the horses. One trooper was examining a saddle sore on his mount. McCabe had walked out the narrow road they had followed and was standing, chewing a twig. Joel was fascinated by the sergeant; under that easy manner, he sensed an alertness and determination, plus a competence that made soldiers trust him.

They all heard the light metal clink of a horse's shoe on a rock. McCabe wheeled with an order. "Over the fence, men, horses and all." These troopers were no strangers to sudden alarms. Less than a minute had passed when all of them were sheltered by the fence. Then came the rush of the mounted attackers, riding out of the trees, yelling and firing revolvers.

The tall McCabe had not crouched down. His carbine shot brought down a horse, sending its rider sprawling, and his firing was the signal for the Spencers to open. A minute of rapid fire from the repeaters broke the guerilla rush and drove them into the shelter of the timber. McCabe spoke calmly. "Spread out. Don't let them flank us." Three dead horses and two men lay out under the oaks.

One of the scouts had been nicked by a revolver bullet and Joel bound up the wound with a handkerchief. The man grinned. "That nick ain't as bad as the kick of them Spencers."

McCabe spoke to Corporal Blaine; both men were leaning forward, peering over the fence. "Most likely one of Mosby's outfits," the sergeant said. "I figger there's upwards of thirty of 'em."

Two-to-one odds in favor of the vicious partisan fighters was mighty strong. Their second rush was made on foot, but they could not pass through the ranging fire of the carbines to get their revolvers at work. The fight settled down to a half hour of spasmodic sniping from both sides. McCabe walked along the line, touching every other man on the shoulder. One was Joel. "Give your carbines to the other boys. This'll be a flanking job."

Crouching low to keep from observation, the chosen men followed McCabe along the fence and through a break into a tangle of blackberry and chinquapins, plus some alders. None of them walked erectly until they reached timber. They were now back of the guerilla line and evidently had not been seen. All stopped and looked at the sergeant. Directly ahead, the stamping of a nervous horse was followed by a man's low voice, trying to quiet the animal.

Another short advance brought them to a growth of high bushes, through which they could see horses tied up, and a man moving among them, talking in soothing tones. "It's Breen," a scout whispered. "That damned moonshiner sicked them folks on us. Trying to make us pay for his whiskey."

The horses had scented danger and became increasingly hard to manage, taking all the farmer's attention. McCabe slipped nearer. Breen, leading a horse, got too close to the scout's hiding place. A heavy revolver barrel crashed down on his head. Mounted on the guerillas' horses, the eight men staged their own charge, hitting the partisans from the rear, sending them flying into the brush and timber. A minute or two later, the battle was over.

Two more scouts had been hit, but not seriously. Six guerillas, all dead, were down; and McCabe was turning away from them when Joel came up to take a look.

"McCabe," he called a moment later, "I know this man, he was with Harne up in Pennsylvania."

After Cord's raid on the Forbes camp, Joel had been sure he had recognized Bill, but a fifty-six caliber slug leaves little of a face to be recognized. There was no doubt in his mind that this dead man, his face untouched, was Harne's Bill. McCabe waited with scant patience for an explanation. "Lee Harne's about here somewhere, sergeant. I'm sure of it."

The officer's only comment was a grunt but, when Joel started away, he said sarcastically. "You do get around, Pender."

The scouts were actually still a part of the Seventeenth but did not camp with the regiment. Their tents, bough huts, and stone cooking places were back of their headquarters shack. This evening, they were making themselves comfortable. Smoke from fires drove off mosquitoes; lanterns, hung high, lighted the scene as men talked. There was the usual grumbling at the weather, the food and drill. Joel had been listening to a discussion of the newly issued carbines when the camp runner approached. "Man up at the shack wants you, Pender."

Some of the nearby soldiers heard the summons and ribbed Joel as he put on his jacket and cap. "Doc's getting promoted . . . Sheridan wants his toe nails cut . . . take your gun, Doc, mebbe it's John Singleton Mosby . . . he's mighty damn mad at the Seventeenth."

Joel grinned at the badinage. He liked it, it made a man feel like he belonged. Outside the lantern light, it was hard to see, and he stumbled over stones and roots. It did not occur to him that this summons could have much importance.

Two smoothly shaven civilians occupied the shed, one sitting at the table, the other leaning loosely against the door lintel. When he moved, the walnut butt of a revolver showed under his coat flap. The seated man offered no greeting, but took out a folded paper, glanced at it, and shot a question. "You're Pender, the Talpo school teacher."

Joel did not answer. After all these months, it was coming, arrest and trial; and the thing of which he was was most acutely conscious was a numb feeling along his legs like a great weariness.

The seated man rose, and his companion closed in as he stepped forward. "Bly and Donats of the Secret Service. I'm Bly. We have a warrant for your arrest; paymaster robbery, arson and murder."

He slipped the paper he had flourished back into his pocket. When his hand came forward again it carried a pair of heavy handcuffs. Joel felt his muscles tensing as they had done at sight of Burley's whip. Then, he had had the old knife as a weapon, tonight he had nothing. Reason kept telling him to go with these men peaceably; but every impulse in him rebelled at being shackled. "Put them irons away," he snapped roughly and Bly grinned.

"Grab him, Donats."

Joel's move was pure impulse, learned from the Cherokee boys. Donat's arms were round him from the back. Joel's longer ones clutched back, and he flung the agent up and over his head with every pound of his lean body in the throw. Donats pitched into his companion and both men sprawled on the beaten ground of the shed floor. Joel's next move was to snatch up the handcuffs and to throw them far out into the brush.

"What's going on here?" None of the three of them had heard Sergeant McCabe approach, and Joel had never heard the man put that much harsh urgency into his voice. Bly was scrambling to his feet.

"Secret Service, sir. This man's wanted for robbery, murder—"

McCabe stopped him with a forward step. "Sonny, Major Colet and Lieutenant Cord told me all I need to know about Pender. If he's arrested, I'll do it; if he's shot, I'll bury him. Get back to Washington. Tell Brady that the Colonel of the Seventeenth is in the hands of guerillas. None of my men have time to be arrested or hanged. We move out in minutes."

As the sergeant talked, men came running up buckling on equipment and, in the rear, others were busy saddling horses. The detectives vanished. McCabe was giving orders. "No sabers, just carbines and revolvers. Bring some of them damn fire grenades and two axes."

In little more than ten minutes, twenty men in column by twos trotted out of the encampment following the tall man who rode ahead of the leading file. Sergeant Sney was along this time and told Joel excitedly what had occurred. Colonel Kellogg had been uneasy about his horse feed. Quartermaster oats were too dusty, and hard on the animals. At noon, about the time the scouts were fighting their skirmish, a woman called on the colonel, claiming that she was from a big farm ten miles from the camp. Her husband, who could not come because he was guarding their place from marauding guerillas, had a quantity of good oats and wanted to sell it. Kellogg was interested, and eager to show up the regimental quartermaster. So with two aides he rode out of camp, breaking his own orders in so doing. One aide returned saying the colonel would dine with the farmers, the Harneys.

"The Colonel ain't back," Sney said. "He'd stretch orders by going out in the afternoon, but he wouldn't stay after dark. General Sheridan won't let even a brigadier do that."

Sney reached over and caught Joel's sleeve. "The aide says this Harney's a tall, kinda good-looking man, except for a scar thet makes his eyelid droop."

Surprise made Joel clutch in his reins, and his puzzled horse almost disrupted the column. "Good God, man, that's Lee Harne."

"Watch your horse, Pender," the little sergeant snapped. "Looks like we're due for some excitement this night. I was in thet house a week back and nobody was living there, then. God, how the regiment will have to crawl if anything happens to Kellogg."

CHAPTER XXV

THE SCOUTS WERE hurrying, but there was no galloping. They rode at a fast, bone shaking trot, keeping their horses to the sides of the road where the sunburned grass partially muffled the sounds of hooves. There was none of the usual creaking of equipment; McCabe's men carried their carbines in saddle boots, not by the regulation snaffle rings.

Joel let his reins hang loose on the saddle cantle and gave himself over to thinking. This night would bring an end to a long and troubled road. The Secret Service agents would be waiting for his return. Colet would be too late to be of any real service.

After several miles, McCabe pulled his men into a small field where a trooper was waiting. They spoke quietly, then McCabe addressed the group.

"Men, we're headed for the Harney farm. Word is, the guerillas have the Colonel. We don't think they had time to slip him south, through our lines. Sergeant Sney was in that house a week ago, and it was deserted. Listen to him, careful."

Sney dismounted, handed his reins to Joel, and stood by his horse, gesturing. "The house goes by the name of Peach Hill, and it's clost to a mile off. It's a big building in a yard full of trees and bushes. There's a biggish barn and three, four good-sized outbuildings. I got in through a window, but there's an outside cellar door.

"Two big parlors in front, then a dining room with a hall that runs back to the kitchen. The cellar opens from that hall. Off the dining room's an office with a big desk. Most of the furniture's still in the house, guess the folks just lit out, quick like."

"No silverware?" a mocking voice queried from the darkness and Sney snapped his answer without thinking. "Not a damn thing." He coughed again and looked at McCabe. "You see how it is, sir?"

The commanding sergeant merely grunted and stood up. "We'll ride ten minutes more, then leave our mounts and foot it to the house. Likely we'll find bushwhackers round that lawn. Go easy, if we jump 'em they'll kill the Colonel. But somebody's got to get inside that house, see what's what, and mebbe get Kellogg loose."

Joel thrust Sney's reins back into his hands. McCabe, who knew about the Secret Service men back there in the camp, would not deny him this one clear chance.

"Sir," Joel said quietly, "I know Harne, let me go into the house."

McCabe rubbed his chin thoughtfully before speaking. "I figgered you might offer, Pender. Sney'll go along."

The Peach Hill property came into view, the loom of the house softened by trees and shrubbery. Barns and outbuildings made indistinct clumps in the thin starlight, but lamplight showed under the bottom edges of window blinds in what Sney had earlier indicated would be the dining room and kitchen of the big house.

The scouts distributed themselves for their encircling job so quietly that Joel was surprised to find himself with just McCabe and Sney. The chief scout handed him a whistle.

"When you and Sney get inside, if you want us to rush the place, blow hard. We'll open fire first, so keep down. Don't be squeamish. You can't take a man like Harne alive, or get word out of him if you did. Kill the man, that's an order. It'll save a hanging."

Joel moved quietly; and he felt a mounting excitement as he and his companion neared the main house, using the cover of each bush, each patch of shadow. Without warning, the sound of a step on gravel stopped them. Sney gestured for Joel to stay. The sergeant's small figure was just a gray shape as he slipped close to his intended victim near the cellar door. There was a flash in the starlight, a dull thump and the hint of a gurgle. Sney returned in a minute or two. "One less," he whispered callously. "Most of 'em are out front. Let's get into thet cellar, fast."

The cellar door was not locked or barred. The two scouts went down into black darkness through which they groped until they bumped into a stairway. Muffled voices sounded from above. Joel took his companion's arm in the darkness. Directly into Sney's ear, making almost no sound, he said, "Sney, this could be my last show; let me go it alone."

"Pender, Lieutenant Cord'll rip the stripes off me if you get hurt. He told me pertickler to look after you."

Joel had taken two steps up the stairs when Sney made up his mind. "Dammit, go ahead. Gimme McCabe's whistle. Do you want my knife?"

"No, keep it and hold your breath."

The next to the final step creaked loudly. Joel fumbled and found the latch, which could be raised with a thumb. The door opened with no noise, and warm air brushed his face as he stepped into a dimly lighted, narrow hallway. The kitchen was to his left, and he heard a stirring there, but the rumble of voices was to his right. Whoever was in that kitchen could come in at his back. He reconnoitered, carefully.

A woman, with her back toward the hall, stood at a table in the kitchen. When Joel had heard the story of a woman who came to Kellogg's office, he had thought of Lisa Milburn and her way with men. His former landlady was somewhere up in Pennsylvania, so he had dismissed the thought. Now, though, there was no mistaking the soft brown hair and the rounded shoulders lifting from a low-cut dress.

Two quick steps and he was up to her. As she turned half way round, he clamped a big hand across her mouth. She struggled for a moment until she recognized her assailant. "Joel," she whispered hoarsely, "he said a man killed you."

For the moment at least, the woman wasn't acting, for the color faded from her cheeks. He shook his head. "The coat didn't work, Lisa. Sam Jaynes got shot for me."

Her eyes were round in astonishment. "You were his wife all along and went off with him."

"He made me, Joel. The man's a devil. He'd kill me if I didn't do as he says. And he's got a doxy over on the next farm, a gypsy woman—" She started to cry. "Take me away from him, hide me somewhere, anywhere, just so he can't trap me again."

His hand dived into his pocket, pulled out what money he had, and thrust it into the gaping bosom of her dress. "Get out, Lisa, clear out of the country or you'll hang. This place is surrounded."

Her eyes searched his face. Suddenly her arms were about him, her rich lips found his. Then she turned and darted out the kitchen door. Joel stood tensed—the rumble of voices from the dining room was louder. His right hand reached to his holster for his service revolver. The flap was loose, the weapon gone. For the second time, Lisa Milburn had disarmed him, and he swore savagely under his breath.

"Damn, dim minded fool." He was unarmed in a house which he was sure sheltered Lee Harne. He looked around. Lisa had been cleaning a heavy iron skillet when he came in. With that, clutched by its long handle, he went into the hallway.

The door to the dining room stood about six inches ajar. Joel could see Colonel Kellogg, iron gray hair rumpled, lashed to a chair. He was gagged with a handkerchief and his face showed the marks of rough treatment. A cigar smoldered in a dish on the floor beside the chair. The candles only dimly lighted the room. Then Lee Harne, brandishing a sword, stepped into view, blocking most of the light. He was taunting his captive.

"So, Colonel, you won't give military information. Hell, man, I don't give a damn for that. My men and I want money." The sword swished viciously past the prisoner's face. "Your aide is locked in the barn. He will go back with a note that says five thousand dollars in gold will get their colonel back in one piece. If they send cavalry, it'll be bad for you. I'd just as soon slit a colonel's belly as a private's."

Grinning, Harne walked toward the darkened hallway, swishing the slim officer's sword against his boot. When Joel thrust the door open, the guerilla's reactions were quick as those of a wild animal. The sword swung viciously and clanged against the iron skillet. The blow wrenched Joel's makeshift shield from his grasp but brought him close enough to drive his fist into Harne's throat, bringing the man gasping to his knees. The guerilla was tough. He staggered but, in falling, caught Joel back of the knees and the two men went to the floor with a thump, Harne on top. Joel had just time enough to twist his head aside and miss the fingers snatching at his eyes. Another twist, and his knee jerked up with force into the man's groin. Then he drove two hard blows to the prostrate guerilla's jaw.

The struggle had carried the antagonists well past the cellar door. Joel stood up slowly. His head was clearing when he heard a sound from the kitchen. He turned to see, then a movement caught his eye. Harne, on his knees, was lunging forward with his sword. Joel jerked back, just out of reach. The guerilla, teeth bared, was getting to his feet, pulling his weapon back for a better stroke, when Sergeant Sney appeared just behind him. His knife whipped up, drove down into Harne's back, jerked out, stabbed again, and Sney let go of his blade as the murderer sprawled on the floor, the buckhorn haft of the steel sticking up between his shoulders.

Sney pulled his knife from the dead man and stepped into the dining room to cut the Colonel free. Kellogg was a big man, and he had been tied so long his legs refused to carry him. "Drag me, Private; damned legs are stiff."

Joel got under the man's arm. "Get to the cellar, Sney. Blow your whistle, I'll get the Colonel." He managed to pull the officer into the hall and down the cellar steps as Sney's whistle shrilled. In another moment, carbine fire raked the house. The three men lay on the cellar floor listening while bullets scoured the rooms above. Revolver fire answered for a few minutes, then stopped. The smell of smoke drifted down, the shooting had wrecked lamps and candle stands. There came the sound of savage yelling and the clash of a melee. Sney said, "McCabe's out there, sir."

"He would be," Kellogg mumbled. "I made a damn fool of myself. But, everything was charming until an hour or so ago, the man's wife was so hospitable."

The outside battle had dwindled to an occasional searching shot, then boots smashed in the doors, and McCabe's men rushed into the burning house. The sergeant reported to his superior officer, who grinned ruefully.

"Thank you, McCabe, until I can do better. I've told Pender and Sney how I made a damn fool of myself." The chief scout started calling in his men.

No one was found alive in the place. Five bodies, plus Harne's, were left in the burning house. McCabe's surprise attack had been so complete he had sustained no losses. "Get the aide from the barn and burn that building."

The way the troopers handled their job showed they were old hands at destruction. Joel stood watching flames break out in the barn and out-buildings; the house was already a blazing mass. He thought of the fire in the Heitel place. He turned away and walked slowly along the graveled drive way toward the barn. Sney could report and supply any details.

So far, Joel hadn't mentioned finding Lisa Milburn in that kitchen. Perhaps he would not speak of it at all. She was a shrewd woman and would get away. He didn't like to think of killing a woman, even—es-pecially—this woman. There had been times—Joel heard the first shot, which snatched at his leg, but he did not hear the second, or feel the sharpness of the crushed limestone against his face as he fell on it. Most certainly, he was deaf to the crash of a dozen carbines searching the shrubbery and the sharp scream of a woman.

When Joel was taken to a field hospital, Colonel Kellogg demanded and got the services of one of the chief army surgeons, Doctor Pomeroy, who personally attended to the muscle tear on Joel's leg and the ugly gash through his side. Two ribs were broken by the pistol bullet. The colonel gave explicit directions to Pomeroy.

"This man goes to the Winchester base hospital, George. That's no reflection on you; they have better facilities." Pomeroy nodded.

Next morning, they prepared to send Joel by wagon. The wounds were pretty painful when he moved, but when he lay quietly, it was bear-able. He let his thoughts drift back to Hylersville. The village would be cool today with a breeze drawing down the valley. It would be nice to sit on the old cabin's porch with Trudie and listen to the light wind whisper in the pines, and the faint chuckles of the creek. He moved, and a twinge brought him back to reality.

The wagon train to Winchester was being readied, and Joel could only wait. Sney came in, resplendent in a new uniform. He turned round slowly to be admired. "Where's your knife?"

"Pender, I traded that sticker off for tobacco." He shrugged. "I was always getting blood on my jacket."

No one was nearby, so Joel beckoned to his friend to come closer. "There was a woman in the kitchen at Peach Hill, did she get away?"

Sney scratched his head under the edge of his cap. "Guess I did hear a woman up there, messin' round. I figger she must have got clean off," Joel frowned. "The boys got the one that did for you. Looked like a gypsy." The sergeant was suddenly very uncomfortable. "We found your pistol right outside the kitchen door."

Joel knew, now, that Sney had heard everything which had passed before the encounter with Harne. They had picked up his pistol; so Lisa Milburn was dead. He looked at the dapper little man and his voice was soft, touched with regret.

"Sergeant, if you were selling me a horse, I'd say you were a damned liar."

"Wouldn't wonder," Sney said, moving away. "Here comes some visitors. I gotta report."

The sergeant departed. Joel closed his eyes. When he opened them again, Bly and Donats, the Secret Service men, were standing beside his cot. He groaned and moved his head from side to side. "Sorry," he said bitterly. "Your hanging will have to wait. Come back in ten days or so."

Bly was shaking his head; both agents looked uncomfortable. "No, Pender, Major Colet sent us, with apologies and news."

"Maybe you'd better explain. Colet's in the South somewhere."

"No, the Major's back, made a quick trip. We met him in Winchester on his way north under new orders. He couldn't come here, sent us. You're cleared, Pender, completely." Bly was talking fast. "George Geis found a Thomas Ellender and took his deposition. Then, Geis organized a search using the Indian boys. Guess they turned over every stone on the Heitel farm. Finally, they about tore that cabin in the hollow down; and there was the government money, thirty-two thousand, seven hundred dollars. Afterward, Geis tried to come North, but there were two raids on Talpo: one by guerillas, one by Confederate cavalry. Geis managed, both times, to save the money and the papers he had prepared."

The agent stopped to get his breath. Joel lay back on his cot, stunned by the good news as much as by any of the dangerous things which had come his way. Bly consulted a note book. "Major had a message to you from George Geis." He peered at the page.

"George said: 'Come back in the spring some time, Joel, bring Trudie. We three will dig sassafras roots together.'"

Joel could almost see George Geis, the hint of a smile on his rugged, lined face, saying "I think some day you will climb the mountain." His eyes prickled, and he closed them again. It was all flat land ahead, at last. One by one, the friends who had helped him marched across the stage of Joel's memory. First was Trudie, with her faith, Tom Ellender, Puffenburger, Sam Jaynes, Tom Hawks, Uncle Thad who was dead. Most of all, Trudie. He could see her face now, oval, framed by her hair, the kindly turn of her lips, the friendship which looked out of her eyes. He opened his own and muttered, "Thank you."

But Bly and Donats had slipped away. He was alone except for an attendant. Joel called, "Brother, get my pants. I don't plan to ride up to Winchester wearing this damn short cavalry night shirt."

"Yes, sure," the man agreed promptly. He knew there wasn't a bit of use arguing with a man with eyes as wild as those. Maybe those visitors had brought whiskey.

"Are you sick or something?"

"Something," Joel repeated. "I'm happy. So'd you be, if a man down in the mountains just took a rope off your neck."

CHAPTER XXVI

THE GREAT NEW base hospital at Winchester was tremendously impressive, large enough to care for all the sick of some great city. As yet partially occupied, it was a grim reminder of the sureness that hundreds of young men would soon be broken, in battles yet to be fought.

He gained strength under the excellent care and presently was hobbling about the place using a pair of specially padded crutches. His trips about the buildings told him this place was a surgeon's dream come true. Outside air could sweep the long corridors, sunlight could come in through properly placed windows. Chloride of lime, hard to find in field hospitals, was everywhere. The ambulance park would have pleased Jake Puffenburger because there were none of the two wheeled carts that jolted wounded to death; here all ambulances were well sprung four-wheeled wagons.

Time hung on Joel's hands. Then at noon on the seventh day, when Joel was sprawled on his cot, with no announcement of any kind, the Reverend Samuel Jaynes walked in. He tossed a small paper bag of apples on the empty cot before shaking hands heartily.

"They're Astrachans, friend. Tom Hawks sent them, and said they're sour, but his good wishes will sweeten them."

Joel was desperately eager for home news, yet could not refrain from blurting out his own. "Sam—George Geis and Colet cleared me. George located the paymaster's money in that cabin in the hollow. Tom Ellender testified for me." He thumped the floor excitedly with his cane. "I'm—" He stopped.

Jaynes' strong face showed no expression. "Yes, you're quite a hero. The newspapers wrote up the story of your saving of Colonel Kellogg. Hylersville is almost ready to make you a hero, almost, I say. And Colet came up for the wedding."

Joel frowned, puzzled. "Wedding," he said slowly, "who?"

"Yes, I married them. Doctor Kenny and—"

He stopped as Joel jerked up his hand. The conclusion had hit him hard. Trudie and Kenny had been friends for a long, long time; Colet was a relative. He got up, put his crutch in place and limped over to a window, where he looked out on the empty ambulance park; nothing there but the always present barrel of chloride of lime. Jaynes said nothing while the wounded man came back to the cot.

In spite of himself and weakened by his condition, Joel's voice was thick. "No need to finish, Sam. All I ever had was hope, anyway, and Kenny's a wonderful man, the kind Trudie deserves—" His head dropped into his cupped palms and, for a long moment he did not feel the hand on his bowed shoulder. Jaynes was talking, but his manner had changed.

"Joel, I did a cruel thing because I had to. You went away with no word to her, in spite of her dreams for you. You let her worry; she had no word of what was happening to you." He cleared his throat.

"When you came to Hylersville, I wanted to know whether there was something real about you; or were you a scared pup hunting shelter. You proved yourself a man. Then, you walked off."

Jaynes sat down, looking intently at Joel. "I had to know if you really loved the wonderful person who is Trudie Quinn. Mayhap I was a bit jealous of you. No, son, I married Kenny to Mrs. Driggs, the nurse who helped with the flu." Relief flooded through Joel.

Jaynes said, "Don't ever hurt that girl again; or I won't marry her to you when we get home." Joel was too relieved, too eager about the prospect to be angry with Jaynes who fished a packet out of his coat as he talked. "Wetwire paid a heavy fine and was released. Little Susan's playing tag with other children. McColl seems to have stopped drinking, and he and his wife have taken in Sallie Briggs' little girl, Lucy." He met Joel's eyes steadily. "Joel, do you regret giving me that money?"

"Of course not, Sam. I never did want it."

Jaynes had his packet open and was laying out paper money. "Five hundred dollars bounty for enlistment, two hundred eighty you left with me. Plus, my friend, Trudie's sixteen hundred dollars, Burley's bragging money. That's enough to finish medical school, and for two young people to live modestly while its being done."

Joel took the bundle, his mind whirling. He passed the whole back to Jaynes. "Keep it, Sam. You've got the cart ahead of the horse. I haven't even asked Trudie to marry me, yet. And school's three years off. I'm in the army for three years or the duration of the war."

Jaynes grinned. "Son, you have some more visitors."

Two men approached. Joel fumbled for his crutch as he saw the dress uniforms, and he tried to come to attention as he recognized Lieutenant Cord and Sergeant Sney. The lieutenant was very military. "At ease, Corporal Pender. Here are orders from General Sheridan, approving the suggestion of Colonel Kellogg, that you be granted an honorable discharge from the armed forces, due to the nature of your wounds."

Cord's lips twitched and it was as though the sergeant had nudged him. He continued. "The General directed us to say: 'Tell that boy to finish his schooling, to help rebuild broken men after this damned war is over.'"

Joel felt a stinging in the back of his eyes as he took from Sney the small piece of imitation parchment. "Sheridan," he said softly, "Fighting Phil Sheridan and his big black horse."

Both soldiers dropped their military formality and shook hands with Joel. Cord grinned. "What worries me is what'll I do if I get a headache; or when Sney gets another bullet in his back?"

"Beg pardon, sir," Sney corrected, "that slug glanced."

Another round of handshaking and the soldiers left. Joel, in spite of his own good fortune, felt a touch of sadness. There would be hard fighting in the Valley soon, and these men would be in the thick of it. He remembered that Cord wanted to be a lawyer—already a bullet had come close to taking his life. This bloody war had taken so much, from so many. He hoped Cord would be fortunate, and live to follow his calling.

CHAPTER XXVII

JOEL FOUND THE train ride north relaxing. He settled back to watch the country slip by. There was so much to think about and remember. When they stopped at Camp Curtin there was no crowd, but four men detrained and walked slowly toward the wide gates. Joel remembered vividly the serious but half comical situation he had gone through in that recruiting office with Jake Puffenburger, and wondered where his friend was.

When he arrived and disembarked, his single valise in one hand, the first thing he saw was Jake, waiting beside a buggy with Sam Jaynes. He wouldn't have to walk to Hylersville after all. He'd been wondering how he would manage. His leg was not up to the trip, but he doubted his ribs would stand up to a horse. The two men greeted him happily, and Jake explained that Squire Wetwire had loaned his buggy for Joel's comfort on the ride. "A bit fancier than I'm used to driving," the young man laughed.

They traded news as they rode along toward Hylersville. Jake had not joined the Army yet, but was working as a teamster hauling supplies. Sam reported that the town was recovering still from the influenza epidemic. So many had died. "Lucy seems to be settling in well with the McColls, and I think that will be good for all three of them. Harry Sholes has even attended church a couple of times. Mrs. Starr moved to live with relatives, after her husband was arrested. I guess she couldn't face the neighbors. Her brother lives in her house, and as far as I can tell, hasn't touched liquor in months. Tom Hawks has largely taken over running Crisp's store, since Darcy had gone back to schoolteaching." The ride passed swiftly as they talked.

As the schoolhouse came into view, an older boy on the steps jumped up and ran inside. All the children boiled out of both buildings and stood waving in the schoolyard as the buggy passed. Mary Talbot and John Darcy, both smiling, began shepherding the children back in for their lessons.

Jaynes had insisted that Joel would stay with him until he was fit to go back to High Valley. "You have a few weeks until you need to report to medical school. I'm sure you'll find ways to pass the time." He looked over at Jake, who grinned widely. They pulled up in front of Sam's little house, and Trudie stepped out, wearing a blue dress.

They were married at the end of the week, at High Valley, with just close friends at hand. They went back to Hylersville, however, where Tom Hanks had set out a wedding supper that nearly the entire town attended. For once, the window curtains hung untouched, no eyes squinting around them. Mrs. Fenemore bustled up self-importantly, exclaiming, "Doctor Pender, it's so very good to see you!" One by one, the townspeople gave Joel the welcome he should have had when he first returned, but he didn't blame them. It had been a difficult time, but it was past. He had Trudie by his side, and soon they would go together to Harrisburg, and he would finish medical school.

* * *

The front porch of the High Valley cabin had been a favorite spot for Joel and Trudie during the four weeks they had waited for medical school to open. This final evening, they sat watching the red ball of sun slip down and hide behind the timbered rampart of the mountains. Tonight, they would be taken to Point Haven and on. Down on the road a wagon rattled. It stopped and there was a sharp whistle.

"Tom Hawks with Doctor McColl's buggy. Time to go, young lady: Point Haven, Harrisburg, Philadelphia."

Trudie got up slowly and slipped a hand under Joel's arm. Tom Hawks' whistle came again.

"Wait," she murmured, "we'll be back." Joel half-turned, puzzled. "I was talking to the cabin." He nodded in agreement. They walked down the steep way, carefully because of the stones, on into whatever the future held, together.

www.ingramcontent.com/pod-product-compliance
Lightning Source LLC
Chambersburg PA
CBHW011347010726
47493CB00011B/2993